THE LIGHT BEYOND THE STORM CHRONICLES

BOOK ONE

A. L. Butcher

First Edition Published 2012
Revised Edition Published 2012
Third Edition Published 2015

With thanks to Oxana Mazur for the cover art.

ISBN-13: 978-1481255622
ISBN-10: 1481255622

Dedicated to my best friend Diana, for all her help and support.

PROLOGUE

The elven mage awoke long before the dawn, cold in the autumn frosts. Crawling from under the thin blanket, she left the small canvas tent and saw that the fire had dwindled in the previous night's rain. Reaching for her staff, the young woman poked the end into the sodden embers to try to get some life back into the fire. The wood she had managed to gather was damp and would not ignite easily. Piling a little of it onto the fire pit, the girl murmured as she held out a slender hand, in which a flame appeared. A small flickering red fire, which glowed faintly in the half-light and made her flame red hair shine, danced above her thin fingers. Smiling, the mage gently blew the flame onto the wet wood, which an instant later smoked into fire enough to boil water, toast bread and warm numb fingers.

Shivering, Dii pulled her old wool cloak around her and looked at the sky, the stars now fading into the grey dawn. Mages could sense the weather, so Dii knew that more rain would follow this day; even now she could sense the pressure in the air. Hunger made her belly grumble, and as she looked at the thin tent, she knew it would not protect her from the late autumn weather much longer, or indeed the many other dangers which stalked the night. Dangers which were very real for one such as her; an elf, a woman and a mage, for as such, she was not free. Freedom in the land of Erana was rare. It could be bought and sold for some, although many did not have that luxury.

Pulling a very stale half loaf of bread from her cloak pocket, the elf toasted it and poured a little water from her water-skin into the metal pot to boil. Food was food after all. Luxury was another rare commodity. Tossing in a handful of dried leaves and herbs, she sweetened the tea with the few berries she had scavenged. The smell of the toast and herb tea revived the young elf's spirits and suddenly the dawn did not seem so cold, or the future so uncertain. The small wooden box she carried contained a few herbs from her previous store, both for healing and refreshment, the land around providing much if a body knew where to look. Such plants could heal and fortify and often were of more value than coin, which one could not eat, nor would fight infection.

Dii was a skilled herbalist, surprising for one of her station, but she was clever and had an enquiring mind that searched until it found answers… She considered for a moment. The only good thing about her Keeper Joset's estate was Malana's herb garden, which was by far the finest in the area and the most bountiful. Regretful for a moment, she thought about the woman she considered her mother, the only one she had ever known: a kind human woman, also a mage and a Kept, or slave, of Lord Joset Tremayne. Malana had taught her a little when she could, including the herb-lore, and loved her a good deal. Education was not the norm in Erana, especially for elves, but somehow it had suited her Keeper to allow her to learn, perhaps it increased her price. Sighing at that thought, Dii returned to her tasks.

Pulling the small purse from her cloak, she examined the meagre coins therein. Dii knew those few coins would not last long, and an elf with a bulging purse would certainly draw attention. She had spent the best part of the small amount she had been able to acquire on the tent and camping equipment, and that had drawn more notice than she had been comfortable with. Dii knew she had been overcharged, but also knew there was little she could do, she had handed over the coins and made her way swiftly from the stallholder's sight.

Dii was well aware her Keeper was a nobleman, and thus rich and powerful. He was a man of influence, but she was also acutely aware of where a lot of that money had come from. So she had taken the few coins she had managed to hide unseen from her Keeper. Dii could have taken more; she knew she had more than earned it, but somehow felt wrong taking the gold of her Keeper, although after all he had forced her to do, she could not understand why she felt that way. Perhaps, she thought, it was simply self-preservation: half of her hoped he would not seek her, but were she a thief, he might be more inclined to do so. The young elf was many things, but a thief she was not. So Dii had left with a few meagre possessions and a small bag of coins. Everything else remained in her Keeper's house. More afraid of what lay within than without, she had risked her life to flee, both in physically doing so and to be out in these lands alone. So far she had been lucky not to have been spotted by anyone unfriendly to her kind, and she thanked the gods for that. Not knowing the trails and roads well, she had nothing to trust but her luck and her skills.

A Kept owned nothing by right, but Dii knew her favours paid well. Her lovers would sometimes give her coin or trinket if she had pleased them, or a grateful villager would pass on a few copper coins for the potions or herb-lore she distributed. Most of the common people had little healing knowledge beyond basic remedies passed generation to generation, and many communities did not have an apothecary. People often turned a blind eye to the local "wise folk," although this was not always the case and many a mage had found themselves in the "hospitality of the Order of Witch-Hunters" due to a failure to heal someone, or from mere spite or fear. To be in possession of magic was illegal and, in many cases, meant imprisonment or even death.

As the herb tea began to steam, Dii shivered in the near darkness and the frost, and realised she would have to seek shelter in an inn or tavern before long, a risky business for an elf and a mage. The young woman was an outlaw, a Forbidden, a Kept, but on the run. She hoped not everyone would see it so. Dii had both talent and beauty and she knew men found her desirable. If need be, there were those who would offer a bed for the night. Dii thought that it would not be the first time she had bargained her body or had it bargained for her. She knew she could never be free, but at least for now she could make her own decisions, at least to a degree.

Malana had secretly given her the herb box and the staff, little more than a sturdy oaken branch found one night after a storm. Everyone knew a lightning-struck oaken branch held Power; the essence of magic. Dii grinned at the irony, such superstitions and facts remained despite the best efforts of the Witch-Hunters. In a land where magic was illegal, magic itself did not know it. It was a risk Dii took to carry such an item, but beyond a small dagger, it was all the defence she could openly wield. Many people would think twice about attacking someone who could wield a large stick, for such it appeared, being a simple item with no ornamentation save the blackness of the wood. At least that was what she hoped. Just being an elven mage out alone was risky enough, she needed some protection from the bandits and other dangers which patrolled and prowled the roads.

Dii searched for the least worn and dirty of her clothes in the recesses of her patched and worn backpack. Changing into breeches and a fresh blouse hastily beneath her cloak, she then washed the clinging sleep from her pale face. It was a striking elven face, skin like alabaster, with almond shaped eyes the colour of the midnight summer sky and just as sparkling. An odd tattoo of pale red circled her cheek and crept down her neck where it met the tendrils of the other mysterious tattoo spiralling and swirling from her collar bone; obscured by her clothing yet offering promise and mystery, an enigmatic adornment of red and black against her soft, pale skin. A face more angular and defined than that of a human, framed by a sea of curls falling to her waist, barely tamed by the ribbon in it, and the sharp points of her ears marked her for the elf she was.

* * *

Dii walked through the day, stopping only to refill her water-skin from a spring. The day had turned out to be overcast and the air was heavy with the tension of a storm hanging over the land. Heavyset big-horned sheep populated the surrounding countryside; hardy and excellent providers of meat, cheese and wool that was surprisingly soft to have come from such tough, belligerent beasts. Trees covered the land to the east, not quite fertile enough for grain or barley but ideal for the orchards and forests that provided for these lands. As she walked, the hills began to roll steeper. The horizon boded storm clouds and any canny folk, Witch or not, could foresee the storm approaching. Every mile she walked was further from her Keeper's land.

As evening approached, the road forked and the rain began to fall in huge, cold drops that chilled the blood and saturated a person to the skin. She was aware some mages could control the weather, calling and dismissing storms and remaining dry in the rain. Dii, however, was young and inexperienced, and did not know such useful spells. She hesitated, unsure; she could try to camp, although she had little food remaining in her bag and knew her tent would not protect her from a storm or high winds. She had passed a farmhouse some way back and contemplated returning to shelter in the barn, yet she did not wish to be caught stealing apples or eggs and, not knowing the sympathies of the farm folk, she was reluctant to beg for food. The other choice was the elf could risk the village she could see on the horizon, which would provide her at least with a hot meal, a warm fire and a bed more comfortable than a hayloft or bedroll. Being a healer, Dii knew the risks of such weather, and of prolonged exposure to cold and damp. She knew also the danger of one such as her seeking accommodation, but at this moment, she was too cold and wet to care; weather such as this could kill. It was worth the risk for a night or two. Hopefully, if she was cautious, the village should be safe enough.

The storm began to rumble and roll, the symphony of the gods beginning to boil like a cauldron. Quickening her pace, the young elf hoped no other souls were out in the storm. Looking around she saw the pear, apple and plum orchards to the east of the village. Much of the fruit had gone but a few trees still bore laden branches amongst the brown and red leaves. The storm would bring death for some of them and possibly ruin the last fruiting for the rest. Resisting the temptation to fill her pockets with the fruit, she simply plucked a couple of the juiciest ones to quiet her rumbling belly.

Dii smiled sadly when she remembered her foster mother's fruit pie. Dii had learned much from Malana, not just some of her magical training, unofficially of course as that was forbidden. Malana was the best cook and best herbalist in the area and although she was the lord's mistress, she was also a midwife. Often the villagers appealed to her when the other midwives had failed or were unavailable. A few times, Dii been given permission to attend, escorted of course. The first time she had marvelled at the sight of new life arriving in such a fashion, the joy, the pain, often the blood. She had watched and then assisted, pleased to be able to help with bringing new life into the light. She remembered Joset had not been pleased she had attended, feeling it unsuitable for her, but Malana had somehow persuaded him. Perhaps it had simply been another use of her skills for which she would receive payment to fill the lord's coffers. The ability to be an excellent cook and a well-trained herbalist, not to mention his favourite bed warmer, were solid reasons why Joset kept her foster mother around. Nasty and manipulative he may be, foolish he was not. Dii knew to her cost that he would not waste a good source of income and entertainment. Malana also believed herself, as bound concubine and Kept, to be in no position to be elsewhere. In her way, she loved him, although Dii had never understood why.

Perhaps he had once been a different man; as a mage, Malana would have been bound in the prison beyond the Enclave, unless she was very clever or very lucky. A mage would be bound with the feared Shackles: cruel, draining of magic and often fatal. Standing at the fork of the road, Dii was afraid and unsure, then a rumble of thunder reminded her of why she must risk her new-found freedom, and perhaps her life.

CHAPTER 1

The village of Dawson was small, just a hub for the local farms and orchards. The small market square, empty at this time and in this weather, was bordered by the Golden Apple, the local travellers' inn, on one side and the Happy Farmer tavern opposite it. A blacksmith lay off to the side, smoke still rising from the large chimney, and a storehouse close by. Trees encroached on the village and the cottages and cabins nestled in, almost as an afterthought.

To the final side of the square was the village lock-up and way-point, rarely filled with anyone beyond those whose tolerance to the local brews meant they found it necessary to participate in matters of a confrontational nature, and the occasional thief or bandit. Those who lived beyond the law mainly did so through necessity, rarely through choice, as Witch-Hunter justice was renowned for its brutality. Those caught as thieves were often executed or subjected to other harsh punishment, although there were many bandits and outlaws who often remained elusive to the constables and Witch-Hunters. There were a few folks who sympathised with them and would keep silent, or even helped out with food and supplies.

Wrapping a scarf around her hair so it covered the sharp points of her elven ears and murmuring a confusion spell, she headed for the tavern with the water streaming from her. Dii knew how to both be unnoticed and to use the shadows for advantage if needed. The confusion spell helped but could be weak, people saw her but somehow forgot what she looked like, or just ignored her; at least that was how it was supposed to work. Dii found it was often unsuccessful, whether it was that she miscast or that the mere novelty of an elf such as herself out in human lands, and a woman looking like she did, was enough to break the spell.

Shadowplay was more successful in the right setting but hard to use. Anyone looking directly at her would see plainly that she was there, but glimpses and half looks often failed to spot. Those very adept in its use could call the shadows and darkness to their advantage, or so she had been led to believe. It was rare that mages should learn this, but she had taken careful instruction from a spy to whom she had been given, as some compensation for her favours. Dii had grown quite fond of him. It was a shame that he was now dead; killed at Joset's hand for displeasing him and to spite her.

Dii entered the tavern as the thunder began to roll close, lightning splitting the sky behind her. The barkeep looked up as the door opened; he saw the small cloaked and very wet figure.

"Come in, traveller, and get you out of that killer storm. You are soaked, lady. Come warm and dry before the fire," said he, concerned to see the small wet figure on such a night as this.

Dii looked around with caution, but the warmth of the fire and the smell of roasting meats and spiced wine overcame her caution. Her belly reminded her it had not been filled with more than berries, fruit and stale bread for too long.

Walking to the bar, she said quietly, "Please, I would like a hot meal and room, if such there is? I have a little coin."

The barkeep, Roderick, smiled at her. "I would not turn away a traveller on such a night as this, and it would appear you have brought the storm on your tail. There is room and hot food available and my wife could arrange for you a bath if you request, there is a small room beyond the kitchen we use for such."

The elf stood, dripping and shivering. She could feel the eyes of the tavern's occupants upon her then looking away. "Er…yes, yes please. I could use a bath and dry clothes. I am hungry too but I am not sure I have enough coin to pay for all that."

A young woman, the daughter of Roderick, came around to take her cloak. "Let me dry this for you, miss? These wool cloaks take some time to dry when soaked right through."

Tired and cold, Dii let her take the cloak. The girl accidentally tugged on the edge of the scarf, revealing the sharply pointed ears. Dii almost felt the intake of breath from one of the tables as one of the patrons spotted her for an elf. "Well, miss, we do not get many of your kind in these parts, certainly not…unaccompanied, or as pretty come to that, however I am not one to judge. Coin is coin. I would not send anyone out into that storm. My wife Elena will fetch you some stew and a spiced cider. The rooms are cheap and basic; you don't get fancy. You have enough here for a night or two." Leaning forward, he continued quietly, "Just keep to yourself and you should be right. They are more mouth than action around here. There is a room you may use, at the end of the hall. Give your damp things to my daughter to dry, when you return my wife will serve you supper."

Gratefully, Dii fled to a room, small and sparse, containing little more than a small bed and a wooden armoire. Setting her staff in the armoire, she removed her damp clothes and boots, changing into a patched long dark woollen skirt and petticoats with a black bodice and a grey blouse. The clothes were not clean, and smelled musty but at least were dry. With luck she could trade for some more, this hamlet did not look like it came supplied with a resident apothecary. Stuffing her dagger into her belt, she hoped she would not have need of it. Barefoot whilst her boots dried, she returned to the common room to find a steaming bowl of mutton stew, fresh rolls, and a warm spiced cider. Dii heard the muttering and tried to ignore the stares and murmuring from nearby tables, and the whispers from behind her, as she began to eat.

A man moved closer to the table and hissed, "Witch, you bring the storm. You are Elfkind, so your magic must bring the storm. Do not think we tolerate your kind here. Where is your Keeper, Witch?" As he moved closer, he took a seat and snarled, "I bet you fetch a goodly price, Witch. Are you trained as a whore?" Reaching across the table, he grabbed her hair and tried to pull the young woman across it towards him.

Resisting the urge to use her magic in such a public place, she tried to squirm away, painfully tearing out a chunk of hair. "Go away! Leave me be! I am no whore, I am just an herbalist." Before Dii had a chance to reach for the dagger, a man intervened and pulled her assailant away.

"Get home to your poor wife, Ranulf, and leave the wench alone. Elf or no, she is not for your taking if she refuses," said the bystander. "He is nothing but an ignorant fool, miss. He will not be a bother again. From what I hear, he could not have made good his threat anyway," continued the man.

Ranulf skulked away, muttering and slamming the door. Dii's protector went and sat alone at his table. Watching the elf, he said, "I like my own company, miss. I am not the social type, but I will not see a woman threatened." He drained his mug and, taking one last glance at the pretty elf, he ventured back through the storm to his own dwelling in the smithy.

The barkeep brought over a spiced cider. "I apologise, miss, for the behaviour of that man. It is unfortunate; he is known to be…rather an oaf with women. I hope he did not hurt you."

Dii looked up at the barkeep. "No, he did not hurt me more than a tug at my hair, and he would not be the first man to try had he done more. Tell me who the other fellow is?" Dii glanced over at the door and a faint blush rose on her face.

Roderick glanced thoughtfully at the door and noted the blush. "That is our blacksmith Dmitri, and they are the most words I have heard him speak for some time to anyone. His woman died five winters ago. He has barely spoken a word to anyone since."

Pausing, he looked around cautiously. "We had a Witch…er…wise woman here for a while, but some…citizens drove her away. Perhaps had she been here, Anneta would have lived. She had red hair like you…maybe that's why he was kind to you. My wife takes the laundry which he does not do for himself, but I doubt there has been a woman in his cottage for some time. He does his work and comes to the tavern now and then." Smiling at the pretty elf, he returned to the bar and glanced at the door again.

Quickly eating the food brought for her, Dii pretended to read. Watching the common room with some wariness, she settled into the shadows and hoped she was inconspicuous enough to be ignored now that the villagers had returned to their drinking. As soon as she could, the mage fled to her room and bolted the door behind her. Climbing into bed still clothed, she put her pack close by and lay down by the light of a solitary candle. Rain drummed upon the roof as the thunder rolled around the hills and across the village. A storm full of fury roared in the night and the candle flickered out in the shaft of wind forcing its way through the badly sealed casement.

Dozing fitfully, Dii dreamed strange dreams of the Arcane Realm, full of magic and weird creatures and voices. She saw mounted men galloping in the night, and blood, a lot of blood. As the storm rolled in her dream, it echoed outside, waking the mage with a start just as a fork of lightning rent the sky and thunder tore it asunder. In the silence beyond the thunder, a great crash boomed and Dii ran to the casement to see a large tree at the edge of the village afire and falling. Flaming branches hit the thatch of one of the cabins and, wet though it was, sparked it into flame. Other branches rained down, and Dii heard frantic movement as the occupants of the tavern rushed out.

Dii grabbed her bag, hastily pulled on her boots, and headed downstairs. The fire caught quickly despite the rain, the wind feeding it, fanning it. One cottage was burning, another nearby smouldering. Smoke curled from the storehouse and someone yelled, "The stores! The winter foodstuffs! Fetch buckets to dowse the fires!"

Spotting Dmitri pulling on a shirt as he ran from the smithy, Dii surveyed the scene and then heard the scream from the burning cottage near the trees. Flames threatened to leap from burning thatch to the next few cabins. The rain made the thatch smoke with a choking, cloying black smoke. Fire clawed from the doorway, low but spreading, and a woman screamed again from within. Dmitri plunged through the doorway yelling, and Dii dived after him, the smoke choking them both. Her eyes watered and her lungs filled with the heat and smoke, making her splutter and wheeze. Pulling the scarf from her bag she tore it in two handing half to the blacksmith. "Cover your face. Do not breathe the smoke!"

Summoning her Power, she released a bolt of white light which formed a trail of ice crystals that hit the flames before them. The ice thawed in the heat and covered the burning floor with water, dousing the flames. Dmitri stared at her for a moment his eyes wide.

"The room at the back, Ranulf's wife, maybe Ranulf also," Dii screamed in the noise.

The water turned to steam in the heat and Dii could feel it singeing her hair and the sweat pooling in the small of her back. The fire was ebbing where her magic hit it, yet it raged still. Casting again, she managed to douse the worst of the flames and then, as Dmitri kicked down the door to the back rooms, she saw the glowing beam above them bow.

"Move!" she yelled and knocked him back into the room with a blast of magic. As the beam fell, she hit the floor and rolled. The beam plunged down, showering cinders and ash, and Dii grabbed at the smouldering edge of her skirt where she'd been hit.

Cowering in the smoky gloom was a young woman with a small child in her arms, the child unconscious and the woman choking and holding out her hand, reaching for salvation. Grabbing the infant, Dii pulled it close and wrapped it in her cloak. Her eyes stung so she could barely see, and her lungs felt painful with every breath, despite the scarf over her mouth. "Where is Ranulf? I see him not," she spluttered. The woman pointed to a shape on the floor. "Get him at least to the other room, or better, outside," she called to Dmitri.

Grabbing the woman's hand, they ran to the room beyond, the floor and walls still steaming. The mage cast another bolt of ice as Dmitri entered, carrying the unconscious man and choking, almost collapsing on the floor. Hearing shouts from outside and seeing hands reaching in, she handed the baby over and dragged the woman into the fresh air, crawling outside into the dark, and blessedly cool night.

Dmitri dragged Ranulf out, then fell to his knees wheezing. Gasping for clean air, Dii calmed the pain she felt and glanced to the blacksmith, who waved her away and pointed to the child. Crouching, she looked at the infant, gently touching his face. She Focused and murmured, "Goddess Syltha, grant me your Power this night to heal this child."

A warm blue light emanated from her hands and bathed the child in its glow, mending until the child awoke and began to cry for his mother. Dii moved to the unconscious form of the father; looking upon the face that had taunted her, threatened her, she could see the man's burns and the singed hair at his temple. Closing her eyes, she drew deep within herself; pulling on her faith in the gods and her Power. "Syltha, again I ask, grant me your sight. Grant me your grace to aid this man."

The blue glow flowed from her hands as again she focused. Dii felt his pain as the healing began to mend, pulling the man back from the edge of death. The magic weaved around her as she pulled his pain within, for a moment the burns appearing on her own skin and she stumbled back with the force. He stirred. Opening his eyes, he saw the elf crouched over him.

"What did you do, Witch! What evil magic have you that brings the storm upon us?" he spluttered.

Dmitri managed to get to his feet. "You ungrateful cur! You are not worthy of the service she has done you; that you live and your son lives is by her hand; 'twas the storm that brought the fire, not she."

Dii sat back on her heels, breathing heavily, trying to stop her head spinning and herself from throwing up from the exhaustion, the sheer effort and the smoke. Magic demanded a price and her swirling head reminded her of that fact

The woman crept over to her. "My son, he lives?"

"Aye, he lives. Come let me heal you, that smoke may have harmed you," Dii replied, wearily.

The woman shook her head. "No, save your Power. You may need it yet for those worse than I."

Dmitri pulled Ranulf to his feet. "Go, man. Take your family to the inn and pray that the gods forgive your ingratitude."

Ranulf helped his wife and limped to the inn, still muttering and complaining.

"I am sorry. You are a better person than I," Dmitri said. "Had I been you, he would not have made it to the fresh air and no loss would that be."

Coughing, Dii replied, "Ignorance does not deserve death. I am a healer; it is not my place to choose who dies and who lives. I must heal all, deserving and undeserving. Magic comes with a price," she sighed. Reaching towards him, she smiled faintly.

"No, I must help the others; the storehouse is not yet safe. I feel a little better now, but thank you for considering my welfare, miss."

Dmitri headed unsteadily towards the bucket chain from the well, thinking he very much wanted the pretty, young elf to touch him, to place her hands upon him. Fighting the desire, he glanced back and found her still crouched, watching him. He swallowed back the feeling and moved to the task in hand.

The mage felt tired. She had expended much Power this night. As the village moved around her, she felt someone take her arm. "Come, Mistress Healer, rest awhile. The fire is as good as out."

Looking around, she saw the daughter of the innkeeper and, almost in a daze, she allowed herself to be led back to the tavern. Dii requested a little hot water in a cauldron. Dropping some herbs and honey, she crumbled in a little arcana dust and stirred it into the water to produce a strengthening and fortifying tonic, drinking a little herself. "Would you take this to the wife of Ranulf and a little for him, if he will take it? The drink will fortify. Please also take some to Dmitri the smith."

The girl looked over Dii. "That I will take to Ranulf as you ask. Perhaps the other you would take yourself. I have seen the way he looked upon you. He has looked upon no woman such since his wife died. Perhaps you may…comfort him a while yet." The girl winked and Dii felt the blush rising. It was not that she was a shy maid, far from it, but still she could not stop her blush.

Dii smiled and wandered slowly towards the smithy. She could easily leave the drink outside, or merely deliver it and leave should he not wish for her company. Dii was tired but the man had been kind to her when she had succeeded in drawing attention to herself and what she was. Perhaps the company of the man who had shown her kindness would not go amiss. Dii meandered silently and thoughtfully towards the building with the small pitcher of the brew. Seeing a candle burning in the window behind the main forge, she carefully tapped upon the door. Dii had not been allowed many choices, but she had entertained many lovers not her own choosing. This man had been kind to her and for once she could choose with whom to spend the night. The novelty and thrill of choice spurred her forward.

"Who comes at this late hour?" was the reply followed by the sound of movement beyond.

"It…it is Dii, the elf. I bring you a healing tonic that may give you strength and ease you."

Hearing the bolt slide back, the door opened to reveal the smith Dmitri, who looked on her with some surprise. "You best come inside. It is raining still and cold now the fire is gone. I would not leave a woman standing in the rain."

Dii entered the small rooms behind the forge, untidy and neglected, yet not unpleasant. The smith was still coughing. Taking his hand, she said, "Drink this, it is a calming brew of herbs and honey. It will reduce the fatigue and the pain in your lungs. Will you not let me heal you properly?"

A fire, now merely embers, still smoked in the chimney. A rug of thick sheepskin lay on the floor before the fire and a small wooden table sat against a wall with a wooden chair, well-made but not fine quality, made by skilled hands but not a craftsman. A screen to the left hid a bed. The rooms were small and simple yet functional.

"I…I am sorry," he stuttered. "There has been no lass here for a while. I am not a fit sight to be seen this night. You should not waste your magic on the likes of me." He tossed some wood upon the fire and stoked it awkwardly, coaxing the embers to catch the log and filling the rooms with the warmth and odour of fresh, dry pine.

Dii looked at him intently as his eyes searched her face when he turned to her. Smiling a deep and alluring smile, she spoke softly, "There are more ways to heal a man than magic and whom I chose to spend my skills upon seems to be my own affair now. I see nothing that would suggest you are unfit to be seen, however if you do not wish for my company then I shall return to the tavern."

Placing the potion upon the table, she turned to leave. Dmitri gently caught her arm. "I would like it very much that you should stay. Yet I fear I will be poor company to a beautiful creature like you."

Grinning, Dii replied, "That I cannot say in foresight; you may ask me in the morning and I may tell you, or I may not. Indeed, you may find me poor company, for all I know, but let us take that risk. I am not a shy, retiring maid and I desire your company this night. Perhaps we may offer each other comfort and companionship?"

The smith smiled a rare smile and, taking her hand, he kissed it. "I have no manners, but may I offer you refreshment, Dii, some cider or ale; a little food? I have some bread and cheese." He fetched a pitcher of ale and some tankards, setting them upon the table. "I should take your cloak... Forgive me, I am an uncultured fool. It is just I am not used to entertaining beautiful and sensual women." He turned to watch her, his eyes on hers.

"You think I am sensual?" she asked coyly.

Dmitri stood close to Dii and touched her tattooed cheek rather nervously, as he whispered, "I think you are beautiful and mysterious. I have never seen such a pattern, or one that trails down so enigmatically."

When she did not pull away from his touch, Dmitri stroked her face gently. As they stood close, he searched her face for reassurance. Not the sort of man to force himself upon a woman, and having none for some time, he found himself unsure in her presence. Dii gave him a smile. Wrapping her small hand over the one caressing her, she led him to the sheepskin rug before the fire. Standing in the flickering glow, her pale skin was almost luminous in the light within the cabin. For a while, Dmitri just looked at the pretty girl before him, touching her skin, seeking confirmation from her that she was willing.

Softly, he took her into his arms and kissed her, hungry for her but not overpowering, giving her the chance to pull away if he displeased her, but he found no resistance; in fact, he found her eager. Her tongue sought his and as Dii tiptoed to reach him, her hands found their way beneath his shirt. Deftly he slid the cloak from her shoulders, letting it drop to the floor. As his lips kissed the bare skin above her bodice, he began to untie the laces, one hand finding its way into her now loosened blouse. Dii sighed softly as his hand found her breasts, caressing and squeezing gently, touching, exploring; her own hands beneath his shirt stroking his back, tweaking the soft hair, feeling the muscles of an active and fit man.

Tracing her tattoo with his lips, following the swirl as it crossed her, he nibbled at the painted skin. Dii arched towards him, bringing her breasts closer to his lips and hungrily he took one into his mouth as she moaned low in her throat. The young woman pulled at his shirt until he slipped away from her to remove it, tossing it to one side. She kissed his skin, teeth nipping, her fingers reaching down to find the muscled thighs. Her hand softly ran across the tightness in his breeches, stroking him through the fabric. Dmitri groaned at her touch, moving forward a little into her hand; all the while kissing her, sucking at her breasts, his hands all over her, yet gentle and pleasing. He murmured to her of her beauty and softness, whispering sweetness in her ear.

Scooping her up, Dmitri laid her upon the rug and pulled away her skirts and underclothes until she lay before him naked. Wrapping one arm around her, he pulled her close, taking in her taste and her smell. The young elf smelled of herbs, smoke and the musky scent of a woman. Dmitri moved his hand between her thighs, gently inserting his fingers into her warmth, stroking softly, enjoying the sensation of her folding around him and taking delight in her moans. He sucked at her breasts as he stroked her, waiting for her to begin moving with him, wanting to bring her pleasure, needing this woman.

Dii began to trail kisses down his chest, down to the belt of his breeches, exhaling slowly on his belly as the sensations filled her. Licking across his muscular torso, she nipped as he moaned with desire. A man of an active profession, he was muscular and strong, smelling of fire, of labour and of smoke. Leaning back, he settled on the rug and pulled her onto his lap, his manhood firm beneath her inside his breeches. He sighed as he turned her face to his and kissed her longingly. Fingers running through her hair, he loosened it, allowing it to fall like a curtain around her. Kissing her neck, he moaned feeling her weight on him. "Mount me, let me feel you around me," he breathed into her ear.

The elf smiled with joy, free at last to take a lover of her own choosing, the choice itself filling her with a kind of ecstasy. Free to lay with a man who desired her and whom she herself found pleasing. The thought of it, being mistress of her own choices, was at once exhilarating and terrifying, here and now it filled her with emotion and desire. This man had been kind to her; he mirrored her own loneliness, the need for the touch of another. Dii knew men found her desirable, she knew how to use their desires; apart from her magic, which of course was illegal, it was one of the few powers she possessed.

Dii moaned softly into his neck, exhaling warmth into his ear, sending desire pounding through him. Nibbling his collarbone, she reached behind her and rose a little to unlace his breeches. Resting on her haunches above him and gently biting his neck, she began to stroke him, her hand firm around him, expert and sure. Slowly at first, listening for his breathing to increase, then she began to quicken her pace as he moaned and writhed. A sheen of sweat built upon him and glistened in the fire as he got closer to the edge. He pulled her down and whispered in her ear, "Let me feel you around me… Let me take you to the edge as you do to me. I need you…"

As he began to pant, almost at his peak, she slid herself onto him, slowly swirling her hips and arching back. Her hands stroked his thighs and played with the hair. He groaned deep in his throat as she mounted him and began to ride. Dii felt him hard within her, thrusting deeply as the sensations and pleasure began to ripple through her as he hit the spot she needed. As she arched her back, he leaned forward and took her breast into his mouth once more, tongue swirling around her nipple. He grasped a fistful of her hair and pulled her head back, exposing her neck. Kissing along her neck and jaw, he moaned as he plunged into her warmth. Dii wriggled and squirmed in his lap, wrapping her arms around him she swirled her nails in the small of his back sending little sparks all over him. Suddenly his arms circled her, rolling her onto her back on the soft rug and pulling her legs around his waist, making the elf cry out in her passion. The thrill of taking this beautiful girl, the comfort and desire of another person, the sounds of her as she moaned beneath him made him quicken his pace until she cried out and trembled. Watching her come under his touch, he let himself go with a deep groan before releasing her. Feeling her legs slide from his waist, he lay beside her on the rug in the glow of the fire.

Dmitri rolled onto his belly next to her, pulling the cloak over them. "You are astounding; beautiful, clever, kind, and…talented. Only a fool would not see that. Will you spend the remainder of the night? I know you probably cannot stay here. I am not a mage, but I know that you travel alone and what that means. I would protect you should you stay, but I feel that you have some purpose far away from here. Alas, there is much ignorance and hatred of your kind, and for that I am sorry. Spend what is left of the night with me, and forget for a while."

Dii sat up and touched his face gently. "You are kind, Dmitri, and could I stay I would, but I will be hunted. My…Keeper is a powerful man, and as you say, there is much hatred here. I know you would not be able to protect me from those who would come for me and I would not have you risk yourself and your livelihood on my account. It would not be long before the Witch-Hunters came and perhaps my Keeper's men. I would not bring that down upon you, or this village. I must be away in a day or two, but I would like stay tonight."

Rising, he picked up the pretty elf and carried her to the bed beyond the screen, laying her gently down and pulling the blanket over her. "Rest here, I will damp the fire. There is not much time left before I must light the forge. I will rest a little in a while."

Leaving, he pulled a robe around him and tended to the fire. By the time he returned, Dii was sleeping and he climbed in to the bed beside her, stroking the hair from her face. He dozed until just before dawn, rising to light the forge and prepare some food.

CHAPTER 2

The village woke to the aftermath of the storm and the fire. In the light of day, the large Elder Oak had tumbled and burned; some wood was salvageable, and enterprising folk were making use of the fact. The cottage upon which it had landed would need re-thatching and repair and the family had lost much, but not that which was most valuable, thanks to Dii and Dmitri.

Dii woke late and dressed quickly, leaving the smith to his work. Slipping back into the tavern, she tried to creep in unnoticed but failed and received a grin and a wink from the barkeep. Fetching her pack and staff from her room, she changed and collected her laundered clothes. The tavern smelt of smoke and she noticed the young woman nursing the small infant rescued from last night's fire.

The woman smiled at her, saying, "See, he lives and is well enough by your grace, mistress mage. We can never repay your bravery or kindness. I apologise also for Ranulf's conduct towards you. Not all are so…vociferous and so forthright in their attitudes. He is not a bad man, he has a roving eye to be sure, but what man does not?"

The young mage gazed at the woman nursing her infant and wondered what else she refused to see. "I would not leave someone to die, mistress. If a roving eye is truly the worst of his faults then you are luckier than some. I will not tarry here much longer; I have…business elsewhere, but could not travel with the storm."

The woman nodded sadly and returned to nursing her infant. Dii quietly approached the bar. "I must move on today. I have business elsewhere and cannot tarry here. I would use what coin I may have left to purchase some supplies that may see me for a few days. I have not travelled in these parts so I am unsure of how many days to the next village."

Roderick nodded and, quickly disappearing to the store and kitchen, instructed his wife to make a basket of victuals. Returning, he looked the mage up and down. Leaning forward, he said quietly, "Well, there is the main market road from here toward Jaeden, 'tis three or four days or so at a brisk walk, less if you can find a wagon to take you. There may be farms that would accommodate you, there are one or two small hamlets off the main track and some way-points. But if you want my opinion, you had best keep away from the main highway. Talseca is in the other direction if you are bound thither, that would be the nearest town that way. Or if you'd chance the city Varlek is many days away by the back roads. There are elves there, in the Enclave. You might stand out less among your own people. Although of course the Order have their eyes there…."

He bent in close, suddenly very thoughtful. "There is a quiet hunters' track, now not so oft used, tis a longer way but will be safer. There are a few farmhouses and a wayfarer's tavern there; they have little trade and would be glad of the business. That path, if you head toward Jaeden, would take you past the old ruins. One of them old temples from before the Plague, now in ruins, but I hear well enough for cover…and exploration for trinkets should a body be inclined. A person could camp there for a few days, there is a river nearby and the remains of a hunters' camp. As I say 'tis a more…roundabout route but less…conspicuous, for the Order of Witch-Hunters rarely pass that way. Of course, miss, you know your business better than I."

Dii bowed her head. "I thank you for your kindness," she whispered.

Handing her a basket and the remains of her belongings, he smiled. "Blessings of the gods on you, mistress mage, for the service you have done us."

Clutching the basket as she left the tavern, Dii looked about the village, glancing to see the smith standing, watching. She felt she could not leave without a farewell.

"I am sorry it should be such that you must leave this place. You will go with my deepest regard. I would not see you go with nothing. I have a little coin, please take it…it's not a payment for--" The smith looked uncomfortable. "--you know.

"It's a gift, a token of my regard for you," he continued, "to see you along the way. To buy food, or warmer blankets or whatever you please, a trinket for that pretty hair. I am sorry, I am lousy at small talk and worse at goodbyes. Perhaps one day you would return here, when your business is done."

Thrusting a small pouch of coin into her hand, he turned away before she could say anything and shut the door. Dii sighed, thinking to return the coin, but realised that the man meant it sincerely and thus would be offended. Besides, she was not sure when she would acquire coin. Dii hesitated but knew this place was not safe for her, so with a slight sense of reluctance, she began to make her way towards the old hunter's trail and freedom from her Keeper's land.

* * *

A few days before the events of the storm, Ulric Tremayne rose early from his chamber in the Tremayne manor. He liked to take his favourite hound Springer for some morning exercise and stretch his legs. His manservant, Nathaniel, knew his habits and had laid out for him a set of rugged clothes and his warm cloak. Ulric preferred to dress himself. Lord's son he may be, but helpless he was not. He could hear the servants moving around preparing for the day as he dressed. He knew it was later than usual as his father was away…on business. In reality, this meant he was visiting the cottage he kept for the purpose of…being entertained by his Kept and orgying with his cronies.

Lord Joset had a stock of Kept at his disposal, occasionally bringing his favourite ones to the main house. This upset Ulric's mother Malana, Joset's official mistress. Ulric loved his mother, but, well, a man needed entertainment. However, Ulric would have preferred his father to be more discrete. He thought of Dii, similar in age and raised in the same household. Malana indulged the pretty elf, treating her like a daughter when she could, and when his father was not looking, fearing his wrath when he was. He knew his "foster sister" was little more than a Kept in his father's eyes, but he also knew what his father had forced her to do, and how he misused her.

He was fond of Dii. It was hard not to be, she was such a sweet and gentle creature, but she was still a servant, perhaps even a slave. He also knew that men found her irresistible, him included. Ulric knew to an extent this was a curse for Dii; she was pretty, clever, charming and talented. Moreover, she was Kept, and as a mage, mysterious. Although he suspected many Kept, in theory, did not have such affluent surroundings, he knew also that their keepers treated them far more reasonably.

Ulric sighed as he dressed. He had tried to persuade his father to not be so abusive to her, to treat her more kindly. Dii had Power, Ulric's meagre drop of magical blood through his mother and his own eyes could see that and her favours paid well. He remembered his mother informing him of the recent argument. Dii had displeased Joset. Ulric was not sure how, although he suspected that she had refused to go to his bed, claiming respect for her foster mother, or perhaps she had refused one of his friends.

Joset had beaten her often, Ulric knew that, and when Malana finally intervened, he had raised his hand to her as well. Dii had done the unforgivable in Joset's eyes; she used magic against him to protect Malana. The spell had knocked him off his feet, and Ulric knew his father's wrath could be extreme. He did not know what he had done to Dii afterwards, but she had stayed in her room for a day and a night now, and Joset had gone to cool his temper at the cottage. Ulric was glad; at least that gave Dii and his mother the chance to recover. It was fortunate, Ulric thought, that he had not been there, as he was not sure how he would have reacted, torn between his father and mother. He had returned that evening after his father had already left.

Dressing and pulling the long jet-black hair that was another legacy from his mother into a ponytail, he threw the cloak on and whistled to his dozing dog. Pausing outside Dii's chamber, he listened but silence greeted him. The dog whined quietly and, concerned, Ulric pushed the door. It was locked, but with a shove, yielded when the lock broke. As Ulric entered the small chamber, he noticed the armoire was emptier than usual, the herb box was gone and the casement window was open. Ulric whistled; it was a long drop for one not skilled in climbing, and he thought the fall alone could have killed her had she slipped. Looking around, he noticed she had only taken the essentials with the exception of the clothes, only those things her foster mother had given her. Pulling up the loose floorboard, he noticed the stash of money she thought a secret was gone.

"Damn!" he muttered before pulling the window closed and heading to the servant's quarters.

He knocked softly on the door of the maid. "Velta, it is Ulric. This is important."

The door opened and the young half-elf servant smiled at him, her hair dishevelled from sleep, still dressed in her night robe. "You know my door is never locked to you, Master Ulric. It is always important when you seek ingress to my room." She winked.

Thrusting her already ample chest out, she opened the door to him more fully. Suppressing the urge to take the offer, he smiled. "As much as I enjoy your arms around me, now is not the time. Dii is gone. You are her confidante; tell me where?"

Velta closed the door behind him. "Indeed Miss Dii trusts me with her confidence, thus keep that confidence I must, even from you, Ulric."

Ulric grabbed her arms. "You foolish girl, do you know what my father, your lord, will do when he finds out she has run away? I know why, gods, I know why. If you are complicit in this, he will turn you out, or worse, send you to the Enclave. Magical may you not be, but pretty and compliant you are. I am sure you would please him as a Kept…passed around among his friends…or perhaps you have not heard the stories of the Enclave?"

Velta shivered. "I knew she was leaving. She climbed out when the house was silent, after dark when the moon was high. She had bid me fetch a loaf of bread and a water skin. I know not where she is bound, that she did not share, I swear it."

"Damn it, go wake my mother!" Glaring, he let the maid go. "Say nothing of Dii's flight. Tell her to meet me downstairs. Go woman!"

She fled to do as bid. Stalking to the solar, Ulric patted the dog absently and muttered to himself about the folly of elves and servants. Malana appeared, hastily dressed, "What calls for you to see me at this hour? What is wrong?"

Ulric took his mother's hands. "Mother, Dii is gone, fled from the house, not that I am entirely surprised."

Malana stood stock still a moment, a sharp intake of breath passed her lips. "I do not blame her, but your father will be so very angry… I do not know what it is best to do. Perhaps she is better free, away from here?"

"Mother, freedom is not something that a Kept can have, you know that. She is a mage and Elfkind, how far do you think she will get? Alone! An unaccompanied Kept! She took little money, perhaps no more than enough for a week. If she returns herself or we can find her before he returns, then perhaps it would be better for everyone. If he must, he will have her hunted… Do we want Witch-Hunters interfering?" Ulric said, looking at his mother and seeing her fear.

"She is safer gone," Malana began to weep. "You know that, but I fear him, his anger. Perhaps you can persuade her to return, she likes you. Your father will be gone some days yet but if he returns before you, I can make some story that you have taken Dii somewhere."

Ulric looked at her, gently wiping a tear from her face. "I would not leave you alone with him and his wrath, Mother. Dii has made her choice. She knows the risk and yet she leaves. She must know she is his best…asset."

"You speak of her as property, Ulric!" Malana replied, exasperated and afraid.

"Mother…she is not your daughter, no matter how much you wish it. She is a Kept, at best a servant…to all intents, property is exactly what she is."

Malana turned away from him. "As am I!"

"Mother, I am sorry, but you at least are loved by him, as much as he can love anyone. Perhaps were Dii his natural daughter, it would be different. You are safe enough and well maintained here. Would you rather life in the Enclaves?"

"No, of course not…but she is not property…nor am I. No, you must go. He will believe me if you are gone. Joset trusts you. Ask in the villages, she cannot get far alone and on foot. Go, go now, my son, and find her. She is safer here than out alone."

Ulric took his mother's hands again and, seeing she was in earnest in her request, nodded slowly. "Mother, if you wish it, I will seek her. I will send word if I am to be gone more than a few days. I can drop it at the way-point and have it delivered if I have need. I should leave at once. In the meantime, perhaps I should leave a note for Father; you can give it to him in a few days. Explaining I have taken Dii…to meet a distant customer?"

With those instructions, he turned to leave, packing a few items of clothing, his sword and shield, a pouch of money and a few items of food. Ulric did not expect to be away from home for many days, however, he knew the roads were dangerous and it would be possible he might have to challenge the odd Witch-Hunter or bandit, although he would rather avoid such an encounter. For himself, he would be not be at risk from the Order, but he was well aware they had the habit of asking awkward questions. Shrugging into the fine leather armour after deciding anything heavier was unnecessary, he patted the mournful hound. "Well then, Springer, you keep Mother safe."

Mounting his horse, Ulric began to trot his beast in search of the missing mage. All the time hoping to find her before his father returned and hoping Malana would be believed, hoping he was pursuing in the right direction. He was to be wrong on all counts.

CHAPTER 3

Dii was grateful to the barkeep in Dawson; the old hunters' track was indeed quiet. The trail was in places rough and bramble covered, but easy enough to follow, winding away from the village, and more importantly, her Keeper's lands. The weather remained damp. The mud stained her boots and the rain fell in short showers, but the terrible conditions had somewhat abated. She walked briskly through the morning. As the sun rose high, the mage found an area of grassland just off the path. The damp grass, flecked through with late wild flowers, was long and green and exuded a sweet smell. She smiled to herself at the sweet innocence of life as a few bees buzzed around the flowers. A yearling goat kid munched a mouthful of grass and watched the mage with that disinterested gaze of a ruminant.

Belly rumbling, Dii threw her cloak onto the grass and settled down to partake of a brief meal. Looking in the basket, she was amazed to see it stocked with half a loaf, cheese, half a ham, a cloth containing apples, a sealed clay bottle, a water-skin, and some eggs wrapped carefully in straw. Beneath this was a pouch of coin, containing exactly the amount of coin she had paid the barkeep. Dii was overwhelmed at the kindness; this food could last her a good few days and perhaps be traded.

She munched thoughtfully as she contemplated the last few days. When she had run from her Keeper's house in the darkness, her thoughts had been simply to run, to flee that place. She had thought to head towards the great city of Varlek and the sea or another such port. Dii had never left the lands of her Keeper and although she had seen maps, knew neither distance nor route. Suddenly she felt a pang of guilt, hoping beyond hope that her Keeper Joset would not have noticed her absence and if he had, his wrath upon the family and the other Kept would not be too dire. Dii sighed and knew return almost certainly meant death for her. Packing away the food, she rose and proceeded onwards, lost in thought.

* * *

Ulric made good time, stopping at the villages within his father's lands. Two days he persevered before deciding he was on the wrong trail. He settled at an inn, the owner of which could barely do enough to accommodate the Lord Joset's son. Nursing a tankard of ale and a plate of surprisingly fine broth, he glanced around, subconsciously appraising that which would be his to manage one day.

Staring into the fire, Ulric contemplated the question which had bothered him since he had quit his father's house. Where would a young elven mage go? A woman as striking as she would attract attention and raise comment, he thought. Ulric slowly sipped the ale and wondered whether he should just let her go. He understood why she needed to run, but he also knew his father. Joset would hunt her if Malana were not believed. It would not merely be Dii who suffered, the servants, the Kept at the cottage, even his mother if Joset was angry enough to call the Witch-Hunters. Ulric was a little jealous; he too partook of her attentions now and then and was fond of the girl. Although not wanting to see her come to harm, it was more, he realised, the thought of her being away from his house and him that vexed him.

However, if Ulric were unable to find her, would his father's men succeed? Ulric grimaced, answering his own question with the notion that if needs be, they had a more…direct and immediate approach. Ulric wondered how far she could get, whether she could use her charms to get herself a protector. Now that he did not doubt.

"Tomorrow, I will head the other direction to see where she might have been bound," he muttered and found himself relaxing as he savoured the ale, away from his father's vision, and influence.

Distracted, he started when the pretty, red-haired tavern wench smiled at him and placed a plate of sweet bread before him. Bending over him, she succeeded in making sure he was eye level with the straining bodice that was losing the battle to contain her ample chest. "Compliments of the house, my lord. Our…services are at your disposal."

Ulric smiled at the young woman, his eyes roving over her well-endowed attributes. Thinking about Dii had made him consider a good many things, including the fact he did not enjoy sleeping alone. "Well, thank you for the…hospitality. I would be quite careful to whom you make such an offer as that. Some men may think more is on offer than is the case." This girl was pretty and obviously flirting and a man of his means could afford a tumble or two with the local wenches. Ulric grinned and decided to test his luck.

The wench returned his grin. "Sir, I know for sure what is offered to those of a generous nature, those who would treat a girl with the respect she deserves. A young man travelling by himself gets lonely of an evening, is that not the case?"

"Sometimes, it is indeed. Now, my dear, I think I will retire to bed. I need an early start on the morrow."

Leaning forward, he brushed a hand across her cleavage and dropped a coin into its depths, then he yawned theatrically and made a show of retiring to his chamber. By the light of the candle, he listened whilst the other patrons left for their own dwellings, or retired to their rooms. Sure enough, after a while, there was a quiet knock upon the door, which upon opening revealed the tavern girl.

"I was sent to see if my lord required…anything else in the way of comfort?"

Ulric looked at the young woman, pretty and flushed, his eyes once again drawn downwards. Licking his lips, he opened the door wider. "Well now, I am sure I could think of one or two other services that would make my stay more…comfortable."

"My name is Teena, sir," she said, to which Ulric nodded slightly, not bothered about her name. Winding his fingers in her red hair, he thought absently of someone else as he began to undress and motioned her to do the same as he pushed the door closed.

* * *

Sometime later, Teena slipped out of Ulric's chamber, turning and blowing him a kiss as he closed the door. As she slipped beyond, her father caught her arm. "What do you think you are doing, Teena?"

Smiling sweetly, she replied, "You told me to make sure the rich lord was comfortable. I did and he is."

Alan leant back against the wall, not seeing the door to Ulric's chamber still slightly ajar. "You foolish girl, his father is Lord Joset, master of the lands hereabouts. You have ears, girl. You surely know the rumours! The Lord Joset's little collection of whore-slaves, his business ventures--" He paused. "--and his parties, the reason why he is so rich but the lands and villages go without.

"You would bed his son? For all you know, a man even worse than his father. Do not let the looks and the easy charm fool you. I hope he paid well enough for your favours, and that he or his father do not decide to keep you for worse pleasures."

Teena looked haughty. "If I pleased him well enough, maybe he will keep me as his mistress."

Alan grabbed her arm and said quietly, "Foolish girl! Have you heard nothing I have told you? If he takes you for his house, it would not be as his mistress, girl, at least not for long… Do you wish to be shared amongst his friends, forced to do… many unspeakable things. Yes, I know you enjoy the odd tumble with the patrons here, but you have a choice if they please you not. Do not throw away that choice."

The barmaid suddenly began to look worried, glancing to the door. "Why does no one confront the lord?"

"Confront him? Do not be daft! What do you think happens to those who defy him? He is the lord of these lands. He has men at his disposal, you think any here would dare stand up to him and risk losing their living, their home, perhaps worse, for the rumours that may be simply hearsay. Besides, most of those that go are elves, half elves, and the like. No one cares what happens to them. Now get you to your own chamber, girl, and hope that the young lord is not his father's son."

Both father and daughter retired to their respective quarters and Ulric quietly closed the door. Ulric knew his father had business dealings and the women he kept at the cottage were common knowledge. However, Ulric had heard the muttering in the bar, felt the undertone, and was astute enough to realise it was fear that managed these lands, not respect, affection or even duty. Joset was disliked, and those were shadows that followed his son. Still, he thought arrogantly, what did peasants know! The girl had been an amusement for an hour or so, but she was just a tavern tart, albeit an enjoyable one. He decided he would spend a few more days leisurely sampling the hospitality of his father's lands and looking for Dii, perhaps use his considerable charm on the peasants, dispel the rumours, sample wares and women. Perhaps dally again with the barkeep's daughter, if only to spite the two-faced barkeep who had been so facetious. Thinking about Dii, he smiled. She would not have gone far…a young elf alone.

* * *

Dii continued on, sensing the rain. The autumn storm which rumbled distantly again threatened to break, and she wondered where the ruins lay. Pausing, she scanned around, suddenly sensing a feeling…almost a sound in her head, a sad ethereal song which seemed to call to her. The song led her forward until she saw before her the old stone ruins. Dark stone, flecked with silver, impressive in days of old but now strangely sad as the mosses and creeping plants pursued their relentless reclamation. Broken down walls now little more than piles of stone surrounded the remains of a tower topped with a tall spiral, twisted through with ivy. A wooden door hung from the stone, thick wood now almost as hard as iron but ajar. Dii hesitated, unsure at first, but as the sad song filled her so did a strange courage, and a destiny unfolded.

The air was cold and smelled of the odd, tin-like residues of magic, blood and the remains of creatures. Once this place had been Powerful, and the residual magic hung like a mist. Dii shivered with the chill and something else, a strange feeling. Perhaps the joining of the mundane and Arcane Realms was thin here… Perhaps it was something yet to happen. Dii looked about her in the darkness and carefully called a glowing ball above her, a small elemental; a mere wisp but with the light of a lantern at its call. This was one magic she had always excelled at, allowing her to study late at night, and it had even provided a little company, like some lonely children would have an imaginary friend.

The flickering light revealed passages and, in places, fallen masonry. Proceeding with caution, she saw the trails in the dirt: the detritus of crawling and scurrying creatures, the edges of large webs, and the carapaces of giant beetles lay strewn around. Alert, she checked the dark shadows, calling another lightwisp and half expecting one of the scuttling creatures to decide to make a meal of her. Yet still she moved on, drawn to do so. Her curiosity got the better of the worst of her fear. Carefully, she searched, finding a few lost trinkets, old coins and tarnished weapons but nothing of significant value.

Then she heard the song. Its sadness enveloped her, shrouding and calling her. As she moved, it swirled around her like a mist and the magical blood within her pounded. Drawn onwards by the sound and the magic, Dii entered the central chamber of the tower and she stopped as she saw it: the Mirror. A Circle of Power surrounded it, but Dii could feel that the magic was weak and the Circle was dim, a mere flicker. Horrified, she saw the enchanted glass cracked and shattered; a twisted mass still reflecting but also corrupted; a dark reflection of sadness, of magic, and of the past and the future. A man's skeleton lay close and covered most of the axe that had caused so much damage.

Dii stood before the Mirror and felt its pain as a strange, deep loss and despair; dying yet unable to die. Gently, she reached to touch the artefact, which shimmered weakly beneath her fingers.

"You poor thing, how may I help you? I give you my magic, that I may ease your pain," she said softly, finding herself upset as though a living creature was mortally wounded.

As she stroked the glass, a broken shard sliced the edge of her hand and Dii started with the sharp pain, her blood dripping down the frame. The song rose around her as the cracks of glass began to glow, the magic bringing it a little life, somehow easing it as the Mirror linked again to the Arcane Realm. Yet she felt that her magic was not of sufficient Power to help the artefact further and, finding the sadness of this place oppressive and almost overwhelming, Dii turned to leave. As she did so, a wisp of hair caught and tore.

Dii decided she did not wish to spend the night somewhere filled with such sadness and probably strange night-time creatures. Stepping out into the autumn light as the thunder rolled, she saw a storm rage on the horizon and hurried onwards, seeking sanctuary in the darkness of the hayloft of a barn.

* * *

The Archmage rested: dozing, replenishing, and dreaming. Archos had spent an active day and night studying and trying to finish the spell he was creating. Even with his Power, something had unsettled him so he had given up and gone to rest. As he dozed in a chair in what he called his "workshop," the Mirror he owned began to sing. Pulled from his sleep, he rose and walked to it. "What is it that you disturb me at such an hour?" he murmured. The Mirror's song began to wail the strange, haunting song of the Arcane Realms. Touching the edges of the Enchanted Silver frame, he watched as the Mirror shimmered and the mists cleared.

Archos watched as the view of the chamber in the ruins flickered into view. The image was weak, so he channelled some magic into the Mirror, and Archos saw the other Mirror in the tower and a glimpse of something red as the image flickered out. "Damn you," he muttered, "must be a weak one."

Concentrating, he channelled another small bolt of magic into his own Mirror. These artefacts had many uses, if a mage knew the correct spell, one of which included finding other such Mirrors. It was almost as though they spoke to one another, communicated in the Arcane Realm. They fed on magic, although Archos was not sure if "fed" was the correct term. Demanded, needed, or desired were perhaps more accurate. His Mirror could be fickle but it was old. It had cost him a good deal some years ago, but he smiled as he caressed the silver. He saw the image flicker back up and as it did so, a bolt of magic, of pain, of Power, and of the most intense desire shot down his arm and right across him. Suddenly his head spun, for just a moment, and the Power made him drop gasping to his knees.

"Gods, what was that, such Power! That cannot have been from the other Mirror!"

He had never felt such intensity as the Power of the woman who called to him across the vast Magical Realms. Breathlessly, he gripped the edges, surprised and deeply intrigued. As he pulled himself back to his feet, Archos saw her: the flame-haired elf woman touching the Mirror in the ruins. He watched as she ran her fingers down the glass and murmured something. Again, he cursed that he had never been able to get the thing to transmit sound. Archos gazed, transfixed, at the beautiful young mage. She could not be more than twenty-five summers, although with elves, it was hard to tell. It had taken him years to learn Mirror magic, yet before him stood this young mage activating an old, dying Mirror.

The image faded and he snapped at the Mirror, "Show me. Do not play games."

The mists swirled and he tried to reach through the unyielding magical fog. "Damn you, so be it!" Archos continued, glaring at the Mirror.

Stalking to the workbench, he selected the necessary accoutrements. Removing a box from the shelf, he crushed some of the contents into the bowl and taking the obsidian knife from the bench nearby, he sliced a long line down his arm, letting the blood run into the bowl and stuffing the kris in his belt. Swirling the blood with the powder, he muttered the incantation and poured the now bubbling contents into the conch shell. The incantation took a while but eventually an odd, red-tinged smoke rose and filled the room with an acrid stench. Flinging his cloak around his shoulders, Archos picked up the staff leaning against the wall, knowing it was best to be prepared and well aware what manner of creatures dwelled in the Arcane Realms. Pausing to heal the wound in his arm, he collected the smoking shell. Striding to the Mirror, he poured the bloody mixture down the glass.

"Show me, guide me, and take me there. I am Archos, Lord of Magic, and you will obey me," he snapped to the fickle artefact and his eyes glowed silver.

The Mirror began to sing and the glass shimmered dark blue. He pushed the mists apart and stepped through, feeling the sudden cold of the Astral Winds tug him and the sharp sting of Power as he entered the Arcane Realm. The other Mirror shimmered weakly, and he quickly pushed his way through the fog. As he approached, Archos saw the portal was weak, fading, and the light slowly dimming. The bolt of Power he sent crackled blue for a moment and disappeared, but the portal brightened.

Stepping through with some difficulty, he caught his breath again in the chamber of the ruins. He scanned the old place quickly, and noted he was not familiar with this particular ruin, one of many remnants of the past. The room was empty save for a skeleton in tarnished armour with an axe, a few empty carapaces, and the skittering of some creature.

The old Mirror stood before him, and he could feel its Power failing. He was alone, yet the Archmage could sense her, even taste her trail in the magical air. The feeling sent a shiver down his spine and a bolt of desire to his loins. A scent lingered above the damp tinny smell: lavender and herbs, sensual like a heady perfume. Yet he knew she was gone, not long, but he could not sense her nearby.

Examining the Mirror, he saw the extensive damage and the softly glowing lines where the girl had tried to repair it, heal it. How could she have known what to do? He could feel the shadow of her Power even now. Archos saw a jagged crack edged with blood where she had cut herself. Perhaps, he thought, the Mirror had called to her; she had replied, feeding it magic and her blood. He wondered if the Mirror had given her anything, or if she had even asked. Touching the edge, a bolt of pain shot across him, almost making him stumble back. The Mirror began to wail faintly, a terrible wail of sadness and pain. Archos saw in the shattered glass a strand of hair the colour of fire and carefully plucked it out; removing a piece of silk from his pocket, he deposited the hair and a small piece of glass, and stashed it in his pocket. For a moment, he shifted his Focus and searched for her. He considered trying to follow her now, but looked back at the Mirror with a sigh.

"No, your Power won't last much longer, my poor broken one. Not even magic can heal you, alas. I need to return, to seek her other ways. I need your Power one last time. The price will be high, but we will pay it. I will end your pain."

Archos dragged his staff over the Circle, increasing its Power. He hoped the magic would be enough. He did not fancy being stuck here, gods knew where, and having to find his own way back or worse, getting stuck in the Arcane Realm for longer than he needed, both eventualities being rather inconvenient. The Archmage sprinkled some arcana dust over the floor to boost the magic even further and emptied the rest into the shell. Beginning the incantation, he sliced deep into his arm, suppressing a grunt of pain as the blade tore deeply through flesh and dripped blood over his robe. Archos knew this would require more blood than the trip here had, for this Mirror was weak. Although he could boost its Power for a while, he needed to be sure it was enough.

He watched as the blood flowed freely down his arm, dripping onto the floor within the Circle until he stood in a pool of crimson, filling the shell from the stream of blood and then, for good measure, he held his arm over the Mirror and let the blood drip onto it, muttering the words he needed.

"I am Archos, Lord of the Arcane Realms, and I lend you my Power by the blood I shed. I am Archos, Lord of Magic, and I command the Arcane Ways to let me pass."

As the incantation ended, the smoke began to swirl up from the shell and the Mirror began to sing faintly with a shrill, keening song. Tossing the shell towards the Mirror, he let fly a bolt of Arcane Power, shattering the shell and scattering its contents. The Mirror screamed, but shimmered deep blue, and Archos stepped into the shimmer. A wave of pain washed over him and it almost floored him. Turning, he pointed his staff at the centre of the portal and pumped a ball of dark red light into it.

"I am sorry, I wish it were not so," he murmured as the screaming stopped, the portal faded, and he hurried back to his own Mirror before the link broke completely.

Stepping through, he collapsed against the wall, leaving a stain of blood and knocked over a case of flasks and empty glassware with a crash, suddenly tired and dizzy. The dying Mirror had demanded much, his own was hungry and Archos was fatigued. Murmuring a healing spell, he managed to cast it just as the door flew open to his half-elven manservant and confidante Olek. "My lord, I heard a crash. Gods, are you all right? You are white as snow."

Olek was used to his master and the blood magic, but usually Archos let him know when he was planning something requiring a lot of blood.

"Yes, yes. I just need to rest," he gasped. "That was more demanding than I thought. I am fine, I just need to get my energy back and perhaps eat something. I am tired. I have used much Power of late and I suspect by the fuss the housekeeper was making beyond the door, not eaten nearly enough. I have seen someone, a woman of great Power and beauty. Her magic called to me. I have to find her! Such Power should be trained and protected. You should have seen her!

"Just bring me some refreshment. I think we need to go on a journey soon, so make to leave. I have found an apprentice, Olek, and what an apprentice, if what I felt is indeed the case. I will watch her, but I suspect I will not be the only one doing so; such Power, such talent will not go unnoticed, and a young elven mage alone is far from safe."

CHAPTER 4

Bailiff Robert looked wistfully at the pile of scrolls and parchment letters that had somehow accumulated again on his small desk at the way-point. Biting into the pie which had gone cold on the pewter plate, he wished he was gaming in the tavern or at home with his wife Leian. The riders collected the correspondence from the way-point stations once a day, if he was lucky. He was not often lucky.

A rider entered dripping wet from the pouring rain. "'Ere extra delivery beyond the usual; some fellow from a village yonder. Says they had a Witch and she is bound for Jaeden. Escaped slave, tried to kill him, burned down a building. Seduced a citizen then fled."

Robert glanced at the dripping man. "Jaeden? There are a number of roads leading there but it is many miles, a few villages in that locale…I wonder. I will send word to the Order. Still raining, is it?"

The rider glared and muttered, "Very funny, haha." He tossed a bag onto the desk and returned to his mount and the rain.

* * *

Dii left the hayloft just before dawn, as the edges of sunlight crept over the horizon. She nibbled the food as she walked, wanting to preserve her rations. The night had been wet and the air hung damp and still. Following the hunter's trail, it widened and joined the road, giving her pause and making her suddenly unsure of which direction to take, not wanting to travel upon the main highway. A sense of foreboding filled the young mage, and a chill of apprehension crept along her spine. The air was heavy and no sound of bird or insect broke the eerie silence, as though the world hid its face in fear. Dark clouds rushed across the sky towards a storm blasted horizon, a foreboding sky indeed. The young mage trembled as icy fingers clawed across her and twisted her belly; she felt alone and vulnerable and very, very afraid.

Thinking she heard something, she turned and looked uncertainly behind her.

Pulling the cowl of her cloak further over her face, she murmured a confusion spell and, trying to regain her composure, walked along the meandering road with a step more confident than she felt. The silence was broken by the sound of hoof beats as three mailed knights of the Order of Witch-Hunters rode towards her. Dii almost froze but she summoned her courage and continued walking, as though she had a right to walk upon the Great Highway unaccompanied. The Witch-Hunters rode past, seemingly ignoring her until one turned about. "It is a dangerous for a young lady to be out unaccompanied. What business have you this way? You are far from a settlement."

Another of the Witch-Hunters dismounted and, letting his horse graze the short grass, sauntered close behind her. His armour glinted dully, a sword hanging at one side and a club at the other. The mounted speaker began to walk his horse close to her, intending to intimidate her. "Answer, you! What business have you here?"

Dii replied quietly, "I am just an herbalist…seeking trade. I was seeking herbs and other such plants and was heading to the villages here but lost my way."

The Witch-Hunter behind her stepped in close and pulled the cowl of her cloak, removing the scarf from her hair and dropping it on the ground, revealing her as Elfkind.

"So a pretty elf out alone, have we? This seems to be the little whore Witch from the village, lads. We have caught ourselves some sport!"

Dii tried to pull away, afraid, the apprehension knotting her stomach. She knew she could not fight three, and she certainly could not out run a horse.

"I am neither Witch nor whore. I am just an herbalist, please leave me be," the elf woman whispered.

A nasty laugh echoed after the tremble in her voice and the mounted Witch-Hunter reined his horse to a stop in front of her. "Is that so…elf? Well, we seek a Witch fitting your description that brought a storm upon a village and nearly killed a man, it seems. I am sure you would agree that such a dangerous individual needs apprehending. What a coincidence that this elven Witch whore we seek is on this path at just the same time as a…herbalist carrying a staff."

Dii tried to look around, seeking escape but knowing it impossible. The second Witch-Hunter produced a Witch-Net, expertly throwing it onto the young mage before she had the chance to run or cast. The ropes twisted into her feet and arms, tumbling her to the ground hard. The Witch-Hunter laughed unpleasantly. Raising a knife, he plunged it into her shoulder, a thin blade lightly coated in Banecrystal poison, enough to weaken and cause considerable pain as it began to crawl through her.

"Now for the perks of the job…perhaps if I am satisfied, I might even let you live," the fellow snarled.

He grabbed at her skirts. In her terror, Dii began to struggle and cry, pleading with her tormentors, but to no avail. They merely laughed and tormented her more. As the fear and anger rose, so did the magic, suddenly bursting from her in a blast of flame, a spell which rose from her before the Banecrystal did its work. The Witch-Hunter took the full Power of the blast and, erupting into flame, screamed and fell back arms frantically trying to extinguish the fire which surrounded him. The sickly sweet odour of charring flesh filled the air, rank, choking, terrible. The horses reared in terror and the mounted Witch-Hunter only just kept his seat, his companion backing away, horrified, while yelling, "By the gods, she roasted Carlo! Bitch…get her! She will suffer for this!"

Angry, the man raised his club as the stricken mage tried to roll away and the other Witch-Hunter dismounted, drawing his own weapon to join his companion. The blow hit her ribs, cracking bone and knocking the air from her. Gasping for breath through the pain, she saw the other Witch-Hunter approach; again, she tried to roll away and summoned her magic, through the clawing pain of the poison, before the club hit her on the back of the head, knocking her half-senseless. As she laid prone, the two remaining Witch-Hunters continued to beat her, clubbing, slashing her until finally satisfied she was unconscious. Thrown onto one of the horses like a sack, the soldiers retrieved the frightened beast of their dead comrade and, knowing nothing could be done for him, the group made haste to the Order's fort.

* * *

Archos had contemplated carrying out the ritual he needed straight away, deciding against the course of action as his head pounded, he was exhausted, and he knew he would do the girl no good as he was. The Archmage had Power and a great deal of it, yet even he needed to rest and relax. Magic demanded a high price and used incautiously, could be very dangerous even to one of his skills and experience. Lost in thought, he walked to his finely furnished bedchamber. He knew he needed to sleep and to meditate, yet he was apprehensive, for he was well aware of the dangers that threatened both elves and mages.

One wall of the chamber was hung with paintings and an antique tapestry he had acquired a year or so ago depicting an ancient and epic battle of times past. A history now long gone. A casement window, of glass both clear and stained a pale blue and set with velvet curtains of deep indigo, looked out across his lands. The Archmage often watched, seeing his people and their lives go by and thought himself lucky.

The fire burned low but still warm in the hearth above which was a beautiful mirror, of the more mundane variety, edged with rare tortoiseshell. Silver candlesticks and glowglobe brackets held scented candles and glowglobes, which cast their soft light, reflected in the mirror, to make the room bright and aromatic. He enjoyed this room, it was restful and quiet, an inner sanctum of peace.

The wooden bed was large and hung with scarlet damask and a black bear fur lay upon it, warm and soft. Cushions and pillows of silk and velvet lay scattered over the top, in blue, black and silver and a warm wool blanket of rich blue peeked out from beneath the fur.

A mixture of sturdy oak and shining bronze, a large carved chest was nestled in a corner, the lock of which could not be seen but to those who knew precisely where to look, and those who did would be wise to exercise caution in opening such a strongbox. A mage could use more than mere lock to protect his treasured possessions. That is, of course, assuming they got that far into his domain.

A set of shelves and an armoire of oak, that matched the chest, contained various small caskets and mysterious boxes, not to mention a large selection of books, scrolls and curiosities. Among them beautiful elven and human antiques and a very rare statue of a swooping eagle from one of the Helmerri troll tribes, a gift from the Shaman with whom he had forged a friendship some years past. Archos was a collector, believing such items should be preserved. The Order often destroyed such historical items, especially if they were of Elven or Trollish origins, thinking them valueless. Many of the rooms were largely uninhabited, save the few that were maintained for the guests he sometimes, but rarely, entertained. Archos mainly kept to his own chambers, the library, the dining room and workshop, which included an area for making potions and medicines if he needed such. The villages in his care were provisioned well enough in the healing arts and the lord of the lands ensured it remained so.

He adored the large gardens, including his beloved enchanted maze; an odd feature, it was said to have a mind of its own, designed by his own hand and the route through known only to a few. The centre of the maze contained a small but airy summerhouse, which was both delightful and very private. The inner gardens were walled, full of rare plants and fragrant all year round. The gardener's hothouses lay within the walls and the man was immensely proud and fiercely protective of his charges.

Behind the manor was a low-walled kitchen vegetable garden, close to the cottage occupied by the housekeeper and gardener. A rather belligerent billy goat named Oscar, his nannies Elva and Mella and kids vied for control of the lawns and the chicken coops with an equally belligerent flock of geese. The large herb garden below the manor's window scented the air with a myriad of medicinal aromas.

The manor was a good distance from the villages but not beyond access, although it was said the route from Harkenen had a will of its own and did not allow those to pass, save those whom it chose. Archos was not remote from his villages and lands, taking an interest in their welfare and providing both wealth and protection for them, unlike many of his fellow noblemen. In return they protected him, and his privacy in a land where a mage could be hunted on a single word.

The paddock and stables lay just beyond the main gardens and Archos had a number of good and well-tended horses, both for riding and to pull the carriage housed in the stable shed. The feisty, spirited stallion of dark grey named Storm was his favourite, a beast who so far allowed no one but Archos onto his back, although Olek was considered worthy enough to lead the proud mount. Olek too had a mount he favoured, a fast young gelding of chestnut, Shadow, and there were a number of others for the use of the household and rare guests. Personally, Archos preferred to ride but the carriage had its uses, especially for privacy. Both the Archmage and his confidante liked animals; Olek always said he tended to prefer them to people. Animals rarely disappointed, did not hate or betray and held no prejudice.

* * *

Archos pulled his boots off and lay upon the bearskin covering the bed, gazing into the fire and contemplated his next move. Olek knocked and entered with a tray containing a dish of stew, bread and a bottle of wine. Setting it down, he scrutinised his master. "My lord, you need to eat and rest. You work too hard. I see something troubles you? Shall I pack to leave?"

The Archmage dipped his bread in the broth and ate thoughtfully. He looked at his manservant and friend, his silver-grey eyes distant. "Yes, although I need divination to find her. I have not seen Power such as that in one so young! So much untrained Power and such beauty! Something calls to me from her… I felt her Power from across the Arcane Realms. I must find her before the Witch-Hunters do so."

Olek nodded. Although not a mage, he had known Archos for many years; owed him his own life and had pledged it to his lord, thus he knew the man's whims and caprices, his desires and needs, better than any other. The half-elf was independent enough to speak his mind were it necessary, a fact Archos appreciated. He had not, however, before seen the faraway look in his master's eyes, but he noted also the look of steely determination.

"I shall prepare to travel then, Master. I will also clear up the…mess in your workshop."

Archos chuckled, "Oh yes, please do! I will need some supplies, I think. I'll write a list for you."

Bowing slightly, Olek left to go about his tasks. He thought back to the time twenty or so years ago when he had met Archos: Olek had been a thief and a good one too, however not good enough it seemed, and he found himself in the cells in the city of Varlek, condemned to hang. The Witch-Hunters had not taken kindly to those who plundered the pockets of others and indeed still did not. Particularly if those with light fingers were of an elven persuasion. Archos had appeared and paid his captors, buying his release and his life. Olek had been told the nobleman needed a manservant whom he could trust to carry out his wishes, to carry out those duties that utilised the skills of one of Olek's…talents. The thief had been in no position to refuse.

Devoted to his master, Olek was deeply fond of Archos. Theirs was a complex friendship, and he believed he could call it that, with respect and affection on both sides and many shared secrets and dark histories. He knew the mage sometimes had odd needs and requirements, and he knew that Archos trusted him beyond anyone else to source certain items and equipment. Olek believed the Archmage was lonely. There had been a few women and now and then a man or two, but most merely passing affairs, and he knew magic could be a lonely art to those who did not understand. If necessary there were always partners to be found for the right price in the more fashionable establishments of the city. Never had Olek seen the look Archos had given when he spoke of the mysterious young mage.

Archos did not see the need for many servants. Being away or in his study a good deal, it seemed rather pointless. He liked to be private and those he employed were trusted and loyal, but his needs were few and he did not like to be fussed over, being an independent sort. The housekeeper Marrissa and her husband, the groundskeeper known to everyone as Old Thomas, were elderly, having served Archos for many years. They lived peacefully with their strange and largely silent but beloved son who, Archos said, could make even barren land grow. Mathias tended to the heavier work his father was unable to manage, happy and simple in his needs. Unaware and unheeding of the world beyond his little part of it, but content and hard-working in the small part of it in which he existed, he neither wanted nor needed more. The young man was gentle, his mind at once both very simple and complex. He spoke little, in a strange language of his own and a series of simple signs, yet those who knew him understood. He had a way with plants that was unparalleled and seemed happiest when tending them, avoiding people but those at the manor. Archos protected the young man from a world he did not and could not understand, and Mathias and his family served his lordship loyally and fondly.

Any other servants needed could be hired from the villages within his domain. The villagers adored him and were a good deal more tolerant of both magic and elves than many from the other domains. An elven village lay within the part of Shimmering Forest which bordered the Tremellic Valley and elves were perhaps more common here than in most other places, and certainly treated with more respect. Trading and a relative peace tended to be the norm, a quiet valley surrounded by forest, river, hills and mountains, somewhat distant from the "mainland" of the plains and hills. In places, the Shimmering Forest crossed the Valley Road and even the Great Highway. Not even the Order of Witch-Hunters could truly tame the ancient great forest, although they tried. Tremellic was prosperous and largely self-sufficient.

Although traders came from the plains relatively frequently, the valley was often left alone, something which suited Archos and villagers both.

Archos did not entertain a good deal. He did not enjoy associating with the other nobles, so a large household was not necessary to his needs. Besides, servants gossiped and Olek knew there were many secrets hidden which needed to remain so. There were the usual, more mundane enemies a man of wealth and power acquired, and Witch-Hunters were what Archos described as "an inconvenience," if and when they were foolish or brave enough to set foot in the area, which was not often, due to the bribes paid and the remoteness of it. Olek was also well aware that Lord Archos had powerful friends to call upon should he need to. Olek himself was not short of contacts and those that owed him a number of favours.

The day to day running of the villages was the task of the Steward. This man had also been one of Archos' finds, a forger and fence of some note, rescued from the gallows of a small border town. Olek grinned. Steward Simon was one of the most trustworthy men he had known, in the given value of trust as it pertained to Archos; of course, the villagers had no idea of the past of their Steward. These lands were among the safest and most prosperous in the realm, thus he doubted they cared. Simon was well liked and a very able Steward, managing the lands with care and discretion. Occassionally his other talents came into play. It never hurt to have a supply of forged papers at one's discretion.

Olek returned to his own rooms, not as finely furnished as his master's, but fine none the less. The walls were polished wood and a few colourful drapes hung around. The bedchamber was warm and comfortable, with well-made, dark furniture. One wall held a small case of books, another with an armoire and cabinet, armour stand and shelves with small wooden boxes, ornaments and trinkets. A bottle of green glass stood on the low rosewood table by the bed, with a pitcher of green glazed pottery and goblet. A few sturdy chests were stored carefully. Locked, of course but Olek was no fool – the locks which could be seen were not the only ones. A thief kept his own belongings secure.

The room beyond the bedchamber was small and filled with the various tools of poison-making, alchemy and weapon craft. A well-stocked desk and bench took up most of the space, an alembic and a number of glass bottles stood on the shelves that lined the walls. There was also a small room Olek used for a dining room and private parlour if he did not wish to eat in the main dining room. Archos could be generous when the mood took him. He had a taste for beautiful objects and things of quality, and had finely decorated the whole house. Olek knew well enough of the Enclaves in which the urban elves were forced to live, and he knew that for an elf to live in such luxury was extremely rare. Thinking back to his years of poverty, his years of having nothing but that which he could steal, Olek was extremely grateful.

The blades of the curved drakemetal swords did not shine; they were the blades of an assassin and a thief. With care, he began to sharpen the weapons, taking his time. He packed carefully, various items being hidden in the many secret pockets of his cloak and his pack. Then removed the drakescale armour from its stand in the corner and checked it over. It was good quality and well cared for but he knew that unnoticed damage could be fatal. He removed the crossbow from its space in the cabinet; small but deadly, it was enchanted and lethal over a short range. He carefully folded back the arms and slid a bolt home, settling it in the niche in the bracers of his armour. He selected the silver flask filled with the strong powerful brandy he favoured and secreted it in his cloak with the other items.

Fetching a travelling chest Olek tossed in a few items they would need for the journey, leaving plenty of space for any magical accoutrements Archos wished to bring. Taking the keys from their secret place beneath a stone before the fire, a stone which looked very much like its fellows, he pulled the panel away on the dresser in the drawing room, rooting around until he found the small drawer and, unlocking it by feel, pulled a metal box from within. Removing several gems, he returned the bag and its box to the secret place. Sometimes this portable wealth was simply easier to deal with than a bag of coin.

* * *

Archos woke after a fitful sleep. Dressing in fresh clothes, he washed and made his way to the library. It was large and well stocked and he immediately headed to the concealed door in a distant corner, selecting a couple of books both for reference and leisure. Furnished with glowglobes and a number of chaise and armchairs, the room was comfortable and light. Indoor plants stood in fine pots around the edges of the shelves. A fireplace sat under a large mantel piece above which was a large mirror reflecting back the image to a mirror on the opposite wall, creating an illusion of a vast room of books and tomes. Books lined the other walls from floor to ceiling, and large bookcases in the centre held scrolls and ancient parchments. The parquet floor was covered in soft rugs and furs. The library was possibly the best stocked and well looked after in the land, and almost certainly contained the most books of magic. Archos had lived a long time and collected a good deal. He liked to read and found the library restful. Books were rare, most people could not read, and if they could were unable to afford books to read for leisure. Archos liked to preserve the past, and he had, more than once, risked life, limb and liberty to acquire these tomes.

A circular inlaid table sat to one side upon which lay a chequered board of black jet and white marble squares. The edges were decorated with ivory and jade pattern-work. The Cs'zibo set lay in mid game, the red pieces of the mages having the advantage over the black of the Witch-Hunters. Nearby to one of the chaise was an Elvish Harp, rarely played but an impressive piece nonetheless.

Setting the books carefully upon the workbench in his workshop, he went to the cabinet and selected another large shell, carved with runes, a small crystal bottle and a ewer of clear spring water. Taking up a polished bowl with a shallow lip, he set it in the centre of the Circle upon a tripod and filled it with water. Fetching the obsidian kris, he laid that next to the other items. Archos walked the Circle that glowed in the centre of the room and dragged his staff along the edges, leaving a trail of pale blue flame. Crossing to the workbench, Archos retrieved the other items and set them on the floor nearby.

Pouring a few drops of the pale liquid from the crystal bottle into the bowl, he took the strand of hair he had collected and coiled it slowly into the water. He sliced into his palm and dropped a few drops of blood into the water. The blood made small scarlet stains in the water that swirled and twisted. "I am Archos, Lord of the Arcane Realms. Grant me the power to seek the owner of this hair, grant me the vision of her, show me, guide me," said he.

The water bubbled then stopped, suddenly turning silver and reflecting like a mirror. Within the reflection, he saw the young red haired elf, alone. A shiver passed across him and he gripped the edge of the bowl. A deep desire filled him as he touched the edge of the water, feeling a spark. Archos saw the Witch-Hunters circling the young woman, he saw them chase her down and the Witch-Net cover her, he saw the Baneblade strike her. Feeling his heart race wildly, he almost felt her pain as the blade tore her shoulder. His fingers tightened on the edge of the bowl and thunder rumbled outside around the hills. As she fell, he saw the Witch-Hunter grab her, try and force himself on her…a circle of flame rippled from the young mage, making the horses rear in shock and the leaves on nearby trees whipped as though in a strong wind as the screaming Witch-Hunter fell in flames.

The Power blew through the workshop, fluttering the leaves of the tomes and swirling the Archmage's robes, making him stagger back. Bottles clattered to the floor, smashing glass and spilling contents. Blue flames roared along the line of the Circle. The water bubbled, sending furious spirals of steam and strange mists around the room. Archos found himself sweating and breathing heavily as he glanced around at the carnage.

Olek heard the crash and arrived at a run, flinging the door open to see the Circle flaring madly. He watched as Archos tried to calm the Circle. Raising his staff, he drew in tendrils of arcane mist as he limped slightly back towards the scrying bowl.

"Show me," he growled, motioning Olek across the Circle as it calmed. The water bubbled again with a bluish steam. Pouring in more of the spring water, he saw a stone tower sited upon a hill. The banners of the Order of Witch-Hunters fluttered in the breeze. Archos clutched again at the edges of the bowl, blood dripping from his fingers and pain shot though him, as the bowl cracked in half, spilling the contents.

He limped to one of chairs and sank into it saying, "You saw the tower? We must find her, although from what I saw she would not fall easily. We must find her! She has much Power, so much talent, so much life and beauty. They will not take it from her if I can prevent it!"

"Master…I know of only one Order prison in such a location as that: Magebane Rock. It is some distance from here, however. We do not even know she is there, I could be mistaken as there may be another." Olek replied carefully, concerned at the chaos of the workshop and the look that had crossed Archos' face.

Archos clenched his hand over the arm of the chair. "She is there or will be. Do you have any idea what they will do to her? Scrying is not a definite art, but we must heed its Power. I need to pack some items, make to leave in three hours. If we can find where she has come from, we may be able to intercept."

Olek bowed and left to prepare as Archos looked around through the devastation of his workshop, picking out a few salvageable items. He dowsed the Circle and packed what he thought he would need. Leaning on the staff and concentrating, murmuring a few words, he grinned as he felt the power of K'hlak course down his arm. The stave was of ancient oak with a demon bound within, a bargain which had been hard fought many years past and of which Archos still bore the scar, now it suited them both.

The staff was tall and held a large, deep, dark blue crystal, which glowed with an odd light, set in claws of silver and with a sharp point. A formidable weapon, even without the magic, it had served him well. As he told Olek, several feet of ancient oak with a spike at one end and a heavy crystal at the other could provide someone with a seriously bad day. He scribbled a note to his Steward to arrange fresh horses on their route and for the carriage to wait by the way-point to the forest roads and the fast route home. They rode through the night, seeking a mage in the midst of a Witch-Hunter fort.

* * *

Ulric Tremayne had travelled for many days and was disconsolate in his failure to find Dii. He had promised his mother to send word and he did. Stopping at a way-point, he scribbled a note: "Mother…the business which takes me from home is proving more of a challenge than I anticipated. I will continue to pursue until it is fruitless to do so. I have a notion of where she might have gone. I am well enough and it does me good to see the lands that will be mine."

A few days later, the way-point rider arrived at Reldfield Manor and delivered the message, handing it to the servant. As the half-elf took it from the rider, Lord Joset Tremayne, Lord of Reldfield, apprehended the servant.

"What is this?" he spluttered. "A message for Malana? What means this that my mistress receives a note?"

The half-elf bobbed a bow. "I know not, my lord. Should I fetch the Mistress

Malana?"

Joset grunted and tore the note open. Recognising his son's hand and seal, he dismissed the servant. Reading, he muttered to himself and strode angrily to the solar where Malana sat. He thrust the note into her face. "So, you have become a liar now? I have here a note from my son. I think you know to what it refers? Ulric has taken Dii away to pursue some business, has he? This note would seem to deny that. I expect you have some other explanation?"

Malana started, "I…I am sorry. I thought it for the best. Ulric will find her and return her. Let him have her for his plaything. You know he desires that. He will need an heir and is not yet married. She is young and clever; let her bear his sons that your house continues in its strengths. She is young and was frightened when you were angry. She thought you would punish her or turn her out. Dii would never seek to offend you but in error."

Joset pulled her up by the hair and spat in reply, "Give my only son to that elf whore, taint my noble blood with that of an elf, you jest surely? He can take her any time he wishes, for she is but property. Perhaps she would be more fertile than you, my dear; only one son living and an infant daughter stillborn. Why is that? Perhaps when my son returns her, I should take the girl in your place…as my official whore… not just the pretty little fuck she is."

"My lord…my love, I have been at your side for nearly thirty years. I have turned a blind eye to your other…entertainment. I have born you a strong fine son and mourned that he is the only child of your blood. Dii is young and knows nothing of the world, where can she go? What can she do but return?" She bit back tears, knowing well his wrath when thwarted.

He dragged her onto her knees. "Perhaps if the little slut returns, I will teach her discipline, teach her who is master in this house. She will obey me, she will submit to me and, by the gods, she will fuck who I choose for her without question. If she does not, I will give her to the Witch-Hunters for their sport and simply find another slave. You, my lying mistress, will also learn that I do not take kindly to deceit. You will make amends to me, in any manner I choose. If I am not satisfied, you will return to poverty in the Enclave I took you from. Do not forget that all you have here is at my whim. I can just as easily remove the fine things which surround you, the freedoms and protections you get from the Order. Now you will please me…bitch."

Later, some of Lord Joset Tremayne's contacts received word to seek out word of a tattooed, red-haired elven mage.

CHAPTER 5

Magebane Fort sat upon an escarpment backed by a rock of black flecked with blue. The fort was relatively small, having once, many generations past, been the ancestral home of a family now long passed into history. The keep remained surrounded by a sturdy wall fifteen feet high, and contained a gate raised from inside. In case there was any doubt of the owner, the Arms of the Order hung above the gatehouse. Arrow slits were sited in each wall and the gate house was guarded. A nearby village catered to any needs the Order requested, whether the village liked it or not.

* * *

The screams of the red-haired mage echoed around the cell. Her blood fell like rain upon the floor and the burn of the Banecrystal Shackles tore through her, a pain like fire which dragged the magic from her in the most painful way possible. The whip that had torn through her clothes, leaving her in mere rags and soaked with her blood, splattered that blood across the dark stone of the cold cell. Her pale skin was torn and sticky, her hair matted, and a bruise marred her pretty face with purple. The wound in her shoulder dripped blood and the poison was slowly creeping through her, weakening, draining. Mages had died from Banecrystal and the Order knew it. This was their most feared weapon for those with magic in their blood. Dropping the whip at his feet, the Witch-Hunter dragged her across the floor to the bench at the wall before tossing her across it. As his companions watched, he snarled, "Bitch… little Witch whore, you will pay manifold for the death of the man you murdered with your filthy magic. We will have much sport with you before we are done."

Holding her down, he forced himself into her, until the darkness finally overwhelmed the young mage. Her Astral Self screamed into the arcane mists, casting her pain into both the mundane and magical worlds.

* * *

Lying on his belly in the shadows of a small copse of trees, Olek watched. The carriage was hidden at the way-point in readiness but was still distant enough to be a damn risky run. It was early evening and the sun was obligingly hiding itself in the low grey clouds. He saw a couple of mounted Witch-Hunters leave the gatehouse to go about their business and as he watched, he noticed a mailed guard slip around the far side of the wall outside. Olek silently rose to his feet and cast a look at Archos waiting amongst the trees. Motioning a circle, he crept forward to the edge of the trees and waited a moment.

Leaning on his staff, Archos looked to the sky, considering the weather with a satisfied grin. A faint blue glow like marsh gas began to ripple just above the ground. Removing the dagger from his belt, he slashed his arm and dripped blood within the Circle until a small pool of crimson had appeared. "I am Archos, Lord of the Arcane Realms. I am Archos, Lord of the Elements. I am Archos, the Oncoming Storm. This night I call to my will the forces of nature, of wind and rain, of light and dark, of wood and stone; that we may succeed in our endeavour."

The sky began to darken, and in the half-light, Olek too grinned. Drawing one of his swords, he melted into the darkness as he pulled the shadows around him. Shadowplay had saved his hide more times than he cared to remember and he was a master at it. Slowly he crept around the walls, pausing at the gate house until the guard focused his attention elsewhere and Olek ran past. Even someone as adept at Shadowplay as Olek could sometimes be spotted if someone looked directly at him, knew what to look for or had an enchanted item that revealed the Shadowplayer but most people simply did not register the shape sliding past. Olek slipped around unseen to discover a small postern door in the far wall.

The half-elf's excellent hearing picked up voices behind the old wooden door. Carefully he examined the lock and hinges, assessing the strength of difficulty of the lock. Silently he stood until the voices moved further away and then, scrutinising the area, he noticed a worn trail to some trees and signs revealing it was a favoured spot for the occupants of the fort to nip out for a crafty smoke of the bitter tobacco liked in these parts. Olek knew from long experience that soldiers were much the same, whether they were Witch-Hunter, mercenary or guardsman, and for this he was grateful.

Olek had wondered if Archos was able to obfuscate the carriage and horses, but had been informed that although theoretically it was possible with a lot of time and a great deal of Power, it would likely scare the horses half to death. Horses were canny creatures and would likely not take kindly to being enchanted. Archos said he was not prepared to risk a difficult and untested spell when they were being chased by Witch-Hunters. Besides, he had a plan. They would just have to risk the run.

As it grew steadily darker, he could see the storm clouds rolling in and felt the heavy air around him. Archos stood in the Circle, the blue flames roaring around him as he called the storm to his bidding. Above him hovered a deep, dark sphere almost black in intensity but interspersed by flashes of light. Even in the gloom it was dark, sucking in what light remained. Archos was dripping blood from the gash in his arm and his Focus was on gathering the storm and holding it. His breath was fast and he was sweating with the effort, such magic as this was far from easy.

"Well, have you found us a way in? I cannot hold this storm indefinitely," the Archmage growled to Olek, who had scurried back to him.

"Postern door around the side, should be easy enough to open. They aren't clever enough to fit a decent lock and don't expect attack in such a manner. After all who has the audacity to break INTO an Order fort, my lord? I heard people inside close by, two maybe three, a smokers' path, nothing special. It is quite a distance, though. You will want me to bandage that arm, unless you want to leave a trail of blood?"

Summoning his Power once more, Archos Focused and the mini storm shrunk to a marble sized ball as the sweat glistened on his forehead. "No… It is fine… I have it contained now. Come, let us do this." Leaning against the tree until his vision cleared, he settled the storm over his staff and absently healed his arm.

"You are sure of this, Master? You know I respect you above all men and I respect your judgement, but we are infiltrating an Order fort, full of Witch-Hunters. You have…looked better. That storm is only just contained."

Archos looked to the fort in the darkness and his eyes glowed silver. "I can feel her… I can feel her pain. She is here, I am sure. Besides…stealing a captive mage from under the gaze of the Order has a somewhat satisfying irony to it, do you not agree? I have been idle in matters too long. If you wish to stay here, I would not force you to go," he said with a grim smile.

Olek grinned. "Stay here? You surely jest? Even were I the sort of man who would let his friend and master do something so utterly reckless alone, I could not resist going for the sheer spectacle of the thing. I am, as always, your friend and your servant, and I await your bidding, my lord. Now it is dark enough that we can cross the way safely enough. Somehow I doubt the Witch-Hunters employ elves or half-elves with night vision to spot us, at least not willing ones. Keep in close to me and go where I go, just to be sure."

The Archmage smiled and briefly gripped Olek's arm, then followed him closely through the darkness. The sky was starless and the moon not yet risen. The darkness fell around them and nothing stirred. An eerie silence hung in the air. Olek thought it was the quiet before the storm, or a forest holding its breath, either way it would serve them this night. He could feel the Power around him, the effort needed to maintain such Power, to contain and control a storm by will alone. Olek knew enough of magic from his years of being at his master's side to know that magic demanded a price. He glanced behind him at the silent Archmage whose concentration was on containing the storm he held. Stopping close to the door, the half-elf gently put his hand on

Archos' arm. "Wait, let me see to the lock. Can you see well enough in this light? Your eyes are better than most."

Leaning against the wall, Archos could feel the pull of the storm he held, he could feel the pain swirling through him, a strange disjointed discomfort at this distance. As Olek began to deftly pick the lock, Archos shifted his Focus slightly to try and search for her. He felt the astral mists, coldly clinging to him.

"Grant me Astral Sight this night to lead me to her, let me find her light in the darkness of the Realms of Magic and this place of pain and corruption," he murmured, using the wall for support.

Archos pictured her in his mind…the flickering image he had seen. His Astral Self touched the trail she left, the pale light like a thread; he let it run across his hand and felt its fragility. It was rapidly weakening. As he felt her trail swirl around him, his heart began to beat faster and his breathing quickened, partly through the sheer Power he was using and partly through the deep attraction that seemed to draw him in. He felt her pain along the thread, a deep searing pain that filled him to his core. He gasped a cry as the agony she felt crept through every muscle.

Olek looked around, pausing as Archos' eyes glowed silver in the darkness and the storm he held began to spin faster and expand above him. "Hurry. I have her thread… It is weak, failing. Time is short," the Archmage murmured.

As the lock clicked, Olek hissed, "Ready?" and swung the door open.

Before them lay a corridor lit by the flickering light of torches on the wall. Ahead lay another, and as the door opened, two mailed Witch-Hunters who were standing and conversing spun round. "Hey, what the fuck?" the first yelled in surprise.

Olek moved like a cat and covered the ground before the man had even drawn his sword, burying one of his blades deep into the man's chest. The other turned around to strike and found himself slammed into the wall. Archos pinned him there, stronger than the Witch-Hunter had anticipated. "Where is she? Where is the red-haired elf?" The growl deep and low, full of the rage of the storm. A terrible sound in the otherwise quiet corridor.

The Witch-Hunter spat, "I know not of any red-haired mage, Sorcerer. One shout and the entire fort will be roused. Can you take us all, you and your elf?"

Slowly, Archos began to release the storm. Lightning crackled, leaping from his fingertips. With a voice that was as dark as the storm he held, and as dangerous, he snarled, "You lie. I can strip the thoughts and the memories from your mind. I can fill you with a pain you could not endure. You will tell me where she is or I swear by the gods I will place this storm within you until it rips you apart. I will get the information I require. How is up to you. As for your friends… Well, that would certainly be an interesting test of my Power…but I suspect the odds would be in my favour. However my time is short and I do not feel like such games this night." Archos pushed him harder against the wall. "If you wish your companions to fall to my wrath, that is entirely your choice; can they fight the Oncoming Storm? Now where is the girl?"

The Witch-Hunter felt the pain in his head, the fury of the elements and the unpredictability of the storm. The man trembled, realising he was no match for what stood before him. "Down…in the cells…in the cells…down to the left…large wooden door…please…let me go. I have a wife…children."

"So? That was a consideration, was it, when you tortured the mages you found? Mercy is not something found within these walls, so here is no mercy from the Storm."

The man shook in the iron grip of the Archmage. The rage of the storm boiled the man's blood, cutting off the scream before it began. Dropping the dead man, he motioned onward. Olek stepped forward, his swords drawn and the shadows playing around him. He had never seen Archos this angry or this hell bent on his purpose. This night, Olek was afraid, but he mustered his courage and moved forward, swirling the shadows before him and aware of the powerful storm at his back. The passage led down steep stone steps and a couple more unsuspecting Witch-Hunters met death at Olek's blades.

"There! A large wooden door," he pointed out. "Hmm, that lock looks rather moredifficult than its predecessor, it will take me a little longer, Master. It would seem at least within they have sense to secure their prison." Olek crouched and glared at the lock as if willpower alone could defeat it. Selecting a long, thin pick-lock, the thief went to work. As he listened for the click, he thought could hear whimpering from inside. He hoped to the gods the girl was here and still alive, he did not relish being in close proximity to the angry storm if it were otherwise.

Archos leaned against the wall, the cold stone cutting through the heat he felt within him. He felt exhausted from the sheer Power of maintaining the storm and splitting his Focus, and the pain that seemed to fill his being. It was a strange dragging pain that was both within him and surrounding him. He heard the lock click in the silence and opened his eyes as Olek opened the door and peered inside. "Bloody hell! I have found her…"

The brutality of the Witch-Hunters was clearly in evidence on the young woman: unconscious, bloody, bruised, molested, what remained of her clothing in bloody rags. Olek began to unpack the bag, fetching bandages and a blanket as Archos crouched next to her, his rage suddenly tempered by concern.

"Can you save her?" Olek asked quietly. Rarely had he seen such a pitiful sight.

"Get those bloody Shackles from her. I can do nothing until then."

Olek began to pick the locks, wincing as he saw the Banecrystal-infused metal burn her skin. His hands were gloved, but as he worked, his wrist brushed them and he felt the burn in his adept elven blood. Eventually he freed her and as the magic draining burn receded a little, her dark blue eyes flickered open for a moment. Trying to flinch, the pain of her wounds coursed through her and she whimpered again like a wounded animal, a terrible soulful sound that cut into Archos as he squatted close.

"My poor broken beauty, what have they done to you? Come to me; give me your pain, now you are safe." As his Power touched hers, he felt the strange, if faint, pull she seemed to have, but could feel her falling away from him. Suddenly the pain hit him full on, making him rock back and almost lose his balance. For a moment his vision swam and he felt close to passing out. As he recovered, he stroked her hair, trying to comfort her and murmuring softly.

The Archmage channelled a healing spell, and wove comfort and warmth into it, surrounding the frail form in his Power as Olek quickly bound the worst of her wounds in silence. The storm he held rippled around them, as his Power and consciousness moved between the spells and the worlds of magic and reality. Splitting his Focus as he shifted to Astral Sight, he touched the thin fragile thread of her trail which hovered weakly in the Arcane Realms.

"Come to me, my petal. I have you now, trust me, I will not let you fall…" Feeling the thread of her unravelling, he summoned up more Power. "Come to me…you must help me. Use your Power…come to me…be mine and I can give you everything."

Slowly he felt the thread gain strength and her form shimmered in front of his Astral Self. Touching her, he felt the young mage's Power. As he began to shift back, he felt it momentarily swirl around him. Slipping his Focus back, he shut his eyes and hoped that would clear the pounding in his head. Archos channelled another healing spell into the young woman and leaned back against the wall, saying, "Give me a moment… I nearly lost her. I have done what I can, but she is far from safe here. The wounds are severe and the magical healing will take time with her injuries and the Shackles that held her. Even now, I am not sure she will live. Gods know how much of that damn Banecrystal poison is in her. We need to move fast. When she is in the carriage, I can work on her there and I can rest. Once we have her safe, drive and stop for nothing. The storm will be behind us. That should keep them occupied. I am fatigued and cannot hold the storm much longer."

The staff hovered nearby; Archos muttered something as it floated to his command. He tossed it across his back, where it was easy to reach and he could release it with a word. Gently, he wrapped Dii in the blanket and lifted her in his arms. For a moment, his vision swam again and he breathed heavily, gasping in air to try and clear his head. Glancing down, he smiled at the soft form and felt her Power, weak as she was, flutter around him. Never had he felt such an attraction and longing for any creature; nor quite such a resolute Power and strength in one so young and untrained.

"Do you wish me to take her?" Olek said with concern, noting Archos' pale countenance.

"No... No, I have her now," Archos replied softly and motioned him towards the door. Olek saw the look on his face, which said nothing would part them now.

Olek stepped into the passage, relieved to be out of the cell. Moving quickly, he led them back towards the door. Archos followed with only a fraction of his attention on where they were going. He was tired and knew he needed his magic for a while longer. As he walked, he trailed the storm behind him and slowly unravelled. Out in the darkness, he let it go and suddenly the full fury of the storm was allowed to rage.

"Run," he breathed. "Run now!" Although by now his muscles ached and were not too obliged to respond without protestation.

They ran as the clouds raged in the sky and released rain in huge drops that froze. Whipping water determined to soak everything it could find, it was a rain that obscured the vision and chilled the bone. Wind roared in from the south, battering the banners and slamming the casements of the upper windows, raining glass in shards. The storm twisted in a tempest in the courtyard, sucking up stones and wood and slamming them into walls, ground and people without prejudice. Angry clouds spat forked lightning, cleaving the sky like the vengeance of the gods and grounded within the walls of the fort and on the roof, splitting tiles and bringing fire even in the driving rain.

As they reached the coach, the horses skittered in fear and Olek pulled the door open and jumped up, almost dragging Archos and the girl inside. He hastily pulled one of the soft rugs onto the floor, then leapt out and up to the seat as the thunder rolled and lightning sliced the air just behind them. Archos would trust no one else to drive in such a situation, and besides Simon had business elsewhere. The horses began to run in fear and it took all Olek's skill to bring them under control enough to steer. Looking behind him, he saw mayhem. The roof burned and he could hear the sounds of panicked men and terrified horses, even at this distance. Three mounted riders rode out of the fort towards them. As the carriage picked up speed, he steered it to the forest trail.

Archos heard the storm rage and the frail breathing of the girl beside him. He flipped up the window and grinned when he saw the chaos of the storm unleashed. He felt a little hollow for having held the storm for so long and he saw the horses panic as thunder rolled close. The hoof beats behind them grew closer and he knew Olek was struggling to control the carriage as it rocked and bucked around him. As they approached the forest path, he looked down at Dii and gently he touched her, feeling her Power even now and it gave him strength.

"I bloody well hope you have a plan, my lord, those riders are gaining on us, our horses are terrified and your storm seems bent on killing everything!" Olek screamed back to him.

Closing his eyes, Archos tried to calm himself and summon the Power he needed. "Just drive for the gap in the trees, off the road," he yelled back.

Olek looked around in the darkness and the mayhem of the storm. "Gap? What gap? Oh gods, if it was any man but you I would think you mad. I hope you have Power enough left for this."

"So do I, my friend," muttered the Archmage.

As the trees rapidly approached, Archos drew his Power and slammed his staff into the floor. "Wood to my will, let us pass where there is no gateway. Wood to my will, hide us from sight!" he cried into the darkness and the rapidly approaching trees.

As the spell ended, a gap appeared as branches turned and trees bent aside. The carriage plunged into the dark wood as the greenery slammed back behind them. With that, Archos blacked out.

CHAPTER 6

Witch-Hunter Commander Robin Thomason stood at the edge of the forest and scowled. "Vanished? Bloody great carriages pulled by four horses do not just vanish without trace. Are you mad?"

One of the Witch-Hunters shuffled awkwardly. "It was there, racing towards the trees, not even on the road and suddenly the forest swallowed it. No tracks, no evidence just beyond the trees, nothing, just gone."

Commander Robin glared at him. "So you are telling me, someone breaks into the fort, steals a mage from the cells, kills a good number of Witch-Hunters, then flees into the forest in astorm from the wrath of the sky gods and disappears. Does that sound like magic to anyone else here or just me?

"Have you even bothered to look for tracks in the forest? It is a bloody carriage and four, I sincerely doubt it can fly, although after the events of this night I am questioning many things," he snapped at the uncomfortable and soaked Witch-Hunters.

One of his men looked nervous. "In there? But there are bears, wolves, elves."

Robin pinned him against a tree. "Oh, bears and wolves and elves! You are a bloody Witch-Hunter, man! The scourge of magic! Not a simpering girl, although it would appear I could be mistaken in that. Trust me when I tell you this. A hungry, blood-crazed bear will be a walk in the valley compared to what I will do to you if you do not go and check for tracks!" the commander screamed at the now trembling man.

He turned and looked at the fort; five Witch-Hunters dead, the horses still panicked, and what remained of the roof still smoking slightly. It had not been a good night. "I would also like to know how they got in. You do know the good name of the Order Of Witch-Hunters has been sullied this night. If word gets out that we were unable to contain one young, inexperienced Witch, how do you think this will affect our reputation? I want to know who did this."

Mounting his horse and leaving his men to squirm, Robin returned moodily to his post.

* * *

Olek finally managed to steer the horses back onto the forest path. He was an experienced coachman, but managing to steer four terrified horses across a path that did not exist was no mean feat. Slowing them, he crooned words of comfort and eventually the carriage rolled to a stop. Jumping down, he leaned against the edge of the carriage and removed the flask from his cloak for a long drink, then pulled open the door. His fear and anger abated with concern as he saw Archos unconscious. "Oh shit…" he muttered.

Clambering onto the roof, he pulled down the travelling trunk. Rummaging frantically for the key, he flipped open the lid and pulled out an assortment of bottles, finally locating the pale blue bottle he needed and removing the stopper. Olek scrambled inside and gently pulled his master's head onto his knees, pouring the contents of the bottle into his mouth.

Archos woke, choking. He felt as weak as a kitten and his head pounded. For a moment, he had no idea where he was, or for that matter 'who' he was.

"Never ever do that to me again! I thought that last spell had been too much," Olek said quietly, his voice filled with relief.

Archos sat up, leaning against Olek. "I am sorry, my friend. I will try not to make a habit of it," he said weakly, grasping Olek's arm with fondness. "We should move… the girl…she needs further attention…take us home, my dear Olek."

Olek looked with concern at the pale Archmage, nodding slowly. "Next time you decide to pull off a trick like plunging the carriage into a gap that does not exist, please inform me so that I may have a spare pair of breeches handy." He grinned as Archos managed a smile. "At least we are on the road now, and that should make things easier. May I suggest we rest up at the White Hare? They are friendly to us and will not ask questions, then perhaps the Steward's, you need rest and food, else you will be no use to the girl."

Archos was too tired to argue the point and waved his hand, then slid onto the floor next to Dii. He touched her gently, easing her wounds and pouring into her the potion that would negate the Banecrystal. "I am sorry, my sweet girl, to cause you more pain, just a little longer then you will be home."

Dii twitched and whimpered, barely conscious and unaware of anything but pain. Slowly the carriage rolled on in the dark forest, leaving no trail.

* * *

A few days later, Witch-Hunter Commander Robin scowled at the man standing before him. "So you say this Witch was the slave…er…the Kept of Lord Joset Tremayne and escaped? He wants her back? Why? What need has he of a captive Witch? Why does he simply not buy another slave?"

The man, a servant of Lord Tremayne of Reldfield, looked the Witch-Hunter in the face. "His woman is fond of the girl apparently, and she brings him in a good amount of gold…if you know what I mean. She is talented and clever. She is no threat to anyone, never allowed off his lands unescorted, never allowed to use her magic. Some of his…er…associates are fond of her and enjoy her, um, talents. She is very alluring and being what she is heightens the attraction. It was rumoured she had been apprehended as a Witch. The Lord Tremayne is wealthy and provides many… services and patronages for the Order."

Robin drummed his fingers on the table, knowing that the woman requested was no longer within Witch-Hunter hospitality. "Lord Tremayne?" he asked. "Hmm… the slaver-lord, yes? Well, we do not have her at present. I will have enquiries made at the other Order facilities. Perhaps you should try looking in the brothels of the city; a talented girl can make money utilising her skills. Tell your lord enquiries will be made."

He dismissed the man and sat in contemplation for a while. So, the little fiery mage was property of the slaver-lord Tremayne. This could bring him in a good deal if he could find her, and he wondered how much she was worth to this lord. Or, perhaps, if her reputation was well deserved, he could keep her for himself until such time as she no longer amused him. Tapping his fingers, he wondered whether the attack on Magebane Fort was linked. No, surely the man would not arrange an attack then request her back. He walked to the map lying on the work desk and contemplated it for some moments. Smiling, he thought to himself, "Lord Archos of Tremellic, perhaps he knows the whereabouts of our little redhead. Tremellic Valley borders the Shimmering Forest. Besides, that man has been a nuisance for too long, it would certainly be to my credit were that bastard removed as a problem. Perhaps I should disrupt his idyllic little valley."

* * *

The village of Harkenen was the largest settlement in the Tremellic Valley and Commander Robin arrived during late afternoon. Witch-Hunters rarely came here and he was unfamiliar with the lands, having had to make enquiries and finding the locals rather unhelpful. "The Steward manages these lands, it seems. Perhaps he may be amenable to providing some information. These provincial stewards are all the same," he said to himself.

The Witch-Hunter rode to the gate in the fence circling Steward Simon Stedfall's small estate. The gardens lay alongside a path of shingle beyond which stood a two storey house of some size. Steward Simon looked out of the window of his homestead to see the mounted man in the livery of the Order of Witch-Hunters beyond the gate.

He was glad Lord Archos and his charge had already safely returned to the manor. Swearing under his breath, he quickly scrawled a note and called his servant. "Take this to the Lord Archos. Use the back ways; don't be seen." He sauntered outside in the afternoon sun, acting as if he had not seen the Witch-Hunter.

"I seek the Steward Simon. I trust you are he?" Robin scrutinised the man before him.

Looking up in mock surprise, Simon replied, "Good afternoon to you, sir. Are you lost? We do not get a visit often from the Witch-Hunters in these parts. They have no need to…trouble our peaceful valley. What is your business here? I am the Steward to his Lordship."

Robin glanced around, thinking this Steward seemed of comfortable means but knowing that such men were often not as honest as might be and open to bribes. "My business is that of the Witch-Hunters; I seek a Witch, a dangerous young elf. She is responsible for the death of Witch-Hunters. Unfortunately, the cunning little whore managed to use her sorcery to evade us. The Order would very much like this individual within our…hospitality."

Simon looked thoughtful for a while, mulling over the words and letting the Witch-Hunter wait for an answer. "A Witch, you say? I know of no Witches here. We are somewhat apart from the other domains and it would be unlikely that she would head this way. Surely she would be better heading to a city where she would be less likely to be noticed and more likely to find employment. I am sure someone would have noticed a Witch in these parts."

"Well, I was hoping to find news of her. The reward for her capture is substantial. Perhaps the lord of these lands will be able to shed some light on the matter?"

"My lord does not often receive visitors. I manage the lands hereabouts in his name, and he is content for it to be thus. He is a man who likes his privacy and does not take kindly to being disturbed. He will not receive you. He would not know of a Witch any better than I. He would not wish for the peace of the valley to be disturbed. If you want my advice, you will conduct your enquiries elsewhere, for you will receive no answers in these lands. There are many hidden dangers for those who are unfamiliar with the area…" Simon said, the threat hovering between them.

Robin raised an eyebrow, yet maintained his composure. "Really?" he questioned. "I thought you said this is a peaceful valley. That sounded like you dare to threaten me."

Simon smiled a smile full of knowing and cunning. "Aye, sir, and we seek to maintain it such, but, well, the Shimmering Forest encroaches close by and a traveller unfamiliar with the roads may simply stray from the path and into danger. That is merely to what I refer. There are ferocious beasts in these regions, we are sometimes troubled by bandits, and the paths can be treacherous. If a man were to wander from the path, it could be many days before he found his way back, or was found…or what was left of him."

Robin was becoming frustrated, "I wish to see the lord of this domain. I am a Commander of the Order of Witch-Hunters, and he cannot deny me!"

"Well, if you say so. Feel free to ride to the gates of his estate and you may tell him that yourself. That should be a most entertaining conversation, if he actually decides to open the gates, that is. Be careful of the path that way, it is somewhat circuitous. Some say its moves of its own accord, sometimes the path does not lie where it seems to." Turning on his heel, Simon returned to his house. Not bothering to look around, he heard the mounted man ride away.

Commander Robin rode for some time along the wooded path, never seeming to get anywhere. In places, the forest seemed *very* close and winding. Eventually he found himself back in the town square. As darkness was falling rapidly, he decided perhaps it would be expedient to follow up the rumours that the attack on the fort was linked to Joset Tremayne and his slaves. The tavern did not seem overly keen to cater to his needs overnight, but Erick the barkeep, being a sensible sort, made sure the man was fed, watered and relatively comfortable. The Witch-Hunter had hoped to overhear some gossip, but news of his presence had obviously gotten around and the tavern was all but deserted. Those who remained were quiet, simply talking about mundane issues. The cloaked figure sitting in the shadows nursing a large flagon of ale made him nervous, although of course the Witch-Hunter would not have admitted that to a living soul. Robin considered challenging the figure, but alone and in somewhere even he noted to be rather hostile, Robin decided against it. Perhaps the watcher was simply enjoying a drink in privacy, he told himself.

The next morning, beginning to wind his way back towards the fort, the Witch-Hunter contemplated a plan, one that suited twin purposes of inconveniencing the mysterious Lord of Tremellic and his precious lands, and also getting his hands on the red-haired slave-girl who was the pet of the slaver-lord. Returning to his quarters at the fort, he settled at his desk and wrote:

My Lord Tremayne,

It would seem you have lost something of value. I may be able to provide some…compensation, far beyond her worth. An elf village lies near the edge of the border with Tremellic Valley and the Jaeden hills, and can be accessed by one of the inlets branching into the Great River or the traders' path into the forest. Easy pickings for a man of your calibre. The only price I ask is that the red-haired Witch becomes my property. She is now damaged and of less value to you. Any mages you acquire are, as always, the property of the Order, but any remaining elves should fetch a good price, more than that whore would. I can be contacted via a note left at the way-point in Jaeden, marked with your seal.

Leaving it unsigned, he sealed it with a plain seal and simply deposited it with the other letters for the way-point riders to collect. Smiling smugly to himself, he went about his business content he had upset the Lord of the Tremellic Valley and secured himself a slave. He had tasted of her charms once in the cells, but he wanted her when she was not bloody and beaten…at least not initially.

Sometime later, the note appeared at Reldfield and found its way into the greedy and corrupted hands of Lord Joset Tremayne.

* * *

Dii awoke from her fever. The strange dreams and visions that had haunted her still clung faintly to her mind, and confusion filled the young mage at waking in a strange place after such an ordeal. She looked around and found herself in a large comfortable bed draped with deep plum velvet. The room was warm and a large vase of white roses filled the air with their perfume. Pleasant light blue brocade draped the walls and a bookcase laden with ornaments and books stood against a far wall. A large chest lay at the end of the bed and a comfortable armchair sat at the edge of the room upon which lay a discarded book.

She found herself dressed in a soft cotton shift and a momentary panic as to why she was dressed as such filled her. Sitting up, she spotted a dark wood dresser, containing fragrant oils and thoughtfully, a bronze comb, a box of ribbons, and other hair ornamentation. The chair before it was comfortable and even in her Keeper's house, she had never seen anything quite so fine.

Desperately thirsty, Dii spied a pitcher of water and glass mug on the table next to the bed and as she reached for it, her trembling hand knocked the mug over.

At the sound, a large elderly human woman entered, her greying hair piled in a large bun pinned atop her head. Simple but well-made clothes with many pockets and a motherly air about her made Dii feel a little more at ease. "Ah, you awaken, my lady. Master will be delighted! I am called Marrissa, I am the housekeeper and at your disposal, my lady. Please let me help you."

Handing her a glass of water, Dii slowly sipped the cool, fresh liquid, noting the sweet taste of it. The woman continued, "There are clothes for you within the chest. I hope they are to your liking, for we did not know your tastes. The master said to set for you a bath if you wish; and then, if you are able, to join him in the dining room for a meal. He asked me to excuse him not being here when you awoke but he is resting. He has watched over you these last few nights until the fever passed into sleep, and he took some rest."

Dii bowed her head. "I thank you for your kindness, Mistress Marrissa. I would very much like a bath, if it does not put you to a great deal of trouble." Slightly overwhelmed, her hand trembled both from the weakness of her sickness and apprehension of her new surroundings.

The old woman smiled in a motherly way. "Of course it does not. Perhaps you would like to finish your water and then see if the clothing is suitable for you whilst I make arrangements. There is a room at the end of the passage containing a bath and I will see it filled and waiting."

Bowing her head, as though Dii were her mistress, the woman turned and left Dii alone to her thoughts and her wonder at the situation. She finished the water and slowly set the glass down. Gingerly, she tried to get to her feet, the room momentarily spinning. Grasping the post of the bed, she waited for the dizziness to abate then walked slowly around the room, her muscles stiff from lack of use, the recent damage and subsequent healing.

Curiosity led her to open the chest to reveal a fine selection of clothes including silk and cotton blouses, wool and calico skirts, and a couple of sets of riding breeches. The colours were bright, and the selection more than she had ever worn, and certainly better quality. Most of the clothes she had previously been attired in were at the whim of her Keeper and his customers as it suited them, or patched and mended hand-me-downs from the other servants. As she took each garment out, laying it on the bed, her eyes widened, unable to believe these might be all for her use as she wished. Breathing a gasp of wonder at such finery for one such as her, she carefully picked out a soft blue blouse, a red skirt patterned with dark blue, and the bodice of crimson, with the soft fur lined boots.

"Your bath is set, my lady. Do you need assistance? When you are refreshed and dressed, myself or Olek, the lord's manservant, will take you to the dining room," Marrissa informed her on returning, smiling broadly when she saw the clothes set out on the bed and the look of astonishment on the face of the young elf.

"These are all for me?" Dii asked, still in disbelief.

"Oh yes, mistress. As I said, I was not sure what you would prefer and the master said you needed new garments. The market here is good and some clothes were ordered from the city. I hope they are suitable."

Dii blushed, no one had ever called her mistress and she did not know what to make of it all. Whispering her thanks, she was led to the bathing chamber.

The bathwater was warm and scented with dried petals, a small shelf contained oils and a small soft bag of oatmeal and herbs. Her fingers ran gently over the rune at the edge and as she touched it, a stream of water flowed. The warmth eased her muscles and the tension she felt ebbed a little. Dii wondered who this mysterious lord was. She had a few vague memories of the last few days, but remembered little after passing out in the cells. What she did remember was pain and the humiliation of the brutal attack, vague and disjointed memories of a handsome man in her dreams

A. L. Butcher

calling to her, soothing her, visions from beyond her fever. Dii shivered despite the warmth of the water and tried to clear her mind of the horror and pain.

* * *

Dii dressed carefully, combing the scented oils through her curls until her hair cascaded around her in a sea of red. She picked a flower from the vase and pinned it to a curl. The scars around her wrists and ankles were still red but the sleeves of the blouse and the hem of her skirts covered the worst. Her muscles ached and she felt weak, fragile like the first snowdrop of the year.

Waiting outside her chamber, Olek smiled as the door opened and a pretty, if nervous, elven face looked out. "I am Olek, miss. I will take you to my lord, who was most pleased to hear you have awakened, as am I." Leading her to the dining room, he bowed his head to the man seated therein and smiled at Dii, leaving her alone with Archos.

Dii saw a handsome human man sitting at ease, his thick, grey-flecked hair was mostly blond and long, falling to the middle of his back. A small neat beard covered his chin and an inscrutable smile played across his lips. He was dressed in a long robe of grey and silver, similar to a long frock coat with many pockets, beneath which he wore a dark grey shirt matching his attractive silver-grey eyes, and deep blue breeches which matched hers, along with a sash of black silk tight around his waist. The large mahogany table was laid with a bowl of soft, fresh bread rolls, giving off a delightful homey smell, a basket containing fruit, a steaming bowl of meat stew, a bottle of wine and a pitcher of spiced cider.

She realised how hungry she was but hesitated as he stood and walked towards her, suddenly unsure of how to behave. Bowing, he said in a soft and strangely alluring baritone, "I am glad to see you up and about."

Gently, he touched her face, tipping it up so he could scrutinise her. As they touched, a bolt like electricity sparked across both of them as Power met Power. Dii gasped and blushed as the Power sent a bolt of the deepest desire and longing through her. Unexpected after all she had suffered.

Archos smiled at the blush and said softly, "My dear, you are well enough, considering, but will be fatigued and sore a while yet. Now it would please me greatly if you would join me for a meal."

Dii blushed again and bowed her head, saying quietly, "I thank you for your kindness and generosity, my lord. What…what should I call you?"

Brushing her cheek, his fingers followed the spiral of her tattoo and made her shiver beneath his touch. He replied, "Archos… You may call me Archos. I am Lord of Tremellic and Archmage of the Arcane Realms. Do not fear. You are safe in my house and my lands. Now, does the pretty elf have a name also?"

"Dii, my lord," she replied quietly, unable to take her eyes from his; feeling the tingle from his touch.

With a soft smile, he tore his gaze from hers and, taking her arm, he led her to a seat. "You should eat. You were gravely ill for some time and you need to regain your strength. Dii? Dii'Athella? It is Elvish. It means Flower of the Dawn…a most fitting name."

Sitting down, she took some bread and a small bowl of the broth as her host returned to his seat. Quietly she replied, "I do not know, lord. I do not remember my elven family. My…foster mother told me that was one of the only words I could say when they…acquired me as a tiny child."

Archos nodded, knowing elven children were often removed from their families, and settled to watch her. The desire for her, and also the pity that such an exquisite creature should be misused and suffer as she had, filled him. After she finished, he walked over to her once again. "I would like to show you around. You cannot have seen anything of the house or gardens."

Escorting her through the house with her hand nestled on his arm, he noticed how his blood raced when she touched him. Dii was quiet and attentive, listening to him speak and looking in wonder at the splendour he showed her. The artefacts, arts and items fascinated her and she asked questions about everything. Unlocking a door, he opened it and showed her inside. Dii gasped and ran forward. Archos laughed with amusement as she spun around with excitement. "So many books, my lord! So much knowledge. I have never seen the like! It is…so beautiful…so wonderful!"

As she smiled and gasped in wonder, he felt he could drown in her smile. This woman seemed to light up the room and he felt another bolt of the deepest desire and affection. Slowly, he walked up close behind her and, with his breath hot on her neck, he said quietly, "I brought you to see this for a reason. All my life I have been seeking a worthy apprentice and have not found one until now. Your Power called to me across the Realms of Magic, drew me to you, yet it is wild and untrained. You have so much Power that you do not know how to use. I would help you to free it, to free yourself. If you consent to be my student and my companion, all this is yours…all I know…everything that is here and more, so much more."

CHAPTER 7

Some weeks had passed and Dii was growing stronger. The Banecrystal scars were still apparent, yet the others had mostly faded. Archos found her to be attentive, clever, and a most excellent pupil. She had a thirst for knowledge that he found enchanting. The young woman spent a good deal of time in the library reading, and sometimes she came to his workshop and sat watching him. Her spell casting was, of course, untrained, yet she had talent and an innate ability that enabled her to learn fast, very fast. Archos taught her many basic spells and techniques, and she absorbed the knowledge easily. They spent many hours together and he was pleased to see her confidence increasing every day.

The first time she had entered the workshop had taken him by surprise, as the Circle flared and crackled when she entered. He realised that his Power was stronger when she was near, but he found it hard to Focus, discovering himself watching her. When they touched, he could feel her Power, and Archos felt a desire and affection for the young elf more deeply than he had ever felt for anyone. Sometimes he saw her watching him, turning those dark, mysterious eyes upon him. As the time passed, she became ever closer, and the touches and glances lingered longer. Dii smiled at him and for him, yet he could still see the pain and slightly haunted look in her eyes. It filled him with anger and sadness that such a talented mage should have been so treated. However, such was the way whilst the Witch-Hunters ruled.

Archos was working late one night. A ritual was needed which he could not quite recall from memory, and he had need of a book from the library. As he passed the chamber where Dii slept, he heard a whimper. He paused and listened. Hearing her cry out, he pushed the door open on the room within. In the pale light of the glowglobe, he saw Dii tossing and turning in the grip of a nightmare. She seemed to be trying to fight with something and crying in pain. Sitting on the edge of the bed, he gazed down at the young mage, stroking a curl from her face. She stirred and awoke with a start.

Dii looked around her, confusion clouding her pretty features as she whispered,

"I…I was back there…back in the dungeon. It was horrible and I was so afraid. What are you doing here, my lord?"

"I heard you crying out and was concerned. I came to offer assistance and comfort." Archos took her hand and kissed it gently. "My dear, you are safe; you have survived. You just had a bad dream, a nightmare. You have nothing now to fear. I will sit with you; watch over you, if you wish." Pulling her closer to him, he let his lips brush hers. He inhaled her scent: herbs, lavender and beneath it the scent of a woman, intoxicating, yet also vulnerable. Gently he caressed her hair, a gesture full of comfort, yet also erotic.

Dii could feel his Power, and his concern, real concern, real Power. His heart beat fast beneath the robe he wore and she was experienced enough to know the desire he felt. Never before had a man held her close like this, comforting in such a way, and the feeling made her tremble with desire and affection for him. Yet, she felt his loneliness, and although he had never said as much, she knew it to be so. The feelings she felt swirled around her; and she wriggled close to him, needing the comfort of another person, the warmth and touch, yet also providing it.

She looked into his silver-grey eyes, eyes filled with many things: Power, desire and concern, knowledge. She brushed his lips with the tips of her fingers, snuggling into him and letting her head fall against his chest. Gently he kissed her hair and ran his fingers through the curls. Dii let her fingers gently caress the back of his hand, sending little bolts of longing through him. Turning over her hand, he saw the red burns on her wrists, fading and no longer raw but still visible. They would never fade entirely, branded for all time as a mage. Gently he kissed them, tender and kind.

As she leaned into him, Archos slid an arm around her waist. Still murmuring sweet nothings, he gently and almost absently stroked his fingers across her arm. He tipped her face to his and searched it with hungry desire. Her eyes were of the darkest blue he had ever seen, eyes like the midnight sky full of mystery and infinitely fascinating. He saw Power yet vulnerability, desire yet shame, and a deep strength. Archos kissed her gently, allowing her the chance to pull away. She did not, but returned his kiss, at first hesitantly and then with fire. Dii pulled away and smiled at him. At that moment, he was completely lost in her spell, her smile almost making her glow in the light of the glowglobe.

"You are so beautiful, Dii, alluring and so deeply desirable. I do not think I have ever desired anything as much as I desire you. Would you let me lie with you this night?" Archos asked, not demanding as so many men had before.

Looking into her eyes, he touched her face. "I know what you were…what the life of a Kept such as you can be. How you may have been…used. I wish for you to give yourself freely, and of your own choice. I would not take from you anything but that which was given by your own will."

Dii looked at him, unused to such remarks, unused to choice. She smiled the enchanting smile and touched the hand on her cheek. "I…I would like to feel you close to me, my lord. I would like the comfort of your touch. I would like to feel you, taste you. I see the desire in your eyes and find it reflected in my own. You are so kind to me. I would like to please you." Her eyes flickered down from his and a blush rose across her face.

Archos touched his other hand over hers and bowed his head to her. "I wish to see your passion and to delight in it, to experience so much with you. Let me distract you from your nightmares, bring you to the edge of ecstasy and beyond." Archos gently ran his finger down the edge of her jaw, sending a little tingle of desire through her, and he tilted her face to his softly brush her lips with his fingers.

The beautiful mage smiled again with the light of desire and mischief lighting her eyes, her confidence returning. Kissing his hand, she sucked on the ends of his fingers. "My Lord Archos that depends on how much of a distraction you can provide does it not?"

He kissed her and laughed. "That remains to be seen. I feel that you would be kind enough to inform me should I not provide suitable…distraction. If indeed this is the case, I pray you indulge me to beg your leave to try again until you are satisfied. Or perhaps it will be the case that you will beg me to take you again."

Dii snaked her hand beneath his clothing, swirling her nails across his chest. "You are sure of yourself indeed." As her hand began to circle, Archos kissed her again, a kiss loaded with passion and desire. He cupped her breast and gently circled her nipple through the soft cloth, gently massaging with the tips of his fingers until her nipple was hard and pointed.

Sighing, she kissed a line down his neck, nibbling at his collar bone and eliciting a moan of desire from him. They were soft kisses, yet full of so much emotion. The hard edges of her teeth sent a shiver across him as he tugged at the edge of her night-robe, slowly pulling it away and revealing her pale skin and the alluring tattoo. Hungrily his hands and eyes took in the soft painted skin against the paleness, softly he murmured as his lips caressed her. Archos lay close and looked at Dii; her red hair bright against the white bed linen, and naked before him, Archos knew he had never seen anyone quite as alluring as the young woman next to him. As he kissed her, the Archmage breathed in her smell and the taste of her, committing it to memory as his hands played, stroking across her softness.

Lips running across her shoulder, Archos exhaled warm breath onto her skin, making her shiver with need of him. He could see the faint red lines from the lash, now fading but still visible. He sighed, murmuring, "I should have got to you sooner."

Fingers carefully stroked the scars as Dii kissed his neck. "Let us not talk of such things, my lord. We are here and this is now. That which is past is not for this night," she murmured.

Nibbling at the edges of the swirling tattoo, he trailed his mouth ever so slowly across her. Dii began to sigh with pleasure as his mouth slid down to her breasts, his tongue swirling around her nipples. He breathed onto the moist skin, making her moan and arch towards him. She crept the hand on his chest around to tickle the back of his neck before she rippled little sparks of magic down him. Slowly she pulled away the fastening of his robe and the shirt beneath, and then moved her hands to explore around his belly, tickling him, teasing him. Scoring softly with her nails, she rippled more magic across him.

Moaning, he pulled her close. "Magic?" he growled. "Naughty girl, using your Power to tantalise me."

"Do you wish me to stop, my lord?" teased the young mage.

Pulling her into a passionate kiss, he circled his hand down to her thighs, stroking her. "No. No, I do not wish for you to stop. Your Power excites me. You have no idea of the Power or the allure you hold. Power and beauty are a dangerous mix… I like danger. You make me feel more alive than I have ever felt."

Dii kissed him with sharp little nips, teething a line down his neck until he began to moan softly. Tracing his chest with her lips and tongue, she circled a line just below his belly. Licking a tantalising swirl, she kissed back up his chest and nibbled the tattoo, the dark arcane symbol etched into his skin. Dii gently stroked her fingers across the edges, trailing a thin line of magic, eliciting a loud groan as the magic rippled over him. She ran her tongue across his chest and around the ring piercing his nipple, tugging as she looped her tongue around it. As he stroked her, she kissed her way back up to his neck. Kissing along his collar bone, she paused and slid up to his ear to whisper, "What pleases you, my lord? I can be slave or mistress as is your desire."

He lay back on the pillows and closed his eyes, hands running through her curls as her skin brushed against him. Sighing contentedly, he opened his eyes to watch her and replied, "Surprise me, pleasure me, do what you will. What I desire is you close to me, your skin on mine, your lips on me, your pleasure to my pleasure. Give me your Power…your passion…and I will give you mine."

Grinning wickedly, she kissed her way down to the edge of his breeches. Unlacing the ties with her teeth, she gently and slowly pulled the garment from him. Pushing him back, she began to kiss and lick her way up and down his body with no particular rhythm, which just tantalised him more. Little sparks of desire and magic rippled across him. Stroking his skin with her fingers, she traced the lightning tattoo on his thigh. Pausing to watch him moan, she licked across him slowly. Beginning to bite him, almost…but not quite drawing blood as he moaned again. Crawling back up, she kissed him deeply, her tongue seeking his.

Archos growled and reached for her, pulling her to him and taking her breast into his mouth, licking, sucking and nibbling until she too began to moan. Rolling so he could stroke her cleft, he tickled her and made her sigh softly; warm and wet she was, inviting and yet tantalising. He began to stroke her harder, circling around her pip until her breathing quickened. His fingers explored, teased, and tickled, and her hips began to move with his rhythm. Weaving a hand into her hair, he pulled her head back to reveal her neck to his kisses, nibbling the tattoo from the side of her face down her neck and again across her breast. Archos trailed kisses almost to her hips, all the while stroking her, listening to her rapid breathing, moaning and sighing, the soft sounds of her pleasure.

Dii moaned as he pulled her hair, sighing as his lips crossed her body, tasting her skin and making her shiver and wriggle. His fingers teased her and as he caressed her breast, she began to slide down him and to slowly lick his inner thigh once more; sliding across to the other leg, she bit softly, swirling her nails softly down his manhood, stroking as he writhed under her touch. Licking until his breath became rapid gasps. Taking him into her mouth, she gazed up as she began to pleasure him, slow and deep. Watching as his eyes closed and he clenched his hand into her hair. Suddenly pulling back, she smiled and dragged her nails across his chest, sparking magic across him as he moaned her name. Dii scored her nails on his skin, tantalising, stroking him firmly, until she knew he was close to the edge. Archos teased her pip like for like until he felt her pulse racing, felt the climax building within her from his touch.

He pushed her onto her back and kissed her soundly, caressing her thighs as he slid into her. Dii wrapped her legs around his middle, pulling him in deeper and tightening her muscles around him as he began to thrust, her hips moving to meet his. One arm around her and the other running over her skin, Archos rolled so Dii was above him and her hair flowed around and over them both, a sea of fiery curls. Deep and slow they moved together, wrapped as one as the magic cascaded over them. Lost in each other, the fire in the grate glowed deep blue and the flames roared as the climax took them. Dii buried her head in his chest and cried his name softly as she peaked.

Archos kissed her deeply, wrapping his fingers into hers. "My Flower," he said, using the pet name, and Common translation of her own name. Something they shared which had grown over the weeks. "You take my breath away. Your Power is great, both in magic and in matters of…love."

Returning his kiss, she gave him a playful push, sliding next to him and leaning on her elbows she watched him with a happy smile that made his heart flutter. "I have many…talents, Lord Archos. I hope I pleased you, although I am not worthy of your attention."

He tipped her face to his and kissed her gently. "My beautiful girl, any man who would not be pleased and flattered by your company is not only a bloody fool but a mad one. As for worth, never let me hear you say that. I do not give my attentions or my Power lightly and you are a great deal more worthy than most, you deserve so much."

Kissing her again, he pulled her hair over her shoulders and let it cascade. "You are so beautiful and your hair is like the rays of the fiery sun. I have never seen the like. You captivate me. I have lived a long time and travelled far, yet I have never seen one as enchanting as you. Now you are still weak and I have fatigued you, lay your head upon me and sleep, rest and replenish. I will guard you from the dreams."

Dii smiled happily and snuggled into his embrace, falling asleep quickly. Archos watched her until he knew she was sleeping and then, extinguishing the glowglobe, lay in the darkness feeling the warm, soft girl in his arms until he too fell into a contented sleep.

* * *

Deep in the forest, the elven huntress Ozena crouched in the undergrowth with her bow nocked, waiting for the opportune moment to let the arrow fly into the yearling boar. She had been away from the village for some days searching for suitable new hunting areas. Just past her nineteenth summer and now a full hunter instead of apprentice, she felt both pride and trepidation at the responsibility. The deep green ink of the tattoo that marked adulthood was still bright on the ivy leaves weaving around her wrist, and the lines of blue were striking under her jade green eyes. Her long hair, the colour of mahogany and woven around her head in braids, framed her face like a wooden crown.

Her former teacher had told her she was the best he had ever trained; quick to learn and with an eye as keen as the hawks which circled above the grasslands. With swift reflexes and a natural aptitude with the bow, he had said when a few more summers had passed he would recommend her to the Elders as a second teacher of bowcraft, which would allow him to focus on producing bows to trade. Ozena was a modest girl and had blushed at the compliment. Many things made young Ozena blush. Life in a small elven village in the Shimmering Forest did not endow a young woman with a great deal of experience beyond the forest, and she was not used to compliments and praise.The village of Szendro was close to the edge of the Shimmering Forest and an inlet which led to the Great River. A small community of fifteen or twenty households which hunted, fished, gathered and grew enough to sustain the village, and more from the forest. The road from Tremellic Valley and the human lands led as far as the village, although in places rough and overgrown, allowing some trade to flow. The elves of Szendro lived close enough to the edge of the forest to consider it worthwhile to trade elven fruit wines, herbs found among the trees and furs for bread, grain and beer with the valley, and gained some measure of protection from its human lord. A man friendly to elves, in a world where elves had few rights and less respect among his kind. The Elders seemed to respect him and certainly did not discourage the trade; and this, in itself, was an unusual phenomenon. Even Ozena knew the elven village gained a good deal from the mysterious human and enjoyed peace and a security that had been rare since the Plague.

Ozena squatted silently, watching the pig snuffle in the undergrowth. As it turned, she raised the bow and let fly the arrow, burying it deep in the creature's chest. Snorting in both pain and surprise, the beast briefly looked around to spot its tormentor before collapsing with a grunt. Ozena grinned at her success and walked to the beast, pausing close enough to check it was dead but far enough away to be able to leap aside. Such a creature could cause injury if so inclined, with sharp tusks and a fearsome set of jaws. The boar was indeed dead. Binding its feet to a suitable branch, she made a yoke to carry it back to the village. It was a good three hours back, as she had gone further than planned in following this creature.

As she returned along one of the old hunter paths, Ozena smelled smoke in the air, wood smoke, but far more than was usual for the cottages and buildings to produce. It was coming from the direction of the village. Beginning to fear that something was amiss, she dropped the boar and set off running. Yet cautious as she neared, she listened and heard nothing; there should have been sound, the laughter of the children and sounds of a village going about its business. Arriving at the edge of the village, a scene of devastation met her eyes.

The Ancient Tree was burning. The symbol of the village and her kin, consumed by fire, a thousand years of growth destroyed. Many generations of Elfkind had played and lived beneath its expanse and now the mighty oak lay fallen and aflame. Fortunately it lay far enough from the ring of trees to not to set the forest alight. Ozena paused. For all she knew, those that committed such could still have been close, so she crept around the perimeter warily, the sight greeting her becoming ever more desperate. Fear gripped her. The warriors of Szendro were well able to defend themselves, however there were but a few. A large force could overwhelm them, and indeed had. Other than bears and the larger forest creatures, nothing had threatened the village for a good many years.

Within the village circle surrounding the Ancient Tree, she could see the bodies of some of the Elders--those who held the lore and traditions and were the core of the village--lying bloodied and slashed where they fell. Amongst them were the bodies of the warriors, slaughtered in defence of their kin.

The eerie silence was broken only by the crackle of the Ancient Tree; she could see none of the women or children, either among the dead or hiding within the village. The silence leaving her certain the killers had left, she crept to the little cabin she shared with her sister Amena, to be greeted by emptiness. She called, but heard nothing. The women, some of the younger boys not yet grown to manhood, and female children were gone.

Ozena fell to her knees weeping, grief cutting her deep and leaving a jagged pain in her guts. She turned her tear-filled green eyes to the scene of carnage and asked herself who could have done this, and why? As she wept, she heard faint cries and ran to some undergrowth near to the edge of the village where lay one of the Elders – an old man named Loresh. As she crouched next to him, she saw the severity of the injuries. Tearing strips from her cloak, she bound the wounds as best she could, shocked by the bloody pool around him and fearful wild animals would investigate the wounded man.

She wondered if she should try and move him. As she tended him, the old man spoke, "Child?" he managed to say weakly. "You live. You were saved?"

He could barely believe his eyes and thought, perhaps, this figure was a spirit or the visions which sometimes came to dying men. The old man had little left but hope and so hope he did.

"Elder Loresh, it is Ozena Lyn. I have returned from hunting. You are hurt so badly…I do not know what to do. The others, they are fallen or gone. What am I to do? Please, Elder, guide me, that I may help you…help them."

Loresh weakly took her hand. "Dear child Ozena, you must go seek help. Do not waste time on me. Go to the village of the humans where we trade, beyond the forest, they will help us. Seek them. Their lord is a good man. He likes elves… Go, child… run…find the women…" He closed his eyes and lay back, exhausted from the effort of speaking.

Squeezing his hand, she vowed with more courage than she felt, "I, Ozena Lyn, will seek the womenfolk and the children. I will avenge this evil… I will find the human lord."

* * *

Ozena paused at the edge of Harkenen, unsure and afraid. She had never visited the place and was not sure how she would be received, despite the Elder's words. What if they were wrong? What if it was this man, close by, who had arranged the attack, Ozena asked herself. Yet she knew choices were limited, where else could a young elf such as her go for help?

The young huntress summoned her courage, and looking about, she spied an elderly matron tending her garden in the early evening light. Taking a deep breath, she said desperately in the Common language, "Mistress, I offer apologies for disturbing you this night, but I beg help. My village in the forest has been attacked and my fellows lie slain… My sister is missing, she is but twelve summers… Please, mistress, help me. One of our Elders lies gravely hurt." The words sounded strange to her and she hoped they had been correct.

The woman looked at the young elf, flushed breathless and clearly frightened.

"My poor child! You look so frightened and upset. Tell me slowly what troubles you."

Ozena bit back tears, frustrated that she was forced to repeat herself. "The elven village…my sister is taken…the women and children are gone. The men…there is an Elder…a grandfather. He is hurt badly, dying in the forest, at the mercy of beasts. I am not a healer. Please, I beg you, I need help. Have you a healer here, men to help search?"

The old woman did not believe that an elf would make up such a tale and come running to a strange human village begging for assistance in such a manner without foundation. She had traded with the village and knew the risks elves ran.

"My son will fetch the Steward, Master Simon, and you can recount to him what you say has happened."

Simon looked grave when he arrived. "You say the village is all but destroyed and the womenfolk missing? We saw smoke but thought no more of it. My lord would wish to know of this immediately. I will ride to him myself with word of this! Do not fret, miss, we will see this dealt with. It is a serious matter." With that, he turned on his heel and quickly went about his task, riding swiftly to the manor whilst Ozena was taken to his house to wait, still unsure and afraid for her kin and her people. And above all feeling helpless.

Steward Simon stood in the parlour as Archos entered with Dii on his arm. "What troubles you thus that you ride at such speed to seek audience, Simon? Another visit from our Witch-Hunter friends?"

Simon shook his head. "No… No, my lord. It seems there may be trouble within the forest. A young elf woman has come from their village with word that it has been attacked. She speaks of the men lying slain and the women and youngsters taken… and an old man lies badly wounded. It would seem slavers have dared to cross your lands, my lord."

Archos looked angry and Dii felt him tense. "Slavers? You are sure of this? They are either extremely bold or bloody stupid. This girl, why was she not taken too?"

"The girl was certain. She was a hunter and not in the village at the time. There was smoke, my lord, but the wind was blowing it away so it did not occur to me where it originated from. My lord, I shall ride with you to view the scene?"

Archos turned to Olek and gently slipped his arm from Dii's embrace. "Olek, we leave at once…I would see the truth of this for myself. This is grave news indeed, but we may be able to do something for the Elder."

Turning to Dii, he kissed her hand. "We must go. You will be safe enough here, my Flower of the Dawn."

Taking his hand, she gazed at him. "You would leave me here? I would ask to come with you, my lord. I can be of use, and if we find the women then I may be able to provide comfort. I know what it is to be in the clutches of a slaver."

Archos looked at her and touched her cheek gently, moved by her words. "Come then, fetch your cloak."

CHAPTER 8

Archos, Olek, Dii and Simon rode swiftly to Harkenen as the evening brought darkness. Ozena was waiting nervously as the Steward fetched a couple of village lads to assist where needed. Ozena hoped this human lord was not angry with her for disturbing him; she was not entirely convinced such a man would concern himself with the affairs of a small elven village.

Dismounting, Archos saw the young elf's apprehension and, wishing to comfort her, said in Elvish, "You would be the one seeking assistance, for it seems I have failed in my protection of your village?"

Ozena gawped in amazement to hear the Elvish tongue spoken by one not Elfkind. She stammered, "Elvish? You speak the Forest Tongue?"

Seeing the fear, and beneath it the surprise, Archos held out his hand, gently touching her arm, and within her head, the young elf heard, "I speak many languages for I have lived a long time and travelled far. You have nothing to fear from me, Ozena Lyn of the Elfkind. I am Archos, Archmage of the Arcane Realms and Lord of Tremellic, and I will assist you. You are safe with me and mine, and we will offer what comfort and assistance we can."

The huntress blushed and replied in Elvish, "Lord, I am ashamed I must beg for help, that I am unable to help my village, and I thank you for the kindness I have received within your land."

"It is not weakness to request help when it is needed, for the strength to see when that is so shows both cunning and resourcefulness. Now, you may ride to the forest with my lady Dii'Athella and then lead us along the path to your village, that we may see for ourselves what tragedy has been wrought upon your people," Archos replied, reverting to Common.

Ozena nervously mounted the horse with Dii and held on tightly, clinging to the beast's mane. Dii slid her arm around Ozena's waist and said, "You will not fall. The horse is gentle and clever. Her hooves are sure upon the track, and she will not let you tumble. I am Dii, and I come to offer what assistance I can to you and your village."

"My sister is gone; she is but twelve summers. She is a Spirit Child – a mage, the first born to the village for many years," Ozena replied, desperately hoping another elf would understand.

Dii squeezed her hand. "We will see what can be learned. My lord has many ways and means at his disposal. Come, let us make haste."

* * *

"I heard what these slavers do to the young wenches, Freddy…use 'em over and over, if you get my meaning. They get made slaves to some rich fellow or put to work in the whorehouses. I do not know what's worse…" one of the Steward's lads from the Harkenen said to the other as they rode in the wagon to the edge of the forest.

"Aye, I heard how as they chain 'em up in the Enclaves like they was condemned, the pretty ones get taken away like you say… Glad it ain't my sister as is gone."

Olek trotted his mount next to the wagon containing the lads. "Have you no respect? Because it is certain you have no tact. Miss Ozena's sister is missing, along with most of the other women. Perhaps next time the slavers will not be so choosy and take your lasses…'tis not only elven women get taken, but pretty human girls and even lads on occasion. Now show some respect unless you want Lord Archos to be informed of your rudeness? I am sure he would be most keen to hear, if he has not overheard your idle chat already."

As the lads muttered their apologies, Olek nudged his mount up alongside the horse carrying the two elves. "At your service, ladies…"

Smiling, he stayed abreast and made idle chat with Dii, asking Ozena about life in the Shimmering Forest, trying to distract her from her grief; however, the canny half-elf was on the lookout for both trouble and information which might assist them. Alert, but at ease, his keen senses watched and listened, even as it seemed he was engaged in chat with the women.

Tethering the horses in a small clearing, they dismounted. Drawing his swords, Olek nodded to Archos before melting into the darkness, scouting around the edge of the village. Searching, looking for signs, because he knew that sometimes such raiders left a man on watch. However he saw no one and returned to the others. "Perimeter is clear enough, no one left on guard in the immediate area. It's a bit dark even for me to find a trail in these trees and I do not know the land here particularly well."

Seeing what carnage lay before them on entrance to the village, Simon muttered in shock, "By the gods, who has done this?" Looking over to the two lads staring at the bodies, he shook his head sadly and continued, "What are your orders, my lord?"

Archos glanced around, taking in the grim scene, and replied, "Check the houses, including outside in the gardens or animal pens, and make sure the dead are, in fact, dead. I doubt we will be that lucky that someone lies wounded but alive, however it is a possibility. Fetch blankets, anything to wrap the dead. We will see to this survivor and hope we are in time."

Dii was saddened by the scene, so much needless death for the greed of slavers, and she squeezed Ozena's hand. "Oh, I am sorry, such loss! Now I should help, see what can be done here, for the dead as well as the living."

Walking to the husk of the Ancient Tree, she sadly ran her fingers along the scorched bark and, calling her Power, she cried, "Spirits grant me this night the strength and the Power to help those that have fallen here. Luna, Lady of the Sacred Moon; turn your light to us that we may provide for the spirits of the dead, and turn your sacred gaze upon those who are taken that they may gain comfort in their fear." As she lifted her arms towards the moon, the clouds in the sky parted, the soft light bathing the village clearing.

"Bloody hell!" spluttered the lad, Freddy, as he left a cottage armed with blankets, and saw the light stream down.

Seeing her cast the spell and graced in the light of the moon, Archos stood transfixed, almost holding his breath. For a moment, nothing existed but Dii and the moonlight, at least for him. As Olek returned, he saw his master mesmerised by the pretty young elf. "Not bad… What now?"

Archos tore his gaze away from Dii. "Indeed…. I will take Dii and tend to the old man; he can be escorted back to the village once healed. Now we have light, perhaps a trail may be more obvious. Take Ozena and scout among the trees beyond where he has fallen. See what you can find. Check there is no one else living among the undergrowth and scout the perimeter again."

The mages headed to the area where the old man lay, after swift instruction to his location from Ozena. Archos hoped it was not too late, that the old man was still living after so much time. Close by lay a human, a sword wound slicing his belly open, spilling his guts upon the ground. The old man had not fallen easily it seemed.

"Dii, fetch me water, please; we need a brew against infection and a tea for fortitude. I know you packed some herbs, poultices and the small kettle. We can heal him well enough that he may ride to the village. We need fire, make it hasty."

Crouching next to the old man, he looked over him: an Elder, rich in years, rich in knowledge. Noting the amount of blood and the torn clothing binding the wound, Archos thought it was a combination of sheer stubbornness and the cold that had stopped him from bleeding out, although the tourniquet had certainly helped.

Speaking in the language of the Elfkind, he said comfortingly, "Elder, I am Archos, lord of the valley yonder. I offer to you my friendship and the Power granted to me by the goddess Syltha to mend your wounds, if you will allow me. We come in friendship, to seek answers to this tragedy, and to find your kin if we are able."

The old man whispered, "Lord Mage…I am honoured that you come…but please do not waste your magic upon an old man. You must seek the women and the young, find where they have been taken."

Dii quickly gathered wood then, lighting a flame in her hand, blew it onto the tinder, weaving her hands until the fire took with a roar. Then she found the herb box, a small black pot and waterskin, and set to work, handing over what was required as fast as she was able.

As Archos split the blood-soaked leather breeches the old elf wore, he assessed the damage: a deep jagged wound in his leg that by a miracle had missed the artery. The old man's ribs were broken and the skin was split and bleeding. He could see the damage was great, however, and the first signs of infection were present. Archos touched the wounds and took the pain within himself, then carefully applied the poultice before closing the wounds with magic.

The injuries knit slowly, even magic was not instant, and he bound the wounds with care. "That should ease you, Elder, although it will be a while yet until you are fully healed. Now my Steward will take you to his home, where you will be well tended and safe. There will be food and rest for as long as you need it within the village. Once we find a trail, we will seek the women. I assure you we will see this evil avenged."

He turned and viewed the terrible sight of the dead and looking to Olek, who had searched among the undergrowth as directed and returned with a brief headshake, the Archmage said, "I know a little of these rites. We need graves and items to offer to the Spirit Guides."

A look of sadness and anger reflected in Ozena's eyes, and her face was white with shock and grief. Dii stood close, offering what comfort she could, although of course it was not enough.

Ozena wiped her eyes. "Forgive me, in my grief I had not thought… Yes, there is a Garden of Souls just to the north, among a grove of cherry trees. They should be taken there and they will need something for each to take to the Other World as a suitable offering… The Elder may know best what is suitable."

Archos nodded and replied, "Simon and his lads can see to that with the Elder's guidance. I think we should seek a trail as I do not believe the slavers left no sign, although it will not be fresh. The Great River flows close to here, and there are inlets, barges could be brought close. The river runs through the land to the coastal city and many inlets and channels lead from it to villages and outposts.

"The slavers must have wagons, or herded those taken to such. Assist Olek, Ozena, you are familiar with these woods."

"Who would do such as this? These men fallen here defended their women and the old, yet it was not enough. What manner of men would slaughter and steal the women, the children?" Dale asked his brother, upset at the sight as they deposited blankets for use by the dead.

Simon gazed upon the scene and looked to Archos. "I do not know what manner of men, but such is this world it is so. Let us pray the women live still and can be recovered. We need to make haste that the dead may pass to the Other World as is fitting. Animals will come and the dead cannot be left. My lord, what would you have us do? I am ignorant of what is correct and in my ignorance do not wish to offend."

Archos looked at his grim face and sighed sadly. "Graves…seek guidance from the old man, but I will leave this in your charge. Send for more help if you need. Afterwards, clear the area as best you can. There is much to be salvaged. I am sure the elves would not want stores to rot. Any elves we find will be accommodated in Harkenen or the other hamlets. We cannot expect them to return to the ruin of this place, at least not initially."

* * *

"Here…I see a trail, tramped down undergrowth and snapped branches as though people passed. This trail leads to the river… Perhaps they have gone that way and we may find them," Ozena stated hopefully, and swiftly made move to follow.

Olek caught her arm and said quietly, "This trail is not recent, hours old at least; see, the blood is dry and we do not know exactly when the village was raided. You said so yourself. You do know we may be far too late to find anyone this night, Ozena?" Seeing the urge to dive forward into unknown dangers in her desperation, Olek continued softly, "You must be cautious, lest we miss something of importance. There is the chance there may be guards remaining, even so."

Looking at him, tears stinging her green eyes, Ozena sniffled. "I have to believe she is alive and I will find her! Let me go and search, if you do not wish to."

Gripping her arm gently, but with enough force to prevent her running, Olek replied, "Archos has many ways of finding people…it may not yet be too late. You know not what lies ahead. A good scout would not blunder forward unprepared into the unknown. You will do your sister no good if you fall to the slavers also. You think I would let you go alone? My lord has set himself to assist you and so then have I. Lord Archos is a man of his word in many matters and will see this through. You have my friendship and my blades. I will help you, but we must be rational and cautious. Men are often far more dangerous to track than beasts, especially men of this kind."

Looking down, suddenly ashamed, Ozena knew the sense of his words; she nodded and fought back tears as the fear within twisted her guts. Olek motioned them both onward and as the trail led on, they picked up the smell of smoke on the air. The sound of male voices, and the crying of a woman, carried back to them. The woman cried in Common, "No! No… Leave me be… Please… No!"

Olek stopped and whistled like a bird, two short and one long note. Archos looked up and, motioning to Dii, plunged into the forest with her on his heels.

Ozena shot forward, calling her sister's name. Olek swore, drew his swords, and plunged after her.

"Stay here. Olek and I will deal with this. If needs be, run. Do not wait for me," Archos told Dii as they stopped at the edge of the trees, before the clearing. He kissed her, seeing the apprehension. "We will be fine, but just in case… Simon will take you home if needs be."

As Ozena broke through the trees, one of the guards chuckled. "Eh, what is this? A little elf slut that got away… Fresh sport, lads!" As he rose from his place at the fireside, his companion pushed away the unfortunate young elf whom had been his recent victim. The young woman crumpled, sobbing, to the ground, but had the presence of mind to crawl away.

One of the guards grabbed for Ozena, catching her arm, and was greeted by a drakesword slicing into his arm and a voice that hissed in his ear. "One more move and I will cut you to pieces. She is not for you…slaver." Olek spat, "Now on your knees."

Trying to swing around, the man reached for his sword and was met by the other drakesword, which cleaved through his chest and dropped the man in a spray of blood. "Well, I warned him." Olek shrugged as the man fell, spurting blood upon the trees and gurgling his last breath.

The injured elf crawled toward the trees and, seeing her, Dii sprang forward, offering comfort and tending to her injuries as best she could. The poor soul was sobbing and shaking. Gently Dii removed her cloak and wrapped it across her shoulders as she led her towards another female elf, bound and trembling.

Archos moved fast holding the guard who had raped the young woman in a grip like a vice. The wind swirled in the trees, wailing and thumping branches, and flames began to rise around his feet. In a dangerously quiet voice, the Archmage hissed, "Enjoy your sport this evening, raping and burning? You dare to set foot in this village on my lands and treat these women as such? You will beg forgiveness from them then you will tell me who dared to send you here."

The guard began to whimper in fear as the Archmage's eyes glowed silver. Trying to wriggle, he slowly slid his hand down towards the dagger at his belt. Suddenly the dagger floated away from his fingers and hovered close to his eyes. "Do not think I will hesitate to kill you, slowly. Your life is nothing to me. You made your choice when you took that woman against her will this night and brought your slavers upon my land. Now you will tell me where the others are, the women and children from the village you destroyed?"

The guard trembled as the flames began to climb around him and the heat rose. Eyes watching the dagger floating before him, and the man whimpered in terror until the ground around him became wet with his fear. "I do not know, Master. Taken to the city slave markets maybe…those two were part of our payment, that's all. We are just here for coin and the…benefits. I am just a guard trying to earn a living. Some man named Rufus hired us, scarred, large man. Just picked us up to be guards, nothing more. He's the boss of this outfit. They were just elves…not real women."

Archos growled a low sound, which was echoed by a sky bubbling with angry clouds and the dagger burst into flame. As the Archmage stepped back across his own ring of fire, the dagger plunged deep into chest of the guard, searing and slicing between his ribs, who screamed and fell, writhing in the circle of flame.

The younger guard, who had been watching the captives before Dii approached, slid into the shadows, trying to avoid notice, a task at which he failed. He turned and fled seeing what had happened to his companions, only to be felled by Ozena. Leaping over, she shook him. "Where is she? Where is my sister? She is but twelve summers old! Tell me where they have taken her."

The lad, not far from Ozena's own age, groaned in pain at the arrow through his leg. "I…I do not know… I was just following the others. I did not touch the girls… please…there were many girls taken."

Ozena stood above him, her hands trembling as she loaded another arrow. "She is small, and young, she has hair like the snow and eyes like jet…a Spirit Child."

He began to cry and beg whilst Ozena stood above him, her anger bubbling and tears running down her cheeks, but she could not bring herself to kill him. She had never taken a human life and as he pleaded Ozena felt confused, a measure of pity mixing with the biting anger. As the boy groaned, Olek appeared next to Ozena. "Go help Dii with the women. It would help them to hear the Elvish tongue."

Ozena turned to him. "I cannot kill him, he is just a boy."

Olek said quietly, "He would not show you mercy…or the women that were taken. Perhaps he did not participate, but he did not prevent what has occurred. You know he cannot live. There can be no survivors amongst the slavers." With that, he slit the boy's throat, turned and walked away, not even casting a look back at the bleeding corpse.

CHAPTER 9

Once the dead were dealt with and the survivors set to return to safe haven in Harkenen, plans and instructions were formed for the salvage of what foodstuff, supplies and surviving livestock could be found. That would, however, be the task for future days. It would be some time before the forest reclaimed the village entirely, as it surely would. The dead slavers were removed from the village and the bodies left to animals and the ravages of nature, as the Steward deemed them unfit for burial.

In the ruins of Szendro, Ozena turned to Archos with tears stinging her eyes. "She was not there! She is gone... They will take her to this city. How do I get there? I cannot leave her there alone, she is a Spirit Child and very sensitive. I am not foolish. I know what may happen to her. Please...again I must beg of your assistance for I know not the way to the city."

"My dear girl, do you think I would leave it here and not pursue the elves further? I promise you this, Ozena Lyn of the Elfkind: I will do everything in my considerable power to find those taken and avenge what has happened this day. However, there are many possibilities as to their whereabouts. Olek will leave on the morrow, after we have made appropriate plans, and pursue several lines of enquiry. There are ways to search for them. I offer you the hospitality of my house. You will be close enough to Harkenen that you may visit the elves there, and Dii may keep you company if you do not care for mine. You could not travel to the city alone, and were it so, I doubt you would find the information you chose. Those in the city would not be as tolerant of a lone elf as people in my valley. Olek has...contacts, as do I, businesses that may serve us well. You must trust me on this." It was said kindly, but allowed no place for argument.

"I am so ashamed." Ozena looked away. "I cannot help my sister. I have failed in my duty."

Archos looked intently at her, letting a comforting spell envelope the huntress. "Ozena, you have not failed. You sought help as soon as you were able. Had you been within the village, they would have taken you also, and we may not have known anything was amiss. Your sister and your fellows in the village would lay unburied and unlooked for. Come, let us return to the manor to make arrangements. The two young women and the Elder will be looked after well enough in Simon's care."

* * *

Once Ozena was settled at the manor, Archos led Dii to the workshop. "You did well tonight and you looked like a goddess bathed in the light of the moon. My pretty Flower, Dii'Athella, I have for you a gift…an ancient staff once belonging to an elven sorceress. I acquired it some years ago, but it does not suit me as well as the one I now wield. You have been an attentive and clever student and even in a few short weeks your Power has grown, but a staff will enhance it and help protect you. It is carved from the branch of an Ancient Tree and set with a silver globe full of sapphires and clear stones of some value. I was told the story that they are the tears of the Sorceress Elthera and some say it contains a part of her."

He handed her a tall staff of black wood carved with many ancient, arcane symbols. The top was adorned as the Archmage had described and as she touched the wood, Dii felt its Power and a sad song filled her head. Although she did not comprehend the Ancient Elvish words, she felt the sentiment. A warmth filled her as the elven sorceress, now nothing but a wisp and a memory, floated once around her then settled back within the ancient wood.

* * *

Archos sat in his parlour and meditated for a while, trying to calm his thoughts and the rage within him. He gazed at the fire, watching the flames leap and twist. Dii was with Ozena and knew to watch over her as Archos felt the young huntress would try and make for the city alone, given half a chance. The fire twisted in elemental fury for a while before settling a little, reflecting his mood in the flames.

The Archmage disliked slavers even more than he disliked Witch-Hunters. Slavery was not illegal; mages were slaves by default, at the whim of the Witch-Hunters to decree their fate, be it life shackled within the Enclave Prison, the possession of someone of power or in what they ironically referred to as the "hospitality" of the Order. Elves who lived within the Enclaves or taken from the Shimmering Forest were used, at best, as servants, but Archos was well aware of the fashion for the rich and powerful to keep an elf as a pretty play thing, to use and discard as they wished. Elves were seen in many places as less than cattle and, having no rights, they were at the whim of their owners. There was, unfortunately, a market for them. Those who were kept shackled were forced to live not only with the Banecrystal cuffs about them, which crippled magical ability and often the wearer through the pain, and branded them as a mage or adept for all to see. Thus if the mage was able to escape, it was virtually impossible for an elf or half-elf mage to hide. Those forced to live in the

Enclaves rarely left, condemned to a life of poverty. An unaccompanied elf without the required papers was fair game for the Witch-Hunters and slavers, or anyone with nefarious intent. Even those which lived within the house of their masters, although often more fortunate in their treatment, still could not move freely, and it was often the case any offspring born to these servants became the property of the master.

Reaching a decision, he smiled unpleasantly and found his parchment and quill, scribbling a couple of notes:

This half-elf acts as my agent. He is to be given all the assistance that you would give to me. He acts in my name and with my authority. I trust you will oblige him and guarantee his safety. It would be unfortunate should I discover he has been denied or mistreated.

Archos Terrian Stormrager, Lord of Tremellic.

Sealing it, he fetched a couple of small velvet bags and set one next to the first scroll. The second scroll was of a more personal nature:

I seek information on the whereabouts of an elven mage child, white hair and eyes of ebony, captured by slavers. Also information regarding a man known as Rufus; he is large and scarred, believed to run a slaver barge, or wagons. I am sure any information about, and disruption of, the slave market would suit many purposes. If, by chance, the child or information of her whereabouts happens to fall into your hands or perhaps any information of a recent consignment of elves to the Enclave, be sure I would be grateful.

The Oncoming Storm.

Calling for Olek, he settled back in the chair. "Ah, Olek…fancy a nice little trip to the city? I am sure you can make use of your considerable talents to seek information regarding the elves. There is a scroll authorising whatever you feel is best…in my name if needed. I am sure I do not need to tell you the pouch is for…expenses. If you would be so kind as to pay my regards to Darius Veltori of the House of Thieves when you are buying supplies for us, he might appreciate the call. I am low on arcana dust and could do with another marble bowl, you know the sort I prefer. Take what you need for payment. Perhaps you could drop in to the Society of Hidden Secrets also and send my regards. As always, I trust your discretion in these matters. It should not take more than a few days, if you wish to renew your acquaintance with any of the more…undesirable elements of the area, you have leave to do so. They can be forthcoming with information and hear many things others do not. Oh, and be careful, my friend. I will do what I can from here…and keep the ladies company."

"As always, my lord, I am your servant," Olek agreed, and with that he left to make his arrangements.

* * *

Dii half woke in the darkness of the chamber she now shared with Archos. The nightmare had sliced through her sleep like a knife. The events within the elven village had suddenly brought back the memories of her ordeal in the Order's dungeon. Although she had been barely conscious for a good deal of it, she remembered enough, that and what Joset had forced her to do…things which sometimes rose from the depths of memory. She whimpered as the images appeared unbidden and swirled around her head as real as they once had been.

Archos stirred as the woman next to him thrashed in fear at the dream. He heard her crying and whimpering. Gently he took her into his arms, releasing a comfort spell to calm her. "Hush, Flower. It is just a nightmare. Hush, you are safe with me, there is nothing to fear in my house."

Dii woke, her eyes wide with fear and remembrance of the dream. As she felt his strong comforting arms around her, she snuggled close and whispered, "I was back again…in the dungeon. I remember what happened…what they did. It was confused, but somehow very real. I remember what my Keeper made me do. Those girls…what they had been through and what will happen to those we could not find. It made me think of it. I…I am sorry. I should be stronger. I am so ashamed of it all."

Gently he kissed her and held her until she stopped trembling. "My beautiful girl, you are kind and gentle. No woman should have endure what you have been through. It will take a while for you to accept it…for the nightmares to cease. There is no shame in that, for you have suffered a great deal. I can help you…ease the memories. I cannot remove them, but I can help you to lock them away."

He stroked her face tenderly. "You are safe here. No one will hurt you again, you are my girl now. You will become Powerful…one day no one will match you, but it will take time. Sleep. Sleep safely here."

As he caressed her face and kissed her hair gently, Archos cast a sleep spell and held her until he was certain she slept. As he searched her mind, he found the memories red and blazing from the dream and he felt the pain she had stab deep within him. Taking the images, the hurt and the pain, the Magelord pulled them into himself, soothing and clouding them. He felt the pain, the humiliation, the shame and fear she had felt and silent tears fell from him. Kissing her softly, he closed his eyes and considered his next move.

Silently he rose and dressed hastily before entering his workshop. Selecting a number of items and picking up his staff, he gave an evil smile and headed to the stables to find his favourite mount.

Archos arrived at the caves as clouds covered the stars. He let his mount wander knowing he would not wander far, even in a storm. As he entered the cave complex, the glowglobes lit and shone with their pale light. The walls were of a black rock in which were many crystals and the whole area glowed like the summer night sky. The cave always made him feel very alive with Power, but even he could not stay here for more than few days or so, as the Power was so great it began to be painful. Idly he wondered if he should bring Dii here, to make love to her on the soft furs in the central cave, intense and surrounded by Power… Now that would be an experience. He smiled before chastising himself that it was a thought for another night, when things were more settled and the missing elves were dealt with.

The central cavern was a vast chamber of ancient stone which arched above him glistening with iridescent crystals. Carefully he swept aside the furs and rugs covering the floor, surprisingly dry from the magic that channelled the water away from the chamber and into the small rock passages which pooled deep below the ground and bubbled to spring further in the valley. The Circle that lay etched deep in the black stone flared to life as he dragged his staff around it and, stepping within, he felt the surge of Power and the cold mists of the Astral Realms around him. He knew what he had planned required a good deal of Power and blood, and he steeled himself to begin the ritual.

Letting his staff go so it hovered within the Circle, he removed the kris and scored deep into his arms. He let the blood flow freely until it pooled at his feet and he felt a little light headed. Slowly he walked the Circle, trailing the blood along its lines until it began to bubble. "I am Archos, Lord of the Arcane…the Storm that Rages… Sky Child. As my blood is shed this night, I summon thee, my demon servant."

The Circle flared again, roaring around him. As he continued to bleed, a dark shape began to form. The staff twisted on its axis faster and faster until the demon appeared; a terrible shape of distorted, twisted flesh and bone that rose on two clawed legs like those of a spider. With flesh torn and hanging in strips, it oozed blood and pus; hands held claws like daggers and dripped into the bloody Circle. The terrible creature twisted what passed for its head and hissed, "There isss a price demanded of thee, if thou wishesss to sssummon me."

Archos caught the spinning staff and leaned on it. "See, blood is shed this night and you will do my bidding as is your bond. You will have what remains of your blood price; it will be paid soon enough. I will walk in the Arcane Realms and you will have your sacrifice."

Leaning heavily on the staff, he slipped into Astral Sight, the cold winds of the Arcane Realm chilling him as he walked the strange, twisted paths and he called to mind the image he sought. He searched the dreams and visions passing before him and the trails which lay there. Weaving one among another, or flitting past like moths. Suddenly he saw the dream, as the Witch-Hunter lay sleeping, reliving his fantasy of the little red-haired mage, savouring what he had done to her…what he would like to do to her when she became his.

As the images of Dii and her torment flickered around him, he saw Commander Robin laugh as he took her. Archos paused, channelling his rage. Slowly he took the edges of the dream and wound it to him, stepping within the man's mind and dream, twisting the images around himself, around the demon.

"Did you enjoy her, Witch-Hunter? The red-haired mage, the girl you took as she lay close to death? She is mine, the girl who wakes crying and screaming in the night because of you. I hope you did enjoy her because it will be your last moment of enjoyment, the last time you will experience pleasure," the voice echoed in the mind of the sleeper.

Robin flinched at the voice in his head, stripping his defences. He tried to summon up his self-control, the resistances he had been taught. They were not enough as he felt the voice, the Power slice into his mind; he felt it open like an orange and full of such pain as he had never felt. Archos reflected the pain from Dii, the pain he had taken from her and sent it back to its maker.

"You think your defences are enough to fight me, Witch-Hunter? You have no idea who I really am, what Power I hold. Your defences are nothing to me, nothing against my rage and my vengeance, nothing against the Power of the Oncoming Storm."

Robin twitched and tossed in the grip of the dream, a dream frighteningly real. Trapped and unable to wake. "She was just an elf whore. A Witch, she belonged to the Order, as do all Witches, mine to use as I saw fit," he thought as the voice echoed around him.

Archos pulled the man close in the dream, his eyes glowing silver and the rage swirling around him like a tempest. "She was a woman! Elf or not, she was neither your plaything nor your slave. You corrupt your own law; the authority you claim to wield is a terrible parody of fear and spite, power simply used for your own gain and your own indulgences. Power without reason and responsibility is not power, it is corruption. All I see is avarice and vice, greed and perversion. That is the legacy of those who claim to protect and fuel the world with ignorance to keep it so. You do not protect, you condemn and destroy."

Winding the images around him, Archos summoned his Power and, with a terrible laugh, he called the demon forward. "So you like pleasures of the flesh, to take things and people that are not yours, to force yourself and your will upon them? Well, let us see if you enjoy the tables turning."

Lifting the Witch-Hunter up, he invoked creatures from the mists; strange arcane creatures that wrapped tightly around his prey, their sharp scales lacerating skin, bleeding the life essence away.

Close, he whispered, "So Witch-Hunter…how long before you beg for mercy… before your will breaks?"

The man tried to pull away. Archos simply smiled and began to warm his blood until it seared in his veins and the Witch-Hunter screamed, blood spewing from his mouth, over himself and the floor. Shifting his Focus back a little, but holding the dream, Archos drew his dagger and sliced into his arm again, dripping more blood onto the arcane ground.

"Demon, feast upon this man and take my blood as gift for your services this night. He is yours to do with as you wish, when you wish, for as long as you wish. He is strong, K'hlak, he will not break easily…but he will break eventually. Until that time, he is yours; after that, you will return to the staff, for you are mine, as is our bond."

Leaning back, Archos summoned the entropic forces to him, twisting them to his will. He enjoyed hearing him scream as the demon took him again and again, tearing at him, clawing at him and into him as it did so.

Archos smiled an unpleasant smile as he watched the man's will break, screaming for mercy, screaming he was sorry, screaming for death. As the demon slid back within the staff, Archos slipped back into real sight and the safety of the cave. He grinned faintly as he lowered himself onto the furs piled in one corner, leaving a trail of his own blood. He slowly healed himself and lay down to rest enough to return before dawn.

Back at the Witch-Hunter fort, Commander Robin screamed in the darkness as his sanity unravelled around him.

CHAPTER 10

Olek made good time arriving at the city of Varlek. Stabling his horse, he headed to the townhouse Archos kept in the Eastern Quarter. Unlocking the door, he entered to be greeted by the half-elf servant Valaria who kept house. She was another of Lord Archos' finds, an old half-elf whore whose looks had faded and who walked with a limp after one beating too many from the human whoremaster who had owned the brothel, a man who had mysteriously disappeared not long after Valaria's misfortune.

The brothel itself had become one of the assets in Archos' not insubstantial business dealings as a more high class gentleman's club. Those employees who chose to stay were allowed to do so, while those less willing were found more suitable employment Valaria was clever, loyal, and above all discrete, and still maintained some friendship with those of her former profession. She managed the small townhouse well enough and lived in her own rooms behind the main house. Valaria was deeply fond of Archos but it was a long time since they had shared a bed. Her ties were of affection and gratitude these days. Olek grinned when she greeted him with a motherly hug. "Where is the master? You are alone, Olek. Is everything alright?"

Laughing, he replied, "Oh yes, Lord Archos is well enough. He has a pretty young mistress to amuse him, a mage. I am here on business, to find some elves taken from the forest close to Tremellic Valley, their village raided and the women and children taken."

Valaria looked thoughtful. "You could try the slave markets for starters, and I can make enquiries. I still have a few contacts, so I will speak to Desiree at the Golden Mask. I doubt they would be taken there as her girls are not slaves, but she may have heard rumours. It may be worth visiting the whorehouses also, but I am sure you are able enough to manage your affairs."

* * *

Olek slipped into the one of the alleys leading to the docks and, cloaked in shadow, he paused at an old wooden door. Tapping softly in a complex series of knocks, he waited until a grill slid aside and a pair of eyes looked out. "What'ya want," said a voice.

"The Shadowdancer wishes to see the Thiefmaster, to discuss some business, business that I bring from the Oncoming Storm, business that will only be discussed with the Thiefmaster himself."

The eyes disappeared for a while and then the face reappeared, which did not improve the day a great deal as it was a cruel and exceptionally ugly countenance. A grunt came from behind the grill and the door slowly and silently slid open. Olek stepped into a dark room and the doorman grunted again, pointing to the far door. Olek went through and bowed his head slightly to the man sitting at the small table. The well-furnished room, containing comfortable furniture and a screened sleeping chamber contained a man industriously writing, his face shadowed in the dim light The man looked up and grinned, the slight point to his ears denoted elven blood some generations ago but to all intents passing as fully human, a Passer, as they were sometimes known. He was slightly built, wiry and fast, the drop of elven blood within him enhancing the adeptness he had been born with, a man who lived by wits, speed and a fluidic moral code when it came to property. The Thiefmaster knew talent and skill when he saw it and Olek knew he treated his employees well enough if they behaved, and ruthlessly if they did not.

"Why, if it isn't the Shadowdancer. I trust this is more than a social call?" he said with a familiar smile. Motioning towards a seat, he poured a drink from the crystal decanter close by and set it on the table.

Olek sat down and waited for the Thiefmaster to drink first. "You think I would poison you? I am well aware for whom you work. I am not a bloody fool. Besides, if I wanted you dead, do you think you would have got through the door?" Darius Veltori said, recounting the words of the games they played with a grin, each using the game as a form of code.

"You are sure of that, Thiefmaster? I could best your guard easily enough, at least the one you allow to be seen. As you say, you are not a foolish man." Olek grinned back, enjoying the game and taking a long savouring sip. "You are correct. As much as I enjoy your company, I come on business seeking information about some elves recently taken from a village within my lord's protection, raided by slavers it appears. I seek information about a slaver known as Rufus, a large man covered in scars. There is an elf child my master is keen to find; a young woman not above twelve or thirteen summers and striking to look at, white hair like winter snow. If you were to discover any information about such, I am sure it would be a profitable venture. Speaking of which, does Harmil the fence still operate, or has he had his long overdue engagement with hangman?"

Darius leaned back in his chair. "It would be possible for me to make enquiries, but there would be expenses. Some of my associates have access to information, access to the houses of the more wealthy citizens. Oh yes, Harmil continues to evade the constable and the Witch-Hunters, although how is anyone's guess."

Olek smiled and emptied some of the gems from the bag. "Good will payment. There will be more if the information is of use. Now I will leave you to gather your sources and I have other places to be. Leave any information you find in a wooden box at the Oaken Barrel tavern, you know where."

Staying in the back alleys, he made his way towards the Enclave, using the shadows to his advantage. Loitering in the doorway of one of the poorer and unkempt shops, Olek glanced around, watching the guard at the gateway to the Enclave, and he slipped inside. The interior of the store belied the exterior, being filled with a variety of goods and well lit by glowglobes set in wall holders. A half-elf stood behind the counter, a sword obvious at his back. Olek wandered around browsing for a while before speaking to the half-elf fence when the shop's other customer left.

"I seek some items of a magical nature: ten pounds of arcana dust, or as much as you have; a scrying bowl of enchanted black marble, if you have one; and a large conch shell from the shores of the Far Isles."

Harmil looked around cautiously, eyeing the back of the retreating customer as the door swung shut. "Those items are illegal. I only sell legit items here."

Olek strolled to one of the shelves and selected a couple of items. "Is that so? Well, it would seem that is an enchanted dagger I see here with the drake's tooth hilt. Oh, and the ewer of silver set with blood gems from the Jagged Peaks of Helmerra is rather splendid. These are now legal, are they? Things have changed since I visited last. I suspect the Thiefmaster would be VERY interested to hear that you refused a sale to a friend of his, the Shadowdancer, and denied some items to a VERY important benefactor. It would seem I should take my trade elsewhere. There are other fences and purveyors of goods in the city who may oblige."

Harmil tried to meet Olek's gaze and, as Olek turned aside and smiled, he replied, "Wait, sir, it pays to be cautious in my line. I recognise you now, sir. I have the items you requested, although not a great deal of arcana dust. I can get some and have it taken to a neutral spot for collection, if sir wishes."

Turning the dagger over in his hands, Olek appraised it and said nothing, as though weighing up the fence's offer.

"Perhaps you would be interested in the drakestooth dagger, it has Power, sir. Good for a mage or those who use the shadows. Browse, see if you find anything else to your liking whilst I fetch your goods."

Olek nodded slightly and after receiving the items and a couple of purchases that took his fancy, he headed cautiously into the docks. Weaving amongst the alleys and byways of the dockyards, he sat in a tavern until dark, then silently he pulled the shadows around him and found his way through the lower docks to the boarded-up warehouse that hid the entrance to the Society of Hidden Secrets, the highly illegal mage underground. The old wooden door was locked and he deftly picked the lock, walking through the darkness and trailing his fingers along the left-hand wall until he found the niche that held the handle. Twisting it, he heard a click and, stepping back, let his feet drag until he found the uneven board in the floor. As he bent down, he felt the board rise a little more and, pulling it up, he felt the cold damp air of the catacombs beneath the city. He dropped into the darkness and landed in cold water in a cavern that smelt like the sea. Glad he had been here before, he hoped to remember the way.

Groping around, he found the hidden tinderbox and lit a torch. Even his eyes were not good enough to negotiate the utter darkness of the catacombs. He walked for a while, counting steps until the catacomb wall became hung with cloth. Pausing, he waited until he felt the cold air on his face move and then pulled aside the drape to reveal a large room in the cavern furnished with furs and fine rugs. A glowglobe sat in a wall holder by the door and cast its pale light across the room.

A Passer mage stepped up to him. "What business have you here? This place is dangerous…secret, how come you here?"

Olek smiled confidently and held out the scroll. "I come from the House of the Oncoming Storm, for I am his and at his bidding. I have been to this place before and as his man, have the rights as the servant of he who owns this place. I bring greetings and a request contained in this scroll. Mage I am not, it is true, but I do the bidding of the Lord of the Arcane Realms."

The mage looked worried and took the scroll, reading it quickly. Olek smiled once more. "I trust my lord's wishes are plain enough? Information can be returned to the Oaken Barrel."

The mage bowed his head. "As my lord wishes, enquiries will be made, and the elfchild will be sought for. I will escort you to the other entrance that leads to the Enclave. You may find your way from there."

Olek returned to the townhouse via the tavern and waited for the information his sources would bring in. He needed to steel himself to visit the slave market in the morning should his contact provide what he required. He had been to the slave markets before, and a sadder and more despicable place he had never encountered.

* * *

The Oaken Barrel was not among the high class drinking houses in the city of Varlek, being owned by the House of Thieves, although not, of course, officially. It was often frequented by those customers who wished to keep their business private. The barkeep was large, sporting a goodly number of scars and several missing fingers. He knew when to listen, and when to keep his mouth closed, useful traits for one of his profession. He was a friendly sort, at least to those patrons he liked, and never drew enough attention to himself or his dealings to attract undue attention from the Order.

Visiting early, Olek found the missive. It was short:

The small one whom you seek has not yet been found within the confines of the city. Enquiries will continue.

As Olek turned to leave, the barkeep merely said, "A gentleman who sent his regards says the scarred man comes late today."

Olek settled to wait, thinking it perhaps wise not to be seen lingering too long in the market district. Besides, the slave market turned his stomach so he slowly savoured a brandy and warmed by the fire before needing to compose himself and head towards that place.

The market district of the city was always teeming, stallholders selling, customers buying, thieves looking for a chance to use their skills, and guards and Witch-Hunters on watch for thieves and magic use, making sure their presence was well noted. He browsed a couple of stalls, seemingly looking for nothing in particular.

A city guard approached him. "State your business beyond the Enclave, elf," the guard demanded.

Olek looked at him, feigning an air of submissiveness. "I do my master's bidding. I have a letter of authority. He seeks items in the city and I know his tastes." He held out the scroll and after inspection, the guard grunted and thrust it back.

"Well, make sure you do not dawdle, elf," he grunted and moved on, but kept an eye on Olek.

The half-elf purchased one or two small items and made to move along until the guard turned his attention elsewhere. Watching from the shadows, Olek knew the slave market was somewhat ad hoc, unless you were a person of means who had the money and influence to buy on request. This day the slave market was quiet; he saw a few wagons, mostly empty, but close to the wall, he spotted a caged wagon containing an elf woman who was with child and some young boys and a guard sauntering nearby. Olek knew pregnant woman often fetched a goodly price as the infant was either sold on separately or the buyer could effectively get the child for free. A child born a slave remained that way. Those nursing infants or pregnant mothers were often more amenable in order to protect their child. He wondered whether they were forest elves and if so, from where. Looking around the side streets, he saw a whore plying her trade and sauntered close, dropping the Shadowplay.

"Fancy earning some easy coin that does not necessarily involve being on your back, girl? Here is a gold piece. That man by the wagons, the human, distract him by whatever means you see fit. Keep him busy for a while"

The woman took the gold, sliding the coin between her breasts and giving Olek a smile, then sauntered over to the guard, flashing her attributes. The half-elf dropped back into the shadows and silently approached the wagon once the guard was suitably distracted, the fellow having been persuaded to accompany the whore down a darker alley. Olek took the opportunity to pick the lock of the wagon and, opening the door, he whispered in Elvish, "Here, come to me, I am a friend and I mean you well. Slavers raided a village in the forest, taking elves, but I do not see them here. Have you information?"

The elf woman hesitated, unsure of this man but knowing she did not wish to remain where she was, she whispered, "I do not know. Some of us were taken from villages in the forest and some simply removed from the Enclave, both from this city and beyond, I believe. Some of those taken had not much of the Forest Tongue and wore the human style clothes of the city, some said they were taken on the road, snatched going about their business for their humans. Children were removed from their mothers, it was terrible, poor frightened little souls."

The woman rubbed her belly, as though thinking of those children taken away. She looked afraid, yet there was an air of determination such as motherhood brings. Deciding to trust the stranger, she continued, "It was so dark, sometimes we stopped and people were pulled from the wagon. There were six women in my wagon, not all from my village, and three children. Only a few of us from the caged wagon I was put in came here.

"My village is gone. I have no hope but that someone buys us, someone kind; I can sew and cook well enough, I am skilled as a potter. There were a few other wagons and some that came from elsewhere, I think, which joined us. I heard a dialect, Elvish but not of our village," she said sadly.

Olek took her hand and, checking they were not observed, helped the woman from the wagon. "You will be free again. I cannot get you out for a day or so, but you can be hidden until such times as my lord can make arrangement for safe passage for you, all of you as we can find. I have further business here, but you will be safe enough with my allies. There are survivors from the village…not many…but there are survivors and I seek more. Please, you must try and recall, anything. Even if it is does not seem important?"

The woman looked at him, tears in her eyes of sadness and gratitude. "I am sorry I cannot remember much. I remember water and darkness…and…and…"

"You must trust me. I will take you somewhere you will not be found. There are many tunnels and some lead to the Enclave. There is a half-elf woman there, Aura;

she will help and be kind to you. If you recall anything, please tell her. One more thing…I seek a man called Rufus, a scarred human."

The elf woman shook her head. "I am not sure… There was a man, a human, he seemed to be in charge. He comes to the market later…it is early. Some of us were… already sold, yesterday, possibly even before."

Olek nodded and picked up the smaller child, motioning the woman to bring the elder ones. He led them carefully through the back streets. "Quiet, cry or draw attention and it will not go well for us. Follow me closely."

Silently, he slipped up to a door and held a finger to his lips, motioning them into the shadows. He picked the lock, then drew a blade and entered. The old warehouse was empty and he hoped the hatch was still loose. Bending down, he pulled. As he hoped, the hatch in the floor opened and he motioned into the darkness. "Here is a tunnel, follow it and pull on the rope at the other end. It will open a hatch to a house in the Enclave, there is a ladder but it is not too high. Find Aura, tell her Shadowdancer sent you."

He pressed some coins into her hand and then watched as she led the children. Shaking his head, he returned to the market and hid in the shadows, grinning with satisfaction to see the man in consternation as he discovered the missing elves.

Olek watched as a large, scarred man approached, accompanied by another caged wagon pulled by a rough looking horse and steered by a burly human. The sound of wailing came from within and someone tried to rattle the bars. The fellow looked as though he could manage himself well enough and Olek shifted the swords under his cloak for easier reach. Contemplating, the half-elf selected a small phial from his belt; he slowly coated one of the swords with the sticky contents and waited.

Seeing his merchandise gone, the scarred man layed into the guard with some fury. Checking the side streets, he spotted a city guard and indignantly reported his losses. Olek crept around unseen to lurk in the shadow of an alley, watching the wagon driver dismount to reprimand the occupants who were causing a good deal of noise. As the slaver Rufus passed, Olek stepped out and clapped his hand over the man's mouth, dragging him back into the dark alley and into a disused building.

The slaver tried to struggle. Although larger and stronger than the half-elf, Olek swept the man's legs from under him, dropping him in the filth with a blade at his throat and then sat on his back and hissed, "This blade contains a slow poison, cry out, struggle or otherwise attempt to make things difficult and I will plant this blade in you. There is a slow paralysis but excruciating pain as your muscles start to burn from within. You will die, but it will take several hours, if not a day or two. If you cooperate, you may yet get to walk away with the same amount of appendages as you started the day with."

Rufus tried bluster, wriggling and trying to dislodge his assailant, only to feel the sharp point of the blade draw blood. "You cannot do this. I am licensed by the city. I break no laws."

Olek leant to his ear. "I do not give a fuck if you are licensed by the gods themselves, for I do not abide by the laws. Keep them or break them, I do not give a damn. I seek some elves, those you stole from the village of Szendro beyond the Tremellic Valley. I seek a girl, small, white hair. I also seek information on the whereabouts of the others, for I see but a few here. Who paid you? Answer me these questions and you may escape the blade of the Shadowdancer this day."

Rufus weighed his chances. He was stronger by far than the half-elf who held him, but usually his prey were women, children, and those much weaker. He was at a disadvantage and suspected this man would kill him before he had chance to get to his feet. "There were many elves, some were sold here…but we had a special order. I just deliver them. I do not remember individuals; elves are elves, simply profit."

Olek hissed into his ear, "You best start to remember…where they dropped, who met them? Why not bring them straight to the slave market. Perhaps a little pain would focus your mind?"

Rufus closed his eyes, realising he would surely die if he held his tongue. "We dropped some at a small village on the river, a couple of the maidens, although I can't remember if the white haired one was there. It was a village in the meander of the White River before it flows into the Great River proper. Some young fellow bought them, paid his bills, took his goods. He said his father was a merchant, sold silk, a rich fellow. Well must have been to afford what he paid. Arlen, Arlec, Arden or something was the village; there is an Order fort nearby. The others…I am not sure…some were reserved by some other rich fellow. Those we dropped with another slaver, after that I have no idea. He paid very well. He has done business before…likes to get fresh ones for his master. We just hand over the goods and don't ask. Gold buys silence. I know not where he took them, a few women and girls, a couple of lads. The pregnant bitch and other lads we kept along with some already sold."

Olek smiled like a snake. "Very good… Now, what should I do with you? Perhaps deliver you to the custody of a friend of mine. The Thiefmaster would certainly be interested to hear you are taking Enclave elves. If your information is good then perhaps, if those I seek live, you may get to choose another line of work. However, should your information be a lie, a decoy or some other falsity or the ones I seek live not, heed this, slaver: I am merely the prelude to the fury of the Oncoming Storm."

Binding and gagging the slaver slowly, Olek scored a line across the man's arms with his untainted blade. Removing another phial, he slowly held it before the man's eyes. "This is a form of that which coats my blade. The ropes that bind you will be covered in it. Wriggle or try to escape and this enters the wound. My friend will have the antidote. Well, possibly."

Very slowly, he dripped the poison onto the ropes, not letting it enter the wounds. Returning outside, he noticed the second slaver wagon had departed. Cursing, he returned to the Thiefmaster, requesting accommodation for the captive and for a look out to be kept for the second wagon. On return to the townhouse, Olek spent the rest of the afternoon writing notes and contemplating which allies would be most useful. The housekeeper informed him she had contacted the whores and was awaiting a response.

Soon after, a rider left to deliver a note to Tremellic:

The little Spirit Child has not been traced within the city; some young maidens were dropped at a village named Arden or Arlen, near to a fort, to a merchant's son. I have not a name but he deals in fabrics and fine silks. The others were dropped with another slaver; I have people making further enquiries. We have an elf woman and three children in protection within the Enclave. The slaver Rufus will soon be enjoying the hospitality of the Thiefmaster. He may be persuaded to remember more than he has done.

I suggest we meet at Arden? The other enquiries will take a few days.

As ever your servant.

O.

CHAPTER 11

Ozena sat in the quarters she had been allocated, a far more luxurious accommodation than anything she had ever seen. The human housekeeper had been kind to her, laughing merrily when she had gasped at the rooms and said it was not what she was used to. The old woman had brought her food and offered her a bath with hot water. Ozena was used to bathing in the river or one of the nearby pools. Hot water was simply not a luxury that existed in her village. She had felt guilty that the woman had been put to trouble, but apparently there was some form of water boiler, like a giant kettle that could be tapped, kept warm by a magical fire. This in turn was controlled by the runes which decorated the large marble bathtub. The housekeeper had said this was one of the perks for having a mage as a master.

Dii had loaned her a soft linen shift and spare wrap, not to mention a set of clothes, although Ozena was too polite to say they were not what she was used to. Scented oils and perfume were available for use and Ozena looked wide-eyed at the selection.

As she lay on the bed, Ozena sunk deep into it. Resisting the urge to bounce, she ran her fingers into the light chiffon drapes of leaf green. There were a couple of chests and an armoire, and set just off from the bedchamber was a small dressing room, containing items for her toilet and a vast mirror; another luxury, as the small looking glass Ozena generally used was rather old, but dear, having belonged to her mother. The small decorated parlour was furnished with a couple of comfortable chairs, a chaise, a small bookcase and a large window looking out on to the gardens. A vase of flowers sat on the dresser, a hasty addition, as the housekeeper had told her the master rarely entertained and many of the rooms were rarely used. The elf had been surprised that such a vast home belonged to only one man and his mistress, plus the small household staff.

Ozena felt lost, her world had suddenly shattered around her. Everything she had known had been torn away, the village gone, her home destroyed or as good as. Everyone she knew was missing or dead, save the Elder and the two rescued elves.

Suddenly she was dependent on the kindness of a human lord and his household. Inside, she knew she had no hope of finding her sister without their help. The huntress had never been far from her village and did not know how to find this city, not to mention she was not a fool, all elves knew they could not travel alone. The two poor rescued women were testament to the unfortunate treatment which would often befall her kind, even without the terrible fate of her village. Ozena felt deep anger, anger that such an event had occurred and anger at herself for her uselessness. Archos had told her he would find her sister and the others, yet with every hour that passed Amena was more lost to her and the chances of finding her alive and unharmed diminished. Alone and weeping with despair, Ozena curled into a ball, lost in misery until she had no more tears to cry.

Perhaps magic could find her sister! Ozena knew the tales of the great mages of old and she resolved to request the help of the female mage of the house, feeling she had imposed much already on the goodwill of Lord Archos.

Olek had already left for the city. Archos was in his workshop, and Dii lay on a chaise, studying from an old magical tome. Much of learning magic was theory and booklore, she had discovered, not that it bothered Dii as she loved to learn.

"If I may have a moment of your time, Dii?" Ozena asked nervously, not knowing what response she might receive.

"Of course. You are settling in well enough? I am still not used to so many fine things, or being allowed to move where I choose. Now, what is it I may help you with?" Dii replied, smiling at her.

Ozena looked at her feet, suddenly ashamed. "Yes, the house is very grand, much more than I am used to, yet somehow lonely in places, I think. My village was always busy, there was always someone about; that is partly what I wish to speak about. I… Well, to be truthful, I am ashamed to always be seeking help and giving nothing. I do not know a good deal about magic but what the legends tell of great sorcerers such as Lord Archos. I was going to ask if you could find a person using magic; if you would be kind enough to try and look for Amena."

"Truth be told, I am not sure. I think it may be possible under some circumstances. My lord tells me he found me because his Mirror sensed my magic and he managed to scry for where I might be. Scrying is tricky and rather haphazard in its results. Your sister is but a child and her Power would be slight, so I really I do not know. Perhaps Lord Archos would fare better as he has much greater Power than I." Dii saw the sadness and desperation and, offering comfort, patted her arm.

Ozena clutched her hand. "No, please… I have asked so much of him already and he has done so many things, I am ashamed to ask again. Please, if you think you may try or ask him to."

"I am sure my lord would gladly help, for he is most concerned to find the elves from your village.

"However I will try myself, then I may ask him…it may be the case it is simply not possible to find her that way. Olek has gone to find information in the city and Archos has many resources at his disposal."

Patting Ozena's arm, she said, "Come let us try and see if anything will be revealed."

Leading her close to the fire, she motioned to a seat and slowly drew a Circle in which she sat gazing at the fire. "I am Dii'Athella, sorceress, spirits of the Arcane Realm, lend me this day your sight to seek a Spirit Child. Reveal to us the whereabouts of the elfchild Amena Lyn."

Pale blue burned the fire, flames weaving like a dancer and the mists of the Astral Realms swirled for a moment, then faded and returned the fire to its normal state. Dii tried once more, trying to boost the Power until, feeling slightly woozy, she ceased.

"I am sorry. Nothing was revealed, perhaps I simply do not have the Power, or perhaps there is nothing to be seen. Scrying can be unreliable and I am not very experienced. She is young, perhaps her trace does not yet show. There are other, more mundane ways to seek a person. I will speak with Lord Archos later and perhaps he knows a better way, or whether it may even be possible. You need not be ashamed to ask for help or to accept it when it is offered."

"I am afraid…afraid we will not find her and if we do, it will be too late," Ozena whispered, her eyes filled with desperation.

The young elven mage wrapped Ozena in her arms and murmured kind words to her, letting a comforting wave of magic slowly wrap them both and let her tears mingle with Ozena's, knowing what could befall a young elven girl.

"I am sorry. I am just being foolish. I need a distraction… I know nothing can be done until Olek returns. Perhaps I may go and walk in the gardens, or down to the village to speak with the elves and see how they fare. Do not worry or give me that look, I know I cannot go to the city alone, as much as I may wish to. I will go and watch for Olek's return. I need a little time alone and close to nature," Ozena whispered, pulling away.

Dii looked at her, seeking the truth of whether she would try and run to the city alone. She saw sadness and despair, but she also saw the beginnings of trust and a resolution to wait. Dii patted her arm. "Well, do not go far or we will worry. Promise me you will not do anything rash."

Ozena smiled sadly. "Alas, it is not within my abilities to seek her in the city. I will just walk, perhaps to the village. I may take my bow and see if I may catch some rabbits. I promise I will not try and run away."

Nodding, Dii watched her go, then turned and headed for Archos' workshop, shaking her head and murmuring a prayer to any gods who happened to be listening.

* * *

Archos had felt the ripple of Dii's magic from his workshop and quietly made his way to the Crystal he had set up on his workbench, touching it so the scene in the library was revealed, although soundless. He watched as she used the fire to scry and saw her comfort Ozena. The Archmage thought it marvellous that Dii, who had suffered so much, could show such sympathy and kindness to another.

He sighed and felt the pang for her within him. Gently he set the Crystal on the tripod in the midst of the Circle and, slashing into his arm, he dripped blood over the item, letting it drip to pool slowly on the floor. Tapping the Crystal, he gazed into it. Shifting his Focus, he tried to find a tiny trail of magic in the swirling mists. He felt the Power from Dii in the library and for a moment stopped and let it wash over and fill him, enhancing his own, and he continued to seek, calling, "I am Archos, Lord of the Arcane Realms, show me this day the thread of Amena of the Elfkind, Spirit Child."

For a while he searched and felt nothing, and everything. Many threads swirled around him, yet he could not distinguish one alone, as though he were blind in the Astral Realm, yet could see everything. He called forth his Power until his vision began to blur, yet still he could not see the tiny thread that Amena held in the Astral Realm. It would be easier if he possessed something of hers, but even so, still extremely difficult. For a while he wandered among the twisting paths and searched to no avail. Archos felt the cold winds of the Astral Realms around him, chilling him as he walked. For a moment he thought he felt something, a slight touch but then it was gone, a tiny tingle, almost imperceptible.

He sighed and tried to search again, reaching to touch what he thought he had felt, the winds roaring around him. Above the manor, a storm began to gather. Straining deep within himself, Archos tried to reach out further. As he searched and pulled the mists around him, he realised either the thread was lost to him or, more likely, had never even existed. Slowly he began to shift his Focus back, finding it difficult, having to follow his own thread back.

Dii felt the ripple of Power after Ozena had left. She had felt such before since she had lived here, but this felt almost like a solid wall. Heading to the workshop, she paused at the door, her own Power suddenly peaking within her with a deep, almost orgasmic blast. She fought down the feeling and the spell trying to cast itself. Pushing open the door, she saw him, slumped on the floor in the Circle and lying in a pool of blood. Dii gasped and ran, leaping over the Circle as it flared around her.

She cradled Archos to her, listening to his ragged breath. She closed her eyes and gently channelled a healing spell into him. As she concentrated and cast, his Astral Self saw her shimmer before him into clear view and he dived towards her, grabbing the thread that linked them. Dii stroked his face, her eyes brimming with tears.

"What have you done, my love? What were you trying to do? Do not leave me… come back to me, my love," she whispered to him, softly kissing his hair.

The wounds in his arm healed and his breathing eased a little, and she held him tight, whispering sweet nothings to him. Hoping the sound of her voice would rouse the unconscious form.

Archos awoke from his Astral Trance as Dii's Astral Self swirled around him, warming him from the chill of the arcane winds that roared furiously around them. His head felt heavy, and for a moment he lay with his eyes closed and felt safe with her. Opening his eyes, he saw Dii, her eyes wide and misted with tears. Gently, slowly, he reached out to touch her face.

"My pretty Flower," Archos said, "I wake from Astral Sight to gaze upon your beauty. I saw you and followed your light. I plunged deep within the Astral Realms, yet it was all so confused. Why do you cry, my sweet?"

Dii bit back the tears. "I feel the Power like a solid wall and then find you unconscious and bleeding. I was afraid you were lost to me, my lord."

Archos sat up and managed a smile. "Oh, Flower, I do not deserve your kindness and certainly not your love. I watched you in the library, trying to search for the young elf, offering such kindness to Ozena. You are a light that shines for me, Dii. You called to me across the Arcane Realms and my very soul became entwined with yours at that moment."

"My lord, I failed in providing her much comfort. My Power is not great enough that I was able to find Amena," Dii confessed with a blush.

The Magelord stroked her hair, pulling the braid gently over her shoulder and untying the ribbons which bound it. "Oh, my pretty, insecure girl, your Power is great. Scrying is something that grows easier with practice. I thought to try and look for her in the Astral Realms, the blood increases the potency of the spells, but I may have over reached myself. I thought I saw something but it seems I was wrong. It may simply be her Power is not yet enough to register, or she may be in Baneshackles or… Well, I am tired and there have been many calls upon my Power of late. I merely need to rest."

Dii smiled naughtily. "Do I tire you out, my lord? And I thought you were a man of great stamina."

Archos laughed and let his fingers caress slowly over her. "Indeed I am and, given the chance, will show you, but serious magic demands a price, and it seems I simply pushed myself a little too far. It is a while since I had a vibrant and demanding young mistress…and less sleep. Now perhaps we should move to somewhere more comfortable. I can rest whilst you study. I like to watch you read. It will calm me and perhaps we can test my stamina when I am rested."

Slowly, Dii helped him to his feet and led him to the library. He settled into a chair by the fire and she wandered the shelves to find the tomes she sought. Archos watched her move and thought on what she had spoken of: her love. Dii became absorbed in her study, but every so often turned her gaze to where he sat and read his own book, or at least pretended to. Whenever the beautiful elf looked at him, she gave a smile which made his heart beat faster and gave him a stir in his loins.

Moving close, he inhaled her scent and ran his fingers down her spine. The tingles rippled and she spun round into his embrace and, pulling him into a deep sensuous kiss, she breathed his name. Archos kissed her hungrily. "My delightful Flower, you study so hard. Perhaps I may distract you…"

Dii turned those captivating dark eyes to his. "My lord, I wish to please you and be worthy of you. I like to learn…there is so much knowledge here and you need to rest."

Stroking along her jaw, Archos chuckled. "I doubt you would ever be unworthy, Dii, but perhaps more…pleasurable amusements could divert us for a while. I hunger for you, for your touch. There are many ways to please me." With a snap of his fingers, the door locked and ensured privacy.

Dii laughed her bubbling, melodious laugh and kissing him, let her lips trail to his ear. "Then I must do my utmost to please you, Lord Archos."

Taking his hand, she led him to a chair close to the fire and near to one of the mirrors. Motioning for him to be seated, she began to very slowly remove her clothes. Unlacing the bodice, she stroked her fingers around her breasts, teasing her nipples until they were hard little points against the soft blouse. Slowly she removed the garment, peeling it down her shoulders until it fell to her feet, revealing soft skin the colour of alabaster and the alluring tattoo that wove and spiralled across her. Running her fingers over her own skin, she leant forward to kiss him, letting her skin brush his but not allowing him to touch. Slowly she stepped out of her skirts and let them pool on the floor. She stood before him naked, reflected in the mirror. One hand slowly stroked a line down to nestle between her legs, which she parted slightly, letting him see her begin to circle a finger there.

With a growl, Archos pulled her close to him, kissing her soft skin hungrily and breathing her scent. Tongue running across her nipple, first one then the other, before sucking them hard. His hand moved down to her cleft to join her own, and slowly he began to tease her. His free hand around her waist, Archos pulled her close and stroked the skin on her back, tickling a spot he knew made her shiver.

Unbuttoning the robe he wore until his chest was revealed, Dii nibbled the skin, teeth hard against him, but in contrast her soft lips caressed. She licked the rune tattoo, stroking it until it glowed from the magic flowing from her fingers, and Archos moaned as the Power tantalised him. Sliding her hands down his body ever so slowly, she untied the laces at his breeches and freed him. Pulling them away and discarding them as she had done her own garments.

He pulled her into an intense kiss as she climbed onto his lap; she let her fingers weave into his hair and leaned back, his mouth at her breasts, tugging and teasing. The bright red curls, glowing in the firelight, fell around her as she arched into him, sighing with delight.

"Pleasure me… Pleasure me by the method of your choice, and then I will take you…slowly…very slowly," he breathed, his mouth sending delightful shudders through her as his lips brushed her skin.

Dii smiled that captivating, seductive smile and kissed him, softly at first then pulling at his lips with her teeth and running her tongue along them. Slowly she began to trail her lips down his neck and across his chest again, pulling at the ring in his nipple as he settled back. Sliding off him gracefully, she began to nip and lick as she went lower and, slipping onto the rug, she sat on the floor in front of him. Pausing as she listened to his breath increase, she ran her fingers across the lightning tattoo on his inner thigh, crackling sparks as he moaned at her touch. Slowly she began to lick and suck at the skin before she very slowly licked a line across to the other thigh, making him groan.

The fire behind her sparked and burned deep red as the passion and desire built. In the warmth, her curls shone like molten copper and Archos buried his fingers in her hair as he watched her wriggle forward and take him slowly into her mouth, her eyes on his. Slowly she began to lick and suck, biting, nipping, watching him writhe as her curls tickled him and the Power sparked around them. Pulling back, Dii rippled her tongue along his manhood and Archos moaned her name. She paused to tickle the tip with her lips.

Her hair and the sparks around them added a new sensation to the experience, seeming to heighten his pleasure. Gripping the side of the chair with one hand, he slid forward as he began to breathe fast under her touch, crying out as she bit him. He growled, "More," as she continued to pleasure him.

Dii pulled back for a moment, returning to bite his inner thighs, dragging the edge of her teeth along him. Wrapping her hand around his manhood, she stroked him, nipping at the skin of his inner thighs. His eyes closed, taking deep breaths as if in meditation, he denied himself release, holding back, waiting. Letting go of her hair, he gripped the chair with both hands as he moaned deep in his throat, feeling the hard rush as his climax mounted.

She paused, chuckling against his manhood, and he fought the release, the intensity filling him. Suddenly she pulled away and slid herself onto his lap, lithe like a cat; kissing his neck as she writhed above him, teasing, not letting him enter her. Still Dii stroked him, now rapidly, then tortuously slowly, then faster; driving him ever closer to the edge, holding him there until he could take it no more. Wrapping his arms around her, pulling her tight, he bit her hard below the ear, stifling his cry as he released over her hands.

"My sweet girl, you drive me wild, you are my heart and my desire," Archos breathed to her, "and now, my pretty, it is my turn to pleasure you."

Slowly he ran his fingers up and down her spine, trailing magic, and settled with them both facing the mirror, one of her legs across the arm of the chair. His hand found her warmth and he tickled her, circling her pip. One hand flicking and tweaking at her breasts as his fingers slid within her. Slowly he began to pleasure her, pulsing magic, watching the reflection of pleasure as she begin to move against his hands. Archos nipped at her neck as she leaned her head back, mouth hot against the tattooed skin and hands busy until he was ready for her.

Archos entered her, arms close about her waist as he slid into a position from which he could plunge deep. He began to move, building the climax slowly and surely, stopping to flick at her pip, skim a hand over her breast, when she came close but never quite enough to send her over until he willed it. He found the reflection of her moaning and writhing deeply erotic.

The air crackled and the fire roared in the hearth as he took her as slowly as he had promised; hands and lips touching, exploring, teasing until she screamed his name as the magic and the passion finally took her over the edge. Still he pumped her until she came again, pulsing around him, and fell trembling in a heap in his arms as he too reached his peak, breathless and lost in the ecstasy of this woman. Both spent and tired, but happy, he picked her up and together they lay on the rug before a fire still sparking and crackling.

"You are mine," he murmured to her.

"My lord, you are a happiness I could never have foreseen. As you saved my life, you are my life," Dii whispered as she snuggled into his embrace.

Archos smiled and as they lay together in the room that held so much Power and knowledge, he thought to himself it was nothing to the power he felt for the girl in his arms.

CHAPTER 12

Ozena had returned from her trip to the village feeling a little calmer. The rescued elves were being treated with kindness and pity, and the Elder was lodged with the Steward who was respectful and kind to the old man. It seemed he would live despite his wounds, but probably would never be strong again. The two rescued women, Ordana and Hannia, were lodged with an elderly matron at the edge of Harkenen, a motherly woman who immediately treated the two young women as her adopted daughters. Ozena had known that the village traded with the elves of Szendro but had not been aware exactly how strong the bond was; that, and the bond between the villagers of the Tremellic Valley and their lord.

Archos had instructed that the elves were to be treated well, as kin to the villagers, and so it was. The flock of forest goats had been settled with the local sheep and the guinea fowls with Ordana and Hannia. Ozena was touched by the treatment of her Elfkind companions among the humans. She had spent the afternoon with the Elder and he reassured her that she should put her trust in the humans which had taken them in. Pointing out that even should she arrive at the city unmolested, but alone, chances were she would be taken to the Enclave, which would achieve nothing in the search for her sister. Agreeing to trust Archos and his not insignificant powers and contacts, she headed back to the manor to find him waiting for her, with some concern.

"Ah, my dear, I am glad you have returned. I had half a mind that you would do something rash, but it seems you are a sensible and wise young woman. I believe Dii tried to search for Amena using magic; I did also, but was unable to find anything. It may be, simply, her thread is too slight to find by such means as she is so young and untrained. I have…contacts in the city and I have no doubt that Olek will not fail to use every means at our disposal to search. I merely wait to hear from him in order to plan our next move. I promise to you I will find who is responsible for this tragedy.

"I fear you may be a little bored in my house. There are a number of Elvish books within the library and either myself or Dii will be around to keep you company, or the elves within the settlements. There is hunting for game in the foothills and the forest edges and you may, of course, come and go from my house as you please. However I request you do not leave the safety of Tremellic Valley."

Bowing to her, he smiled and waited for her to pass him. As she entered, a voice echoed in her head. "We will find her. We will avenge this tragedy. You have my word."

* * *

The rider arrived at dawn a few days later with the note from Olek. Archos walked to his workshop and mused for a while. Taking a large tome from the shelf, he browsed for a while and then grinned, and the storm clouds gathered. Swiftly he packed a few items and sought out Dii and Ozena. The girls were in the library, warm in front of the fire. Ozena was telling Dii elven legends and Archos was relieved to see she seemed more relaxed.

Dii had turned to see him when the door opened and she bounded to him when she saw the determination in his face and the travelling clothes he wore. "My lord, you dress for travel, have you word from Olek?"

The Magelord held his hands out to her and looked over to Ozena. "I have, indeed. We are still pursuing many…leads, but it would seem a couple of the elf maidens may be in the possession of a cloth merchant in a village named Arden. I say 'may' be in his possession as the information was rather vague, however I intend to check the validity, perhaps this man may be of use. It would seem the Slaver was rather…reluctant to talk. I will be gone a few days, however you will be comfortable enough here."

Ozena stood up and walked over to him. "I am coming. One of those girls may be Amena, she will need me."

Archos smiled dismissively. "You and Dii will be safe enough here. Olek will meet me there. We should not have any difficulty dealing with the matter."

She folded her arms. "I doubt not your Power, Lord Archos, yet you do not know Amena. If it is her, she will be frightened. She is unlikely to go with a strange human, whatever her situation, she is a shy creature. I would see for myself she is safe and whole. I have been useless in seeking her thus far, you would deny me this? If it turns out to be other elves than she, they may feel more comfortable with a female elf of their acquaintance than a human stranger, Magelord or not. I am not a child, nor as naive as you suspect. I know what I may find, or not find. Yet still I will go to seek my sister."

He looked at the young huntress, her green eyes set with determination, a burning fire of resolution that made them shine like emeralds. "I have a feeling I have little choice, for you will attempt to go anyway should I refuse. Believe me, I *could* keep you here, but I am no slaver and you have my word that you are free in my lands. I only seek to protect you. However, as you so rightly say, you are not a child. I think this is one argument I may lose, so will simply say this: it is not guaranteed we will find anyone, let alone your sister. You must trust me and let me deal with the merchant should the need arise. Pack what you will need for a few days travel. You and Dii can ride in the coach, I will drive until we meet with Olek." With that, he left to prepare the carriage.

Dii looked at Ozena and said quietly, "That was quite the speech, Ozena. You are courageous and loyal. I think he sees that and that is why he acquiesces. Perhaps we should pack to leave?"

* * *

Arden was a moderate settlement to the east of Tremellic. The buildings lay clustered around a central square that was linked by crossroads to the Great Highway which ran the length of Erana. It also lay close to the River Sinawe, also known as the White River, a tributary of the Great River. A small dock served for both trade and fishing. There was little order as the village had sprung up as a trading post and then expanded. It was still a matter of some days to travel to the larger towns and the city in the south of the country, but many merchants liked the quieter life of the village and kept a country house in such settlements. The Witch-Hunter fort close by ensured the village was secure, both from magic and the more mundane risks which often befell trading areas.

Niall Versann was a trader in silks, velvets and other fine cloth; his business was successful as a number of influential persons purchased wares from him. Only the wealthy could afford such fabrics, and so the coin flowed freely in the House of Versann. He kept a warehouse within the city and a couple of ships that traded along the ports of the Silver Sea, but he lived primarily at the country house, preferring the peace and security of a village to the noise and relative risk of the city. The house lay beyond the village, just off upon the hill, far enough to be private, close enough for convenience.

Olek had appeared the night before and kept himself to himself, booking a room in the tavern under the proviso his master would be arriving shortly. As the afternoon progressed, he waited for the carriage, appearing soundlessly to take the reins as Archos disappeared within to join the women. As evening approached, Archos and his party arrived at the manor of the merchant and Olek went to deliver the message that his lord required accommodation because the lord's mistress had been taken ill. His lord and his women had been travelling for some time and did not wish to stay in the local tavern.

The merchant Niall was obsequious and overly polite to the possible new customer, obviously a man of means, offering the hospitality of his household. Archos was polite and aloof, but watchful of this man; judging his moves, even occasionally sifting his surface thoughts, he found him obsessed with money and the honour of his house.

* * *

Olek sat content in the dining hall, his belly full. He looked around the room and thought, for a trader this man liked weapons. Archos and Dii had retired to their guest chambers; it had taken a good deal of Archos' charm to convince Niall that Dii was not merely a servant. He yawned and noticed the son of the house staring at him, searching his memory for a name after the hasty introductions.

Gamal sauntered over to the half-elf. "Enjoying the hospitality, elf? My father is a wealthy man used to entertaining. He owns a fine fabric business, silks, linens, things of that nature. The business does well enough, as you can see." He swept his arm around, showing off the trappings of wealth. "I hope your master's…whore…er…woman is comfortable. She is a pretty creature, and much indulged, it would appear."

Olek had not been alone in noticing the young man's eyes on the elven women. Feigning an impressed look at the wealth openly on display around him, Olek replied evenly, "Yes, thank you, young sir. My master and his lady were tired. She has not been well and we have been travelling for some time."

The young man looked around almost conspiritorially. "You seem to manage the…affairs of the Lord Archos; he trusts you, yes? I would deal with you about arranging certain business affairs?"

"Business? My lord is not in the same line of business, as your father what do you propose?" Olek said, intrigued, and hoping to gain some useful information.

"The elf girl, the brunette, I wish to have her. What price for her?"

"Pardon?" Olek choked on the remnants of his wine, "You think the girls are for sale? You are mistaken. Both women are with my master. They are not for sale."

Gamal shrugged in a show of nonchalance. "As you wish, my gold is welcome elsewhere, but perhaps I can ask your master on the morrow and the reply will be different."

Olek resisted the urge to floor the man there and then, and laughing, replied, "That I sincerely doubt, but it should be entertaining to watch. My master will require me early tomorrow, if my lady is well enough."

He slipped out of the room and stepped into the flickering shadows of the passageway, pulling the darkness around him and waiting. He thought Ozena may have gone to bed but was unsure. She had left with one of the house servants but had mentioned attending to the horses and some of the baggage before retiring to one of the empty servants' beds in the small quarters beyond the kitchen.

Gamal smiled nastily and rose, walking quietly past the passageway as though to retire, but then turned and headed back through the kitchen and out to the stables. Seeing a lantern lit, he grinned unpleasantly once more, pleased to have privacy and illumination for his pleasure. There would be no disturbances and he liked to watch the reactions of his conquests. Gamal quietly entered the stable and, turning the key, locked the door. Viewing the elf woman Ozena, fetching down a saddlebag, his eyes filling with lust, he licked his lips and felt himself go hard at the thought of plucking that pretty cherry from the tree. Even if she had been bedded by the noble guest and was no maid, he would enjoy her fresh-faced charms.

Ozena heard the click of the lock and, starting slightly, thought perhaps the stable hand thought her in the house and had unsuspectingly locked her in the stable. Inclining her head, she caught the view of Gamal and gave a sharp intake of breath. "What mean you to disturb me? If I am required within, would a servant not come for me?"

He slid up a little too close to her. "Well, I was concerned, a pretty young elf woman alone in an unfamiliar house. Your master and his…whore…er…lady, have retired for the evening and the man Olek also. The servants were not expecting company and have been sent to rest after the upheaval. I like to retire late and sleep late and am not so much an impolite host that I would not make sure all the guests are comfortable."

"I thank you for your hospitality. I should not tarry here much longer. Why is the door locked? I heard it as you entered," she replied nervously.

"Do not concern yourself. The lock is faulty and father has yet to get it mended. I have a key to every room in the estate, so do not worry yourself, my pretty." Gamal moved his hand to touch her face. "Do not think I was unaware of those coy looks… those eyes on me."

Ozena backed up to find herself against the wall. "You are mistaken, sir… Please let me past…"

Gamal smiled like a snake, his hand moving quickly from a tender caress to grab a handful of hair. Pulling her onto her knees, close to her he snarled, "I think not…you know that all elves in this household are mine to do with as I please? Have the other servants not told you? Well, it is no matter, you will find out soon enough! I have a special place I take them, where I have taken the others, you see. A place where none can hear and no one will come to your aid. You will join their ranks soon enough. I can do as I like, use you as long as I like, however I like, until I am sated. If you displease me, you'll suffer for it elf-bitch."

* * *

Olek waited, expecting the man to pass him or Ozena to return if she had indeed gone to the stable to fetch what she needed. When she did not, he decided to check on her welfare. It could simply be she was lost within the strange house. No, the woman was a scout and hunter so that was unlikely, he thought. Slipping out into the yard and across to the stable, he could see the door closed and wondered if the door had simply closed after her. Likely as not she would be unfamiliar with such a building as Szendro had not held more than an elderly donkey and pony used by the traders.

Approaching the stable, his excellent hearing furnished him with the sound of two voices. In one, he could not mistake the threatening tone. Cursing beneath his breath, he assessed whether it would be quicker to pick the lock or kick in the door at the risk of panicking the beasts. Olek felt around his sleeve and found the small silk bag containing his lock picks. The night was dark and cloudy, even the goddess of the moon was not favouring him with her light this night. Usually he would appreciate the darkness in such situations, but not now. Crouching, he scrutinised the lock in the darkness. Feeling silently and carefully, he selected a small, thin lock pick and began to work, trying at the same time to listen for the click he desired and to eavesdrop on the conversation within.

Ozena tried to twist away, almost ripping her hair out. "Leave me be, get your hand off me!"

Gamal pulled her head down painfully, beginning to unlace his breeches with his free hand. "Struggle…oh, please. It makes me harder when they struggle. Not too much, though…or I will make it much worse for you. You will pleasure me. I may let you up if your mouth has satisfied me… I may not."

After opening his breeches, he slid his hand close to her throat and fumbled to remove the leathers from her. "I like to see what I get, little elf whore…"

He thrust her face into his groin. "I wonder why Lord Archos keeps you for himself when he has the other elven whore to amuse him. Perhaps he cannot manage you both; or does he keep you for something special? Perhaps you need the attentions of a real man. Elves are very acrobatic and have a good deal of stamina, is that not so? So much the better!"

Pulling hard at her leathers as she tried to struggle, he succeeded in opening the bodice and ripping away the light cotton garment she wore below. Thrusting his hand into her cleavage, he groaned with lust, grabbing, twisting at her.

Ozena tried to pull herself away with a cry, "No, get away from me!" before finding herself pulled back towards his groin.

Olek heard the lock click just as he heard Ozena's cry. Drawing his blade, he slipped into the stable and saw the scene. He slid in silently behind Gamal and placed the blade at his throat, hissing, "The lady said no." Glancing down, he continued, "Not that you have much to offer her even if she were compliant. As she is not, I suggest you desist."

Gamal froze as he felt the blade at his throat. Pushing Ozena back roughly, he tried to turn but Olek's blade dug into his flesh. "Be gone, servant. This is not of your concern. Or is that you want her for yourself? Master not allowing you to take her… or the other little whore?"

"I have killed better men than you for less," Olek snapped, then looked at Ozena. "Are you hurt? I swear if he has hurt you I will cut him to pieces. Go into the house… find Archos or Dii. I will deal with this cur. Go, I will be along shortly."

Ozena looked at him in shock and, almost weeping, ran for the house. Olek turned his attention back to Gamal. "Now we are alone…is that not how you like it? Away somewhere no one can hear the screams? Why should I not kill you here and now? I am sure my master would be interested to learn of this night's proceedings, trying to touch one of his girls when it had been made clear they were not for you. I assure you he will not be impressed."

"Remove your blade…servant. Neither you nor your master frightens me. However I am sure we could come to some…arrangement. I am sure we could keep this between us? I can lay my hands upon a fresh young girl, no man has touched her; could be moulded to your wishes. Let your master keep his two whores and get your own…" Gamal managed, feigning bravado.

Olek moved the blade down, resting it just below the man's privates. "I find charm and respect provides me with all the tumbles I need. I do not want a…slave. As for fear…you lie as badly as you pick up women. Your whole body tells me it is terrified, all except your mouth, for that seems to know as little sense as your brain.

"You have no idea with whom you deal…whom you offend. I do not need to be bribed, for I am not in need of coin or other…incentives. For the first, I have plenty of, and the second, when I am in need I make my own arrangement. Now what to do to you…seems somewhat ill mannered to kill the son of our host, at least without him and my master being acquainted with all the facts," Olek said, his voice as sharp as his blade.

Olek leaned back and pulled a rope hanging upon a peg. "If you wish to live until morning, I suggest you comply. I at least give a choice." Binding the man tightly, he continued, "We should be comfortable enough here until the household wakes. If you draw attention to us, I will remove that part of you which has caused such offence then I will make you eat it. If you behave, you will at least remain whole until my master decides how to punish your offences."

The half-elf grinned and sat back on some hay; taking the small flask from his pocket, he took a swig. Settling and making himself comfortable, Olek simply watched Gamal wriggle and try to free himself. "I wouldn't try that unless you can guarantee to be faster than my blade, which I sincerely doubt. Of course that would give me cause to kill you in…self-defence, which would be a shame now, would it not? It might happen to upset the horses too. Besides, my knots are good."

Gamal glared but ceased to try and free himself. "My father will have you flogged. He is rich and will ruin your master and his whores," he retorted.

"Oh, well, that could provide some entertainment whilst he tries. The women are not whores and as for ruining my master…no, I do not think so. Now would it not be far better for your tongue and my ears for you to button that insolent lip? It would be such a shame if I was forced to cut your tongue out after all."

* * *

Ozena bit back her fear and tears, and pulled her armour together as best she could. Grateful, she fled to the house and slipped into the kitchen. As the shock hit her, she began to cry and fled to the chamber allocated to Archos and Dii, banging on the door. Trembling, she wept and fell to the floor.

Hearing the noise outside and the subsequent thump on the door, Dii gracefully slid from the bed and, quickly dressing in a black silk robe, opened the door to see a terrified and distraught Ozena.

"My dear, oh Ozena, what is wrong? What has happened? Come inside."

Ozena fell into Dii's arms, sobbing as she was led into the room. "Oh Dii, that man, the young lord…I was in the stable…he locked the door…he tried to…I am so ashamed…"

The young mage pulled her friend close, whispering quiet comfort and letting a calming wave radiate from her. Archos rose from the bed and stalked to the women, belting his robe. Gently, he touched Ozena's shoulder, and grimaced when she flinched. Quietly, he asked, but with a dangerous edge to his voice, "This man, did he hurt you?"

"No… No not really," Although her hand slid to her hair and it's missing chunk. "He tried to make me…do something…He said he had a place he…took the others… no one to hear. Olek came in and saved me." She began to cry again.

Dii shot Archos a look and he nodded. "I should go…assist Olek…and call the servants to bring you something. Or, if you prefer not to wake the house, perhaps Dii can find you something warming and soothing. She will stay with you."

Ozena turned her tear-filled green eyes to him. "No, Lord Archos, please, I am so ashamed, please… Do not raise the household, so that everyone knows. Dii may fetch something. I…I am sorry, I was frightened."

Archos nodded and gently touched her shoulder. "You will be safe enough here. I will see to the man in the stables."

Dressing swiftly, the Archmage managed to contain his anger in front of the women, and stalked from the room. As he left, he touched each side of the door to ward it. He knew Dii was able enough to pass through and reset the ward, for they had been practicing such magic.

"Here, dress in these until we see the state of your armour. I will see to fetching you something from the kitchen. Now we are alone, are you sure he did not hurt you?" Dii said kindly, handing over some clothes.

Ozena wiped her eyes. "He did not…do that, even though he tried. He wanted to…he said I was a whore and it was his right. He rubbed himself into my face. His… you know. I am so ashamed. I was so frightened. So powerless."

Dii took her hands. "Listen to me…you have nothing in the world of which to be ashamed. You have done nothing wrong or to encourage that man. I know more than most that many men think women, and especially elven women, are simply there for their…pleasure… Their property. Not all think this way. Many, but not all. Some men are kind and tender. Until recently I would not have believed it but Archos is kind, Olek is kind, and he protected you. Not all men are like the merchant's son here."

She settled Ozena onto the bed and wrapped a coverlet across her like a child, gently kissing her forehead. "Come now, rest a while. Lord Archos and Olek will deal with it. We can investigate the missing elves and then leave. I will fetch something else to calm you. Try and sleep. Once I return, I will be here to watch over you, sit with you, whatever you wish."

* * *

Archos glided through the dark house, tempering his anger to a deep slow burn. It was quiet as he passed through the yard, and he could hear the horses moving in the stable. Archos thought he must remember to temper his rage until they were away from the beasts. Opening the door quietly, he walked inside. Pulling the shadows of the Arcane Realm around him, he stepped behind Gamal. Close, he allowed the shadows to creep around and chill the air. "So you would be the young man who deems it acceptable to force himself upon women?" he said menacingly.

Gamal spat, "I have no need of force with real women; these whores are merely elves, less than human, less than animals. Just some easy pussy to sport with. You were busy with your little red-haired whore. I just took the one you were not using as your man seemed not to be able to take her. I see you do not like to share. I offered your man here a price for her, even offered him the chance for a sweet little virgin, not been touched. A powerful man like you…surely could handle three slaves, trade her for the one I damaged perhaps. A sweet thing, barely fourteen summers; just imagine the taste of her as you take her." Gamal licked his lips at the thought. His bravado returning, he assumed Archos would punish his servant, or be amenable to Gamal's offer.

Olek clenched his hand on his sword but stayed his blade. Archos looked over Gamal's head to Olek and, smiling a smile that would have made Gamal tremble in his boots, said, "Yes…that would be acceptable. You will take me to her and you will do so quietly. I wish to view this…merchandise. Perhaps my servant was too hasty." As the dark shadows swirled, the lantern flickered out. "My…slave is asleep and did not please me tonight; I am in need of some further entertainment."

Gamal ignored the little knot of apprehension clamouring for attention in the part of his brain that was more aware of danger than the rest. He held out his arms. "Your foolish servant has tied me; I would have him flogged if he were mine. These elves need discipline."

Archos smiled. "Olek can be impulsive. He was merely trying to protect my assets. I am sure I will think of some suitable punishment for his behaviour. Now you have raised my interest in this young maiden. I think we should tarry no longer. Olek may accompany us to see what he may not have."

The rope dropped from Gamal's wrists. "Now show me this sweet little thing. Perhaps we can come to some…arrangement. Do not worry about the lantern. I have good enough night vision and my man does also."

Gamal opened the door and the three walked across the yard. "What have you planned, master? I would have slit his throat for this evening's work; if it were not so inconvenient to your plans," Olek whispered.

"You do not trust my judgement after so many years? It would seem he will lead us straight to our quarry. Do not fear. I will think of a suitable punishment. Ozena wants to keep this between us. Killing the master's son is not the way to do this… Well, not immediately."

Olek bowed his head and fell silent. Entering through the kitchen, Gamal opened a hatch and led them down into the cellar of the house. He had picked up a candle from the kitchen and the meagre light flickered in the cold darkness. Leading them through the barrels and crates, he grinned. "Such a little fresh creature as she should certainly satisfy you, sir. Cost me a deal did she, but as you seem to be attached to that brunette I touched, perhaps we can make a deal. That elf of yours has taken my fancy and although I was…interrupted, I am sure she could please me with enough… persuasion. But then one elf whore is as good as the next."

Archos could feel Olek tense next to him and mutter something. He murmured, "Easy, my friend, let him lead us and himself." Archos himself closed his eyes, briefly biting down the rage and the urge to boil this man's blood.

Seeing a curtain partitioning off a corner, Archos heard a whimper and quiet sobbing. He began to breathe deeply, settling his mind against the fury circling within him. Gamal pointed. "There…my little alcove. No one can hear…even if the household is above. They are so much more enjoyable when they struggle. Do you not agree?"

Pulling the curtain aside he revealed, on filthy bedding, two female elves. Both were naked. One, beaten and bleeding, was curled into a ball, whimpering. The other was young, perhaps fourteen, and her wrists were tied to a rope that linked around her throat, so when she struggled she choked.

Archos said, so that only Olek's sharp ears could hear, "Fetch Dii, and blankets, and clothes. Do not wake the house." Olek nodded angrily and disappeared.

"Is the young one not a pretty little flower…a sweet cherry waiting to be plucked? The other has been taken, but if she pleases you, allow the virgin to watch…take the other, do what you will to her and let the maiden girl see what is in store." He licked his lips, oblivious to the temperature drop around him as his mind was filled with thoughts of pleasure and lust. The candle flickered out as he suddenly slammed into the wall, the breath knocked out of him.

Holding the man fast in his spell, Archos stood close as the mists of the Astral Realms swirled around him, eyes glowing silver in the gloom. He said in a voice that echoed with doom, "I should boil the blood in your veins. I could make you beg over and again for your miserable life. I could make you suffer a thousand hells for what you have done to these women."

In the darkness, Gamal finally realised the danger. "Take them both, they are yours. I am sorry I offended you, touched your woman. No harm done, these here will make amends," he gabbled.

Heat coursed through him painfully, searing his skin, a burn within that twisted and gnawed. "It is not I to whom you should apologise; the women with me are neither whore nor slave. As for these girls, you will tell me where you acquired them," Archos snapped, the commanding voice searing into Gamal's mind.

"I…I will not betray my source…I will report you to the Witch-Hunters…" Gamal stammered, half doubled in pain.

"Oh, I assure you, I will have the information I seek…one way or another. It depends how much pain you can endure. As for the Witch-Hunters…I think not. Firstly, they would not believe you, and if they do, they pose no more than a mere inconvenience to me. However I promise you this…if I or my lands or households are so…inconvenienced, I will hunt you down. I will drag you to the edge of madness and beyond. I will ruin your house and I will enjoy it. Now perhaps if you tell me what I wish to know, I will not have to strip it from your mind myself and flay your sanity to the four winds. I may decide to turn my wrath elsewhere and decide that you are beneath my notice. What is it to be?"

Gamal whimpered in fear. "I will talk…let me be. There is a man, a slaver, large and scarred. He runs a barge and a stable of slaves…er…I mean elf girls. I swear I know not where he gets them. He works from the port near Darsi but serves the city of Varlek."

Archos snarled, a primordial snarl of anger that chilled the blood. "And this slaver, who does he work for?"

"I do not know. I just buy the merchandise… The slaver said he has a contract with a rich lord…runs an exclusive…establishment. Only the very wealthy are able to buy in. Not even my father is willing to pay that; slaves to do whatever you like to. He has a place but I know not where, I swear."

Archos removed the spell and let him drop into a heap, swirling a confusion spell in his mind. He fell on the floor, retching and gasping, as Dii clambered down, followed by Ozena. Olek handed down some blankets and an armful of clothes. For a moment, Ozena stared fearfully at Gamal, then stepped over him, planting a kick as she did so.

Dii surveyed the scene, seeing the semi-conscious Gamal on the floor, Archos standing now serene and calm, waiting, and the two elven women. "See to the girls… it would be better if you healed them, comforted them. One appears to have been raped…the other I think is just frightened. Tend to them, discover what you can. I think myself and young Gamal here may need a word with our host. If needs be, take the women to my chamber. Olek will remain close by should you need anything."

Pausing, he squeezed Ozena's shoulder gently as Elvish words echoed in her head, "They are safe now, as are you. I vow to you this business will not go unpunished." He picked up Gamal and dragged him up to the kitchen; pulling out a few bottles of spirits as he did so.

Dii looked around at the unsanitary conditions; the cellar was dark and very cold. There were crates around and a few barrels. She concentrated for a moment and produced a ball of light that floated just above her. Crouching close, she turned to the women. "My name is Dii and I wish to help you. I can heal you and we have brought some clothes and blankets. Please trust me, we will not hurt you. Ozena, could you see to the younger girl, talk to her. Comfort her. This young lady needs healing."

Ozena nodded, tears stinging her eyes, shame for these women and pity at their ordeal mingled with the shock and realization that this might have been her. The young girl was weeping still, but as Ozena viewed her, she saw that this girl was not the elf she sought, not her sister.

"Please let me see your injuries. We will see you safe from this place. My lord is a powerful and influential man…he will ensure your safety and he will not harm you." Dii held a hand out, offering comfort.

The woman looked at Dii, fear and shame in her eyes. "My name is Varya. He took me…forced me to…do things. The girl he made watch, said she would be next. Just leave me to die…take her…get her out before he returns."

Dii gently touched her, letting a healing spell flow into the woman. "No, you will not die. That man is gone and my lord will not allow him to touch you or any woman again. I can heal your physical wounds. You should not be ashamed, for it was not of your doing. It may not seem so now, but the pain and the shame will ease eventually… believe me when I say that. That young lord is an evil man; he does not deserve to live. I am sorry we could not have found you earlier. We are seeking some forest elves taken from villages in the Shimmering Forest. My friend here seeks her young sister."

As the warm healing magic filled her and began to ease the pain, Dii sat on the floor next to the poor woman. "If you wish, I can make fire and warm the room. You are welcome to come to my chamber if you prefer and are able. It is warmer and safe and I can see to you better there. The household is still sleeping, so no one will see you. There is no need to be frightened now." Gently she wrapped the woman in her arms, quieting her tears and holding her close.

The woman nodded weakly, pulling a blanket over herself, as Dii continued, "Take what clothes you need. If you feel you cannot walk, Olek can carry you."

She shook her head vigorously and slowly began to dress with Dii's tender assistance, Ozena helped the younger girl, and they moved to the warmth of Dii's chamber, to heal and comfort.

* * *

In the kitchen, Archos tossed the spirits over Gamal and growled with a voice that allowed no disobedience. "Let us see what your father has to say, you will cooperate with me."

Gliding to the door of the master's chamber, he listened. Hearing nothing inside, he put his hand against the lock until he heard the bolt slide back and, dragging the boy, he stepped inside. Tempering his anger to a serene countenance, he leaned back against the wall and pushed Gamal forward. "Wake him, tell him…tell him you have offended his guests and their master seeks explanation and recompense. We will leave as soon as the others are fit to move."

Gamal found himself unable to refuse and staggered to his father. Shaking him awake, he fell to his knees. "Papa, wake up…I have done something…something I should not…I have given offence to this man, our guest and his party."

Niall woke to hear his son stammering his sins, and picked up the stink of spirit upon him. "What have you done? Why you reek of spirit, boy!"

Sitting up, he looked at Archos leaning against the wall. "Is this true? What offence has my son caused?"

Archos cast his silver-grey eyes over to Gamal. "Firstly, he offered my manservant gold for possession of one of my elves, and when this was refused, he attempted to take her anyway. My women are not for sale, this was made clear yet still he pursued attacking my young companion. Thus, he has caused harm and offence both to one of my women and to me. We come to seek hospitality and receive insults and offence within your house. Something I would not expect from a man of your…standing."

Niall looked to his son. "You foolish boy, insulting this man. I hope your elf is not unduly harmed, sir. It is unfortunate perhaps my son misunderstood this woman was not available?"

Archos smiled a dangerous smile. "Perhaps…but I would have thought being told the girls were not for sale is reasonably clear, would you not agree? Does your son often take that which does not belong to him? This would not be an admirable trait in a trader and one not good for business. Also to insult a man of my means and influence, one who was contemplating becoming a customer, is not good for your house. Perhaps he makes a habit of this?"

Gamal's head was cloudy and, as if his mouth was making its own decisions, he whispered, "Perhaps a bribe? These rich fellows always want more…maybe the deeds of ware for the *Anna-Louise*? He might be content with that, they are merely elves." As the confusion spell began to ebb and the man's brain began to catch up, he continued quietly, "Be careful, he is a mage…he threatened me, Father, although it is all a little unclear. I saw him cast a spell. His servant bound me, and threatened me also."

Niall glanced around the chamber, his mind working; perhaps he could bribe this man. He was angry his son had been threatened for mistreating an elf woman…an elf! Obviously, this rich lord was not eager to share his slaves and was selfish to keep them both for himself. He understood well enough the veiled threat. "Perhaps we may come to some agreement; some payment for your trouble and disturbance, for the inconvenience?"

Thinking hard, he rose from his bed and strode to the dresser. He selected some papers and a small purse of gold, papers which related to a ship lost recently. Niall smiled, hopefully the man would believe the cargo existed and would bring in a fair price, when in reality the sea had claimed it. Once the man had gone, he could send a rider to the Witch-Hunters. Even if the fellow was not a mage, it would be an inconvenience to him and insult him to be questioned by the Order, perhaps Niall could even arrange to have those pretty elves sent to him as a reward.

Archos smiled slightly as he read the thoughts from Niall. So that was the game the man wished to play. He would find out to his cost that when it came to games, it helps to know your opponent and to know whose rules he uses.

"Sir, I have the deeds of ware to a merchant ship, due in port within a week. These deeds account for the cargo of fine linens and silks. They should fetch a good price, also a small portion of gold, perhaps to buy something for the young lady?"

Archos smiled a deadly smile as he took the offered deed and pouch, making to leave but turning at the door. "How can I be sure the steward of the ship will allow me access? I am not so used to dealing with the fellows who manage and sail ships. If this cargo is as you say, I should get a fair enough price for it. Not that a mere bribe can compensate the insult. I think we will make to leave shortly. My lady is recovered and we need to make good time back to my manor."

As he stepped through the door, he smiled again. "We will be taking the two elves you had bound and raped in the cellar. I will ensure they come to no further harm." For a moment his eyes glowed silver and he left the room, returning to Dii and the women.

Niall said, "Idiot boy, I told you to be careful with those girls. Now we have lost their price too. No matter if he is indeed a mage, an encounter with the Witch-Hunters should teach him not to threaten me and my son. Now I suggest you make yourself scarce. I will make sure they leave, play the attentive host, and hopefully he will think all is well."

Archos returned to find Dii and Ozena still comforting the elves. Entering the room, he bolted and warded the door. "I am sorry for the misfortune that has fallen upon you here. I can promise you that I will do my best to make sure the boy suffers. Now we are due to leave shortly when the horses are ready. Have you a place to go, a home to be safe? I would see you delivered there if you are able to travel?"

Varya sniffed, "I have a home in Sethla, near the sea. I am ashamed to return home. I have been gone many weeks. My mistress is a seamstress, and she will think I have run away. I cannot tell her, she is a virtuous woman and will turn me out, thinking me a whore."

"Good reliable seamstresses are hard to find, it is quite a skill so I understand. Why would she turn a well-trained girl onto the streets for something that was not her fault? Perhaps you will find she will be happy and relieved at your return. If you wish, I can give you a letter of reference or the like. If you receive any problems from your mistress, you may use those to seek another, more understanding position. If you wish, I can arrange for a letter explaining your absence, perhaps an illness or unavoidable delay?"

Wide eyed and tearful, she looked up. "You would do that for me? I am but an elf and a stranger to you."

Archos laughed. "Why should I not? I would not let you shift for yourself after your ordeal. I have seen the Enclaves and I would not allow you to return to such a hell if it was in my power to prevent it. I have many contacts and would see you safe enough and in gainful employment. This reminds me, half of what is in this pouch is yours, the other half for the forest elf. It is little indeed, I am afraid, for the virtue of a woman, but you may find it of use. I will escort you to my manor and arrange for an escort to your home."

Turning to the young elf, he smiled and said in Elvish, "You are from Szendro village? Were taken in the raids? I will see you returned to my lands; some of your fellows were rescued and you will find companions and safety. The rest we seek still; unless you have somewhere else to go, kin elsewhere?"

Eleyena started when she heard the human lord speak in Elvish, unused to humans who bothered to learn the language of the Elfkind. Whispering she replied, "I would not be a burden to you, sir."

Archos chuckled, "My dear, were you to be a burden to me, I would not have rescued you or offered what I have offered. You are surprised I speak the language of the Elfkind? Well, you speak the Common Language? I have studied the Elfkind and their history for many years and I speak many languages. It pleases me to do so. There was an Elder elf surviving from the village to preserve your lore. You have my guarantee you would be delivered safely and treated kindly, for your fellows are to be settled within my villages, though you may go about your business as you wish, not as servants or slaves but as citizens."

Eleyena nodded slowly, tears in her eyes. "I would like very much to return. I am not...hurt as she was. I was just frightened and ashamed I was unable to help her."

"Once these ladies are fit to move, Olek can go prepare the carriage and I will ride with him. You ladies may ride inside, where it is safer and more comfortable. We will make good enough time to the manor; it will be easier to collate the information we have from there. That bastard gave me a little information and with luck, our contacts will have provided some."

CHAPTER 13

The morning after Archos and his party returned from the merchant's house, the Witch-Hunters visited Tremellic. "Are you sure this is a good idea? I mean, chasing down Witches within the villages is one thing, but this lord could make life…difficult. A man of influence and power can stir up local politics," said one.

One of his companions glared. "We are Witch-Hunters, and our word is law. Or have you forgotten? I do not care if this man is the Lord High Commander himself, if he is indeed a mage, he is ours. If not, then perhaps we will get some decent hospitality."

The third Witch-Hunter merely grunted and approached the house of the Steward, knocking on the door with a decisive tap. Simon himself opened the door, having had word of the arrival of the Order in Tremellic once more. Simon made sure he was aware of what went on within the villages and thus ensured Archos was fully updated.

The second Witch-Hunter, who looked to be the leader of the group, looked the man up and down with some disdain. "You are Steward of these lands? We seek audience with the lord of the valley. We will not be denied. We seek some…property stolen from a merchant, a man who was threatened; some elves, and we have heard there are elves residing in this valley."

Simon crossed his arms in the doorway. "So what if we have a number of elves here? We are close to the borders of the Shimmering Forest. It is profitable that we trade, elves are good craftspeople. Sometimes one of our menfolk will take an elf woman for companionship or servant. They earn their keep; we have no need of an Enclave here. They are not mages so, therefore, none of your concern. They do not move unaccompanied beyond the valley without the required papers if they leave at all. As for your merchant and his missing…property, then you best look to the House of Thieves, if you can find them that is."

The Witch-Hunter snapped angrily, "You dare to stand against the Witch-Hunters, Steward? We have cause to believe there are mages here. We have the Rights of the Order, unless you care to step into our hospitality? Now you will inform the lord of our arrival!"

Simon merely smiled and bowed. "As you wish, I doubt he will see you. I am not a mage and know nothing of any hereabouts. I am not impeding your…enquiries I am merely pointing out a few minor matters. Our ways are apart from those of the main country. I will ride with you myself; the route to the manor can be tricky if one does not know it."

* * *

They slowly rode to the manor; the route was indeed circuitous and difficult. As they approached the gates, Simon turned. "I will go and announce your arrival." Dismounting, he walked up the path muttering, "Assuming he has not already seen you."

Olek answered the door and they spoke in low tones. Watching as the Witch-Hunters dismounted, he nodded and said, "Go and make sure the elves are kept inside. We should be able to handle three of the Order well enough."

Simon gave him a look of understanding and returned to the group. "You are in luck, my lord feels like company today," he said sarcastically and, mounting his horse without another word, he turned and left, chuckling to himself.

"How may the house of Lord Archos assist the…noble gentlemen of the Order of Witch-Hunters?" Olek bowed and said, keeping his voice even.

"We seek some…elves stolen from a merchant and are following a rumour of mages within this valley, but that is a matter to discuss with the master himself and not his elven servant," was the haughty reply.

Olek showed them inside, making polite conversation, while Archos locked and warded both the workshop and the library, hastily casting a spell of obfuscation over them. He pulled off the robe he favoured and quickly dressed in a plain shirt and frockcoat. Warning Dii and Ozena to stay out of sight, he sauntered to the parlour to wait.

"Ah, gentlemen of the Order of Witch-Hunters, to what do I owe this rare visit?" Motioning to seats, he waited for them to be seated and made a sign to Olek to fetch refreshments.

"My lord, we have…intelligence that mages or a mage reside in this valley, magic appears to have been used against a merchant and he has made a complaint. Some property was removed from his house and threats were received by this man," recounted the leader.

As Olek arrived with a plate of refreshments and a jug of spiced cider, he said, "If I am not required, Master, I will make myself scare. I doubt these gentleman would appreciate the presence of a servant. Besides, I have the task you required of me to carry out."

Archos waved dismissively and pretended to turn his attention to the Witch-Hunters as Olek left and slipped into the shadows, settling himself into a hidden niche to listen. Archos settled back with a smile, letting an aura of confusion slowly emanate from him. "Mages? I am not aware of any mages residing in the valley. But my Steward surely told you that? This merchant, why should I know him? I have not much to do with merchants."

The first Witch-Hunter rubbed his eyes absently, saying, "You sought hospitality from this man."

"Ah yes…I do remember a brief stay at the house of a merchant. I have an elven woman who…warms my bed and she was taken ill, so we were obliged to stop. I decided to purchase some items of his, but we disagreed over price and quantity. He wanted significantly more than the items were worth and I refused to pay the price. His son tried to bribe my servant over something, after insulting him. Needless to say no business was done; I can only think he was dissatisfied with the result. We left at first light to continue our journey. As for the removal of property, this man has the audacity to call me a thief or a person of my household such after this behaviour?"

Smiling as they helped themselves to the sweetbreads and refreshment, he leaned back. "Now, to me these sound merely like hollow accusations, do you not agree?" Archos said charmingly.

The second Witch-Hunter looked around the fine items in the room, absently stuffing his mouth with cake, and the third merely grunted. "What of the elves that live here? We noticed one or two as we rode through the lands."

"What of it? You would not deny elf women have their charms. So some of the men of my valley choose an elf companion or elf servants, is that not common practice? We have some dealings with the forest elves now and then. It is a profitable trade as we are apart from the plains and the roads for merchants beyond my boundaries can be dangerous. It suits us all to trade with the local elven villages, who keep the wolves and bears from our borders and livestock. The elves that reside here are not mages and, as I am sure my Steward told you, have the papers necessary if moving beyond the Tremellic Valley. That is all. Now, if you will excuse me, I have a number of pressing matters to deal with, for you have disturbed me in my business. Once you have finished your refreshment, my servant will see you out. I would watch the road back to the villages; the route can be rather…treacherous to the uninitiated," Archos said in his soft, yet commanding baritone. Convincing, charming, he smiled at them, concealing the distaste he felt at their presence in his house.

Bowing, he turned and rang a bell, at which Olek appeared and he instructed smoothly, "See these…gentlemen leave safely. It would be most…unfortunate if some accident were to befall them. I have warned them of the dangers of the road. Please escort them to the gates when they have finished refreshing themselves."

Olek bowed and saw that it was so.

* * *

Returning to his master, Olek found Archos brooding. "You heard?"

Olek went to the cabinet on the wall and removed a bottle and two goblets, filling them generously and depositing both on the parlour table. "Yes, indeed, my lord. That merchant fellow is either astonishingly stupid or astonishingly brave. Now what is to be our next move? Ozena's sister is not yet found, nor many of the other missing elves. I shudder to imagine what may have befallen her."

Archos took a slow drink of the brandy and then said nothing for a while until finally replying, "I think a visit to my privateer might be start, and some increased bandit activity; disruption of certain ships and caravans. They may be able to throw some light on any contacts this slaver may have. As much as it pains me to let the Witch-Hunters leave, I suspect it would be considerably more inconvenient if they failed to return home. Ask Simon to keep a good eye out, perhaps have a word with that bandit leader who patrols the roads beyond the valley with his gang."

"We need further intelligence on this slaver nobleman and his 'exclusive club.' Dii may know, but I would prefer not to make her relive that part of her history. She may only know her old Keeper's ways, not the names of his…associates. I think a trip to the city may provide some information of use. I am unwilling to leave the ladies here unprotected, a day or so is one thing, any longer and that invites risk. Besides, I have a feeling Ozena would refuse to be left behind."

Olek swirled the brandy around. "You wish me to return to Varlek, Master? Or would you prefer to deal with that yourself? If this 'club' or similar exists in the city or among the nobles, I cannot see a half-elf gaining entry. Even one as handsome and charming as myself, I am still merely a servant."

Archos smiled fondly at him. "My friend, you ceased to be 'merely a servant' to me a good while ago as you well know, or you would not be drinking my fine brandy in such a casual manner. However, to the world beyond this valley, you could never be more, nor could any elf. You may have a point about this exclusive club, should it exist. He may simply have been speaking about one of the higher class brothels; there are a few of those. Somehow, though, I sense he is not speaking of this. We have intelligence of some and that perhaps does not seem the style. Certainly the reputable ones would not take one as young as Amena. That is more…a private arrangement. However, that could be within one of the houses in the city, or beyond."

Olek nodded, sipping his brandy. "I agree, but it has been known in the past for such a temporary establishment to appear. There are plenty of old warehouses or, as you say, in the large townhouses. Without further intelligence, it is hard to tell."

"Not that I think for one moment you would bother asking permission to attend and simply make your own arrangements for entry to such a place. There is substantial risk. I would assume the place would be well guarded, if merely to make sure the slaves do not decide they prefer freedom. I am sure you would be able to infiltrate adequately enough. It may be worth visiting the lesser brothels and other such establishments. It never ceases to amaze me what a man will reveal when he is…otherwise occupied. Ask in the Golden Mask, Desiree or her ladies may have heard rumours. We should check the Enclave too, new…servants taken there or elves simply held there until such time as a suitable position is found. Besides, Enclave elves tend to be close knit. They may know something."

Olek returned his grin. "Then there will be many guards to meet my blades, Master, should we find this place guarded. I expect I could be persuaded to visit the houses of ill-repute if that is needed. In fact, I may need to go back several times." He chuckled before continuing more seriously, "You know I would do anything for you, my lord, my life belongs to you, thus it is yours to command as you see fit."

Squeezing his arm affectionately, Archos smiled. "Oh, Olek, my dear Olek, you have earned your life back from me many times over, do you not know that? But I am flattered you still hold me in such esteem."

"My lord, you saved me from the scaffold those many years ago and I pledged my life to you, nothing has changed in that. I am more than content to be your man, I am proud and honoured to be such, that you trust me so. As for esteem, well, in that you and I are similar in that it is not given unless earned. You are the only family I have known for a good many years and are more to me than anyone else living. Now perhaps we should move along from these sentimentalities and come up with a plan?"

Archos laughed and drummed his fingers on the desk. "Indeed and, for the record, I am honoured that you still choose to assist and serve me as you do. I know I can be difficult to live with. Now perhaps we may both use our respective skills in this matter, if needs-be we can simply let the ladies amuse themselves at the townhouse, although I would rather not leave them unguarded. The thieves may be able to provide some security. However, Ozena will be of use in that she knows the elves from her village, speaks Elvish and may be a familiar face. If we do find anyone then she will be an asset in many respects. If her sister is indeed there, it might be hard to persuade a young, frightened forest elf to trust a strange man, elf or human. Dii may need to heal and comfort the women, and can do so much better than I. She is quite the healer and her gentleness is very calming. She is such a sweet girl. Besides, I am not leaving her here alone. Although I know Simon would watch over her, I wish for her to be by my side. I doubt she has ever visited the city, and Ozena definitely not."

He paused in contemplation before continuing, "I would suggest we make arrangements; go and visit the bandits. I will speak with Simon and we can make preparations. If needed, Simon is well able to make sure that nothing untoward occurs here. Perhaps that would give you time to amuse Ozena. She is clever and fast, but she needs…a wider view, I think. Life within a small elf village does not prepare one for life beyond the Shimmering Forest. Besides, I have seen the looks you throw her way. Distract her, take her hunting; take her to the hot springs, perhaps. We will have a good couple of days before we leave. I may need to…arrange some papers for our journey. Simon may be an excellent forger, but he still needs time to work."

Olek gave an uncharacteristic flash of a blush and said, "Ozena is a pretty girl, my lord, and her sweet innocence of the world beyond the forest gives her an extra charm. She is strong yet vulnerable, like a young sapling in the wind. When that bastard whelp of the merchant's laid his hands upon her in such a way, it took every reserve I had not to cut him into pieces. I would protect her from the likes of him, if she would have me, but that is for her to say. If not, then I shall simply be content to be her friend and guardian." He dropped into silence and gazed at the bottom of his goblet after emptying it.

"Women are odd and mysterious creatures, Olek, but who knows what will happen. That is something even not I can foresee or predict. She may yet need your comfort when we find her sister."

"I hope that the young girl is still living, yet as every day and hour pass, it becomes less likely. I wish I could have found out more information, Master. Perhaps I should have waited," Olek replied.

Archos looked at him with those endless silver-grey eyes. "Olek, we have done and are doing what we could with the information we have. She cannot be found by magic, so slower, more mundane methods are needed. We saved those two girls, another from the village among them. Amena may have been there, as it happens, to my lasting regret she was not. It could be she is already…gone from us. We will find her or, at least if she does not live, what has happened to her; if it takes everything I have to bribe and buy the information to save her, then so be it. Her life, safety, and that of the other elves that fell under my protection, a protection in which I failed, are my concern, along with you, Ozena, and Dii and, of course, my people within the valley. Slavers have been known to take human woman as well as elves. We will do what we must. If she is gone from us, then she will not go un-avenged. By the gods, those who harmed her will feel the wrath of the Oncoming Storm."

Olek looked at him, the rage smouldering and his eyes shining silver. "I know. I just wish we knew whether she lives. I do not like to see the pain in Ozena's eyes."

Archos sighed. "I will scry, see where the ship lies and make to leave. Go speak to the bandits, and I will speak with Simon. The carriage is slower, but Ozena is not a good horsewoman and we may have to transport anyone we find. Besides, it can be useful for privacy."

* * *

Archos woke early and, careful not to wake Dii, entered his workshop. He set up the blue scrying Crystal globe and gazed into the swirling mists, the soft blue light bathing his face. He called the Power from within him and murmured, "I am Archos, Archmage. I call upon you to locate the ship *Gathering Storm*, be she at sea or in port, for she belongs to me, thus is my right as Lord of the Arcane Realms."

The mists rippled and then parted to show the small but extremely fast and manoeuvrable sloop. She was settled in the cove known as Bladecove, close to the Bay of Blades.

Jagged rocks deterred larger ships and those who did not know the region, which meant that the bay was used primarily by smugglers, privateers and the fast local fishing and small trading boats. The route was circuitous, but less observed, to the Far Isles and the other coastal settlements, where the locals fished in the bays and nearby rivers, and the lack of attention from the authorities meant a good source of income was derived from the less legal merchandise which often appeared. The Witch-Hunters did not have the hold on such trade as they thought. Tariffs on many items were high, and the poorer and more remote settlements begrudged taxes to a lord, or worse a distant fort. In a land of martial law many lived beyond that law. Fortune smiled as the cove lay close by, less than a half a day's ride away.

The small ship lay at her ease and Archos smiled. It was a while since he had paid a visit to one of his more…profitable ventures, but was familiar enough with the area. He packed quickly and dressed for riding. Stuffing the kris into its belt sheath, he threw the cloak over his shoulders and, scribbling a note, left it wedged under a half drunk glass of wine in his study:

My dear, I have been called away on a business matter which may provide us with some useful information regarding the elves. I will return after dark but we set out for the city in a couple of days when preparations are complete. In such matters we cannot rush blindly in, particularly in the city. Please pack for travel and take Ozena to buy suitable clothing to travel and not appear at first as a forest elf. Olek will accompany you. If you need anything for yourself Harkenen should be able to provide the basics. Take whatever money you need.

My love,

A.

Archos slipped out and taking a fast ride on his favourite and swift mount Storm, made Bladecove in good time, arriving at the sign of the Drunken Fisherman in the small smuggler village. The tavern was old and of the usual dark stone found in those parts. The common bar was occupied, as it so often was, by the type of sailor that preferred his ale cheap, his wenches friendly and his customs men far away. Archos looked around, seeking one sailor in particular. As he entered, a few heads turned to him then looked away strangely uninterested in his presence. "A tankard of ale, if you'd be so good, and I seek Eadgar Remils, Captain of the *Gathering Storm*," he said mildly to the wench behind the bar.

The bar tender duly plonked a tankard of what apparently passed for ale onto the bar as a one-eyed, largely built sailor gruffly replied, "Who be you that seeks the *Gathering Storm's* captain?"

Archos smiled beneath his cowl at the man's brusqueness, not recognising the sailor immediately, from among those he had seen before; "Someone who will only discuss business with its skipper, sailor."

The sailor looked him up and down, the persuasive baritone ringing in his head. Archos was not a sailor and was dressed better than most here. "Aye, that's as may be. Captain is still aboard, we have been docked less than a couple of hours, rich man."

The mate, recognising the cloak and deep soft accent of his master, walked up. "Erm…my lord, I know you sir. You've been here before. Olivier is new and he means no disrespect, sir. It is as he says, Captain Eadgar remains aboard. I can escort you to the ship. "

Smiling, Archos laid a hand on his arm. "No, I think I will take a walk along the harbour to stretch my legs after the ride, Harald. If Captain Eadgar is aboard still, then I can simply conduct my business there. You seem to have an empty ale pot, I prefer wine." He handed the man his flagon.

Turning, he sauntered slowly through the village past the few ships docked in the small, but busy harbour. Climbing aboard his privateer, he noted the cargo being unloaded bearing the crest of the Order of Witch-Hunters and he grinned evilly. The captain's door was locked but that posed no difficulty to the Archmage. He simply touched the lock and it slid aside.

Captain Eadgar sat at his writing desk making notes and started, grabbing for his sword as the door swung open. "Who enters unannounced? Oh, my lord, I was not expecting the honour of your visit. May I say how well you look? How long have we known each other and I swear you never look any older! Can I offer you some refreshment? We have some fine wine that has recently come into our possession."

Archos settled himself in the comfortable chair opposite his captain and nodded. "This is not merely a social call to see how my favourite sea captain fares. I require use of your intelligence and the speed of this deft ship."

Opening the bottle of wine and pouring two large goblets, Eadgar handed one to his master, who smiled again to see the sign of the Order of Witch-Hunters on the crate containing the bottles. "At your command as always, how may we be of assistance?"

Sipping the wine slowly and savouring it, Archos smiled his easy, persuasive and--more importantly--knowing smile and replied, "Indeed, this seems a fine wine. Such a loss to its…intended owner, alas. Aging is…an inconvenience I try and avoid."

Learning forward, he continued, "Now, enough of the pleasantries. I seek information on a number of matters. Firstly, there is a slave ship I seek, picked its cargo from the Great River barges, and operates out of Darsi and Sinawe and is headed to the city of Varlek. If you could use your contacts or happen to discover such a barge and…have it removed it from service, I would be most appreciative. The slaver himself is currently in the custody…er…the 'hospitality' of the House of Thieves. It would be most helpful if any 'cargo' found on such a craft was removed intact and deposited in a safe location. If this is the case, I can arrange safe transit of said cargo. There is a young woman in my protection whose young sister was taken, a young elf child of about twelve summers, a striking child with white hair and eyes like jet. Now I think we both are aware what may befall an innocent young maiden in such a situation. We seek information of her whereabouts. Perhaps should you be moored in the city, you may overhear conversation in the docks, taverns and whorehouses."

Archos swirled the wine around the goblet, thinking knowing its intended recipients made the wine taste all the better, "Also any craft belonging to the merchant Niall Versann are to encounter pirates, if there are any of your acquaintance, of course. What happens to that cargo, either on the ships or arriving in port, is of no concern to me. Understand this: I want his ships to fail. He has offended me and someone under my protection. If by chance any of your…associates should happen upon any wagons or warehouses of this man, it would be most agreeable if they were emptied of their goods. I hear bandits and thieves are much on the increase these days.

"Also any information on ships or related caravans of a slaver-lord; a rich and powerful nobleman, although as yet I have not a name but any information would be most useful. I am sure you would find my gratitude appropriate."

Eadgar nodded. "We have disrupted Versann ships once or twice. He is an arrogant bastard. I will see to it the word spreads. In the meantime, it would honour me if you would take a crate of this wine. It may interest you to know there have been more heavily armed and aggressive Witch-Hunter vessels recently. We do our best to disrupt trade routes, but they seem to be more…challenging than usual and we are but one ship, although that is something which I'm working on."

Archos drained the wine and replied, "I have business elsewhere and an enchanting mistress to return to, so I should not tarry."

"My lord, you would prefer the company of a beautiful woman to that of an aging pirate…how odd. I could be offended."

Archos laughed and selected a crate of the wine. Turning, he casually tossed a pouch onto the table. "You know how to contact me, should your investigations prove fruitful. I would put off sailing far for a day or so for there is a storm due."

Leaving, he rode into the night, stopping merely to rest the horse at a wayfaring tavern on route. On the horizon, dark clouds full of the rage of nature and the fury of the elements began to gather.

* * *

Olek left the manor and rode swiftly to the edge of the valley and out onto the Great Highway. He rode for an hour or so, and his keen eyes picked up smoke on the horizon amongst the sparse trees which still grew as a remnant of the forest, through which a small river ran. As he gained the ground, he dismounted, tethered the horse and moved cautiously. Before him lay a temporary camp: several tents, a chest or two, a few crates, a barrel, and some fish strung out to dry in the air. Beyond the camp was a hastily built paddock with a number of horses. Olek counted seven men that he could see and looked for the man that sat slightly apart. He stopped, thinking how best to approach, and pulled the shadows around him, although there were not many on this fine day.

Slowly he slipped around to the edge of the camp to where the lone man sat and then stepped out of the shadows behind him.

"I trust you are the chief of this band, sir, for you seem confident enough to sit apart from your fellows?"

The bandit spun around, sword drawn, to see the figure standing at ease near to him yet beyond sword reach, cloaked with the shadows swirling around his feet. "Who are you, that you come here? You yourself are confident sir considering I am armed and you do not appear to be."

Olek laughed and somersaulted with lightning speed over the bandit's head, kicking the sword from the fellow's hand, toppling him in the dirt and landing with his own sword against the man's throat.

"Appearances may be deceptive, my friend, but I do not come here as an enemy, for if it was so, you would now be in pieces."

The other bandits formed a circle, weapons drawn, as Olek sheathed his own sword and held his hand out to help the man up. "As for who I am and why I am here, I will discuss that with you at the fire, as a friend and not surrounded by a ring of swords. Believe me in what I say when I tell you that a good deal of you would fall to my blades before I lay slain and those who did not would feel the wrath of him whom I serve. But as I say, I come here in friendship."

The chief nodded reluctantly and the bandits sheathed their blades. "You have balls, sir, I give you that. Now perhaps you would care to join me and my companions in a beer from the barrel." The man gestured to the fire, walked to the barrel and fetched some beer.

He sat and motioned Olek down. "You know I have killed men for less than you just did."

Olek smiled and took the beer, saying, "I do not doubt it, but if I wanted you dead you would be now lying in the dirt with your head removed, or simply you would not wake to see the dawn. I am not honourable enough to feel remorse for killing a man in his sleep should it suit my purpose. I am known, amongst other names, as the Shadowdancer, and I come from my master with a business opportunity." As he sat, the cowl of the cloak fell enough to reveal his pointed elven ears.

The bandit chief smiled and held out a hand. "I am honoured to meet you, your reputation precedes you. My name is Tholin. I lead this band, but what could the Shadowdancer want with a band of rogues and outcasts such as us?"

Olek waited until the man was sipping his beer before drinking his own. "Ah, well, that is a good question. I have…other business to deal with and not even I can be everywhere, thus I find it useful to have contacts…eyes and ears around that I may use. Shadows in the shadows, you might say."

One of the other bandits approached. "How do we know this elf speaks the truth, Tholin? He uses the name of the Shadowdancer yet it could be a lie. Elves lie."

"Well, perhaps you should take it on faith, unless you want a personal exhibition of my skills…human," Olek said with a smile like a cat.

The man drew his sword. "Sure, I have not shed blood for a few days, and yours will do nicely, elf."

Olek simply laughed at the man and as he charged, side stepped and drew both his swords. The bandit charged again and Olek stepped back and disappeared into a patch of shadow beneath the trees to reappear behind the man, bringing his swords down a millimetre from the fellow's face and a lock of the bandit's hair fell past his eyes. He kicked the hand holding the sword and the weapon spun away. "Move one hair's breadth and you are a dead man, bandit. I am the Shadowdancer, if you doubt me further perhaps we can continue this…entertainment, and after I leave you scattered for the wolves, I will take my business elsewhere."

The bandit paled and held his breath until the swords were removed. "Apologies, sir, for the insult," he managed with a squeak.

Olek nodded and shrugged, pulling the cowl back to shield his face. "It is best to be cautious in your dealings. Now after so much dawdling, perhaps we may talk business, my time is short. Witch-Hunters pass these roads. It would please my master if they were to be delayed…removed…inconvenienced. The Witch-Hunters seek not only users of magic but those of us who, through choice or necessity, live apart from what they term as law. If you are caught, you will hang, if not worse. The 'hospitality' of the Order is well known for its brutality. Now do you not think it would suit us all for them to be inconvenienced?"

Tholin looked at him in awe. "The Shadowdancer has a master? This man must be truly great or truly to be feared. What you ask is dangerous."

Taking a slow swig, Olek merely replied, "The man I serve is both, for he is the Oncoming Storm. Now I can easily take this request elsewhere. You are bandits; you are supposed to be tough outlaws, the menace of the highways. It seems, however, that this is not the case."

He got up to leave and Tholin stood quickly, moving to stop him. "We accept. We patrol the roads from the edge of the Tremellic Valley to the bend in the Great River known as the Blasted Oak Crossing. I am sure the Witch-Hunters can be inconvenienced."

"Good will payment," Olek said, holding up a small bag of gold coins. "I can be contacted at the Sign of the Moon on the road from Eleiry to the Tremellic Valley. There is a box there, of bleached wood. You may leave a message there, and proof if needed. The message will get to me. If you please my master, there will be extra payment."

Olek walked away from the camp and took a circuitous route back to his mount, then made the journey home.

Collecting the two elven ladies of the household, they headed into Harkenen. It was market day and the town square was bustling with people, both humans and one or two of the braver elves who had been rescued, including the young woman taken from the House of Versann. The market square was crowded as often villagers came from further down the valley to buy and sell, Harkenen being the largest of the Tremellic Valley settlements.

"Archos tells me you are to buy suitable attire for travel to the city plus whatever supplies may be needed. The townhouse is stocked well enough for food, but I think Ozena certainly should purchase…more appropriate garments," said Olek, looking around absently for a stall or shop selling women's clothes.

"What is wrong with what I am attired in?" Ozena asked, looking at the leggings, woollen tunic and the sturdy leathers she wore and glaring at Olek.

Olek grinned. "Oh nothing, if you are hunting in the valley or tumbling about in the forest, but you will stand out as an elf from the Shimmering Forest in the city. Not that that is a bad thing, of course," he added hastily when he saw her look.

"We need to blend in, or at least try and draw as little attention to ourselves as possible. Elves are…treated at best as servants or Kept, whether that is their position or not. A forest elf will look out of place and may be questioned, but a female elf that is viewed as a servant may not be. Heed this, the city is dangerous, especially for an elf woman, but you will be safe enough with myself and Lord Archos. Now perhaps the vendor there can assist whilst I go purchase some…herbs."

Dii took Ozena's arm and led her to a small booth. "Let me find you something suitable. I am not sure of city fashions but perhaps a skirt and blouse and a more suitable coat? If you prefer, you could wear your leggings beneath the skirt. You are a pretty girl, Ozena, and I think perhaps dark green, or a soft blue, or even brown or black would complement you. I know Olek likes green and blue and he favours black for himself. My love likes silver and blue, red and black and dark blue. I have seen human woman wear men's breeches and have them tailored so we could buy those too, they are useful for riding. I think the human women and city elven girls prefer the longer skirts than those of the forest. For in amongst the trees and undergrowth, a skirt may snag and tear. I know the forest elves favour leggings but they are a little unusual unless they are the tailored breeches. I am sure we will find something that suits; if needs be, I can adapt it."

Ozena blushed and whispered, "I have no money but a few copper coins, which will not cover such items. I must go without."

"Nonsense! That does not matter. My lord gave me some money with which to buy supplies; we will find you something suitable. I could use some riding breeches and some ribbons and pins for my hair."

She wandered over to the stall holder, leading Ozena by the hand, and began to look through the items carefully. "Here, Ozena, how about these?" She selected a long embroidered blue skirt sewn with green leaves and a soft pale green blouse. "The colours of the forest and pretty like you; perhaps something plainer also."

"Mistress Vendor, what have you for my friend, something simple and comfortable in which to travel?" Dii asked the stall holder, who was suddenly nervous that the lord's mistress was browsing her goods.

The middle-aged woman bobbed in curtsey and selected a plain black skirt of wool and a white and black patterned blouse, another of simple white and an emerald cotton bodice laced with black ribbon. "Perhaps this, my lady…and perhaps the paler green bodice yonder to complement the other garments. Maybe this warmer woven shawl top for the evenings? It can become cold these nights. It is brown and soft like the young lady's hair, woven from the good wool of these parts by my daughter. I have another in a rich black if my lady wishes, or white if that is to my lady's taste."

Ozena looked awkward for a while, then curiously took a closer look and touched the clothes. "They are so soft and fine…and what about those, and that beautiful blouse? I have never seen such a garment!" she cried, suddenly carried away by the excitement and the array of goods. Dii fetched the breeches of light and dark green diamonds and a long flowing blouse with long bell sleeves. "Oh and that hat, I have never had a hat that isn't armour, not even in winter; not a hat just for…er…putting on your head for no reason, and may I have some gloves, like those ones of cloth?"

Dii wrapped her arm about the young elf's shoulder and laughing, replied, "Of course, my dear. Well, I suppose that stocks you with clothes for a while…and you need to replace your garments from the village."

She selected a soft cotton blouse of deep red, another of dark blue, a long flowing dress that laced at the back, a black and white bodice, and two pairs of riding breeches, plus the black wool wrap. She too bought a small fur hat, some black velvet gloves and a set of pale suede ones and handed over a large handful of coins to the delighted stall holder, having purchased a good quantity of the woman's stock.

"May you wrap them and send them to the manor for this evening?" Dii asked with a pretty smile.

Olek watched the two women with amusement, especially Ozena's suddenly becoming excited. It was good to see her smile and focus on something other than recent events. He wondered how much they had bought when he saw the woman bundling up the garments. He bought his herbs and poisons and checked on the new arrivals, paying his respects to the Elder lodged with the Steward. As Ozena and Dii moved off to look elsewhere he spotted a dark green triangular scarf. It was sewn with small, pale green glass beads and a tasselled hem of silver. The fabric was soft chiffon, impractical for anything of use but decoration. He grinned and handed over a few coins and folded the soft scarf into his coat.

CHAPTER 14

Olek awoke early, well before dawn, as was his habit. He dressed and slipped outside, patrolling around the manor and the nearby grounds, pulling the darkness around him he moved silently. Archos had often told him there was no need to patrol, however Olek felt it his duty to check that the lands were safe. As he patrolled, he contemplated the recent events; Archos had seemed less alone and more content since Dii had arrived and Olek had seen the way they looked at each other, as though no one in the world existed but they themselves. She also made his master happy and even after such a short time, he knew they would not be parted. Olek liked Dii. She was sweet and kind, but there was an air of vulnerability about her, an air of pity that filled him with a little sadness and anger. To have been treated as she had been, he shook his head, never understanding how someone could be so cruel.

He thought about Ozena, the young forest elf he found so fascinating. He thought her rather pretty, in a fresh kind of way, like a forest pool or the first flowers of spring, a soft and natural look, a true creature of the forest. She had an innocence about her that he found endearing, the innocence that arose from youth and what he considered a sheltered upbringing. Olek knew she was far from stupid but she had a sweet and rather charming naiveté. Yet in her he saw strength and independence. He had laughed when he heard she had defied Archos in refusing to remain behind. Determined and loyal, Olek knew not many would have the courage or fortitude to refuse him. She had courage yet she was young and rather impulsive, and he hoped with careful training that could be overcome. Olek saw the fear and hurt in the young elf huntress and it pained him. He had seen what life in the Enclave could be, especially for an elven woman, and he knew that many of the women from the ruined village would be unlikely to survive. Ozena brought out his protective side. Olek was devoted to Archos, but he knew the Archmage could, for the most part, look after himself.

Ozena had been upset and restless that her sister remained missing and she seemed, he thought, uneasy too. This situation was alien to her, relying on the generosity and hospitality of a human, even if it was Lord Archos. Her village was all but destroyed and she was reliant on the kindness of strangers, in an unfamiliar house and lands.

Olek thought for a moment what would cheer the young elf's spirits. He had caught the sideways glances in his direction and grinned to himself, thinking a young elf from a small village could not have a great deal of experience in matters of dealing with the opposite sex. Perhaps he could make her easier on that score as well as amuse her. She had her mind on matters other than love but perhaps he could distract her from her sadness and worry with pleasant company and show her not all men were cruel and selfish, and that some would treat a woman with respect and tenderness. He thought to himself, as he returned to the manor, of the anger and protectiveness he had felt in the merchant's house when the son had tried to molest her. Olek leaned against the wall as he remembered how he had felt: rage, deep concern, shame for her, a deep affection, a stirring within him. Perhaps the young woman would not care for his attentions, but if needed, Olek would be content to be her friend and protector.

Olek paused in the garden and looked for something suitable. Entering the hothouse, he found a pale blue and white alpine gentian, its bell-like bloom soft and fragrant. He knew the gardener would have his hide if he caught him, so he endeavoured not to be caught. Gently he cut the bloom from its fellows and then selected some small white autumn wild roses from the porch. He wove them into a small garland and slipped the blue flower at the centre before slipping back inside unseen, just as the sun was rising on a fresh autumn day. He fetched his long bow and quiver from the stand in his chamber, and gently wrapped the flowers in the scarf, taking care not to crush them and laying the bundle on his bed he headed down to the kitchen. Marrissa was making preparations for the day and Olek approached her with a smile.

"Mistress Marrissa, I seek to take Miss Ozena out for the day. Lord Archos is busy in the workshop and Miss Dii is likely to spend the day in study so I thought to amuse Miss Ozena with some hunting up at the Crystal Falls. Make her feel welcome and a little more comfortable in these lands. If you could fix us a picnic of sorts that would be most agreeable."

Marrissa fetched him a basket of suitable refreshments and, handing it over, said in a motherly tone, "You watch your step with the young lady. I'll warrant she is inexperienced in matters of the heart. Do not push her to do something for which she is not ready."

Olek took the basket and replied in a tone laden with mock affront. "I? Would I push a woman against her will? Perhaps you presume too much. I am not after a mere roll in the hay, not that it is any business of yours anyway. I am a perfect gentleman. Besides, it is just a picnic and hunting trip, perhaps to get some rabbits for your stew-pot. I am under orders to entertain and mind the ladies and so I shall." Grinning, he gave her a nod and darting back to his room, placed the scarf and the garland in the basket and set out to find Ozena.

Ozena sat in the dining room eating the breakfast food laid out. The housekeeper had been kind and motherly to her, but Ozena still felt slightly awkward. The woman seemed happy in her position and devoted to her master, but the forest elf was not used to living in a house with servants and she felt slightly guilty, as if she were a burden. She felt sad, Olek had returned from his trip having no news of her sister Amena. Archos had promised her the girl would be found and apparently was making plans to take them to the city to make enquiries. She knew Dii would go where he went and was happiest either reading or with Archos and somehow she felt alone. Ozena felt useless and somewhat unwanted. Archos had been kind and generous to her but still she felt she was asking too much on his hospitality and time; unable to search alone for her sister, relying on help from this man yet awaiting on him to decide when and where he wanted to search. She found she had missed Olek's easy banter when he was away. Ozena knew nothing of magic and although Archos was kind to her, she felt somewhat intimidated and rather ignorant and uncultured around the two mages. Confused and unhappy, she was unsure what to do, how to proceed. She decided she needed to relax and turn her mind away from her worries before they consumed her. Knowing there was nothing she could do here and now.

She saw Olek enter carrying a longbow and quiver, and a laden basket, and she wondered what it was about. She had not seen him with such a weapon before, mainly being equipped with the long-swords and the evil little crossbow pistol he had shown her. She liked the way he moved, like one of the Great Cats of the forest, softly and with a good deal of grace. Ozena had found herself looking at him when she thought he was not watching. Trying to think about something other than Amena, she had found herself thinking about the mysterious Olek.

Ozena thought him handsome with his hair long and braided tightly down his back. It was the colour of the Shimmering Forest soil-a deep black, but flecked with auburn and brown and thick like the fur of a bear. His almond shaped eyes were amber like honey, alert and clever with a light that shone within them when he laughed, which was often. His ears were more rounded than those of a true elf yet still tapered to points denoting a good deal of elven blood. A mite taller and stockier than an elven man yet he walked like an elf, with poise, and had a confidence she had rarely encountered, a confidence she found strange for an elf living amongst humans. Ozena knew he was a servant but felt the deep affection between the two men, and somehow she knew that to an extent the service he held was so much more than mere assistance.

She sneaked a look at his body. The shirt he wore was tight and showed his fit, muscular chest and the breeches he wore were also tight and she fought with the urge to check how tight. His cloak hung over his arm and he was wearing the grin she had come to find attractive. Ozena had never quite felt such attraction for a man before and something in her said she should be focussing upon her sister and village and not this man she found so interesting. This morning she ignored it, knowing she could do nothing this day for her sister and knowing that the stress and worry would overwhelm her should she let it.

Olek saw her staring at him but pretended he had not noticed and sat down easily in a chair next to her, pretending he did not see the blush that reddened her pretty face as well.

"Good morning to you, Miss Ozena. Lord Archos is busy today making preparations to leave, thus I am not needed until this evening. So I thought to go out hunting, the game is good in these parts – rabbits, pheasants, grouse, deer, forest pigs on occasion. I think I could use some relaxation and…distraction after the recent events. I could do with training with my long bow. It is not a weapon I use often and I need to keep my skills honed and desire the practice. Would you care to join me?

"The weather is fine and I thought you might care to see the lands hereabouts, beyond the manor and gardens, for they are wonderful lands. I cannot practice archery in the gardens without getting filthy looks from Old Thomas in case I damage something. I am convinced that man cares far more for plants than people, except the master of course. Anyway, I thought it might be a pleasant distraction to be away from the house and out in the fresh air? I expect Dii will be content enough within the library in study." He gave her a smile that made her blush once more and waited for an answer.

Ozena tried and failed to stop the blush. "I…I would like that very much indeed… My tutor said I was the best pupil he had but I think he probably said that to them all. The gardens here are not…natural…beautiful, indeed, but somehow wrong…too neat and ordered. Nature does not grow that way; she is wild and disordered and goes where she pleases. I would like to see the lands, the hill and fields, I would like move beyond the house and gardens. I am not used to being within doors as much."

Olek chuckled. "I would not say that too loudly, the master is very fond of his maze and it's the finest in the land. But yes, I agree, it is ordered and tamed, certainly not what an elf of the Shimmering Forest would know. Come, I know just the spot I think you would like."

He pulled her up by the hand, burying a smile at the blush she again failed to suppress. "That is, of course, if you trust to be alone with me?" Olek said with a teasing glint in his amber eyes.

Ozena looked at him with her green eyes laughing. "My mama warned me against men such as you. It is a shame she is not living that I may thank her for the warning and the information that such exist. But I think you are gentleman enough not to take advantage of a girl like me. I…never thanked you for coming to my assistance the other night at the house of the merchant. I was so ashamed about what occurred, however, I talked to Dii and she reassured me quite a bit. You are kind. I seem to know you would not hurt me."

"Well, I am flattered you think so. If you wish me to have an ulterior motive then I shall. If you wish merely for a pleasant day out and a picnic, then I will enjoy the pleasant weather and the charming company and be content with that. I would not expect more from a lady than she would be prepared to give. As for…what happened, I was pleased to assist you. Men such as he deserve not to live, in my opinion. A woman should be treated with honour and respect. If she is unwilling, she is unwilling, and a man should know when a women does not want him and turn his attentions elsewhere, or find other amusements."

He walked over close to her and looked into those deep green eyes, his own eyes golden in the morning light streaming through the window as he touched her cheek, saying softly, "Were you MY lady, I would treat you with respect and honour; I would not force you to do that which you wished not to do. I would be your servant and your protector. But let us not dwell on what happened that night. I assure you that man will pay, one way or another, and although we did not find Amena, we found those two women and saw them safe. Let us forget that for today, let Archos do what he must and we will enjoy the sun."

Smiling, Ozena was flattered by the compliments. "Then let us go enjoy the day and the places you know. Let me fetch my bow and my cloak."

* * *

They rode to the high rolling hills beyond the manor, the hills softened and rounded by the rains and many streams that proliferated in the region. Beyond the hills lay the Jagged Peak Mountains and the cold plateau lands of Helmerri and the trolls which lived there, a tough hardy people who occasionally traded within the valley when it suited them. Although a distance from the main edges of the Shimmering Forest, copses of short sturdy trees dotted the green hills, fruit and hazel, a few elderberry from which the locals often harvested fruit and flowers, and here and there a large sturdy oak of ancient years towered above the rest or a young sapling sprouted, looking for its chance. Birch and ash grew, although shorter than those of the forest itself. In the distance she could see the vineyards that provided the local wines and the main orchards as they passed by. Valley folk grazed their hardy sheep, cattle and pigs on these hills, and Ozena was heartened to see a few of the forest goats that had either wandered in or been rescued amongst the sheep, finding the new pastures to their liking. Ozena had seen the many farms and Olek had mentioned the small holdings that produced many of the foodstuff and wines that supplied the valley.

She had been persuaded to ride her own mount, Olek saying it would do her good to learn, selecting the small and friendly but rather elderly bay mare from the stable. This mare was apparently the mother of his own mount and sometimes used by the old housekeeper, although she had a pony she preferred. His own mount was the fine and mischievous gelding of chestnut. He led Ozena's mare, Rana, and instructed her how best to manage the beast. Ozena had found an affinity with the horses. Although she was still far from a horsewoman, the beasts trusted her, even the proud and feisty mount of Archos who suffered neither fool nor fear. She had spent a lot of time in the stables since she arrived, petting and grooming. Olek was glad Ozena was helping with the horses. There were many to manage, although Old Thomas and Marrissa assisted and the almost mute boy Mathias helped with the heavy work.

Olek pointed out areas he thought would interest her and recounted stories of the lands. Evidently he knew these lands well and was proud and sure of the terrain. Even mounted, he moved with ease and grace but maintained alertness that, as a hunter, she found familiar. However it was far beyond anything she knew, as though he was aware of everything around him but was able to appear utterly fixed on the conversation. As they rode, she wondered who he was, really was. What was this man's history? She found herself intrigued that he could move from the amiable and easy going riding companion to the ruthless and utterly focused blade-master, the man who had calmly slit the throat of the young slaver and simply walked away.

Ozena had hesitated in the trees that night, found herself unable to do it, and that was weakness she decided. Olek and, even more so, Lord Archos were able to do what needed to be done without hesitating. Ozena realised then that the entire village of Szendro had been complacent. Although there were the warriors, they were few and merely used to fighting with the few forest creatures that occasionally wandered too close. Although the elves had known risks, it appeared that knowing and accepting had not been the same thing. A tear rolled down her cheek and she suppressed a sob. Olek looked at her and reined the mounts to a stop. Gently, he touched her cheek and wiped away the tear. "What is this? My company is so odious that you cry?" he said with a concerned smile.

"No, no, I am just being foolish. I got to thinking about Szendro village, what happened, how unprepared we were... Everything that has been lost."

Sighing, Olek replied sadly, "Yes, it is indeed a tragedy, so much lost, not only the lives of the elves, but the lore, the culture too. I do not think you could have been prepared. Szendro was far from the usual slaver routes. It could not have been foreseen. However we have managed to return some of the elves, your Elder lives and the stories and traditions will continue. Lord Archos tells me he will arrange for the elves to have their own cottages, within the villages but near to the edge of the forest. The elves will be part of the village life but can maintain their links. I think he was going to meet with the Elder, discuss recording the lore of your village so that it will be remembered. Much indeed has been lost, but it will be ensured that not all. Closer ties with the elves have been forged."

Pausing, he took her hand for a moment. "If it had not happened, I would never have had the honour to meet you, Ozena. Every day I thank the gods that you were not taken."

Ozena blushed as she listened to him, not drawing her hand away as he took her small hand in his. "I had not seen it that way. It is easy to lose oneself in the sadness and overlook the good things, things that have been found, new friends, new…er…"

Olek smiled and patted her hand, sensing her awkwardness. "Come along, we are nearly there. My belly tells me it seeks the contents of the picnic baskets. Do not dwell on the past, for that cannot be changed, merely avenged and remembered. Look to the future, for that is not yet written and for some part, we make ourselves."

They rode on until Olek led them to the edge of a copse of trees. He dismounted and let the horses wander; he knew they would not stray far. The trees were not high, but stout and well weathered. The grass here was long and a deep green speckled with wildflowers among which bees and butterflies flew even on this autumn day. Busy collecting their food before the winter took away the flowers and let icy fingers crawl across the land. There was a deep gurgle of water and she detected the fresh smell of a nearby stream or pool. Birds sang in the trees and there was a buzz of insects, and the inexorable hum and squeak of small life going about its business mainly disregarded and unnoticed.

"There are rabbits in the banks yonder, and sometimes pheasants. I have seen the wild pigs hereabouts but not often. We might be lucky though, they come for the apples. Not bad eating if you can snag one. There are wild hives up here, in the trees. Now I am very rusty with the longbow so I will let you instruct, Mistress Hunter." Ozena hesitated, not sure enough to dismount. As the horse shuffled, he smiled and gently lifted her down with his hands strong and sure about her waist. He placed her carefully on the grass and pretended he had not seen her blush.

"Thank you, Olek. I am not yet a confident horsewoman. I am not long past my apprenticeship as a hunter, as you would call it. You are a weapons master, Olek, what can I teach you?"

"Aye, but I am rusty with the weapon. Besides, I like to watch you," Olek replied with a wink.

Ozena looked around and a grin lit up her face as she breathed in the fresh air, scented by the wildflowers and the smell of the earth. "It is beautiful and so peaceful, I have never seen the like. The forest was beautiful, but it was dark from the trees. Here there is so much light and it is so open."

As she smiled with the sheer wonder of the place, he took her hand gently and said softly, "Aye, indeed it is…an excellent spot for relaxing." Olek smiled as he saw her smile, thinking he liked to see her happy and had not seen much of it.

He gave her his grin and said, "Well, this is your day. I am simply escort; hunt as you wish, amuse yourself as you wish. The water in the pool is warm and fit for swimming. It is heated by the fire that lives within the earth. We have food enough to stay our hunger. Show me what you can do…for the long bow is not my first weapon of choice."

Ozena drew her bow and crouched, waiting. Patiently she sat, aware of Olek watching her but focused on the rabbits. One hopped by unaware and suddenly the arrow shot from her bow. The rabbit tumbled over, an arrow in its flank. As the rest fled, she loosed another arrow and another until three small furry bodies lay in the grass.

"Hmm not bad, very good in fact; you have a good eye and very fast reflexes." Olek let fly an arrow but the rabbits, already panicked, rapidly ran for the safety of the warren. For a while they practiced and enjoyed the freedom of the place, adding a few game birds and one or two of the more foolish rabbits to the pile.

Laying the blanket on the grass, he set out the food and sat. "Sometimes I come here to think…just to be alone…away from everything. It is a good place to relax, to simply be. The blanket is soft and we have good food and I purloined a bottle of the master's best wine. We can sit and chat, get to know each other. We can swim in the pool, or just lie in the grass and watch the world go by; whatever you wish."

Ozena did not know if she should ask, but the curiosity was drumming in her head so she took a chance. "Olek, may I ask you something? Your skills are great and I would like to know how you came about such."

Olek laughed good-naturedly. "Aye, well, I am sure the tale would bore you, for it is not very grand."

"Please, I would like to know about them…and about you." Ozena blushed enchantingly.

Smiling, Olek shrugged and replied flirtatiously, "As you wish, I am not the sort of man to refuse the wishes of a pretty girl."

She blushed again, unsure what to make of the comment. Olek grinned and kissed her hand, making her blush even more.

"My mother was a whore. Oh, do not look like that. She was an elf from the forest like you, or so I was led to believe. Taken in a raid, she was settled in the city Enclave with many other elves. Mother was neither mage nor adept, but she was pretty and the career choices for an elven woman are rather limited. At least she was not forced to live in Shackles as the mages are. She was a whore and, from what I remember having heard, a good one and sought after. I have no idea who my father is or was… I doubt she did, either. The Enclave was, and still is, poor and life was cheap. Although she did better than many there, I remember days when we were cold and hungry. I was always quick with my feet and my wits even then. I was fast and my small hands could find things hidden in the pockets of the men she would entertain; supplementing our income, as it were. Life is hard in the Enclaves and, well, choice is not a luxury many can afford. You do what you must to survive.

"I have no idea how old I was when she died, perhaps twelve, maybe less. She was with child again and as is often the case, the infant came into the world stillborn and she followed a day or so later.

"I made my living as I always had, only now I would stalk the human parts of the city at night, picking pockets, opening locks, taking what was not guarded. I made enough to survive and enough sometimes for the few luxuries that can be bartered in the Enclave. Time passed, in such a place one day is the same as the next, and I know not how many months or even years went by. I made a living of sorts as a thief. It was hard and dangerous, but such is the way for many who live in the Enclave or even beyond its walls in the poor human quarters; some of those as bad as the Enclave itself. One day I had managed to acquire some trinkets, now I cannot even recall what they were, when I was caught by the city guards. It seemed a human thief knew that I was reasonably successful and seemed to take offence that I was working in what he claimed to be his area; a half-elf who did not know his place beyond the Enclave walls. I was arrested, condemned to the gallows. Not even I could escape the city gaols in those days.

"Lord Archos appeared and paid I know not what to have me freed. He simply told me he had a need of a man with my talents that he could trust to serve him as he had business he did not want made known. Well, I was hardly in a position to refuse. I guess that is it, not much really. The rest of my life has been here, serving Lord Archos. He has been the only family, or as near to it, that I have known for a good many years. I have no idea to this day why he chose me and not simply another thief, of equal or greater talent. I asked him once. He just smiled and said he saw talent and loyalty and prized both. There are many secrets to be maintained and thus it suits us both to be as we are. He is generous to those he is fond of, and educated me far beyond what one may learn on the streets. He encouraged my talents and skills. He is a remarkable man and it is an honour to serve a man such as him. Archos knows how elves are generally treated and does not treat me or any elf as though we are slaves. I find often his motives for actions are not what one would expect.

"Aye, well, that is enough of my history for it is nothing special. Sorry to disappoint you, but I am not the heir to the kingdom or some such," he finished with a smile.

Ozena listened, raptly attentive to him. "It is more interesting than mine. I am a simple forest elf from a small village."

Olek rolled onto his belly and looked at her for a while, his amber eyes bright and playfully searching her face. "Well, perhaps you never before had the chance of anything more. Do not underestimate yourself. You saved many of your companions by your swift action. You have talent; you are good, excellent even, with a bow. Sometimes destiny needs a little push in the right direction. Anyway, there is nothing wrong with a peaceful life. You could be many things, Ozena. Your village has fallen, but yet you live and many choices are open to you."

"I am nothing special." Ozena blushed and muttered, "I am an elf and a woman. As you say, there are not many choices."

"That is true for the most part, but within this valley, those restrictions do not apply. Beyond that, there are skills one can learn to make life somewhat easier. Elves will never be equal, so we must be better and apart from the laws when it suits us. Besides, you have the protection of Lord Archos and that counts for a great deal."

Gently, he stroked a lock of her mahogany hair that had come lose from the braid and poured her a cup of wine. She blushed again and thought a man had never before poured for her a drink. Elves drank a little ale and wine but were not, as a rule, heavy drinkers and she was not used to anything beyond the fruity wines of the forest.

Ozena watched him, fascinated. Everything he did was smooth yet calculated, even at ease, he was alert and she saw the muscles beneath his shirt ripple as he moved. Ozena suddenly felt a little warm and a flutter in her belly that she had not felt before. She thought she had caught him glancing at her but was not sure what that meant. Her experience of men was limited and she had never been courted before.

He lay back upon the blanket and watched the clouds pass, then got up and sauntered slowly to the pool.

Undressing quickly, he dived in, like a sea bird, deep to the bottom of the pool. Surfacing, he called to her, "Come join me, the water is warm and relaxing. I can feel the tension just flow away. If you wish to swim, you may use my shirt to cover yourself if you are shy."

Ozena blushed a deep red to the roots of her hair, but found she was watching him swim and dive like an otter. Standing up, she decided that she had never done anything reckless and Olek's words about choices echoing in her head, she turned her back to him whilst he was diving and stripped, scrambling into his shirt. Finding it was shorter than she anticipated, she pulled the blanket around herself and crept to the edge of the pool. Dropping the blanket so she stood just in the thin cotton shirt, she jumped into the warm water. Olek had disappeared and suddenly popped up behind her.

"See, do you not feel better? It is a warm mineral spring fed from the fires of the earth," he breathed in her ear.

Ozena was trying and failing to not look at the naked half-elf, noticing his muscled torso and the ivy leaf tattoo that circled across his arm and over his chest. She saw a red scar bisecting a leaf and wanted to ask, but did not dare, and a long thin scar just above his belly. As she swam, he swam beside her and dived beneath her to playfully splash her when he surfaced. Ozena was fascinated by his body, wanting to touch him, to stroke the tanned skin. She found herself drawn to looking at him below the water and blushed again. She forced herself to look away, intrigued and curious yet shy. She had never met anyone so comfortable in their own shape. Forest elves tended to be more modest, even when swimming in the rivers and pools when bathing.

Olek gazed at the young woman before him, the wet shirt clinging to her curves and her moves graceful. As she surfaced, he thought she resembled a water nymph or spirit of the pool, rising from the water as she did. Again he felt the stir within him, more than just desire, a protective and profound stirring.

The huntress found the tension ebbing away from her; a combination of the pleasant company, the warm mineral water, and the distraction from her worries. For a while, she almost forgot the recent events. Olek dived deep then swam away from her, reappearing later with green fronds of the water plants draped over his head and shoulders. He roared like a beast and splashed towards her, yelling something about the monster that lived in the pool and chasing her. Playfully she screamed and swam away slowly. The Swamp Monster splashed after her and wrapped her in green slimy clutches.

"Ahaha, who be it that comes to my pool. It be a tasty elf maiden. Yum yum," cried the Olek monster.

"Oh no, help me, what is this foul beast that has me in its clutches," she yelled back, laughing.

Olek pulled her towards him and kissed her gently, wrapping her in his arms. Softly he held her, treading water, letting her pull away if she desired. She felt his warm skin close to her and felt his desire just brush her beneath the water. As he kissed her, she felt a shiver of longing, an unfamiliar but very pleasant stir within her.

Ozena accepted the kiss, leaning into him, then blushed and pulled away, suddenly nervous.

"I…I am sorry, Ozena, I have embarrassed you," Olek said and pulled back, but still with his arms around her.

"No… No, Olek, I am not embarrassed. It was nice… I am just not used to attentions from a man. I feel so easy and safe with you and you are so handsome and worldly, but I am just a foolish maiden with no experience. I am sorry," Ozena replied, shaking her head.

Olek took her hand and kissed it. "Well then, if it does not displease you, perhaps you will allow me to continue with my attentions, at whatever pace you decide. I would not rush you into anything, or expect something that was not on offer. Surely you know that? Perhaps I can teach you, if you will let me. You are a very pretty young woman, clever and strong of will. I confess I want to…know you better, but I leave the choice to you."

Ozena nodded and pulled the pond weeds from him. "I do find you very attractive and I would like you to continue with…your attentions, but I am nervous. I have never been courted, or lain with a man."

She plucked up her courage and kissed him, letting her tongue find his for a moment. Blushing, she looked down and swam to the edge of the pool before glancing back at him. As she pulled herself out the water streamed from her and silhouetted her form through the shirt like a second skin. Olek swallowed and dived away until he was fit to leave the water. Ozena quickly dried herself on the blanket and then dressed, then held the blanket for Olek to climb out.

He grinned and shook his head, watching her blush. Eventually shaking off the remaining weeds, he clambered out and took the blanket to dry. Dressing in just his breeches, he fetched enough wood to light a small fire and setting his cloak to sit on, settled comfortably.

"I…I have a gift for you. I hope you do not mind." He took the scarf from the basket and held it out. "I found this in the market, after you saw the clothes. It is green like the ivy that covers the oak, and the beads shine like your eyes. It is not much, but I thought it might please you. Look inside, there is something else."

Ozena stammered quietly, "I have never been given such a gift before!"

He took her into his arms and kissed her again, one hand caressing her neck, softly, tenderly. "Then we shall take it slowly, if that is what you wish. Just snuggle in close and relax, let the afternoon just pass by and rest. You are safe here with me, and I will not rush you to anything. Let us just enjoy each other's company and see what happens."

Ozena snuggled into his embrace and set the green scarf around her shoulders, soft and fragrant from the flowers. Tired from the swim, they lay quietly enjoying the peace and the company until she fell into a light sleep. Olek shifted so she lay in his embrace and gently kissed her hair until she woke an hour or so later.

"We should return before dark, Ozena. Marrissa will have my hide if she thinks I have been up to no good all day with you, and we should get those rabbits back to her kitchen." He helped her mount the horse and together they returned to the manor.

CHAPTER 15

Lord Joset Tremayne entered the house he kept for entertaining his cronies. It was a large cottage and converted barn area which now served as a well-furnished hall. It was not within his own lands but close enough to be a few days travel, in Bornlea, one of the small hamlets that served the city of Varlek and was a half day's ride from the town of Jaeden. Bornlea was a small village near the river and a waterfall that made a meagre trade by fishing and farming the river clams that were found close by. The house comprised a few private chambers, a drawing room, a large parlour and beyond, some guarded quarters that housed the elves. A middle aged female half-elf curtsied as he entered.

"There will some new arrivals shortly. I trust you will make them comfortable and at ease. Lord Soren, his sons, Lord Petric, old Lord Rundin and his son, Lord Renfrew and his young son and Commander Oscar Fayden of the Order of Witch-Hunters, with one or two of his colleagues, and myself will be attending. You know most of their…needs and preferences," he ordered the woman.

The woman nodded. "As you wish, my lord. It will be excellent to have some new stock in," she said, knowing her master's taste.

Joset licked his lips lustfully, anticipating the pleasures he believed would be forthcoming. "Oh yes! Perhaps one of these can become talented and sought after and make me more money, earn her keep and repay the…service I have done her. I am told some of these girls are indeed striking to behold," he mused, eyes distant as he imagined the twisted pleasure and the piles of gold.

The Lord of Reldfield turned on his heel and left to refresh himself. He half wished Dii was there to provide amusement to his friends, then the anger surfaced that she had dared to use magic and dared to run. The ungrateful little bitch, he thought. He wondered if any of these girls would be suitable enough to replace her. Joset was still angry with Malana. She had been very contrite after her punishment, yet still she defended that little witch whore. Ulric still had not returned but had sent word he was heading to the city. There were not many options for a lone elf; he had mentioned searching the brothels. Joset grinned. Ulric was becoming a chip off the old block. It was a shame the boy was going to miss the entertainment, he thought. Still, Ulric had always been overly attached to Dii, had even once mentioned having her only for himself.

* * *

Archos and his party made good time to the city, arriving just before dark. A message had been sent ahead to prepare the townhouse for guests. Valeria could manage Olek arriving unannounced, but for the lord and his entourage to arrive, she needed more notice. The townhouse was not as large as the manor, but it was comfortable and spacious enough to accommodate the group. It had a small private chamber Archos used when he was spell casting, a comfortable parlour and a small library and workshop, not nearly as fine as the one at the manor but fine nonetheless. There were a number of comfortable chambers and a small dining room that was kept finely decorated. The house was set aside from the main group of dwellings and surrounded by a high wall topped by broken glass, not that thieves would be foolish enough to try. The few that had found it a fatal decision. There was a garden filled with fragrant herbs and a few fruit trees, a patch of green within the dark city.

Once everyone was settled, Archos approached the two elven women. "Ladies, you must remember that here elves have not the freedom or respect you would find in Tremellic. You must keep close to myself or Olek, or remain in the townhouse. We have some friends here, the thieves and…others, but also many enemies. There are Witch-Hunters, guards and slavers, but hopefully if we are cautious and discrete, our investigations will prove fruitful. I would suggest, for a start, a visit to the Enclave. Ozena will hopefully recognise anyone from her village and it may do to make enquiries there. We will, I hope, hear further from some of the contacts Olek dealt with before. Now, I think we should make ourselves comfortable."

Later when they were alone, Archos wrapped his arms around Dii's slender waist and drew her in to a kiss. Gently he murmured, "The city is a dangerous place for you, but I want you close to me, where I may ensure you are safe, my Flower of the Dawn." He kissed her with fire and picking her up in his arms, took her to bed.

* * *

Olek slipped out at first light and checked the message box at the Oaken Barrel, fetching from it a scroll simply sealed with black wax and the sign of a cat. He smiled and slipped it into his cloak, returning to the townhouse to deliver it. As he entered, Valeria informed him that she had discovered from her contacts that some of the lower class brothels had acquired new recruits and a surprising number of elves seemed to be going missing from the Enclave. Archos dressed quietly and, with Dii still sleeping, he stood and watched her from the doorway, still and safe. The nightmares seemed to have eased a little but sometimes she would still wake in the night and he had seen her crying when she thought he was not there. He hoped that he had not made the wrong decision to bring them all to the city.

He sat on the edge of the bed and kissed her. As she woke, he said quietly, "I have to go out shortly. You and Ozena may rest today after our long journey, but I would like you both to do something for me. When I come here, I try and take medicines to the Enclave, just a few herbal remedies. They may have herbalists, but last time I was here, they were rather rare, education is not encouraged unless it suits the masters' purposes. Besides, potions are good for trade. The elves may buy at the apothecary but the more complex remedies are too expensive for many. Whilst we are there, we can speak to the elves and look for those from the village. See what Ozena knows of herb lore and teach her some, it is always useful to know. Now as much as I would wish to return to your embrace, I must resist and make enquiries and preparations." He kissed her again as she agreed to do as bidden.

Heading down to the parlour, he knew Olek would already be up and about. The half-elf recounted what the housekeeper had told him and handed over the scroll. At first glance it appeared blank, but Archos ran his finger over the edge and the writing slowly appeared. It simply said:

Sources tell me there are some new elves just arrived in one of the Red Lantern brothels and more than usual missing from Enclave. The slavers are being watched. The man under our hospitality attempted to escape and had an unfortunate accident, but was quite forthcoming with the names of his colleagues in transport of slaves: Loren, Sardak, and Renfrew. Warehouse of Versann was lost to fire, after mysterious disappearance of most of the stock -Northern Docks. Wagons of linens and silks will be left in the care of a friendly merchant in the booth behind the White Horse Inn. Versann house will suffer a mysterious robbery.

Thiefmaster.

Archos smiled an unpleasant smile and nodded slightly. "Excellent, some information to follow and some vengeance. Now I will visit the merchant district in the Northern Docks, see the extent of the…unfortunate losses of the house of Versann. There may be more mischief to be had there. I may see if I can find the whereabouts of these slavers mentioned, it might be worth you doing the same. I should go and pay my respects to the Society of Hidden Secrets also. Perhaps you would like to check out the houses of ill repute. If memory serves, there are some of the more…varied establishments in that district. The ladies have instructions to prepare some medicines for the Enclave, hopefully that will keep them out of mischief until I return."

Olek nodded. "The docks are often a good source of information. If I remember correctly, there is a tavern in the Street of Red Lanterns. If I need to, I can loiter around there. I…er…I thought to take Ozena to look around the city at some point also…if you permit me. She will never have been to a city, but I suppose that depends on what we find."

"You are…fond of her, are you not, my friend? I have never seen quite such attention so soon to a woman." Archos grinned. "Yes, of course…depending on what our enquiries lead to, we can always return here when things are more settled. Hopefully I should not be too long. Be careful."

Archos sauntered out, slowly making his way to the merchant district in the northern docks area. The buildings were mainly warehouses of the wealthier merchants, guarded and better secured than most. He wandered around, observing and unobserved, until he found the burned out warehouse, now a mere shell. He noticed with a smile that the fire had seemed to be complete, however the neighbouring storehouse to the left had been empty and the one to the right had managed to avoid the blaze. Archos stopped and leaned against the door of another building, watching a half-elf servant pick through the ruins.

"Seems you may be investigating a lost cause there, my friend. I doubt you will find much to salvage."

The half-elf looked around to see who had spoken. Spying a well-dressed fellow, the servant did not wish to appear rude so replied grimly, "Oh yes, would seem that way, sir. My master will not be pleased, and it was some significant losses he suffered. Have you business here, sir?"

Archos smiled beneath the cowl of his cloak. "I have been known to dabble in certain business when the mood takes me. I was seeking somewhere to store goods for a new venture, but it would seem that security here may be lax. Your master, who is he?"

The half-elf, hearing the soft, mellow and oddly enchanting baritone of the Archmage, replied, "Indeed, sir, it would seem that way. The warehouses were guarded but it seems the guards were…elsewhere. My master is a trader of linens and fabrics: the merchant Niall Versann. Hopefully these will be the only losses his house suffers. He is awaiting arrival of a ship, *White Star*. Once that vessel docks safely, he should manage to recoup some of this. I am tasked to investigate the whereabouts of the guards and the person or persons responsible."

Archos sauntered over to the half-elf. He smiled casually and let his voice echo in the man's head. "Oh, I doubt you will find anything of use, looks to me like thieves or possibly an accident. As for the guards, well, maybe they simply sought amusement elsewhere. One cannot get good help these days. They were probably in a tavern or the arms of a whore; I find guards are often not to be trusted. It is simply a misfortune."

The servant nodded. "Oh yes, seems like just a misfortune to me. I will suggest he hires better security. Perhaps gets a warehouse elsewhere. I hope your business is more fortunate, sir."

Archos grinned unpleasantly and, walking away, simply replied, "Oh, that I can guarantee."

He wandered for a while, watching, listening, and taking in the sounds of the district. He watched as the ships docked and noticed the banner of the Order of Witch-Hunters fluttering above one or two. Noting names, he wandered back through the merchant district, pausing to make a couple of purchases.

As Archos passed the stalls and booths, his discerning eye caught a gleam as he paused to browse. He saw the bracelets of golden feathered serpents, flexible and well-crafted from trollish-mined gold, with eyes of dark blue sapphire that blinked and turned as though alive. One had a spine of small emeralds, the other of small garnets. The tight coils twisted and turned, the fine etching making scales which shone in the light. As he picked them up, he felt the faint tingle from the enchantment. He smiled broadly as he recognised the finest troll craftsmanship and he knew they would be the perfect gift for his love.

Alongside lay a long gold, silver and bronze snake, with finely crafted scales, each with filigree alternating between the three metals, the eyes were deep red bloodstones and the jaws clasped the tail and held it secure. Archos picked up all three and looked them over carefully.

"They are very fine, my lord. The large tricolour snake would be worn as a torc about the neck or an armlet. The lady would indeed be graced with much beauty when wearing those," said the vendor, proud of his fine wares and eager to make such a profitable sale.

Archos merely smiled and paid for the items to be wrapped in silk. He moved on and found a shop that sold all manner of the more intimate type of clothing. He selected a long trailing gown of soft Shimmering Spider silk, dyed a pale red, almost translucent, and that would cling in all the right places. The cut was low and edged with a fine lace. The skirt of the gown was slit to the thigh and the whole garment made a soft sigh when it moved and felt like the petals of a rose in his hands. He purchased that and one in a dark bluish black and edged with a pale fur. He had them wrapped around the jewellery and placed in a fine wooden box, carved with leaves and flowers and scented with lavender. Carrying the box, he moved along as if merely shopping. The city guards and Witch-Hunters paid him little attention. Silently and casually he made his way to the hidden entrance of the Society of Hidden Secrets, after a while returning home.

* * *

Back at the townhouse, Dii dressed quickly and combed scented oil through her long red curls. She thought about what Archos had requested. She had never returned to the Enclave since she had been taken from there, but she had heard stories. One of the other elven servants used by Joset had come from the Varlek Enclave, and he had told her sometimes of the conditions; the poverty, the sadness, and restriction of the mages that lived chained and bound in the prison side. The elves and half-elves who lived within the Enclave walls traded and bartered amongst themselves and with the kinder humans, yet many basic needs and items were lacking. Those who worked for humans and were treated well or lived in the masters' houses were better off than most. The servant had told her the elves were close-knit, as such communities often were. She thought taking medicines and such remedies as she and Ozena could provide was an excellent idea. Dii sought out Ozena, who was eating breakfast in the dining room, and sat next to her, piling food onto a plate.

"Good morning to you, Ozena. I believe the menfolk have gone out, and about and my lord bids us a task: to make some remedies and potions to distribute in the Enclave. I have some knowledge of herb lore, perhaps you would like to help me. I expect you know of the forest herbs and basic remedies?"

Ozena smiled to see Dii. "Oh yes. I was wondering how to spend my time. There is a garden, but no hunting, and I am afraid to be in the city alone. Olek seems to have gone out, as you say. I know some herb lore, enough to make a few recipes at least. I would ask for your help later with the new clothes, the bodice and the skirt. I would ask for your advice as I am rather unfamiliar with such garments."

Dii patted her arm. "Of course, my dear, I will help you with anything I am able. I shall look in the small library here. There may be something to assist us. My lord tells me there are many herbs in the garden but it's rather late in the season. There may be dried ones in the kitchens. Come, let us go look."

She led Ozena to the library and then they spent a pleasant morning gathering herbs and making remedies, boiling and crushing herbs, mixing poultices and steeping leaves and roots for potions. They worked through the morning and to mid-afternoon, producing a goodly selection of suitable potions and salves. Later, as they rested in the library with a small tray of refreshments, Ozena decided to take Dii up on her offer of assistance. She knew the elf mage had greater experience in matters of love and how to please a man, and Ozena wanted some advice. She liked Olek, and found him very attractive, yet she had no experience and knew that Olek was a man of the world. Ozena was afraid, afraid that she would disappoint him or shame him, or herself.

Ozena looked awkward, and sitting next to Dii, fell silent from their easy chatter, nervously twisting a lock of hair. Ozena always felt a little out of place in the library and around the clever mages; she could read a little Elvish, but just a little and could not read the Common trade language at all. Education was not something the Order of Witch-Hunters encouraged and did not promote free thinking or universal literacy, believing ruling with fear and promoting ignorance and hatred proved more effective. The forest elves generally retained an oral tradition of storytelling, song and lore. Often only the Elders and any mages or scholars were literate, the general populace not needing the written word in their everyday lives. Ozena was ashamed to admit to

Dii that she could not read, even though such was commonplace. The mages were so clever and educated, and Ozena again felt apart from the household.

Ozena blushed and picked up the book Dii had found on the herbs and medicines, looking at it wistfully. "I cannot read, Dii; I am not as clever as you," she whispered with embarrassment.

Dii looked at her and replied kindly, "Yes, yes, you are clever, just in a different way. You are a hunter, you know the ways of the forest, the ways of the animals, herbs I have never seen or used. You can track and follow a trail. I am fortunate that one of the few kind things my Keeper ever did was allow me to be educated, to read and write, to learn. Not often but he did allow it. It was useful to him, I suppose, to have an educated slave."

For a moment, her eyes filled with tears and the young woman murmured, "Yes, perhaps it suited him to have a clever slave, to torment further, to fetch a better price."

Turning back to Ozena, she took her hand in friendship and continued, "Perhaps you have simply never had the opportunity to learn other than that which you need. I had no need or opportunity to fend for myself, for I was not allowed out unaccompanied and I was fed and had access to the good kitchens, thus had no need to hunt or provide for myself. Although in theory, I know what is good to eat and how to forage for such. I cannot hunt or know exactly what I must do to provide it. I can cook, of course, and sew, but that was more my foster mother's influence. I learned much from books, tales and the few walks and journeys I was allowed to make, plus what others told me. My foster mother was kind and clever. She would read to me and encourage me, at least when he was not around.

"I am sure my lord would not mind you learning. I will ask him if I may teach you, if you would like that. I am sure there is much of which I am ignorant. I know Archos is well taught and well-travelled. He encourages me to learn, to improve myself, and I am sure he would be happy for you to do the same. It is not just magic I learn, there are so many other things, so much within the world to see and understand!"

Ozena nodded slowly, but blushed. She had seen the look in Dii's eyes when she spoke of her former life and felt a little guilty having been the cause of such recollection. Quietly she said, "I would like to learn… I feel so stupid, so useless here. Lord Archos is kind, but I am not a mage. I bring nothing here. I am sorry that I have given you cause to remember that which you did not wish to."

Dii took her hands. "My dear, do not apologise, for it was not your doing that made me live as I was forced to. The memories are there and sometimes rise unbidden. Lord Archos does not give his friendship and his protection lightly. If you were no use, nothing to him, we would not now be in the city looking for your sister, for the elves from your village, and you would not have the hospitality of his house. You have many useful skills. It may simply be that you must adapt those to the new environment. I will happily teach you to read and write. I cannot speak Elvish so you could teach me that, or to use a bow perhaps, for I have no means of defending myself other than magic and I cannot use that openly. We could start perhaps with that book on herbs--you know the names and see the illustrations--it will be easy enough to learn the letters. Perhaps we may learn together." Dii smiled at her, eyes shining with the thought of learning and helping another to learn.

Ozena shuffled her feet as the blush coloured her pretty face, wanting to ask another question but shy and not knowing how to ask or how it would be received. "May I ask you a personal question, Dii? You have lain with men, taken lovers. You and Lord Archos, you…please one another?"

Dii gave her an amused smile. "Yes, we are lovers. There is neither secret in that nor any shame, and yes, he pleases me greatly and I hope I please him. Why do you ask?"

"I…would like to know about…er…men…um, how to please a man; that sort of business. I know the theory, of course, um, what bits, um, go where. I helped with birthing sometimes. I know what the…procedures are, as it were. But I have never… er…you know…lain with a man."

Dii grinned innocently and said, "And you would like to know about how to please and gain pleasure from a lover? Have you a fellow in mind?"

Ozena blushed again and said nothing, suddenly examining the floor. Dii smiled teasingly and replied, "I have seen the looks you have given Olek and the glances he has thrown your way. He is a good man, and handsome. I think also he will be patient. Now let me see, how do you please a man? Well, really, I suppose that depends on the particular man and on what you are willing to do for one another; for men like a variety of pleasures, as in many things. If the man is selfish, he will care not for your pleasure, but if he is generous and kind, he will want you to enjoy yourself, to get pleasure from him also. This will heighten the experience for both of you. Sometimes the pleasure is in giving pleasure itself; to be close to another, to provide such joy and such intensity, and if you love someone, well, that is exquisite."

Ozena listened and continued to blush, but began to ask questions. "I am told it hurts, the first time."

Dii patted her arm. "Yes, often that is the case. And there will be blood, but that is normal and nothing to be afraid of, as some young women are. I suppose it is…a sharp pain, a little soreness, but if your lover is kind, he will be gentle. The pain is short-lived and should soon pass, and if you enjoy your lover and he pleases you, then you only think about it for a moment. It soon gets bypassed by the pleasant feelings. Men like attention, they are much like children in that respect... They like to think they are the only man in the world, the best lover, whether this is true or not. Often they like to think of a lover as a conquest of some sort."

Ozena widened her eyes and said, "So I am to lie?"

Dii laughed. "Only if he does not please you. Men have fragile egos. They like to believe they are a good lover, and virile. If he pleases you, then let him know, tell him what you like, show him, and let him hear you cry out. Men like to be kissed and petted. They like to be stroked and touched and squeezed gently around…certain areas, and some like pain but some do not. You could simply ask him what he desires…"

"I would be too shy for any of that!" Ozena cried and clapped her hand over her mouth.

"My dear, you may find you are not and you will learn not to be soon enough. In my experience, most men like you to use your mouth, sucking, licking, biting, although not too hard. As I said, it really depends on the man himself. I am sure I have seen some…um, educational books in the library at the manor. They are mainly… er…pictorial, so should be of use."

Ozena nodded gratefully. "You are kind and wise…I would like to ask another question, if I may… When you, um, you know…get your peak…when you are with a man. What does it feel like?"

Dii laughed her soft bubbling laugh. "Now that is a question I am not sure how to answer!"

She leaned back thoughtfully, then a swirling ball of light appeared, shifting colours, dancing and pulsing. "Sometimes it is a slow build like a ripple on a pool. Tiny at first, then slowly getting wider and wider until it is everywhere. Sometimes it is fast and furious like a rapid torrent, everywhere at once, overwhelming. Sometimes it goes on and on and on, leaving you almost helpless with pleasure. Sometimes it does not happen at all."

The ball of light spun and the flickering, colours grew brighter and swirled faster, blues turning to purple, to pink, to a deep burning crimson that glowed and then spun around the room and burst with showering little stars of light that slowly fizzled out.

Ozena sat with her mouth open in amazement. "That was beautiful… Is it really that way?"

"It can be. Olek is a kind man, and will take care of you. Not all men are unkind, selfish and abuse women. If you care for or even love a man, it is as if…I suppose warmth within, a comfort and strength. To love a man is the deepest, most profound feeling; almost a kind of madness, yet at the same time so right. Nothing else in the world matters. It hurts, but at the same time, it brings such comfort and joy."

CHAPTER 16

Olek had dressed carefully that morning in greys and blacks, the colours of shadow. Before returning to his duty in the streets, he had carefully attired his swords beneath his cloak, set the small crossbow, and lined his belt with various phials of poison. He contemplated wearing the drakescale armour which he had brought, but decided it was a little too…obvious should he be spotted. He picked up a coil of the strong, thin rope he favoured, a pouch of money, and the scroll of authorisation Archos had given him earlier.

Slipping out, he headed silently to the poorer area of town, noticing as he did so a number of thieves who seemed to be operating around the boundaries of the Enclave. Olek disliked the Enclave; it held too many memories of being hungry and cold, of his mother and the price she had paid to feed them, what she had to do to survive. Despite what he had told Ozena, he felt the burn of anger that still tugged within him that his mother had felt she had no choice but to work in one of the whorehouses. Like many elven women she had been purchased in order to earn money with her body. Perhaps that was why Olek felt such sympathy for Dii. There were other dark memories he thrust down with a grunt. Absently he wondered if the small shack they had lived in still existed, and if there were inhabitants. He paused, tempted to look, but always persuaded himself it did not matter now, as that life was long past. He also, he admitted, did not know what he would do if he found it.

The Street of Red Lanterns was familiar to him, being an excellent place for thieves to operate as the customers of the whores were not likely to report being robbed when exiting a whorehouse. The street itself was narrow and the dwellings ranged from shacks to the tenements that Varlek was full of. He sauntered and watched, seeing a city guard loitering at the end. Casually he entered the tavern and bought a flagon of ale, making sure he sat where he could see the end of the street. After the guard had passed, Olek finished his drink and sauntered into one of the whorehouses close by. He was known here and, after a few pleasantries were exchanged with the now somewhat elderly madam, he asked her, "I seek some information about your neighbouring bawdy houses. I need to know whether you all share the dark alleys at the back. Do you know how well guarded it would be? I know some offer a…wider service than your girls provide and I seek someone who may have been taken to one against her will."

The madam considered for a while. "Aye, most of the buildings this side share the backstreet yonder, which can be entered from either end or through the tiny alley. The sewers lead under also. The Mermaid is guarded and has been increasingly so these last few months. The others have the usual security to stop the customers getting out of hand…or leaving without paying. My girls reside mainly in the Enclave or the poorer side of town for the humans. They say they have heard…screams, and one saw a girl being bundled in bound to the bawdy house yonder. It was not worth telling the city guard for they care not about the plight of whores, especially elves, although they are happy to use the services they provide. At least my girls are clean and fed. Here they get a bit of coin for themselves."

Olek nodded, sadly agreeing this was indeed the case and wondering which house had taken the girls. He paid the madam for the service she had provided, then wandered along the street and found the small entrance the woman had mentioned. He contemplated his next move and sat thoughtfully in another tavern that served the street. Olek bought a small bottle of wine and sat in a shadowed alcove. As he watched and listened, a group of rowdy young men entered and settled at one of the larger tables; well-dressed young men, perhaps in their early twenties. Olek shifted and pulled the shadows close around him, disappearing from view unless actively sought.

The three young men sat drinking and laughing until after a while another entered to be greeted by a rousing cheer. "Hey, Petrus, how was she? To your liking, my boy, has the Mermaid satisfied you once more?" Janik, son of the Lord Soren of Argen, asked.

"That little red-haired one, she was feisty. I had to strap her down and flog her into compliance. I took her, though, sweet little cherry she was. Made her elf lover watch too… He was screaming as I rammed her hard. Damn elves, they should know their place! Looked quite like that girl Dii, you remember her? That little slut could be made to do anything, although sometimes she had to be…persuaded, if I remember, but such a pretty fuck. At least you took her to your bed too, Janik, did you not? But then again, so did we all! She was hardly in a position to refuse! Lucky Ulric, he could take her whenever he wanted," said the one called Petrus with a snicker at pleasures remembered.

The young men laughed and nodded with their shared reminiscence. "All those little flowers to pluck, so little time, my boy," one of the other young men replied, with a conspiratorial wink. Petrus raised his flagon of ale. "To flowers ready to be plucked. There is something satisfying about taking a maiden girl, being master of her. That elf girl was a good fuck, screamed a lot though which just added to the fun." The man licked his lips and took a slow drink. They laughed and bragged about women, recalling with amusement the young women and girls whom they had taken.

Olek sat and listened carefully, his attention drawn when he heard the names spoken and the reference to the girl. He knew it could not be Amena, but nonetheless he would not leave a young girl to be molested again in such a way. He moved his hand to his sword and sighed, knowing he could not kill any of them here. Who was this man who spoke of Dii such? Olek smiled knowingly when he heard the name of the Mermaid. Perhaps it was not the place he sought, but it was a good place to start. He noted appearances and the few names he had been given for a later date. Archos would certainly be interested to know this afternoon's proceedings.

He waited for a while longer then walked past the group. Stepping out into the street, he vanished into the shadow of a doorway. One thing Olek possessed in abundance was patience. After a while, he saw the one named Petrus leave and for a while, Olek stalked him until the man entered a street heading towards a small townhouse. Olek stayed in shadow and walked in silence, forever gaining upon his prey. As Petrus stepped towards the door, he was suddenly grabbed with a gloved hand across his mouth. He saw the edge of a crossbow bolt in the sleeve attached to the hand now gripping his hair as he tried to turn his head and was dragged back behind the house. As he struggled, a voice said close to his ear, "At this range I reckon I can hit the door yonder. Your brain will merely impede the speed it hits. Struggle, lad, and I will test my theory."

The young man was forced into a small empty courtyard with no windows overlooking it, as it was full of rubbish and refuse. The voice in his ear said, "How nice privacy…"

The hand was removed from his mouth and Petrus blustered, "Who do you think you are, common thief? I will see you flogged through the streets then hanged. My father is an important man! Unhand me."

Petrus found himself with a sharp blade pressed against his groin, the deadly edge close to his privates. He could feel the weight of the blade pressing into him. The shadows played around him and the voice in his ear softly replied, "Unhand me? Please, could you not think of less of a cliché? Move or scream and your balls will be rolling in the gutter before the cry is finished." The young man tried to turn and felt the edge of the blade press against him again and the voice hissed, "The city guard would never find me, for I *am* the shadows. Now who would this illustrious father be that I am to be so afraid of?"

Trying to look down and as he moved, the swift edge of the blade split the silk of Petrus' breeches. "My father's men will hunt you down," he managed, now feeling distinctly less brave.

Olek yawned loudly. "By all means, call his men. They will be hunting a shadow, a ghost. Much expense will be used, to no avail. How much is your life worth to him, do you think? Not only do you deem it suitable to rape young women and brag about your prowess to your friends, but really, you are extremely dull in conversation. If you answer my questions, you might yet live. Believe me when I say I could take you to a man who would not be as…merciful as I, for what you have done and said. A man who could no doubt keep you alive for some while, although I doubt you would be in much of a state to enjoy that life. Now who are you? This young lady whom you found so…enjoyable, where is she?"

With the blade against his skin, Petrus' courage failed him. His voice trembled as he whispered, "I am Petrus, son of Lord Renfrew. The girl, the little virgin whore, she is in the Mermaid. She was just an elf. I paid the price thus she was mine."

There was a hiss from behind him and the blade moved yet closer to his balls. Suddenly there was sharp pain as the edge scratched him, not quite breaking the skin. He whimpered and tried to back up. The voice continued, "There was mention of an elven girl called Dii. How do you know her? The other fellows, who were they?"

Petrus swallowed and whispered, "Just a little slut…er…I mean, girl that I had a while ago, a Kept of Lord Tremayne, used to share her around. Little witch warmed his bed too when that human witch bored him. Just an elf Kept, no one of importance, just some fun for the menfolk…the others…oh…er…fellows I just met."

"Oh, now, lad, you were doing so well… You seemed too intimate to be mere acquaintances." Olek smiled beneath his cloak.

Petrus felt the blade against him and with a whimper and a squeak, he felt the skin break and a thin trickle of blood begin to flow, soon joined by wetter warmth as he pissed his breeches. Suddenly the only focus was the blade against him and he squeaked, "Just a little Kept whore, I swear, merely Tremayne's girl. The others, oh, just Janik of Argen; Edwaen, son of the House of Andert; and Reflin, son of the House of Sardak, the merchant."

Olek twisted his wrist and drew his blade deep into the man's private parts and as he fell screaming, drew the sword across his throat, cutting off the scream to a gurgle. Crouching, letting the blood flow away from him, he hissed, "Women are not yours to use, elf or not. I do not like a man who betrays his friends. This information will be most useful."

As the man lay dying, Olek removed his purse and rings. Wiping his sword on the fellow's cloak, he stepped back into the shadows. Listening carefully and hearing silence, he moved in shadow back to the side streets and then walked unseen and unheard to a small booth before selling the rings. Finding the small temple that catered to the needs of the poor and the Enclave, he entered slowly, still shadowed and hooded, and dropped the pouch and the money for the rings in the small box for donations to the needy.

Olek returned to the Street of Red Lanterns and secreted himself within a dim doorway. He watched for a while whilst people moved past and went about their business. The street was busy, not only the whorehouses stood here, but the more exotic and less legal shops, booths and carts. The taverns and the Houses of Pleasure were popular with the sailors and the passing traders. He muttered to himself, unable to find a suitable opportunity at this time of day. He would achieve nothing for either the girl or Archos if he were in the city dungeons. For a while he sauntered along the street, forever watching and listening. Olek waited for a lull and entered the whorehouse. Remaining hooded and pulling around him the shadows, he approached the guard who stood inside looking bored. Keeping his voice even, he asked, "I am informed by…an acquaintance that this House caters for more…specialised tastes?"

The guard looked him over and shrugged. Often the men who visited did not reveal their names, or indeed their faces. "Indeed, but the price is high."

Olek's hand disappeared inside his cloak and produced a purse. "I have coin."

The guard shrugged, indifferent to the plight of those within. "Aye, well, the… special has been finished with for tonight. There is nothing on offer at present. The lamp is not lit, thus we are closed. The…rubbish has been returned to the Enclave. Return when the lantern is lit."

Olek turned on his heel and left, resisting the urge to kill the guard. He thought perhaps the girl could be sought from the Enclave. Returning thoughtfully to the townhouse, he found Archos, who had returned from his day's business. The women were still busy packing up the potions and seemed occupied with their task. Archos was at ease in his small study, writing letters, and as Olek looked uncomfortable, Archos poured them both a drink from the small bottle in the bureau and motioned him to the armchair. "So why the…nervous look? What have you discovered that you think will displease me?"

"My lord, I found some…information, some of use to our task to find the elves and also some of a…more, um…intimate nature…about Dii."

He shuffled as he felt Archos tense and the Archmage merely replied in a dangerously even voice, "Go on, Olek."

Olek shifted and took a large sip of the brandy. "I went to the Street of Red Lanterns and talked to one of the brothel madams to ascertain security, whether any of the Houses had new…attractions, that sort of thing. I stopped in a tavern within the street and overheard some young nobles. This young man…he knew Dii, spoke of her in, well, unflattering terms which I will not repeat. Either that or it is a remarkable coincidence, but I doubt very much there are two such red haired mage elves that were Kept as slaves named Dii. It is not a common name. It would…er… seem this Tremayne…um…shared her amongst his friends." Draining the goblet, Archos merely sat in angry silence and Olek sighed and continued, unhappy he had to relate such information.

"Unfortunately, I was unable to follow all of them and it was the Renfrew whelp who was the one bragging about his…conquest over the young elf…who, it was mentioned, looked like Dii. I have some names to look into and descriptions, but they're rather vague: Janik of Argen; Edwaen, son of the House of Andert; and Reflin Sardak. This young lording of the Renfrew House had…an encounter with the Shadowdancer so will cease to be a problem. This man had, it seemed, amused himself with a young elf virgin, flogged and tied her down. Now, by the description it is not Amena. The poor girl was apparently returned to the Enclave."

Archos leaned back, breathing heavily, trying to get his anger under control. His hand clenched on the arm of the chair and eventually he calmed himself enough to answer. "Indeed? Perhaps, when we have found these elves, this Tremayne should receive a visit. I am concerned that Dii should not know, she has suffered enough… We can deal with Tremayne later, and the Lord Renfrew. I seem to recall the Thiefmaster mentioned such a man as one of the slavers responsible for the attack on the village and Sardak is a slaver. I have some…business with a ship of the House of Versann, if I can find her. It would seem she might encounter a storm, most unfortunate after the loss of his wagons and warehouse."

He took a long, slow drink. "So this injured girl was taken to the Enclave?"

"Yes, that is what I was able to learn, this beaten and molested girl thrown back into the Enclave like so much rubbish. It makes me so angry. I am sorry to recount what I heard, my lord, but I assure you that whelp of the Renfrew house lays with his throat cut after his words and deeds. This lad seemed to have first-hand experience with the elf virgin in the Mermaid. I should perhaps…get changed. I thought to take Ozena out this evening, if you do not require me. I need the distraction after today's work."

Olek bowed when Archos moodily waved his agreement and left to change, leaving his master to contemplate and brood. Dii herself, not having heard Olek come in, passed the door and overheard him speaking of the injured girl. As luck would have it, she had not heard the beginning of the conversation. She entered the study. "What is this about an injured girl from the Mermaid? Now I am guessing that establishment would be a whorehouse?"

Archos rose and, moving to her, wondered how much she had heard. He had not heard her leave the workshop or, distracted, felt her little ripple of Power. "Yes, it is such an establishment; one that offers the more varied services. It would appear deflowering a young virgin is one of those services. Olek seems to have dealt with the man."

Dii moved close to him and her eyes looked into his, a look of determination within them. "We must go, tend to this poor girl. Can we not go to the Enclave?"

Archos looked at her, saw the earnestness on her face. "It may be hard to find this girl. Are you sure? The Enclave is not a pleasant place, certainly not for an elven mage. I should go alone."

She squeezed his arm. "A rich human in the Enclave searching for a young woman? Would I not be better? This girl will be traumatised. She may not accept a man, certainly not a human, mage or not. I would like to help, to see the Enclave. I would not have a young woman in such a state left to suffer. If you will not accompany me, I shall seek this girl myself," Dii said, determined and knowing what it was to be abused.

"You are so kind… You are also right. Perhaps we should go. We have those medicines to take, but I will accompany you. I would not let you…or, in fact, any elven woman, go to such a place alone."

* * *

Archos took Dii and the bag of medicines, leaving instruction with the housekeeper to prepare a room. They made their way to the Enclave. The walls were high and the gate guarded by two burly looking city guards. Dii held tightly to Archos, yet she was resolute to go inside. The guards gave her a lewd look and one licked his lips. Noting the glances his lady was receiving, Archos rested his hand on the small hand on his arm and paused at the gate, saying in a commanding manner, "I require entry to the Enclave."

"What is your business in the Enclave?" the other guard, who was a little more inclined to keep his eyes from Dii and on the task assigned to him, asked.

"Well, I seek another servant, for I find one is not enough. I merely wish to see… what is available."

The lecherous guard gave a filthy grin. "Well, sir, take your pick. There be a few fine flowers within, my lord, although not so much as the one on your arm. Perhaps if you tire of that one, we could find a use for her." He gave a dirty laugh and nudged his companion. Dii felt Archos' arm tense and she looked down, away from the gaze of the guard.

"Well, am I to be kept waiting?" Archos asked with an edge to his voice.

The guards opened the gates and the two mages walked through. The Enclave was crowded, as such slums often are. The elves within stopped to look at the newcomers and then simply moved on, hoping the attention was not directed towards them. Rats ran through the streets and a couple of small elven children looked fearfully at the human as he passed. Archos stopped and, crouching, spoke to one of the small children of apparently indeterminate gender, clothed in well-patched garments a size too big. He held out a silver piece before the child's eyes.

"Child, do you know the woman Romolin?"

The child's gaze never left the coin and he nodded. "Yes, she is busy."

Archos smiled. "Go tell her, the Storm knows where the East Wind starts."

The child gave him a strange look and scampered off, returning a short while later saying, "She is in the small dwelling behind the trader's booth." Small fingers reached for the shiny coin and the child ran off, yelling with delight.

Smiling grimly and moving on before they were swarmed by beggars, Archos led Dii to a small hovel close to the aforementioned trader's booth; a simple stall selling many items, pots, bottles, a few daggers, items traded by those with little left, or items of which the owner was yet to discover the loss in the human houses. Entering the hut, they saw a one-eyed elf woman sitting behind a desk on which lay a pile of old clothes, and a few small trinkets and boxes. The old woman scrutinised him long with her one eye, the other milky and misted. "And what can I's do for you this day. The likes of you's not be here to buy or sell from Old Romolin."

"We will not remain long. I am looking for someone, a young woman, perhaps below eighteen summers. Red hair, recently disappeared and returned, almost certainly injured. Know you of such a girl?" Archos enquired.

Romolin looked out of her one good eye. "There be several such red-haired women, but I's hears of one, a young woman named Celine. She disappeared perhaps some three or four nights ago; ran off with her young fellow, or so they say. Today, I hear that she returned, or leastways there be someone in the hut other than the dying woman. I's would tries there. The mother be with the spirits soon enough."

Archos sighed and held out the bag of potions. "You will take us there. These are to be given to those who need it, for no charge. Trust me on this, I will hear if you take profit from these. Now perhaps we may see to this girl and see if anything can be done for the woman."

She led Archos and Dii to the far edge of the Enclave. There were the multifamily dwellings that housed several families, just a large central cooking fire in the communal hall and the shared sleeping rooms that ranged off them. The streets were littered with rotting rubbish and a sewer ran down the central street. The stench was overpowering. Even larger rats scuttled under foot and feral dogs snapped at them, and passersby. Between the shabby brick and wooden housing were crammed shacks and huts made from wood, cloth, thatch and whatever else could be salvaged or stolen. The shacks were often worse than the communal homes; small, cold, damp, rat infested. Celine's home was close to the midden and the rear gates, gates which were meant to be opened frequently so the middens could be removed, however in reality, the gates were rarely opened. The elves who worked beyond the Enclave were allowed to pass the well-guarded gate, a few occasionally tried to climb the high walls; walls topped with glass, nails and caltrops. Dii's eyes widened at the sheer poverty, at how anyone could live this way. Her life had been hard and full of pain, but she did not remember ever feeling as cold as these shacks or as hungry as many of the elves here.

"Can we not do something?" she whispered. "There is so much suffering here."

Archos touched her face and said softly, "I do what I can. There are a few extra supplies that arrive every so often. Too much would, alas, draw a great deal of attention. I have seen it worse but, for now at least, this is unfortunately the law. The thieves try to help, and the temple, but most humans do not or will not see."

They approached a small shack, a tiny wooden hut roofed with planks stolen or washed up from the harbour, driftwood being a tradable commodity here, and a bit of stolen thatch. Romolin pushed the door to the dark dwelling. "Tis the healer," she called and nodding to them, left to go about her own business.

The interior was one room divided by a screen. A tiny wooden table and two chairs sat in the centre of the room on which stood a couple of candles, now nearly spent but spluttering weakly. Shelves covered, and in fact supported, one wall, and a few pots and plates and a few items of meagre foodstuff sat thereon. A small chest sat just at the edge of screen and a bucket containing water was situated near to the door. Close to the fireplace lay a pile of blankets on which a bloodied young elven man sprawled. He sat up painfully when they entered. His shirt was bloody and stuck to his back, and his arms were bruised and raw. Across his face was a livid bruise and his eyes were shadowed and haunted. As they moved into the dark room, he tried unsteadily to get to his feet. "Who are you? I know you not. We have nothing and Celine lies bleeding yonder, is that not enough?" Seeing only the shape of Archos in the poor light, he was afraid but still willing to challenge this newcomer. No fire was in the tiny hearth and the shack was terribly cold.

Dii murmured and a small orb of light appeared above them, illuminating the room. Archos walked slowly to the young man, holding out his hands. "I am a healer. We do not come to harm, but help. I seek a girl, who was misused and injured. I see you are hurt also, may I help you?"

Motioning beyond the screen, Dii moved carefully, laying the bag she had brought and what remained of the potions close by. Approaching the two small cots behind the screen, she heard whimpering and the cry of someone in pain.

Archos touched the young man's arm and spoke softly. "I am Lord Archos and I am, amongst other things, a mage and I can heal you, and the girl. Is there not also an older woman here? How came you to this state?" Helping the man remove his shirt, he saw the young elf man's back and chest: bruised and bloodied where the skin was broken, with marks from clubs, boots, and a flail criss-crossing the flesh. The bruises were at least a couple of days old and as he touched him gently, he felt the cracked ribs beneath. The young man's wrists showed the marks of ropes, where they had been tightly bound.

"I am Istvan, master. Celine, my betrothed, or as good as, is lying beyond the screen. I was…trying to light the fire when I passed out, master. Please help her first, and her mother who lies gravely ill, but we have no money to pay for healing or remedies."

Archos looked grimly around the room and, seeing a few coals and logs in the unlit hearth, he snapped his fingers and the hearth kindled into flame. "My lady is a healer also, and I feel she may be…better dealing with the women. As for payment, I am not in need of coin, nor would I charge one who had nothing for something that should be freely given."

Softly and with great care, he channelled a healing spell into Istvan, watching the bruises fade and feeling the bones knit. For a moment, the bruises appeared upon Archos himself and he felt the pain of them. Examining the boy's face, he suspected a concussion and probably a level of internal bleeding from the beating. He muttered something and increased the Power of the spell, entwining it with a spell of comfort; bathing Istvan in a pale blue light, warming and mending. Archos closed his eyes, letting the pain and dizziness wash over him, taking it from the boy. For a moment, he swayed, and then the pain ebbed from them both.

Istvan felt the pain and the fog in his head ease slowly, and as the comfort spell and the warmth of the healing and the fire reached him, he felt better. "We were taken, master. Celine she is a seamstress, I am a scribe, or was before I lost my position. We were returning here from the trade quarter. I do not like her walking alone. Some men, I know not how many, leaped upon her, tried to drag her away. I fought them as best I could, but I am just a scribe. When I woke…I was chained up, beaten. She was… She was tied down and naked. The man, he did terrible things to her, master. I was unable to help. Even when she started screaming, I…I failed her." The young man sank to the pile of blankets and began to cry. "I could not help her. I should have fought harder. I have failed her…"

Archos crouched next to him and took the weeping boy into his arms like a father. "Listen to me, Istvan. You did what you could; it is not many men who can fight off a larger group, especially if they are armed. I have many powerful friends and I assure you, the man who took your woman against her will lies dead. Not by my hand but by a man whom I trust implicitly and who does my will; a man who is my right hand. Had I found this man myself, he would be as dead as he now lies. Your lady will be healed, and you can leave this place should you choose it. I will endeavour to find the slavers, for I seek others who are taken: elves from the Shimmering Forest. Now you need to rest, for magic cannot heal all wounds. If you want to be of use to us, to her, then boil some water and fix some food for her and yourself while I assist my lady, if she needs it." He gripped the young elf around the shoulders and held him close awhile. The powerful Archmage held the weeping boy in his arms until he calmed.

* * *

Two small beds lay beyond the screen, covered in blankets and cushions. One bed contained a frail form, a thin elven woman, deathly pale and her face was etched with the lines of pain. She had been beautiful once, but disease and poverty had robbed her both of dignity and looks. The second small cot contained a young elven woman, perhaps sixteen or seventeen. She lay beneath a blanket, crying softly and trying to stifle her tears in order not to awaken the woman beside her. The blanket was stained with blood and beneath the blanket, she was naked.

Dii moved her hand to create a small ball of light which hovered above her, granting them extra light. Moving to the beds, she crouched between the cots. "I am Dii, and I am a healer. Please, I wish to help you, ease your pain. My lord is yonder tending to your man. You are safe now."

A small tear-stained and slightly bloodied face peeked out from under the blanket. The red curls were matted and the hazel eyes were full of fear. "Mama is ill…but it hurts so much. I am so ashamed," the young woman whispered, her eyes flickering to the other cot. "Please do not wake her, she must not know."

Dii fetched the bag and a small pitcher of water from the bucket. Holding it in her hands, she warmed it and cleansed the water then tossing a handful of herbs, she left it to infuse for a moment, the water not boiling but very warm. Gently she took a soft cloth and pulled the blanket away slowly, soothing as she tenderly cleaned the girl. Swirling the cloth over the wounds, she saw the lash marks and the rope burns, and other injuries of a more intimate nature. Murmuring, she weaved a healing spell into Celine. Dii was kind and gentle, comforting and speaking softly, until the wounds faded. She closed her eyes, feeling the lash on her back and the searing pain within her. Dii had a flash of memory of her own treatment in the cells of the Order of Witch-Hunters, still recent, and tears rolled down her face. She almost passed out with the pain and the memories, and yet forced herself to concentrate on her task. As the pain eased, she wiped the tears away.

Celine managed to stop crying and whispered, "Thank you, mistress healer. Istvan, is he hurt badly? And mother, she is so very ill."

"I will see to her, but I need a moment… Have you clean clothes here?" Dii asked eyeing the tiny hovel.

Celine pointed to the small chest and Dii fetched her clean clothing, helping the young woman dress. "The pain will lessen…so will the shame. You have done nothing wrong, not ever. Some men, especially humans, just see elves as property. That does not make what happened easier to bear, but not all are such. It will fade, what has happened, and you will find happiness, as I have. Do not let it destroy you. I will rest a moment and then tend to your mother. Perhaps your man would like to see you safe and tended?"

As Celine walked slowly and still somewhat painfully into the main room, Archos had moved to assist Istvan, talking to him in soft, low tones. He glanced up to see the young elf woman now healed and was glad for it. For a moment in the light of the lightwisps, Celine looked a little like Dii, curly hair of red although shorter. Her face more rounded and her figure plumper, her eyes less almond shaped and hazel, ears less pointed from her human heritage, but yet still a resemblance in the jawline and structure of the face. Archos paused a moment longer and then shrugged. Perhaps it was coincidence, a trick of the flickering light. He knew red hair was a little more common amongst elves than humans.

"I am pleased to see you healed, my lady has done well as always. I am Archos, and I...we seek to help you. See your man here is healed also, perhaps you would like some private time. I will go and check on Dii."

Archos walked behind the screen and saw Dii crying silently. "Oh, what is it, my dear?" he said, taking her into his embrace.

"The girl...she has suffered much...and these places, it just made me sad. It made me remember things. I wish I could help them more." Dii looked into his face, searching for reassurance.

Archos soothed her and murmured words of love. "My sweet, kind girl, I did not think how this would affect you. I am sorry. Perhaps I should not have brought you here. Yet that young woman is healed and will recover, or as much as she is able. Look what you have done for her, despite your own pain. Flower, you are strong and the most courageous woman I have ever met. Despite all you remain such a tender and loving soul."

Dii held close to him for a moment, his arms around her, as he nestled her close. "May they return to the valley with us? I would not like to see them left here. I know they are not the elves we seek, but are they not worthy of the same safety as those from the Shimmering Forest? The girl she can find work, the same as the other women, perhaps easier as she is more accustomed to humans. The young man, he could work for you perhaps, or the Steward. Or find work in the village, perhaps one of the traders could use a man like him"

He sighed. "We cannot take the whole Enclave with us, Dii." Yet he had already considered the same.

Dii looked at him, her dark eyes brimming with tears but resolute. "I am not asking for everyone. I know that cannot be so. Could you leave someone to live here, like this, after everything? We know they were attacked by slavers, the same slavers who raided Szendro and took Amena perhaps."

Archos stroked her hair softly. "You are kind and gentle...room shall be made. I would not leave them here as such, but I suppose we have elves already and two more will not hurt. As you say, it may be easier for them to integrate than the forest elves.

They will find a place well enough. Istvan is literate and clever, perhaps I could use his skills. Yet they will not leave, I think, whilst the woman yonder lies sick."

CHAPTER 17

Beyond the screen, Dii returned to the older woman lying in her cot. Archos moved beside her, stroking her back tenderly and asking, "Are you alright?"

Dii nodded, although it was clear she was finding it difficult, and steeled herself to help the poor creature. Archos saw the strength and resolution in her and gave her shoulder a squeeze of reassurance.

Celine walked to the screen and said quietly, "Ma'esa, her name is Ma'esa. Can you help her? She has been so sick. I do not know what to do. Please, she must not know what has happened."

Dii took her hand. "I will try…"

Archos looked at the frail elven woman lying before him and saw a hint of red between the grey curly locks, and even beyond the pain was a face that had once been beautiful. He saw the resemblance to Celine and for a moment to Dii, then it seemed to fade. Ma'esa awoke and turned to look at the newcomers weakly, her hazel eyes widening as she saw the young mage, although whether from surprise at visitors or something more was unclear.

The Archmage walked over and sat on the floor next to the bed, saying gently, "Mistress Ma'esa, I am Archos and I offer assistance to you." Pausing when he saw her eyes fixed on Dii, he continued, "That is my lady Dii'Athella, who has offered your daughter much kindness."

Celine sat down close to her mother with concern and sadness etched on her face, next to Dii, who had settled close, and Istvan waited by the screen.

"Mistress, we bring medicines for you, your daughter is safe and returned to you." Dii held out her hand and took Ma'esa's in her own, feeling the frailty and slightness of the woman. Gently she rubbed the cold and thin fingers, warming and comforting.

The sick woman looked at Celine and then at Dii and whispered, "My daughter returned to me. I see her again before I die."

Dii softly stroked Ma'esa's hand and put Celine's over it. Looking at the girl, she smiled sadly and said, "See, your daughter is here. She is safe now, Mistress Ma'esa."

Celine grabbed her other hand. "Mama. No, you will live."

Archos looked at Dii and shook his head slightly, confirming what Dii already knew. Taking Celine to one side, Dii gently touched her arm in comfort. "Celine, you understand? There are illnesses that even magic is unable to heal, mortal illnesses. I am sorry, we may…ease her pain a little, but beyond that, not even my lord can heal her. If we could, we would. I promise."

Celine gazed at her, eyes misted with tears. "I know… I hoped… When she is gone, I have nothing here, nothing but Istvan. Please, can you help her? I cannot endure to see her suffer, she has such terrible pain."

Dii softly squeezed her arm and held her close. "I will do what I can, we both will. Perhaps you could find us more blankets. I will make a tonic for her…something that will ease her pain. Would Istvan stay with you? We will stay with her if you cannot stand to see her end."

She began to prepare the tonic; herbs, poppy oil, and a little honey from the bag. Archos went to speak to Istvan, but watched her. She heard Istvan and Archos talking softly and she returned to the bedside with the concoction. Celine went to search for blankets as the door was flung open by a man. Archos and Istvan stood up abruptly and went to deal with this newcomer.

"What is it that you disturb the sick bed of this woman?" Archos demanded.

The man glanced around the pathetic hovel and crossed his arms, looking the two men up and down. "Come to collect on debts. Woman owes us… Heard she was at death's door. Not that she has much of value here."

Istvan glared angrily and shouted, "No! The lady was forced to sell what little she had!"

Archos raised an eyebrow and said smoothly, "This debt, what would it be for? Food, this…pile of wood you call a shack, the furniture? Her daughter has…been unwell and unable to work."

The man sneered. "Well, just debts for this and that…money she borrowed, debts left unpaid. I am just here to take what I am owed. That daughter can work for free to pay what is left," he said with a wink.

Archos smiled a faint smile full of disgust and tossed him a small pouch as he said with a dangerous evenness, "That should cover it and more… Now I suggest you take the opportunity to remove yourself, before I change my mind and remove you myself. Be gone, debt collector! Can you not see this woman has nothing and her daughter is not for sale? I suggest you find a new means of employment…that is, if you wish to live."

The man heard the threat in the voice and decided to be elsewhere. Istvan turned to Archos and said, with eyes wide at the continued kindness, "You did not have to do that, master, pay her debts, for she is a stranger to you."

This time, the smile filled with warmth. "My boy, it pains me to see anyone in such conditions as she. If the man returns for further trouble, I will remove him permanently. What will you do? Celine will not wish to remain here, surely? I can arrange for you to go somewhere safe, safe and free. Both of you, at least until such time as you decide what you wish to do. There are elves that live in the human villages within my domain, forest elves but perhaps you could do well enough. There are farms and orchards, and a market, gainful employment for you both, as citizens not slaves. You will not be molested or beaten again."

Istvan bowed deeply. "My lord, I do not know what to say. Celine would not wish to stay here, but we have nothing to repay your kindness."

Archos smiled once more and said, "Well, Istvan, I do not ask for repayment… merely loyalty and discretion. I have…a number of business dealings and contacts that need to be maintained. A literate man can be of much use, perhaps my Steward could use assistance. I am sure we could find a use for you. Your lady can find employment well enough…sewing, cooking, farming, trading, whatever she has been doing here. My valley is safe, think on it. The humans and the elves live well enough together, at least I am not informed otherwise."

Behind the screens, Dii sat and began to help the woman drink slowly from the beaker; the soft aroma of the herbs and the warmth eased a little pain. As the spell she cast progressed, Dii grew pale from the effort and the intensity as she took the pain into herself. She began to shake and Celine saw her after returning with blankets, and cried, "Stop, you cannot continue… It is too much. Is there another way?"

Ma'esa took Celine's hand and said, her voice a whisper. "My girl, fetch the chest, please. I wish to see the items one last time, and speak alone to the healer."

Looking at her mother, Celine nodded slowly. She headed into the main room and began to unlock the chest, fighting the tears. Istvan held her and Archos moved to watch Dii, resisting the urge to help as he saw her rocking with pain. He sighed, wishing he could do more for this woman, but not even he could save her from the illness that had taken her with so little remorse.

Within the sick room, Ma'esa smiled weakly and reached to touch Dii's hair. "Such pretty hair you have; mine was long and red like yours once, and I was beautiful like you. You have his eyes…such dark mysterious eyes, dark blue like the night sky."

For a while she lapsed into silence as Dii eased a comfort spell into her and murmured kind and soothing words. Wondering what she meant, she said nothing, not wishing to cause the woman more effort. Suddenly with surprising strength, Ma'esa grasped Dii's hand. "There was a ring…an ancient ring of amber…the ring. So like him…so kind." She took a sip of the tea and eased back slowly. "Help me, please ease my pain, my daughter…my daughter is here."

Celine entered just at that moment and Dii motioned for her to sit. "Mama, I have the chest…all we have left. What do you want from it?"

Ma'esa slowly put her hands into the small wooden box, "My life…my two lives and loves…all I have left…you must take it, keep it safe… The journal, you must read it…"

With that, she slipped into sleep and Celine closed the box and watched as Dii held her hands over the woman. She murmured softly, "Spirits, I ask you to help me ease this woman, take her pain and guide her to the Other World. Syltha, I ask your mercy to watch her journey and to comfort those who remain." A faint white light began to flow and then suddenly brightened and filled the room before fading. She touched Ma'esa gently and pulled the blanket up over her face, now peaceful and unlined.

Celine began to cry and Dii said quietly, "Do you wish me or Istvan to sit with you, or would you rather be alone with her? She is no longer in pain; she spoke of you at the end. I can make you something to drink…to help with the grief and the shock."

Eyes red with grief Celine, pushed the box into Dii's hands. "Please take the box. There are a few of mother's things, elven things. My father collected some. Not much, but payment for your services."

"I ask no payment. I would not take from you your mother's valuables or yours. I have no need of such nor would I deprive you of what is rightfully yours."

She left the box on the bed and, slightly shaking, walked into the main room, tears in her eyes. Archos pulled her close as she said to Istvan, "Celine needs you…sit with her. We will make the arrangements."

Archos kissed her hair and murmured, "You did what you could for her. She is eased and no longer suffering. I think Celine and Istvan will return with us. I can use a man of his skill and she… Well, she will find her place within the villages."

After a while, the two younger ones returned and Istvan said, "My lord, if the offer stands for both of us, we would accept… There is nothing for us here now, and you and your lady have shown us great kindness. I will do my best to serve you in whatever capacity you choose." He bowed and held out a hand.

"You will find your place, both of you. Now perhaps you would pack to leave. You may stay at the townhouse in safety until we are due to return," Archos replied, gripping his hand.

Celine bowed her head and whispered, "You have shown us kindness. We can never repay what you and your household have done for us, my lord." Slowly she began to pack her few belongings and the small chest her mother had held.

* * *

Olek felt tense. He was angry and needed to relax. He wondered if Ozena would fancy a walk in the moonlight, to see some of the city. He knew there was an inn in the Eastern Corner that had a flat roof and looked out onto the docks, lit even at night. It was not a hard climb onto the roof and a person could listen to the music playing from the inn below. Olek fetched a small bag of refreshments. He packed a couple of small glowglobes and two soft blankets from the kitchen and storeroom, then slipped upstairs where he changed into a soft silk shirt of dark green and a pair of blue breeches. Letting his long hair flow down his back, he strapped one of his swords on, a sensible man being prepared. He fetched a woollen cloak from the wardrobe and pulled it around his shoulders. He stuffed the blood-stained cloak into a bag, hoping Valaria would arrange for its laundering, and headed down to find Ozena. The woman he sought was carefully packing glass flasks and phials into straw.

He grinned, watching her intent on her task. She and Dii had apparently been busy and he saw the leggings and tunic she wore in the house covered with an old apron.

Silently he walked close to her and said softly in her ear, "Perhaps you would care to join me in a walk to a little spot I know for a picnic? I can show you some of the city, if you wish, and entertain you after your work today. I have borrowed some glowglobes so we will have light. Lord Archos is out with Dii and I am not needed."

Ozena started and then nodded, smiling broadly. "I must change. I am not fit to be seen."

"Oh, I would not say that. You are certainly pleasing to look upon, Ozena, even in a large, elderly apron two sizes too large and covered in…something green."

She blushed and hastily removed the apron, folding it and pushing the offending article away. "Let me just go and change into city clothes."

Olek waited, inspecting the potions and medicines with interest. Ozena re-entered wearing a dark green skirt and the soft pale green blouse and bodice. Her cloak was about her shoulders and her hair was tied in a loose ribbon with the scarf around her shoulders beneath the cloak. Olek grinned and held out his arm. As she slid her arm into his, he kissed her hand and led her out into star lit city.

* * *

Ozena held close to Olek. She was unsure of the city, never having experienced such a mass of buildings and people. She could not believe so many people could live in such a way, with no trees or greenery. The smell assailed her senses and she whispered to Olek, "It smells, so many people smell! It is like the air is replaced with stench and one cannot breathe but breathe the air of others. How can people live such? Is this how humans like to dwell?"

Olek squeezed her hand on his arm. "Not really. Well, some do, but many people have business and lives here, or cannot afford to leave. The merchant and noble districts are not as bad as some districts; places like the master's house have gardens or courtyards. I know the master much prefers the valley and its rolling hills and close proximity to the trees. There is much money here, passed around the merchants and traders and, of course, the thieves and whores. I will take you to the docks before we leave, show you the tall ships. Some much larger than the Great River craft you would have seen. But look, the sky is clear and starry, and I have your company this eve. What more could a man require?"

As they walked the streets towards their destination, Ozena noticed Olek was always alert, always watching and listening, yet able to split his concentration to have a conversation and mean what he said. She felt safe with him, safe and wanted. This man wanted her company and she found she did not have the feeling of uselessness in his presence. She was almost afraid to ask, "Olek, did you manage to discover anything today? Is Amena here?"

Olek pulled her close. "I found…some information which may or may not be of use. I do not wish to say what, in case it turns out it is a false lead. I do not know if she is here or not, but chances are some of the elves were brought here. In fact, we know that to be the case. But let us not speak of such this night, suffice it to say Amena and your elf companions are being sought for and avenues of enquiry are being pursued. Now let us enjoy the evening, Ozena. Let me walk with you and enjoy your companionship. Let us relax and take in the evening."

For some time they walked, Ozena could not tell how long, so focused on his company was she. Olek pointed out areas he thought would interest her, stopping to buy a few small items for her at stalls open at even this hour: a small comb of horn carved with leaves, and a silk sash of a dark green and black diamond pattern. She blushed when he gave the sash to her and as his lips brushed hers, he murmured softly, "You are so pretty, like a clear crystal pool."

As his arms went around her waist, tying the sash, she melted into his embrace and for a while, he stood and held her, enjoying the cuddle.

He led her to the street behind the inn, looking to check no one was watching and clambering up onto the wall behind, he pulled himself onto the roof. "Up here, come, Ozena," he called softly. "It is high but the climb is not hard."

By the time she had scrambled up, he had lain out the blanket and the glowglobes and carefully set out the pasties, spiced juice, bread and fruit he had brought. "We can enjoy the music below, the musicians within are excellent. We can see the harbour and even now, look, the ships come in. We can watch those who pass below and not be observed. I can look at your pretty face under the starlight." With that, he set the comb in her hair, gently brushing it with his fingers.

Ozena blushed and stammered, "It's lovely, you can see all around! Look yonder at that tall ship with the huge sails!" Laughing at her enthusiasm and wonder, he kissed her hand and bowed to her.

"It is beautiful. I have never seen it so, like a mist in the sky. Even in the forest, the sky does not look like this."

"It is the smoke from the city chimneys distorting the light a little. I will take you to the high hills beyond the valley. You can see for miles and the stars are many colours. In the late autumn and early winter, sometimes there is a blood moon."

He laughed once more and poured her a drink, offering her some food. For a while they ate the food and talked, just chatter about everything and nothing, the way lovers do. Ozena found he was easy to talk to and listen to. She wanted him to kiss her again, but was nervous to make the move herself. As they finished the meal, the lutist below began to play an old love ballad.

Olek lay back on the soft blanket and pulled her close to him, feeling the tension ebb away. Somehow the company of this woman made him easy. Picking his goblet up, he tipped it to her lips then gently wiped the small trickle which escaped as she drank, his thumb gently caressing her skin. As she drank slowly, she looked around her. Then her gaze returned to him and, half with amusement, asked, "I expect you have brought many girls here. Most, more experienced than I?"

Giving that intriguing grin, Olek replied, waving his hands in a non-committal gesture, "Yes, hundreds of woman, sometimes many at once."

Ozena pushed him. "That is not what I meant and you know that well enough. But there have been others?"

He returned her look. "Well, I am older than you, perhaps twice your age or nearabouts. I was in the service of the master before you were even born. Would you expect me to have no…dalliances in that time? But there has been no one special… well, not until now. They do not matter; I want the girl who sits before me now."

Ozena looked down. "I am inexperienced… I wish to please you, but I do not know how."

Sliding even closer to her, he kissed her, softly and tenderly. Ozena melted into his embrace and slowly he ran his hands down her back, feeling her shiver at his touch. Gently he caressed her breast, his thumb playing across her nipple, circling and teasing it. Ozena wrapped her arms around him, pulling him into an embrace and she let her hands wander into his long hair. As his thumb crossed her breast, she gasped at the spark of desire. A spark the like she had not before experienced filled her and with a sudden urge that surprised her, Ozena moved even closer to his hand, leaning into his neck and sighing. She was not sure what to do and thought of what Dii had told her. Slowly she kissed his neck and nibbled at the skin. Hearing him sigh and give a slight moan as she did so, she felt another spark.

He kissed her once more. A kiss full of soft passion, a flame burning within. "Experience is learned and it is fun trying. Exploration and learning what your lover likes is part of the thrill, enjoying yourself and each other. Ozena, are you sure of this? You know what I am...what I do?"

"Yes. Yes, I know. You do what you have to do... You have the courage to do what you feel is right. You have done so much for me."

Olek trailed kisses down her neck, pushing back the cloth of her blouse and nibbling across her collarbone. Ozena sighed as the soft kisses made her skin tingle. She ran her fingers through his hair and pulled him up to her. Kissing his mouth, she let her tongue explore his. As his hands softly caressed her, he brushed her nipples again though the blouse, little circular motions that made her moan. Ozena slipped her hands under his shirt and ran her small, soft hands over his chest. His flesh was warm in the evening air and she felt the muscles under his skin. He moaned as she touched him, and taking her hand, he slowly dragged it down his chest to his belly and further down. She hesitated, then began to rub and caress him through his breeches. With his free hand, he began to unlace the blouse and the bodice. Sliding down, he kissed her exposed breasts. The cool night air played over her, making her nipples hard and sensitive. Taking her breast into his mouth, he sucked and flicked his tongue across her until she sighed with pleasure and arched towards him. Softly as she rubbed, he moaned into her, feeling the sensation building.

Ozena felt him beneath her hand, firm and warm, and slowly she unlaced the breeches to take his manhood into her hand, hard yet velvet skinned, surprising her with the feeling of it as he moaned and moved his own hand to her skirts. He rolled the skirts up and stroked her thighs, soft and pale in the starlight. He began to caress her softly, then pulled away from her touch and slid down, kissing his way from her knees to the skin just below her cleft. He kissed and sucked gently at her soft skin as she wriggled and sighed with the new sensations, then he licked across her cleft very slowly as she gasped. He flicked his tongue across her slowly, then faster, then slower, tasting her, savouring her. Ozena began to writhe, her breath increasing, the sensations and the lights Dii had shown her filled her. Burying her hands in his hair, she wriggled and squirmed, unable to control the feelings, so unfamiliar yet so pleasant. Suddenly the light burst within her and she cried out, unheeding if anyone could hear. Olek pulled away and crept up, watching the flush in her face and whispering in her ear, "That was just the beginning... Let me teach you."

She trembled, still overwhelmed by the climax as she whispered breathlessly, "Teach me; take me there."

Gently Olek kissed her neck, nipping her ears, licking along the edge as he murmured sweet nothings. He slid his arm underneath her hips and tilted her as he entered her slowly, trying to be gentle. Ozena gasped with the pain, and he whispered gently in her ear, "The pain will pass. Kiss me, do not think about it, think of the stars, the lights you see, and the fire within you."

Slowly he began to work her and after a short time, the pain was eclipsed by the delightful feelings and the pulsing fire of passion. Faster and faster her breathing became, matched by that of her lover as he moved within her and with her. Caressing her with his free hand, he stroked her hair and tipped her face to his as the fire within them both began to build, slowly, surely and as the climax exploded once more within her, he moaned her name and reached his peak.

Gently he pulled out, wrapping her in his arms. He whispered softly, "I hope that did not hurt you too much. Let me help you clean up and then we may lie here awhile yet."

Ozena rolled close him, kissing him and snuggling into his embrace. "That was… amazing…so much like little explosions within me…although I confess I am a little sore."

Olek kissed her softly. "I am sorry… Perhaps this was not the right time, or place."

"No, it was lovely…perfect. May I come to your room tonight? But I would like to stay longer here, just lie close."

* * *

Gis'Ellah had cried and screamed with anger when her young daughter Kaia was taken from her. She had fought and struggled and pleaded, offering herself in the girl's place. The slaver had been cruel, twisting Gis'Ellah's arms roughly, and putting his boot into her midriff. The human had leered at Kaia, saying the girl would suit being some rich man's plaything, whilst she herself would not please any man. She had fought for her daughter, yet had been no match for the large human and his cudgel.

She had no idea of how long she had been unconscious. The room in which she had awoken was tiny and cold but she was not bound, as she had expected to be. Part of her wondered why, perhaps she had not been expected to wake, or maybe the slaver simply had not cared. The elf was bruised, sore, and alone, but determined. Ribs broken by the cudgel ached, her breath was more laboured than usual and her head spun when she rose. Sliding back to her knees Gis'Ellah held her head until the feeling ebbed a little and she was able, rather painfully to walk to the door. It was locked but she did not expect it to be otherwise. Outside she heard movement and she called out in the Common Language, "Where is my daughter? Where have you taken her? Let me out!"

The small grille in the door slid aside and a voice said, "Shut it, bitch elf. Your child is gone. She will be the play thing of many men. Such a sweet little thing was she. You will never see her again. You may as well forget her, forget your past life, you are a slave now."

Gis'Ellah replied with incredulity, "Forget her? How can I forget my daughter? She is just a child, whatever her fate I offer myself in her place. Have you no mercy, no kindness?"

The man replied with a sneer. "I do not care about mercy or kindness. Young ones like her fetch quite the price. As for you, perhaps if you are obedient, forget about your brat and please whoever buys you, you may yet live. You should fetch some gold for us. Perhaps you could amuse us later, elf woman."

He slammed the grille shut. Gis'Ellah was a resourceful woman. Her husband had died not long after Kaia had been born and she had elected not to be paired again. She looked around the small room: just a small sleeping cot with a mangy blanket, an old wooden chair, and a bucket. On the floor was a lit candle. So she was confined but alive. She thought, possibly a holding cell or some such.

Gis'Ellah looked up. She had felt a breeze when she had awoken, the flame of the candle flicked and she saw a shuttered window. It was high and small, but she believed she could reach it, with luck and determination. The elf woman turned the bucket on its end and balanced the candle in the saucer upon it. She carefully looked around and found, rolled under the bed, another stump of a candle. She searched again and saw another. Grabbing it, she stuffed it into her pocket. She lit one of the stubs and melted it until it stood on the bucket. Dragging the chair to the wall, she climbed on to it. Not quite being able to reach, her fingers brushed the wall. Thinking for a moment, she climbed down and moved the candles to the floor, taking care not to extinguish them. She fetched the blanket and, ignoring its smell, threw it around her shoulders. Balancing the bucket on the chair, Gis'Ellah climbed. The makeshift ladder was precarious but gave her the extra height needed. One of her hands clasped the edge of one of the shutters and she pulled. She was not a strong woman, but the sheer determination of motherhood and the fact that the shutter was not in the best repair meant she did not give up.

Again she tugged, with both hands now, balanced on tiptoes on an old wooden bucket and a rotting chair. Her ribs sang with pain, but she continued. Gis'Ellah knew if she was unable to escape her daughter would die. Suddenly the shutter gave way with a crack and opened to reveal a hole in the wall. As the shutter went, she smelled the city, the stench of people in a city with limited hygiene. The mass of humanity and Elfkind, horses, dogs, rats, rubbish, the docks, rotting food, rain, mud, shit, such a myriad of odours. Gis'Ellah had never seen a city, had never seen the sea or anything beyond the village, their part of the Shimmering Forest and occasionally Harkenen when she had gone to trade the cheeses and breads she made. The elf took a deep breath. Her ribs ached and the effort made her head spin. She stretched out her arms and leapt upwards. Scuffing her hands on the rough stone, she held on. Although the skin was torn, she managed to pull herself up through the hole and dropped heavily onto the ground outside.

The fall was further than she had expected and she landed awkwardly. She heard a snap and an excruciating pain shot up her arm as the bone broke. Gis'Ellah lay on her side in the filth, her ribs hurt and her arm felt like fire, her hands were bloody from the rough stone and her head swam. With her good arm, she tore some strips from the blanket and her skirt and bound her arm, then made a sling. This was a narrow, dim backstreet, which was like nothing she had seen before; a twisting passage, filthy and dark, and instead of trees, it was lined with wooden and stone buildings, warehouses, and small dwellings, many built onto each other, crowded in and creating a strange shadowing darkness. The resourceful and brave elf wondered how these humans could live this way, without the trees, without the beauty of nature. She was afraid, she was lost, cold and in pain, but she was determined to find her child.

Gis'Ellah kept to the edges of the streets as best she could. Not knowing where to go, she crept slowly, listening. She heard conversation, Common Speech, and she pulled back into the shadow of a building. Two human women walked past and she crouched unnoticed, afraid to approach a human, thinking they might turn her in.

Her arm pounded with pain and hunger twisted her belly, but Gis'Ellah waited before creeping on. Before her, the elf woman saw a turning branching from the street in which she stood. Indecisive tears began to sting her eyes. She was lost in a strange place, out of her depth, and she was hurt and hungry. What use was she to Kaia like this? She looked down the street she was in currently and then to the side street. Her captors may have realised she was gone and would be searching. Taking a deep breath, she chose the side street. It was an even darker alley, but fortunately her elven blood allowed her good vision in low light so she was not as hindered as she might have been.

The thief watched. This was not her usual patch, but she had managed to draw a little more attention to herself than she liked in her usual hunting grounds. This area was poor but there were small unguarded warehouses and a few dwellings that were easy pickings as it was less rigorously patrolled. Marna was officially an Enclave elf, or at least had been, but now she usually found somewhere to sleep in the main city; being resourceful, agile, and not above providing a couple of compliant guards with her favours if needed. Marna scrutinised the human women pass the end of the street; they could be easy enough pickings if she was careful, but then something else caught her attention. She spotted the elf woman, filthy, bloody and limping, creeping in the shadows. This woman looked frightened, alone. The Thiefmaster had requested to be on the lookout for some forest elves that had been kidnapped from their village. She studied the woman, her clothes torn and filthy were not city clothes, even amongst the

Enclave elves. Her skirt was goats' wool and shorter than city fashion, as not to catch on undergrowth. Many of the forest women, she had heard, sometimes wore leggings or breeches beneath skirts, or some without skirts at all. The woman wore a strange woollen top, over a linen shirt.

Marna made a decision as she saw the pain and fear etched face of the woman and she stepped out of the alcove where she waited and said softly, "Mistress, you are hurt and you seem to be lost, a stranger here. May I help you? Are you an elf from the forest?"

Gis'Ellah started. "I am looking for my daughter. She is lost…taken. She is only a child. I must find her." Could she trust this elf? What choice had she?

"I have seen no elf children hereabouts, but it looks like you need assistance. Your arm needs setting and you must be hungry. Come with me, I will take you somewhere safe," Marna replied, with pity.

"No, I must look for her. Where are the…houses of ill reputation…the brothels? My girl is taken, the guards said to be a plaything for the human men. I will not stop until I find her," Gis'Ellah said, shaking her head firmly.

The woman swayed with pain and the elven thief took her good arm. "There are people who will help you. We are tasked to look for any kidnapped elves. I will take you to the Thiefmaster; he will know what to do. Listen, even if you can get into such a place, do you really think either of you would be able to leave? Come with me, the Thiefmaster will help. He will get you somewhere safe, arrange for your daughter to be sought," Marna told her.

Gis'Ellah nodded, wanting to find her child so badly but now realising she was in no position to do so alone. Almost in a daze with pain and the reality of her situation, she allowed herself to be led away to a building that, at first appearances, was a rundown shack containing not much beyond a table, a single chair, and a small pot of something on the rather meagre fire. A screen concealed a small cot bed on which lay a rather moulding blanket, the wall behind was covered in another old blanket and pulling this aside, a door was revealed. Marna tapped on the door in a complex knock and the bolt slid aside. Inside was a set of surprisingly well-furnished rooms, with a well-made table and cushioned chair, in which sat a human man, a small ink stand and parchment lay on the table. A warm fire warmed the room and with cooking pots above and a wooden larder to the left there was food to be had. A screen hid a couple of cots; beyond this were a couple of small rooms containing a bed each and a small chest, a pitcher and a small basin.

Gis'Ellah looked worried when the man approached her and, seeing her fear, he turned to Marna and asked, "Who is this Marna? Would this be one of the missing forest elves?"

Marna nodded. "Indeed. I found her wandering in the Shades, injured and alone. She says her daughter has been taken. I brought her here to be cared for and the Thiefmaster to be informed, as was his request."

The man looked over Gis'Ellah, noting the injuries and the desperate look. "Come, Mistress Elf, you are hurt and need assistance. You may trust me. My name is Stefan, a scribe for our group of …companions and we have a number of contacts. I will have someone tend to your injuries--we have an arrangement with some mages--then I will send word of your arrival."

Gis'Ellah replied quietly, "I thank you for your offer of assistance, Stefan, but I must find my girl. We were separated. I must seek her out. She is barely fourteen, just a girl; never been beyond the forest village but once. She will be very frightened. She is a pretty girl, fresh like a stream, her hair is dark brown like mine but she has blue eyes like the summer sky. She is tall for her age, but slender, like a sapling."

"I will have enquiries made. We are tasked with seeking out and assisting any forest elves that are found. Hopefully we can find your daughter before any harm befalls her. In the meantime, I suggest you get healed. There is food in the larder and you may take your rest in any of the beds, or one of the private rooms beyond. I dare say there are clean women's garments in one of the chests you may use. This place is guarded and no one will hurt you." Stefan nodded, noting down the description.

"I have nothing with which to pay for my fare."

Stefan smiled. "Oh, do not concern yourself. The Shadowdancer has paid for any expenses on behalf of his master. Now go and rest before you fall down. We will find your daughter."

After settling her and sending word to the Society of Hidden Secrets for the use of a healer, Stefan returned to the desk and scribbled a note:

Female elf from forest found, hurt but alive, seeks her daughter; brown-haired, blue-eyed maiden of fourteen summers or thereabouts. Mother is in the care of the House of Thieves in a safe house.

What are your instructions?

He sealed it with a seal of black wax depicting a cat and handed it to Marna. "Take this to the Oaken Barrel and let it be known that we seek this elf child, ask in the…er…docks regions. Ask the pirates, the other thieves you know, and the whores. Someone would have seen her if she is here. Any…bribes will be covered by the House of Thieves, if the information is good."

Marna nodded and left to go about her requests.

* * *

Archos instructed Dii to help Celine and Istvan sort through what little they had and to make ready to leave this place of sorrow. There was a small temple beyond the

Enclave, which also catered to those elves who wished to attend and had permission to be beyond the gates. He spoke to the priestess and arranged for Ma'esa to be lain in the burial yards beyond the walls of Varlek. For those elves that could pay, a corner was set aside, a small Garden of Souls within the dark city.

Returning, he passed by the Oaken Barrel and collected the notes, leaving one that simply said:

Cargo behind the White Horse to be traded for more suitable items; I leave to your discretion.

O. S.

Receiving the missive from the thieves regarding the rescued elf, he pocketed the information intending to send Olek to investigate. He scribbled a further note merely saying "Expect further arrivals" and with that, he issued instructions for the letter to be sent to his Steward in Tremellic and then returned to the Enclave to escort Dii and her new friends to the townhouse.

CHAPTER 18

Kaia was afraid. She had been afraid for some time. The slavers had come to her village and a terrible fight had occurred. Screams had filled the air, blood had spilled open the earth and that day the village had fallen. Apprenticed as a hunter Kaia, had nonetheless, spent much time assisting her mother with the goats and cheese making. When the slavers came that terrible day Kaia had thought to run and hide, the men of the village had been cut down, her uncle among them. Her bow had been left in the cabin she shared with her mother. After all no one was expecting an attack. The humans had begun searching among the cabins, and among the trees and so, frightened, Kaia had sought her mother. As she ran a hand snatched at her hood, twisting the young elf off her feet. Although much smaller than her assailant Kaia was not about to be taken easily. She bit, she kicked and she scratched. An arm squeezed her throat, choking. As the world began to darken Kaia hit the floor in the horrible wagon.

There had been three other children: young Amena the Spirit Child and sister of the huntress Ozena, Roshi whom was an age with Kaia, and a girl of thirteen, Qizina. She tried to remember if the lads had been there too, but it was dark and cramped. She thought perhaps they had, but was not sure. Her mother had pushed her to the back, shielded her even though she knew her mother was as afraid as she.

She had no idea how long they had travelled and eventually she had fallen asleep, waking some time later covered in a mouldy blanket. The other children had been forced out and the mothers were crying and pleading. Gis'Ellah had whispered, "Hide, Kaia, hide! Do not make a sound and they will not see you." Gis'Ellah had moved in front of her daughter, refusing to leave the wagon, even though the new slaves were allowed out to eat, drink and relieve themselves. No one would buy starving, stinking or indeed dead elves. Injuries could be disguised. She had been given a crust of bread and a water skin and allowed to remain in the wagon. What difference did it make to a slaver whether the merchandise ate their rations inside or outside the slave wagon? Kaia had heard water close by and smelled the stink of fish. Peeking out from under the blanket, she had seen the scattered shells of the local river clams. She had only a moment to glance but remembered the red shells scattered on the ground, striking against the green and brown. Gis'Ellah had waited until the guards had moved away and, breaking the bread in two, had given her half and a drink from the water skin.

"You must stay there for now. I know you are stiff and sore, but if you are seen, you will be made to go with the other girls... Poor Amena and poor Roshi. We will stay together, I promise!" her mother had whispered.

The wagons had rumbled on and eventually arrived at the city where the humans had discovered Kaia hiding. She was now to be "a private sale" as an extra after the "main cargo" had been dispatched. Gis'Ellah had fought her captors when they found Kaia and dragged her off. The human had said she was to be a "plaything" to entertain men. Kaia had realised enough of what that meant to be very afraid. She had watched her mother be clubbed to the floor by the human slavers as she herself was dragged kicking through a tiny hall to a small locked room. Pushed inside, a human woman grabbed her and held her fast whilst another looked her up and down.

"Very nice, so young and fresh but just becoming a woman. We need to get those forest clothes off her, though, and wash her. Those wagons stink. She stinks," the old crone sneered.

Leaning close, the woman said, "Well, little elf child, you will make for us a goodly coin. Dress you up all pretty and not those disgusting forest breeches and that rough wool tunic, and you will be quite the young lady; ripe for plucking by a well-paying man."

Struggling, Kaia said in as much Common as she could muster, "Let me go! I want to see mother! Where is she? I will not do as you ask... I am a hunter apprentice, not a slave! I will not do what you ask! I am a maiden and will remain so!"

The woman holding her laughed and hissed in her ear, "Your mother is not 'ereabouts child, but she is alive. Now you belong to Auntie Feldia and I. You will do as we say and if you be'ave and are obedient, then we will take you to see her."

Kaia was not a foolish girl. She was neither willing to throw away her life nor the chance to be with her mother. Glancing around, she saw a small bed, a chest, and some clothes set out. The door was narrow but she could hear movement, the sound of the streets close by. She nodded and the woman behind her pointed to the clothes. "Get into those clothes. Give me yours to burn. Good girl, little elf. Be a good girl for me and Auntie Marla and you will see your mother and the daylight again."

She moved to dress in the clothes, looking for her chance of escape. Feldia went out to fetch the customer and Marla remained, watching Kaia closely. "Good...such a pretty thing you are." She kissed Kaia on the mouth and murmured, "Perhaps I will teach you myself."

The door opened and in walked a large elderly human man. "See what we 'ave for you, sir, such a nice young lady," Feldia said ingratiatingly and then returned outside. Closing but not locking the door, Marla watched as the man walked to Kaia.

"Oh yes, yes indeed, she will do nicely," he said, licking his lips and adjusting the bulge now appearing in his breeches.

As the man reached for her, Kaia kicked him hard right between the legs and with a grunt of agony, he collapsed to the floor. The young elf moved fast and leapt over him. Avoiding the grabbing hands of Marla, she pulled open the door just as Feldia rushed in from outside, clutching a filthy hand over her mouth. Kaia bit down hard, tasting blood, and as Feldia swore and without thinking pulled her hand away, Kaia dived into the street and ran away as fast as her legs would carry her. Not knowing where, she just ran until she could run no more and found herself in a district with carts and wagons packing up for the day. It was dark and her legs and lungs burned from having run so fast. She edged into the overhang of a building and hid. Kaia was lost...lost and afraid. Having escaped one danger, she was now surrounded by humans and in a strange place. She thought of her hunter training and crept along quietly. She looked about her for elves. Seeing one or two assisting with the packing, she hesitated. Creeping to a stall close by, she stole a couple of apples whilst the stall holder was packing up his wares. Quietly sneaking along further, she saw two elves walking slowly arm in arm. Plucking up the courage that had served her well thus far, she ran out and up to them.

"Please...please, you must help me..." Suddenly she recognised the female elf. It was her friend Amena's sister. "Ozena? Oh, thank the gods."

Suddenly she began to cry, the ordeal of the last few days and hours overwhelming her. Ozena looked in surprise at the young elf. "Kaia? Kaia, are you alright? Where is Amena?"

Taking her hand, Ozena pulled her close. "Shhhh shhhh, you are safe now. There are some more from Szendro that have survived and been rescued. We have a safe haven," she said in Elvish.

Kaia stopped trembling. "Are the others safe? What of my mama? We were separated. I do not know about Amena...some of the others were taken away. Mama hid me beneath a blanket, but the men...took her. Two Elder women tried to hurt me and an Elder human came and wanted to...um, you know. So I kicked him in the...er...and ran away."

Olek asked her, understanding enough Elvish to follow, "Where was this? Are you hurt? Come, we should return... Lord Archos would wish to know this news."

The young elf gazed at Olek, suddenly wary of the stranger. Ozena smiled a broad smile. "Do not be afraid. This is my al'melda Olek. He will not hurt you. Now if you ran, there will be people after you. Lord Archos may know more."

"At your service, Miss Kaia. This place you were taken, can you remember it?"

As they walked, Kaia shook her head. "No… There were two human women, old and fat. I think the names were Feldia and Marla…strange human names to me. I am sorry, I do not know… I just remember when Amena and Roshi were taken out… there was water…and fish; stinking fish."

Ozena whispered, "She is not here. Olek, where is she?"

He replied quietly and kissed her softly. "I do not know. I will see what the contacts have found… Maybe speak to the slavers again in the market. Someone must know. I promise you, we will find her."

* * *

They escorted the young elf back to the townhouse with Olek watching, checking around them as they walked, watching for any sign the girl had been followed. Ozena had fallen silent, worried about her sister. Would the thieves know or indeed care about the fate of an elven child? Despite what Olek said, Ozena was not convinced. As they entered, Kaia looked afraid and Ozena comforted and reassured her. Celine and Istvan were with Dii, who was gently helping them settle in, arranging a bath and suitable sleeping arrangements with the housekeeper. She had taken some food to them and was sitting with Celine, making sure the girl did not need further healing.

Archos was sitting in the parlour writing when Olek and Ozena returned with Kaia. Archos rose as they entered, raising an eyebrow as he thought of the description of the missing elf child. Olek bowed and reported himself and Ozena encountering Kaia. When Archos walked over to the elfchild, she grabbed Ozena's hand and whispered in Elvish, "Who is this man? Where have you brought me?"

Quickly Olek repeated what she had said about the other children, Amena included.

Ozena squeezed her hand. "Do not fear. This man is our friend, our saviour; he is a Magelord and our guardian. He has done much for us."

The man in question scrutinised her and, in Elvish, said softly, "I am Lord Archos, you may trust me. You are safe with me and mine, child. You are unharmed? Olek tells me the other children were removed elsewhere."

Kaia looked at the floor, suddenly nervous and surprised that a human would speak the language of the Elfkind. "Lord, I thank you for the kindness to me. I am unharmed although the two ugly Elder humans wished for the man to hurt me. I kicked him in the, um, you know and ran, sir. Yes, Amena and the others… I could not see very well, but it smelt of fish and I saw upon the ground red shells of the River Clams. I apologise I could not see more, nor know how long we travelled. Have you seen Mama? She was taken also."

"You have spirit, child, and courage. I am pleased to see you are unharmed. A woman has been found and will be brought here this night. It would seem she is from your village, whether it is your mama, I know not. Go with Ozena, child. She and my lady will see you to some food. You will be safe here; no harm will come to you."

Turning to Ozena, he said, "Take her and see her settled. There are two city elves that Dii is tending, would you help her? Olek will fetch this other elf woman and pay a visit or two. I will go…make enquiries about Amena. Tomorrow morning we leave. It would appear Amena may not be here."

* * *

Olek saw Ozena upstairs then returned to the parlour to converse with Archos. "My lord, you wish me to fetch this elf woman? I will speak to the thieves whilst I am there. You wish an…escort?"

Archos leaned back in his seat and drained a goblet of wine. "Indeed, it would seem the girl Amena is not within the city. An area stinking of fish, with clam shells, is not a good deal to go on. I think perhaps another trip to the slavers might be worth a try. Does not the merchant Sardak keep a house here? Perhaps he is at home. I think I may pay a social call…I recall his father and grandfather; honest men, not slavers but farriers and traders of horses if memory serves. The boy grew greedy it seems, found his coin better served in stock of a different kind. I dare say he can be persuaded to talk one way or another." He drummed his fingers against the table and as his eyes briefly shone silver, he murmured softly, "Indeed, perhaps it is time to renew my acquaintance with the House of Sardak."

As Olek ventured out on his tasks, unseen and unheard, Archos moved off to find Dii and, calling her away from her ministering to the new found elves, said softly "I have to go out. I wish to…pursue a line of enquiry regarding the slavers. Olek has also stepped out and will shortly be returning with another elven woman from the village. See to it, with Ozena, that she is comfortable. I plan to return the elves to Tremellic tomorrow, or possibly the day after if we cannot gain escort tomorrow. Depending on what I learn this evening, we may need to leave quickly to follow my line of enquiry. I suggest you and Ozena pack tonight. I do not intend to be a long while."

He kissed her softly at first, and then with fire. Tearing himself away, he murmured, "I must go… Lock the door when I leave, allow no one but myself or Olek past the threshold. If anyone else tries to enter, defend yourself and the others, by any means you can."

As he pulled away from her, she touched his arm. "I will be waiting for you, my lord, my love. I will make sure the others are comfortable and I can fight if I need to. I will not fall to a slaver or Witch-Hunter again."

* * *

Olek went about his business with his usual care and stealth. Speaking with the thieves to arrange escort, he then went and collected the elven woman. As he was there, the thief on guard passed him a note. "*White Star*, Versann vessel, expected." Olek smiled and pocketed the note, intending to pass the information to Archos when he returned.

Gis'Ellah was still nervous and upset, but had been well looked after by the thieves. Olek bowed to her. "I am Olek. You are the elf from Szendro? I am bid to return you to my lord's house here from whence you may, if you choose, be conveyed to Tremellic Valley. It is close to your former village, which I regret to inform you lies abandoned. There are, however, some survivors currently residing within the security of the human village. We also have an elf child rescued in the safety of my lord's townhouse. She is unharmed and seemed to have used her cunning to escape from her captors and, as the gods blessed her, she ran into the custody of my lady, Ozena, and myself. A girl named Kaia."

Gis'Ellah gasped. "Kaia? You have Kaia and she is safe?" Eyes filling with tears of gratitude, she ran to him and gathered him up in an embrace. "I owe you, and your lord, everything…my child is safe!"

Olek smiled broadly. "If you would accompany me, you shall see her for yourself. It was her courage and tenacity that saved her life and her virtue, for she escaped those who would harm her."

He led her back to the townhouse and opening the door, showed her into the parlour and then left the note for Archos to find on his return. Fetching Kaia, Ozena and Dii, he brought them to her. As the door opened and Kaia spotted her mother, she sprang forward. "Mama! Mama! I was frightened but I did not let the human man touch me. I bit and kicked and fought!" she cried as she folded into her mother's embrace.

Gis'Ellah pulled her close. "My daughter is safe and returned to me," she murmured, tears pouring down her face, not having thought to see her alive and certainly not unmolested.

For a while they stood together, just relieved and astonished to be reunited. Even Olek, ruthless assassin as he was, turned and wiped a tear from his eye. Moving to Ozena, he said, "See…a family reunited and a moving scene indeed." He wrapped his arm around her shoulders and Dii, watched and inwardly hoped to see a similar scene with Ozena and her sister.

After a while, Gis'Ellah turned to Ozena. "I thank you for returning to me my child. Olek informed me on the journey back that it was you that ran for help when the village was stricken? We are then, all of us, in your debt. For had you not, my daughter would be lost to me and those survivors, I am informed, in the safety of the village would not be in such care."

Ozena blushed. "I would not let my kin and friends go unburied, unlooked for and unavenged. I hope to find Amena as you have found your daughter, for she is still lost."

Gis'Ellah nodded slowly. "Yes, she was taken from the wagons before we arrived at the city. I know not where. I am so sorry."

Ozena bit her lip, fighting back tears. Olek took her hand and led her upstairs. Softly he kissed her, saying, "Lord Archos goes to seek further information, and there are other paths to follow. We are doing what we can. Stay with me this night. I will keep you safe and warm and hold you close to me. Dii can see to Gis'Ellah and her daughter. Tomorrow, they return to Tremellic. For now, take strength with me, in my arms for a while. Then I will wait for the master to return, but I will, I hope, find you still here when I return." He kissed her again, stopping her tears and comforting her. Hoping that Amena would be found alive but somehow doubting it. Closing his eyes, he rocked her softly and kissed her gently, hoping to the gods that they would have a joyful outcome also. He knew, however, that gods are often fickle.

CHAPTER 19

The House of Sardak was a fine dwelling located in the richer end of the merchants' district. The Sardak family had not always been wealthy. Original horse breeders and traders the family had earned respect. Hard work did not always ensure wealth, but after several generations of hard working but basically honest men, the House of Sardak now made not insubstantial coin through slavery. The family now lived in luxury, paid for by the bodies, blood and liberty of Elfkind and human alike. Those wealthy enough to keep a slave for…simply pleasure were prepared to pay handsomely for the privilege.

As the servant answered the door, Archos smiled, a confusion spell clouding his features as he said in a voice that did not counter refusal, "I seek audience with Master Sardak; a business matter."

The servant looked him up and down, somewhat bemused. Something was not right, but he could not quite see what. The fellow had never encountered such magic before. Archos simply appeared a well-dressed man, whom the elf would not be able to remember in any detail. "The master is dining, sir. May I have a name and the nature of your business? He does not like to be disturbed at such an hour."

Archos smiled his charming and persuasive smile. "The business I wish to discuss is of…a special nature. I assure you, I am a man of means." With that, he held out a pouch of coin.

The elf looked at the bulging pouch and said quickly, "Master would nearly have finished by now. Please come in and wait. May I fetch some refreshment, sir?"

Archos nodded, replying vaguely, "Oh…yes…spiced cider or sweet wine perhaps." As he entered, he murmured something as he passed the threshold.

The elven servant showed him inside to a parlour, bedecked with arts and rare silks. A statue of dark marble depicting a naked elven maiden stood before the fire, and above the hearth were large daggers of dragon ivory, wickedly sharp and extremely rare, not to mention highly illegal. Archos noted the large number of elven items:

pretty trinkets, weapons, a few small statues of the Elvish gods looted from villages and individuals alike…even a book of lore in Elvish, which he was sure the man would not be able to read. A wooden box carved from the ancient wood of a sacred oak sat on a fine table of rosewood. The inlaid box opened to reveal an assortment of beads: amber, polished horn and stone jewellery. They were the sort with which the forest elves often adorned themselves; woven, carved, polished. A goodly quantity laid within and at the bottom, some silver and even gold; trinkets grabbed or worn when taken. He sighed and closed the box, thinking there sat the adornment and possibly the only heirlooms of many families. He was certain these were trophies and examining a bow that was set on the wall opposite the swords, he thought to himself that slavery paid too well, certainly better than breeding horses.

Herlin Sardak entered and motioned his guest to the larger, finely made table of dark mahogany as the elven servant brought a jug of warm spiced cider, a fine bottle of wine, two goblets and a plate of sweets. "I see you are admiring my elven trinkets, just a few small items I have collected over the years. Pretty things, do you not agree? My servant informs me you wish to discuss a business matter, sir."

Archos sat down slowly, pretending to be impressed. "Yes…indeed, you seem to have a fine collection. I may be interested in acquiring some of my own. It is not that I wish to discuss, however."

The merchant pointed out some trinkets and items he thought the visitor would find of interest and, once the elf had left, Archos smiled and said smoothly, "I am more interested in your other line of pretty elven merchandise: your slaves. I am after some elves. You are the man to provide such a service?"

The slaver grinned like a snake, the prospect of gold lighting his eyes. "I see my reputation precedes me, sir. Would my lord prefer slaves of a younger or older variety, male or female? There are many tastes around these days and I seek to cater to all. The Enclave houses some rather fetching individuals, my lord."

"No, I do not want the dirty city elves. I seek some elves from a village recently raided, young girls mainly. I am led to believe you may have…information as to their whereabouts. I wish to acquire these elves."

Sardak leant back in his chair. "Well, sir. I had some recently in my possession, however, unfortunately, another customer has acquired my stock. Perhaps I could put your way other such…merchandise?"

For a moment, the fire spat and crackled as Archos stared at him, as though in contemplation. In a voice edged with command, he asked, "Oh, well that is a shame. Now where would these elves have been taken? Perhaps I may bargain with the current owner. There is a girl I have heard about that I would be most eager to get. I do not wish for other merchandise, at least not at this time."

Sardak shifted, suddenly uncomfortable. "I cannot divulge my other customers, it would not be suitable. Would you care that your…tastes were told to others? No, I am sorry, sir. I can fetch for you other such goods… In fact, I am planning an excursion to acquire some more goods next month. If my lord will wait until that time, I could see my way to giving a discount, for the inconvenience."

Archos rose from his seat and slowly walked past the fireplace. The fire spluttered again, spitting sparks up the chimney, but strangely the temperature dropped. He stopped as if to admire the daggers.

He spun around in anger. "No… Not acceptable, for I will have the information one way or another!" Lifting him out of his seat, Archos slammed the man into the wall.

"Tell me…who bought the Szendro elves. I swear to you if you lie or deny it, your death will be very slow and very, very painful. If you cooperate, you may live," he hissed menacingly and with a tone that allowed little resistance. "Tell me or I will simply take the information for myself, torn from your mind, thought by thought… I am told it is extremely unpleasant. I look for a girl, young, with hair like snow and eyes like coal, her and the others of the elven village you destroyed."

Sardak tried to bluster and made to shout for his servant, only to find the cry come out as a mere croak. "I would not recommend calling for help. Unless of course you wish this household to be destroyed also. Besides, do you think I would neglect to lay a ward on the door, which now only opens at my will? Now what is it to be?" Archos growled, his eyes glowing silver and the fire spitting and swirling green.

Seeing his own death if he did not comply, Sardak was neither a brave man, nor indeed a fool, and decided at that moment that customer loyalty was much overrated. "The elves… They were taken to a village named Bornlea, small fishing village, near Jaeden. That girl was there…pretty, unusual, fetched a good price. A man collected them, paid, and then we left. Man named Ordis; after the goods are delivered, I do not know where they go. I swear…" he whispered croakily.

"Nor did you care what happened to the elves," Archos snarled in a voice that filled the man with such dread. "Now what should I do with you, slaver?"

Sardak whimpered in fear and whispered, "I have answered your questions, sir. Take what you wish from me, there are many items of value here. Elven things… ancient things…that box you admired…take it…just let me go. I have a family…"

Archos gave him a smile full of malice. "You mistake me for a man who can be bribed. Perhaps you should have considered your choice of commodity and stuck to horse breeding like your forefathers. Why should I care about your family? You cared not for the elves you stole, the men who lie slain, the woman raped and these children sold to line your pockets. I know very many ways of keeping a man alive but wishing he was not so."

Holding the man fast against the wall, he simply watched him for a while. As Sardak tried to break away from the spell, he simply increased the Power. Holding him firm, beginning to crush, tightening, squeezing until the breath of the man was painful and pitiful. His eyes bulged, his throat tightened, and he tasted blood as it ran down his throat. Suddenly Archos spun around and wrenched the dragon blades from the wall, impaling the man through the bones in his arms. Sardak tried to scream, but found himself unable, partly from his crushed and bruised lungs, yet also unable to make a coherent sound. Hanging him bleeding and whimpering from the wall, Archos snapped, "Now, slaver, I suggest one of your sons take over your business, although not the one who frequents the whorehouses in the Red Lantern district and delights in raping elven women. If I discover this is so, perhaps I will pay another visit to your house. Maybe you should consider returning to the old ways of honest horse trading. After all, your health appears to be somewhat weakened. Do not think of recounting tonight's events, for you simply will not remember who did this. That is, of course, should you live and should you regain the power of speech."

The Archmage smiled to himself and looked around the room again, noting items. He murmured as he walked through the door, locking and re-warding it behind him. Pausing, he closed his eyes and muttered, "I am Archos, Lord of the Arcane Realms. Let the household sleep this night, a sleep that cannot be broken until the rising of the sun; the entire house but the room yonder where the man therein will never get another night of unbroken sleep. By the Power within me, I curse this house such."

For a moment as the powerful spell circled from him, he felt its drain, and briefly as the Power left him, he swayed with effort then quietly left the house, silent and still as death. Outside the rain poured, yet somehow the Archmage remained dry. He made his way via the backstreets to one of the houses kept by the House of Thieves. Entering, he left a missive:

Thiefmaster,

House of Sardak to suffer this night a robbery, removal of such elven items as can be found: - wooden box of beads, stones etc., statuette of female elf, elven book – also two dragon daggers – these will be found inconveniencing owner. Deliver these to me. All other suitable items dispose of as wished. Find information of slaver, or servant named Ordis of Bornlea village or thereabouts, check local noble/merchants.

The Oncoming Storm.

He paid a sum to the thief on duty, an elderly human with whom he had dealt before and who bowed when he saw Archos. The Archmage then returned home to find Olek waiting for him. Ozena had fallen into a restless sleep and he had left her a short while ago.

"Your business is concluded successfully, Olek?" Archos enquired.

The half-elf nodded. "Aye, my lord. There will be escort for the elves on the morrow as you ordered. The elf woman Gis'Ellah was indeed the mother of the girl Ozena found. Seems a brave and feisty sort, the girl fought off her would-be attacker and the mother tried to fight them, climbed out of a window and ran off. It was a most touching reunion. Oh, and a message: the ship of Versann would be due in shortly. How were your enquiries at the house of the slaver? "

Archos nodded, committing the information to memory, and then replied, "Successful, at least I hope so. It would seem an elfchild fitting Amena's description was taken to a village known as Bornlea, close to Jaeden, then collected by a man named Ordis. I left that slaver bastard in somewhat of an awkward situation and his house might suffer some further misfortune this night. He has a house full of stolen elven items. Hopefully, these can be returned to the elves.

"I am not intending to take Ozena with us… It may prove a false lead and I think we both know what we may find. I would prefer her not to see that. She is a good girl, but her judgement may be…compromised in favour of finding her sister beyond all else. I think it best she returns with the elves. Go to her, comfort her, use that charm on her.

"The Versann ship, you say? Interesting…." He paused thoughtfully. "Perhaps I can do something to ensure it does not arrive. I have further business in the workshop before we go, it would seem."

Olek nodded and returned upstairs to Ozena. Archos looked at the map he kept, being unsure of the location of Bornlea. Two or three days fast ride hence, he knew they could make good time, but whether it would be good enough remained to be seen.

Silently he rose and entered the small workshop. He stoked the fire, warming the room, and walked the line of the Circle until the edges glowed. A couple of small glowglobes were set on the floor and walking to the shelf, he selected a small tripod and a Crystal of misted stone. Placing an obsidian bowl beneath the tripod and Crystal, he filled it with spring water. He scored a line into his palm with the dagger and dropped a few drops of blood over the Crystal, gazing into its misty secrets as the glow began to rise. Slowly he passed his hand over the top, the lightning coursing from his hand down to the Crystal, making it spark and crackle, and the water to boil and produce an odd swirling blue steam.

"I am Archos, Lord of the Arcane Realms and Lord of the Storm. I am Archos, Skychild, and I call upon the Power within me to seek the vessel *White Star*. I call upon the storm to find her. I call upon the storm to vent my vengeance upon her, and her alone. I ask the grace of the Lady of the Sky and her fury as Skychild blood is shed this night."

Outside on the docks, the sailors were filled with unease as the air grew heavy and oppressive. Out beyond the harbour, the clouds rolled low over the sea, an eerie mist descended and thunder rolled around a cargo ship named *White Star*. She was fully laden and low in the water, trying to weather the storm as it began to rage. Lightning shot sideways and hit the sails, igniting the canvass and rope. The sailors yelled and screamed to one another in the maelstrom as timber began to crack and sails burned. The ship was sluggish and slow to respond, and the cargo suddenly became a burden, a dead weight in the water. The sailors tried and failed to save their ship, their cargo, the storm had other ideas and in rage, threw down its fury upon the vessel. A storm that the survivors would later tell of as the worst in living memory, yet was oddly localised upon the patch of sea containing a single ship, as though the wrath of the sky goddess herself was called forth.

As the sailors abandoned their craft and prayed for deliverance, the ship sank below the rolling black waves and the other ships in harbour bucked and twisted in their moorings. The storm suddenly disappeared as quickly as it had appeared and in the odd calm, the sea became peaceful with a glasslike stillness. From its berth, a small fast ship, flying no colours, shot out to offer assistance and save those who could be saved with the eternal choice of "join us or die."

The *Gathering Storm* acquired some new crew members and as the sailors thanked the gods for their deliverance, the fast privateer slipped back into her mooring at the far edge of the docks and settled as though she had never moved.

Archos grinned evilly and, after tidying away the evidence, sat back in the parlour with a brandy and contemplated a great deal, then he headed to his chamber. He felt the magic pounding through him from the high magic use of the evening, and with it the deep urge that often went alongside. Magic demanded passion, energy, stamina, and the Magelord was graced with those attributes in abundance. It did, however, come at a price and he felt the fatigue of it. Dii was awake, having felt the ripple of Power. As he entered, she noticed the healing gash in his hand and raised an eyebrow, but declined to ask. Instead, she got up from the bed and glided towards him, the fire beginning to twist and glow a pale blue. Dii could feel the tension and fatigue in him, and slowly she let her fingers play across his chest, rippling a little warm comfort into him.

She kissed him softly and whispered, "You are tense. Let me soothe you, calm you." He kissed her hungrily, thinking she always made him feel very alive, banished his fatigue and the aching muscles and pounding head. Almost as though her proximity, her Power, invigorated him. Archos spun her in his arms before walking to the armoire.

"I have a gift for you. I was going to wait until we were back in Tremellic, but perhaps now would be a good time."

Opening the box, he removed the dark blue silk robe. "Put this on, let me see and feel you in the soft silk," he growled with desire.

Dii took the robe and walked towards the mirror, slowly dressing herself and letting him watch. She pulled her hair from its ribbon so it fell around her. The soft silk clung to her like skin, complementing her pale form. The train of the skirt dragged behind her like a dark wave. The skirt was split to the thigh and the whole thing swirled about her as she moved, her beautiful legs just visible. As she glided towards him, she let the magic slowly drift around her in little stars and sparkles of light.

"It is beautiful, my lord. What have I done to earn this?"

Archos pulled her close and whispered huskily, "You do not need to earn gifts, but I can think of a few ways to show your gratitude. You are so beautiful and my need of you is great. I hunger for you, Dii'Athella, Flower of the Dawn! Does the gift please you?"

Slowly he ran his hands over her, taking in her shape and softness beneath the silk. As he caressed her, she sighed and reached to kiss him with passion. Smiling, she pulled away from his lips and replied softly, "It is beautiful, impractical beyond the bedchamber perhaps, but beautiful."

"Oh, I can think of a few situations in which it might be useful," said he, guiding her to lean against the wall and the mirror.

Hungrily his lips found hers once more, one hand in her hair with the other slowly caressing all over. Bowing his head, he kissed the soft skin framed in fur around her breasts. He breathed in the scent of her: lavender, rose oil and her own soft smell. As he nibbled the skin, she moaned slightly and let her hand run down his back, tickling a small patch of skin with sparks. One hand began to slowly unlace his breeches and he growled as she slipped her hand inside and scored her nails across him. Pulling the soft silk down, he sucked her nipple hard. One hand pulled her hair back, exposing the skin as he dragged his lips and teeth across her, listening to her soft moans. In her turn, she began to stroke him, slowly caressing his balls, squeezing, making him groan. Very slowly, Archos' hand slid up her thigh under the silk, dragging his nails, and she shivered with delight. Dii moaned and kissed his neck, pulling the skin into her mouth as he slipped his fingers into her and felt her fold around him.

As she stroked him until his breathing quickened, he plunged his fingers into her, deeply, flicking her pip with his thumb until she began to move her hips into his questing fingers. Writhing under his touch, her hips following his rhythm, she stroked him slowly and then faster, then more slowly, making him gasp and moan for her. His breath misted the mirror behind them. Yet he held back, the climax was close, but he was not ready to ride its wave, wanting more, wanting to give more. Dii bit his neck, sighing, moaning into him as the magic began to pulse around her, heightening the feelings for both of them, deep, sensual and erotic. Flicking her nipples with his tongue, thumb teasing her pip, he felt her tense for a moment then explode into orgasm. He growled and bit her neck below the hairline as she came, crying out for him.

Turning so his back was against the wall, Archos lifted her onto him, and as the silk cascaded around her, he plunged deep, hard and fast. The sensations built again as Dii tightened around him and leaned back, slightly tilting so every thrust was intense, bumping against her pleasure spot deep inside. Nibbling and sucking her beautiful breasts as he drove into her, he listened to her cries, the sweet symphony of passion. Focused on the beautiful, sensual elf, the light around her pulsed and the ripple of Power from her made him growl, deep in his throat. It filled him with such a deep desire and need of her, heightening his pleasure to almost painful levels but so incredibly intense. The whole of his being became centred on this woman, her Power and warmth around him, and the pleasure he gave and received. As she buried her face in his neck, wildly breathless, writhing, unable to stop the trembling, she cried his name over and over as she came close to her climax. He crackled sparks around them, little shocks that sent them both over the edge. He released his warmth into her as the fire roared in the hearth and the light around her rippled and spun. Carrying her to the sheepskin rug by the fire, he slowly ran his fingers down the now crumpled silk. Watching her lie there clad in exquisite silk and still flushed and glowing from her orgasms, he kissed her; a long, slow kiss that made her sigh and him stir again for her.

"You are my light, my beautiful. You are the most astonishing creature I have ever seen. You fill me with such desire, and calm the rage within me. I have never loved another as I love you." Wrapping her in his arms and snuggling into her hair, he murmured sweet nothings. The scent of lavender from her intoxicating as he very slowly peeled the silk from Dii, kissing every part of her as it was revealed.

CHAPTER 20

The household woke early and the rescued elves packed the few items they had. Celine and Gis'Ellah had been given a few clothes by Dii and the housekeeper, and Archos had supplied all four elves with a little money. Having packed a few items with which to travel, those that were pursuing Amena had arranged to send the remaining luggage on the carriage. The chests were loaded onto the carriage as the Thiefmaster himself rode into the small courtyard accompanied by two of his companions.

"Good morning to you, my lord," said the Thiefmaster, dismounting. "I thought to provide your escort myself, for I grow tired of the city and wish to see these elves that have had so much of our attention safely home."

Bowing, he handed the reins to Olek and, fetching a small travelling chest and some smaller boxes, he added them to the roof of the carriage, letting Archos see one was the small box from the House of Sardak along with one or two other items wrapped in a crate that he nodded to slightly. Celine seemed overcome by the situation. Still rather in shock from her ordeal, she began to cry.

Istvan held her in his arms as Dii went to comfort her. "My dear, do not cry. You will be safe enough. See, there is an escort and Ozena will be with you. My lord has provided money for your journey and the man yonder will see you come to no harm. There will be papers for your journey, should they be needed. Tremellic Valley is safe, no one will hurt you there and you will not live in poverty. Istvan is clever and you can easily find employment. We will return in a few days or so and see you settled."

"You have been so kind to us, you and Lord Archos. A kindness we cannot repay, we will not disappoint you. Please, I wish you to have something. It is just a token of gratitude. The only item I have of my mother." Celine held out a cloak brooch.

"Oh, I would not take your heirloom, Celine. That is a valuable item. I need no payment for kindness given," Dii responded with a pretty smile.

Celine took her hands and pressed the item into them. "Please, I insist. That part of my life is over and it is something my mother acquired from my father before I was born. She told me once it was elven and reminded her of someone. Even when we were starving, she would not sell it. Mother would want you to take it, for I have no use of it and you would please me if you would take the item as a gift. It seems to me more worthy of you and your beauty and kindness."

Dii kissed her forehead and softly replied, "Then I accept your gift and that of your mother, I hope to be worthy of it. Now go and I will see you soon."

Istvan assisted Celine into the carriage and turning to Archos, bowed. "I am ever at your service, sir, for the kindness you have shown to her, to both of us. I hope to prove myself worthy of that kindness."

Patting Istvan fondly, Archos smiled and replied, "I choose those I help and who serve me with care. I am rarely mistaken in those choices." Giving him a small scroll and patting his arm, he continued, "See my Steward receives this."

With that, Istvan joined Celine inside and Kaia and Gis'Ellah entered after, making their thanks and farewells. Thus all those rescued were safely within the carriage with an armed escort, to begin the journey to their new home, away from the horror they had endured.

Archos watched with interest, smiling warmly at the elves and noting the glint of the item as it passed between Dii and Celine. He wondered what item could be of such sentimental value that a desperately poor and hungry woman refused to sell it.

Turning to Ozena, he took her hand and said gently, "Ozena, I need your familiarity with the elves and your knowledge of what may be required to escort them home to Tremellic and once there, see them settled as appropriate. You have done so very much for your fellows, yet this will help them settle and belong in a place unfamiliar to them. You speak Elvish, so the service you can render them may be invaluable. They will see a friendly and trusted member of their community assisting them among the humans and on my behalf. Now we have a number of elves, extra provision is needed. You have been instrumental from the start in assisting and saving your companions and so I give them to your care until we return. Discuss with the Elder and the Steward if you wish, but I leave it to your judgement."

Motioning to the thieves, he continued, "There will be escort from the House of Thieves as you see, but I feel your keen eyes and swift bow will see them safely home. We will seek Amena and the others of your village. I hope we will return shortly."

Ozena looked at him for a moment and then nodded, slightly grudgingly. Olek having mentioned something along those lines, they had spoken and even argued for some time about her accompanying them. Eventually she had relented, as a dutiful scout to her village. Knowing that, although Amena needed her, this lead could also be on the wrong path and these elves and those already rescued needed her here and now. Amena would be in good hands if she was found. Sighing, she reached up for a kiss from Olek, who whispered, "Thank you and I will see you soon. I hope to find you waiting for me on our return." He helped her climb up beside the Thiefmaster, who had decided to drive, her long bow and quiver beside her.

"I trust to your good care my lady. She has keen eyes and a fast arm with a bow should you encounter any difficulties," he said with a smile and gently caressed her leg, feeling her hand on his for a moment before she made herself comfortable, yet in a position to use the bow should there be need.

Archos patted the horses absently, then said, "The box of jewellery is to be delivered to Ozena's care, to be dealt with as she sees fit. The rest, deliver to the manor. I trust to you and your thieves the transport and care of these elves. Should they not be delivered to Tremellic, I will hold you personally responsible. Take the back roads, now go! My housekeeper will accommodate you."

With that, the carriage rolled away and Olek went to fetch their horses. Archos sighed and shook his head slightly, muttering, "I just hope we are in time."

He pulled Dii close, sliding his arms about her waist. "Ah well, I guess we should move soon enough. We have a day's hard ride before we need to stop." He kissed her and softly stroked her hair, now tied back in a braid for riding. "May I see the item Celine gave to you? I am intrigued by it. To keep an item of value when in such a position as they were, it must have been dear indeed to her."

Dii held out the brooch, a pretty clasp made of enamelled silver, old and Elvish in design; shaped like a flower known by the Elfkind as dii'athell or Dawn Rose: a beautiful and rare Shimmering Forest rose with petals of deep red that softly faded to a pale yellow as they neared the stem. This flower was often the first to open its petals in the morning and last to close in the evening. This brooch held some value, certainly to someone in dire need; ancient Elvish items often fetched quite a sum of money from collectors. Archos looked at it thoughtfully, thinking it must have held significant emotional value to Ma'esa. Turning it over, he saw the Elvish inscription, obviously added after the item was made. He ran his finger over the words and now his interest was truly piqued when he read: Dii'Athella Ar'thina.

Archos smiled at her and, musing over what he had just seen, he clipped it to her cloak. "It is pretty, like you. The name of the flower is dii'athell, Dawn Rose, or a similar translation. It is very rare and deemed the most beautiful of flowers. I think a very fitting item for you, my beauty. Now we should make haste, my love."

* * *

Back in Tremellic, Marrissa the housekeeper headed to market. The master and his household were away, but she needed supplies for their return. She wondered how the new arrivals were settling in after their terrible ordeal. So sad to have lost everything, and some had suffered such indignities, or so she had been led to believe. She contemplated asking the master to allow one of the women to work at the manor, now that the household was larger and there were two women to attend to. Both ladies were independent, but Marrissa would appreciate the help. She assumed the elf women could cook, sew and keep house as much as any other women.

Marrissa thought, as she rode her small pony to the village, of the changes in such a short time; the young woman that had enchanted his Lordship so much, this girl who seemed to have enchanted them all with her beauty and kindness. For so long it seemed it had just been the master and Olek. Marrissa minded her business, but she could see how lonely that he had been. Olek was devoted to him, but there were some things only a woman could provide. Now and then there had been women, but not often, or at least not that she knew about. Archos was kind to her and Old Thomas, and generous to fault, but they were not mages and she had lived with a mage as her master long enough to know that magic in the world as it stood was a lonely art, spoken of behind closed doors and practiced in secret. She had seen the way the master looked at Dii, how much he smiled when she was near, and Marrissa was happy for them. She wondered if there would be a child.

She had made a batch of honey cakes, as the master was away and she liked to keep occupied, and was intending to take them to the elves as a sort of welcome. Marrissa was a kindly soul and knew that the elves had very little, and the local children loved her honey cakes. She had heard they were, at present, lodging with kindly villagers, but Lord Archos had told her cabins were to be built, near to the forest edges but within Harkenen itself. She left her pony to the care of the farrier's boy in the paddock at the edge of the village, and wandered slowly around. She took a number of the smaller items into her basket and arranged for the larger items to be delivered to the manor. As she strolled in the morning sun, she spied a small elven child crouched alone at the edge of the village, watching the people come and go through the market. He looked afraid. His clothes were ill fitting, obviously passed on from one of the human families from a boy larger than he. Marrissa stopped and walked slowly over to him, and he cowered away from her. She was old and not in the prime of health and her knees creaked as she crouched close to him.

"Good morning, child. Have you nowhere to go?" the old woman asked him gently.

Dai'Rohdin looked at her with big, frightened blue eyes and chewed the end of the woollen shirt that was too large.

She held out a hand, containing a cake, and talked to him softly. "This is a honey cake, it is soft and sweet and it's for you, lad. What is your name, child?"

The child looked at her, then at the cake, and back again. Slowly, he held out his hand and took the cake. He did not understand many of the words she spoke in the

Common Language, as he was too young to have learned much, but he understood kindness. Having been raised to be polite to Elders and those who gave him gifts, he bowed his head and replied in Elvish, "Thank you, Elder, for your kindness."

As she gave him a blank look, he sat and thought of the words he had sometimes heard the adults speak, and the one or two times he had accompanied his father to trade.

"Thank Grandmother," he managed.

Marrissa smiled and held out her hand, which he took, munching on the honey cake, and Dai'Rohdin clung on tightly as she moved amongst the stalls. She stopped at a stall selling fabric, and purchased a square of calico and some woven wool cloth. She thought to sew something more suitable for the boy, and seeing a small furry cap for a child, she purchased that too. Browsing amongst the items on a stall from beyond the Tremellic Valley, the woman saw a small wooden carved pig and paid the few coins asked for it. She led him to the edge of the market square and sat him on the flat stones that often were used to rest one's weary legs.

Sitting next to him, Marrissa held out the small pig and said, "Pig, wooden pig, a toy for you, boy. Also this small hat to keep those long ears warm, these chilly nights."

Eyes large and round, he looked around to see for whom these fine gifts might be, then realising, he pointed at the gifts and asked in Elvish if they were for him. Marrissa smiled and pointed to the pig and then the child, "Pig, for you."

"Pig, hiirki!" the boy cried, then put his two fingers next to his mouth like the tusks of the wild forest pigs and made a snuffling 'oink.'

Marrissa laughed, "Yes, hiirki, piggy."

Patting his head, she set the cap on him, chuckling at his wide grin as the hand not containing the toy felt around the soft fur cap. He saw some elves from the village and, waving, he ran to one of the women and chattered in Elvish, pointing at Marrissa. The woman approached the housekeeper, bowing her head slightly for a kindness done.

"I thank you for kindness, Elder, to this boy when he was frightened and alone. He would like to thank you."

Marrissa smiled and replied, "He is very welcome, and I do not like to see a child so forlorn and frightened. This boy, what is he called, and does he belong to any of the women here?"

The woman looked down sadly. "No, mistress, for his father was a keeper of the forest goats and a hunter, and fell to the slavers. He died bravely defending the women and the Elders. His mother went to the Garden of Souls the spring before last…giving birth to his stillborn sister. He has no one now. His name is Dai'Rohdin."

Marrissa looked at the little boy, all alone in the world, and her heart swelled.

The elven woman continued, "The human family he is lodged with have been kind, but it would seem they have young ones of their own. He is too young to have learned the Common Tongue past a few words. He was to go to one of the farmers if no one else would take him. The other children found are brothers and older. This little one is sensitive after the loss of his mother."

Marrissa made a decision. "I will take him. He can run errands for me, assist Olek with the horses and stables, and my husband in the gardens. I am sure we can find plenty to keep him out of mischief. I would not see a boy all alone in the world given to a family who had not the room. Would you tell him?"

In gratitude at this kindness, the elf bowed her head, carefully informing the child of his luck. His eyes widened and he smoothed down his oversized clothing to try and smarten himself. He replied in Elvish and asked how to express his thanks, as a polite boy should.

"Thank you, Mistress Marrissa. I would work hard and please you," he was told.

The boy repeated it as best he could and smiled, holding out the small toy pig he managed, "Hiirki, pig toy, thank mistress."

Marrissa held out her hand for him and looking to the elf woman, she said, "I have brought cakes from my kitchen. Not much, I know, but for the children and the elves here if they would like them; just a token from myself and the master's kitchen." She held out the bundle and tried to say the young boy's name in Elvish, struggling with the sounds.

"Hiirki!" he said and held up the pig with great enthusiasm and Marrissa said, "I shall call you my little piglet, Dhordi."

The elf woman smiled. "That is close enough. He will learn from you as you will learn from him. Again, I thank you for your kindness."

She returned to her own business as Marrissa packed the wares she had brought on the pony, which came when called. She put the boy on in front and as he clung to the pony's mane, she climbed behind him and returned to the manor. As she rode, she contemplated what she would tell her husband about the new arrival.

Old Thomas had returned to their cottage after his morning with Mathias, their largely mute but strangely gifted son. They had tended to the horses that remained behind and in the absence of Olek, Old Thomas had walked the grounds with his old legs and his old crossbow, although this particular morning he had found the long walk more tiring than usual. Mathias was busy tending to the more physical task of the midden and compost heaps. As Thomas sat in his chair before the fire, he thought about the boy. No, he was a man now, but a man with the mind of a boy, to some degree. Mathias did not speak and what sounds he made were understood by few, but he was, loving, dutiful and hardworking. Still, he thought, it would have been nice to have had a son who would be able to tend the grounds as they so needed. Old Thomas loved his son, and felt blessed to have him nonetheless. He knew the boy could make even the most barren ground sprout with life, but in many ways, he was so very simple. The gods had not seen fit to bless them with other children after the difficult birth of Mathias. Old Tom knew his son was safe in this lands and in this estate, away from an unforgiving and ignorant world.

His wife returned and he heard voices, a small child's chatter in words he had heard before but was largely unfamiliar with. Getting up to greet his wife, he strolled to the kitchen to see her unpacking the baskets and bags with a small elven boy. She was saying the name of the item and pointing to where it was stored, and the lad was happily running back and forth. He looked at Marrissa's face and saw the joy there. Somehow she looked younger, still a handsome woman, but for a moment he saw the woman she had been so many years ago on their wedding day.

"What is this, Marrissa? Who is this lad?" he asked, wondering if his wife had done something rash.

The lad stopped when he heard Old Thomas and hid behind Marrissa. "This is Dhordi. He is one of the poor orphan boys Olek found. I thought he could come and live with us, he can help me."

Old Thomas crossed his arms. "And where is he to sleep? What is he to do? He is very small. Does he speak Common? We are too old to be raising a child, especially one not our own."

"Oh, don't be so mean, Thomas…look at him. He has no one in the world. Would you turn him away?"

"Can he not live in Harkenen with the other children?" Thomas asked, knowing he had already lost this discussion.

Marrissa, in her turn, crossed her arms and looked at her husband defiantly. "No, he cannot. The family he lodged with have not the means or space to keep him, and he would just be another mouth to feed. The elven women have suffered enough, would you place upon them further burden? We have space enough. He can sleep in the room with Mathias, or above the stable or in the servants' quarters in the manor. As for too old, you speak for yourself. Besides, it is true, there is more to manage now with the ladies here and if there…are children from Master and Mistress, then there will be even more to manage. Mathias… Well, he will never marry or have sons, he is but a child himself for the most part. This boy can help us. He is young. He will learn. His father was a hunter and keeper of goats, so he is used to animals and outdoors."

"Children? What do you know that I do not? You have set your heart on this, have you not? It is true that a lad would be of use, I suppose, and we can hardly turn him away, but what will the master say?"

Marrissa looked at her husband and took the little boy's hand. "The master will understand. He can hardly expect the villages to accommodate these newcomers and then turn one from his own door. We will just keep the lad away from his private chambers. If the master refuses, then we will have to send him away of course, but I doubt he will, and Mistress Dii and Mistress Ozena certainly will not."

Thomas looked at the boy and beckoned him forward. "Let me look upon you then, lad."

Dai'Rohdin crept out from behind Marrissa. He held out the small toy and said, "I work hard and please Grandfather. I pig get. Hiirki. Grandmother get."

Thomas suddenly felt a tug within him when the boy called him grandfather, even though it was not, in fact, the case. He looked the boy up and down. He was small, but seemed eager to please and was polite.

"So you will do as told and shown, and be obedient?"

The boy looked blank then nodded, unsure of the words. "Work hard," he said, hoping that was what had been asked and, extremely pleased with his toy, showed Thomas again.

"My lad, that is a fine porker indeed. Did Mistress Marrissa buy this for you?" Thomas asked, shooting an amused look at his wife, who turned and continued unpacking the basket.

Thomas watched the boy help Marrissa tidy away the last of the shopping and listened as she showed him and talked to him, trying to teach him the words in the Common Language. As the two of them worked around the cottage, he crept out and back to the sheds he kept to find a suitable piece of wood from which to carve another pig. He hoped the master would not be angry and let the boy stay. He hoped the boy would learn and not be frightened of Mathias. And a little voice deep in his head said he hoped the boy would continue to call him grandfather.

CHAPTER 21

Lord Joset Tremayne had been raging for a few days. He had returned briefly from the cottage and forced Malana into the carriage. She did not know what had upset him this time. Perhaps it was her speaking of Dii, or voicing her wish that Ulric would return. She felt safer when her son was around, now she was unhappy and afraid. They had arrived at the cottage at dusk and she saw a number of horses and a carriage nearby. Malana had been taken to the cottage before, but not often. This time, her hands were tied and she knew Joset had Shackles in the carriage if she protested. So, closing her eyes, she resigned herself to what was to come. She knew, for herself, it was not worth fighting and after so many years, she was not sure she had the strength. They had loved one another once. She still loved the man he had been, but not the man he was now.

Joset pulled her down roughly. "So, my Witch, as Dii is not here, perhaps you will take her place after we have amused ourselves with the...new stock. Maybe my friends will get some pleasure from you. I grow weary of you, you no longer please me as you used to. If you shame me, displease any of us, I will send you to the Enclave Prison, where all mages belong."

Dragging her inside, he saw preparations had been set as he had requested and his companions in vice had arrived and were taking refreshment. Joset pushed Malana into one of the side rooms and hissed, "Stay inside."

After greeting his guests and dispensing with the usual small talk, he boasted about the quality of his merchandise and the special treat he had planned.

"Unfortunately, Dii is not available, but I have a replacement. Not as young or beautiful, but talented in her own way. Malana has...consented...to attend. I tire of her, but I know Lords Renfrew and Rundin like the more mature woman as well as the young virgins."

Lord Rundin raised an eyebrow. "Malana is here? You say you tire of her, a fine woman like that?"

Joset snapped, "She is disobedient and pleases me not. I think I will seek a replacement, one who is compliant and will not run away or defy me."

With that, he pointed to the drawing room where the girls were waiting. Opening the door, he motioned them in to find Malana inside standing in front of the girls therein; two young elven girls, one a striking girl with hair like snow and eyes like coal, the other a little older, but young and fresh. A terrified human girl cowered behind Malana. One of the girls had unbound the woman who now stood guardian over them.

"No! Joset, I will not allow it! You will not use these girls as you used poor Dii. Take me for your sport, they are but children. You surely cannot expect me to allow this whilst I live. For my shame, I stood by whilst you mistreated poor Dii, but I will not stand aside now," Malana said defiantly, finding her courage if not for herself, for the others who stood frightened behind her.

Joset snarled, "Oh, we will take sport with you, my defiant mistress, but we will take our fun with those too. You will not deny me my pleasure, bitch! I warned you! You think you can defy me. Mark this, there are Witch-Hunters here. Perhaps I may decide to remove my patronage from you and you may spend some time within their…hospitality. Stand aside, woman!"

* * *

Ulric Tremayne had been away from home for a while now. Seeking Dii and staying in taverns and inns was beginning to lose its appeal. He began to long for the comfort of the manor, the good cooking and the soft bed. However it would be useful, he thought, to learn about the lands beyond Reldfield and the manor as well as his own lands. His father would not be around forever and he would be lord. So far, he had managed to find a number of red-haired girls…some of which, of course, he had bedded. Briefly he had met up with some acquaintances in the city, and he had visited a number of the houses of ill repute, but so far had not found the woman he sought.

Still, Ulric thought, she was a sweet, kind and clever girl, who, had things been different, would have made an excellent wife. He dreamed about her often…tasted her in his dreams and sought out those who resembled her, although he didn't realise that was what he was doing. Ulric liked the company of women, especially subservient ones, and he grinned as he thought of the conquests of hearts and virtues he had made, even on this trip beyond the lands.

As he returned the room he had been allocated, suddenly her saw her: Dii, the girl he sought. She had just left another room further along the hallway from his own and almost passed by him in the darkly lit corridor, although he knew her shape anywhere. Ulric grabbed her arm and as she started in surprise, he spoke to her with more venom than was intended, "I have been looking for you! It is time for you to return

A. L. Butcher

with me, back to Reldfield. Mother is upset that you have fled. She bid me seek you and I have been away for some time. It has been quite the inconvenience and expense to find you. Return with me and I will see you are not punished. It is very dangerous for you to be travelling alone. Come with me now."

Trying to pull away, Dii was shocked and afraid, this vision from her past suddenly before her. "Go away, Ulric, leave me be. I will not return to that house!"

Ulric sighed but still gripped her arm, his fingers painfully tight around her. "Do not be foolish, girl. You are an elf and a mage. How far do you think you will get alone? The Witch-Hunters will find you sooner or later."

Dii gazed at him with a strange light in her eyes that slightly unsettled him. "Oh, I had forgotten I was an Elvish mage when I was being tortured in the Witch-Hunters' dungeon. Who is to say I am alone?"

"Well, I see it did not take you long to find a new…protector. Be that as it may, you are not free to make your own choices. Do not make me force you to return," Ulric replied, rather annoyed. Then for a moment, concern flickered across his face, concern for her, and concern for himself should he return without her.

At that moment, the door to the room Dii was sharing with Archos opened and the Archmage saw the scene before him. The temperature perceptibly dropped and an open shutter further along the hallway slammed shut. In a smooth but dangerous voice, Archos said, "Is this…man bothering you, my sweet flower?"

A man who had just left his own quarters and caught the edge of the threat in the Magelord's voice decided to return to his chamber, locking and bolting the door, wishing he had chosen to lodge elsewhere. Ulric looked over Archos, standing behind Dii with his arms crossed, dressed in the riding breeches and shirt he had worn that morning. Seemingly unarmed and a good deal older than Ulric, this gave the young Tremayne an ill-advised arrogance.

"I suggest you remove your hand from the lady's arm, boy," said the Archmage as the chill wind swirled down the corridor.

Finding himself obeying, Ulric said, "This woman belongs to my House, sir, and I simply seek to return her."

Archos said softly, "Dii, go wait within our chamber. I will be along shortly." He never took his gaze from Ulric and the young man suddenly felt uncomfortable.

Dii hurried into the room, breathing heavily, and threw herself onto the bed, trying to hide from her memories and her past; suddenly thinking her new life seemed so fragile. She knew that Joset would never let her be free or happy. She also knew that Archos could well defend himself, but Dii was afraid Joset would call the Witch-Hunters, send his thugs into Tremellic. Memories she had tried so hard to bury raised their nefarious head and as the tears came, she lay sobbing on the bed, afraid, ashamed, and haunted.

Archos continued to stare at Ulric. "It would seem the young lady does not wish to return. I suggest you leave," he snapped.

"Well, sir, if its compensation you wish for, to buy another…companion, then I have money. My father is a wealthy man. I will pay to have her returned," Ulric replied, returning the look.

Outside a storm rumbled and the candles flared in the wall holders, although Archos refrained from using more obvious magic in such a public place. "You wish to buy her from me? Pray, boy, who would this wealthy father be?"

Ulric glanced at the candles, a little knot of worry being overruled by his arrogance. "I am Ulric Tremayne, heir of Reldfield. She belongs to me, to my father, for she is the Kept of our house. She is our property and we seek her back."

Archos said evenly, dangerously, "Are you now? How fascinating… Perhaps I should pay a visit to the Lord Tremayne and deal with him, not his…bastard whelp."

"How dare you speak to me such! I would have your name, sir!" Ulric demanded, angry at the insult.

Archos merely smiled and replied, "Lord Archos Terrian Stormrager, Lord of Tremellic. As for daring to speak to you such, well, you have just offered to…purchase my lady like a common whore. I suggest you do not speak of insults…boy. I suggest also you do not attempt to bother the lady again." With that, he turned on his heel, briefly paying Olek a visit to make some further arrangements, before returning to the bedchamber to comfort Dii.

Dii lay curled in a ball on the bed. Suddenly the years of hurt and shame had overwhelmed her with this vision of her former life. She had fought so hard to escape, and yet here he was following her. Sobbing, she trembled with fear and emotion. Archos entered and saw his love weeping and shaking. Swiftly, he moved to hold her, taking her into his arms. He held her close, murmuring to her, letting a comfort spell flow over her. "Shhh, Flower, my sweet Dii'Athella, he is gone. No one will ever hurt you again, my love."

Kissing her hair, he softly caressed her and held her close. Gentle and comforting, he embraced her until the crying stopped. "You are my girl now. I will keep you safe. That life is over," he murmured over and over to her, reassuring.

Dii gazed up at him, her dark eyes rimmed red and shining with tears. "I am sorry. I am just foolish. I thought I escaped that house and yet here it is, pursuing me. I was afraid. I would rather die than return there, my lord. Please…promise me you will not send me back."

Archos kissed her and then asked, "Send you back? Why would I do such a thing?

You think I will tire of you and cast you aside? Oh, my poor sweet girl, how much you have endured. Listen to me. I will never cast you out, or tire of you. I would never send you back to such a place. Surely you know that? Do you not know how much I adore you?"

Dii looked down and whispered, "I am sorry. I have never been loved before. I have been used and cast aside so often. I am so ashamed, so unworthy. But you do not understand, he will not let me go. Joset will send men after me simply to punish me, if needs be. He would never allow me to be happy, or free. His men will come to Tremellic. He will send Witch-Hunters!"

Brushing his lips across hers and stroking her hair, as he had the first time they had lain together after her nightmare, Archos looked deep into her dark eyes. "My poor, sweet girl, you have nothing of which to be ashamed. His men would never reach Tremellic and as for Witch-Hunters, you think after all this time, all this Power, I fear those bastards? You have a great Power, if only you could see it. One day your Power will be unrivalled. That man will never find you, or hurt you again. Once we have found Amena, he will be dealt with. Dii'Athella, I love you… Do you not believe that? How much it is so? I do not give my Power or emotions lightly. You are my light and love."

Rising, he walked to the small wooden box and beckoned her to him. "I was going to save this for another day, but perhaps that day is now. I have something for you."

Slowly he slipped the gold serpents onto her arms. "These are for you, those poor pretty wrists are scarred from the Baneshackles. I do not care, for I love every inch of you, but perhaps disguising such obvious marks of a mage would be a good idea. They are enchanting and beautiful, not to mention rare and mysterious. Just a small token of my love for you, my pretty Flower of the Dawn."

Dii's fingers followed the line of the twisting gold, stopping with awe on each gemstone; the spines of emerald and garnet dark contrasts to the bright gold. She had never been given something of such exquisite beauty or such value. The coils twisted close around her wrists and as the enchantment took, they settled around her pretty arms, sapphire eyes blinking.

She whispered, "I have never seen anything so beautiful, my lord. Thank you. I have never had such as these. I am sure I do not deserve such wonderful gifts."

Holding her close, he replied tenderly, "Oh, I see something more exquisite every day when she wakes next to me. You deserve so much, Dii. I will not send you away. You are not just a pretty toy to amuse me. I promise you, I will never let anyone harm you."

Arms around her, close, comforting and safe, Archos murmured to her, whispering kind and loving words until she fell asleep. Then he lay in the darkness, contemplating a visit to the House of Tremayne as outside thunder rolled around the hills.

* * *

Angrily returning to his room, Ulric began thinking of a way he could, perhaps, get her back, take her from this arrogant lord. A little later, the Shadowdancer moved silently and, watching from the shadowy alcove in which he had seated himself, saw the meal being prepared for Ulric Tremayne. Unseen, he removed a small phial from his cloak and added a few drops to the wine. Swirling it a little, he smiled beneath the cowl of his cloak and disappeared back into the shadows.

Ulric left at first light, feeling a little light headed. He had not slept well, his head pounding and a restlessness plaguing him. Still he wished to get even with this arrogant Lord of Tremellic, and he planned to speak to his father when he arrived home. Sometime later that day, he began to feel a weakness and then a terrible pain in his limbs. Stopping at a wayside tavern, the paralysis began to creep up him. The owner fetched the apothecary and then the local healer, risking the wrath of the Witch-Hunters. Both were unable to aid him, or even diagnose the Creeping Death...a poison known only to the Shadowdancer and, briefly, a few of his victims. As the poison crawled through him, he found himself unable to move, unable to breathe with a pain like fire in his veins that left his final moments screaming...until that ability also failed.

CHAPTER 22

Bornlea was not an easy place to find, as small fishing villages were common in that part of Erana and it was not on the main highway. It was a poor village, scratching a living from the Great River and the White River tributaries, finding the red clams and the fish that inhabited thereabouts. Although it served both the City of Varlek and Jaeden, it suffered from apathy and fear in the residents and bad management from the local lord, Fordan.

The residence kept by Lord Joset was apart from the village on a small hill. The village was, however, close enough to serve the residence, and be aware of its goings-on. The constable of the village, Martis, had long ago learned to turn a blind eye, especially when a bag of gold appeared to join the others in his drawer with a promise not to take members of his own community. It would seem that silence and pretended ignorance paid well enough indeed to ease what little conscience the man retained. Besides, he thought, they were merely elves. No one cared about elves. He often sat in the way-point office, his rooms close to the gaol building behind, or at his usual spot in the ironically named Jolly Fisherman tavern.

Archos and his group arrived in the late afternoon. It was not yet dark, but the autumn light was beginning to fail. A few fishermen were packing up for the day and the tavern was filling up, but apart from that, there was the usual sombre and apathetic air that pervaded the place. They rode past the village and tethered close to the cottage and its buildings.

"I suspect this would be the place, unless this man is brazen enough to keep a dwelling within the village itself. Let us investigate," Archos said, assisting Dii from her horse.

The young mage looked around, some nagging bit of information was trying to gain her attention. For some reason, this place looked familiar, however she had been taken to the houses of various men, usually under guard or bound. She scanned the area as she tried to remember, troubled by the thought, and then moved off to follow the men. As a Kept, she had usually not been informed of the name of the locale, and of course, never allowed to wander unaccompanied. Often she had been locked up until such time as her services were required, bundled in and out during darkness, or simply too afraid or put upon to take in much of her surroundings. Dii had tried to block what had happened to her from her memory and thus, although she hesitated, she could not quite recall what was bothering her.

"What is wrong, my love?" Archos asked, seeing the strange look.

"This place seems familiar, perhaps I was brought here. Sorry, I am not sure. You know how it can be, a niggling thought of something. When I was…taken beyond the manor of my Keeper, I was bound, even blindfolded on occasion, and guarded, even sometimes drugged. There were many places… I do not remember." Dii looked down with shame colouring her face and filling her eyes with stinging tears. She could barely meet his look.

Archos sighed sadly and pulled her into a close embrace. "I am sorry to make you recall such memories. You are safe now, that life is over. You could be mistaken. These fishing villages look rather similar." He kissed her softly, whispering words of love to her, then said, "Be strong, my love. Let us follow Olek. If these girls are here, we will find them."

Olek drew one of his swords and, pulling the shadows close in the failing light, glanced behind him. He had moved further forward than the two mages and intended to head for the cottage on the hill. He pointed at the sky and then motioned a circle. Archos nodded and took Dii's hand, leading her to a group of trees close by. He looked skywards and taking the kris he habitually carried, sliced his palm and dripped the blood upon the ground. He raised his arms. Still holding Dii's hand, he raised her arm with his and smiled. "I am Archos, Lord of the Arcane Realms, I call from the sky clouds to cover the moon and the stars."

Dii hesitated and then took the kris, scoring her palm and letting the blood drip onto the ground. "I am Dii'Athella, by the magic granted to me, I call this night the mist to shroud us. Let us not be seen by the eyes of men. I command you to my bidding this night." As the blood dripped around her and she felt her Power call the mist, the young mage swayed. The spell was powerful and even with Archos' help, she felt the drain.

As the mages cast together, dark clouds rushed across the sky from the east and darkness fell like a stone. As Power combined, a clap of thunder rolled and the strange darkness enveloped all. Back within the village, the residents muttered about strange autumn weather and hurried to the warmth of the tavern or their own homes. It would be said, sometime later, that the mist had a life of its own. Archos smiled at her. "Well done, see how your Power grows. Now focus on controlling it."

As the mist descended, Olek stopped and waited until the others had caught him up. "Follow me close," said his voice quietly from the mists. He was only a white shape in the eerie shifting darkness; streams of mist running from him like ribbons. He whispered to Dii, "Not bad."

They approached the gate surrounding the compound and heard voices of the hired guards muttering, "What is this mist? Hey, Oliver, I can't even see my own hand. Fat lot of use we will be guarding tonight."

"Aye, but then again, ain't none going to attack us 'ere. Folk is all in the tavern, lucky sods," said his companion.

Archos motioned for Dii to stay back and Olek slipped forward unseen. Shortly afterwards, there followed a grunt, a gurgle and two thuds. A moment later, the gate swung open and Olek whistled for them to follow. Dii smiled with delight and success as a passage in the mist opened before her. Tunnels and paths opened around the mages and the assassin, as behind them it swallowed sound and vision in a strange, cloying fog.

The cottage and the building beyond were, just large white shapes in the dark mist. Olek slipped to the door and, after listening to check that all was clear, picked the lock and pushed it open. The corridor was dimly lit and the household quiet. Archos frowned, concerned by the silence within the house. As they followed the corridor, the housekeeper exited one of the rooms, a half-elf matron carrying a cloth and a bucket full of dirty, bloody water. Spotting them, the woman screamed and dropped the bucket to find the scream stifled as Olek moved like the wind and clamped his hand over her mouth.

Olek hissed, "I suggest you stifle that scream, mistress. We seek information about some missing children, elves. Where are they? Tell us and you might yet see another dawn."

The woman tried to struggle, but found a blade at her throat. "Do not think I would not kill a woman. Where are they?"

She tried to bite the hand over her mouth and pull it away, and again felt the edge of the blade against her skin, not quite drawing blood but knowing it would soon pierce the skin should she move.

Olek removed his hand to allow her to answer. "Get off me. I know nothing of any elf children. I am just a housekeeper. How dare you come here and treat me thus."

Archos stared at the woman, letting his mind sift hers. Pulling from her mind the images she had seen, the things she knew. She began to whimper in pain as he pulled the thoughts from her. The sweat beaded on her forehead and unable to break his gaze, she wriggled in pain as blood dripped from her nose. Olek's blade drew blood, not deep but a score along her neck that sprouted beads of blood. Dii clutched his arm. "Do not kill her. Please, she is just a servant."

Archos growled, "Tie her and gag her. If she calls for help, she dies. We will find what we seek yonder but not what we wish to find. We will deal with her later. She lies that she knows not what has occurred, although who she protects, herself or her master, I do not know."

Olek bound her roughly and as he did so, the woman heard a voice in her head. "Your life is spared, for the love of a woman. Do not make me regret that decision. A servant you may be, innocent you are not. I suggest when we are gone, you seek employment elsewhere in a more mundane role. If I ever hear anything of you again, not even her kindness will save you."

The woman was thrust into a handy store cupboard and the door locked. Slowly he opened the door to the room indicated to reveal a tragic scene: The evidence of the orgy that had ensued. Empty wine bottles and a barrel lay in one corner, and blood was splattered across the rugs and drapes. They lay now piled in one corner to be scrubbed or destroyed. Archos walked through and barely managed to control his rage as he looked around carefully. The room was furnished with a couple of chaise and a number of chairs, even some of these were stained with blood and one had rope bound around the legs and left casually over the seat. There was a large table littered with food stuffs and torn rags. A man's waistcoat lay tossed over the back of one chair and a bloody flail with some more rope was cast aside on the floor under a chaise. A cupboard against one wall stood with doors open and inside were a number of items to be used for both pleasure and pain.

One of the chairs held a shape covered roughly with a blood-stained cloth, and the chaise held a similar shape. In one corner lay a larger shape, and beside it, an odd smaller shape under a large bloody cloth from which a small white arm poked out. Outside, the sky split with lightning, and thunder clouds spiralled furiously over the house.

Olek stepped through, followed by Dii, who clapped her hands to her face in horror. "Oh, by the gods, no!"

Tears stinging her eyes, Dii moved to check the covered heaps. Time seemed to slow for her and the sheer horror of what she knew would lie beneath almost overwhelmed her. Memories and fears of what she realised must have occurred made the bile rise in her throat and she gripped the wall; a memory swirling in her head made it pound, and her breath was shallow as she tried to deal with what was before her.

"Bloody hell," Olek groaned. "Who has done this, to whom does this house belong? What sort of monster could partake in such terrible practices? I have seen many bad things; somehow this seems to be the worst." Even his amber eyes filled with tears of anger and pity.

Archos leaned against the wall for a moment, fighting his rage and biting back the urge to simply burn the place, to vent the rage of the storm upon this house and the village yonder. He had feared something like this, but being faced with it made even his stomach turn.

He moved to the shape on the chair and carefully lifted the cloth to reveal a young elven girl; her face bruised and her hair matted with blood. Her wrists were bound and bruised, and the marks of a flail were on her poor broken body. Blood clotted around her thighs and the evidence of the terrible treatment she had suffered made him growl angrily. Outside, lightning rent the sky and arced down to crack the tiles, shaking the house; the candles spluttered and the glowglobes tumbled to the floor. He checked for life, but felt the coldness of death over her.

Dii fought back the urge to be sick, or to just turn and flee, and made to assist, calling all her inner strength to help these poor souls. Heading to the chaise, she suddenly saw movement. The cloth over what lay below was rising as though with breath. Springing forward, she pulled it back to reveal a human girl of perhaps fourteen. She was tied to the chaise, bleeding and barely alive, but alive nonetheless.

"She lives! This girl lives!" Dii called and quickly made to heal her, knowing time was not a luxury.

Crouching next to her, Dii looked the girl over carefully and assessed the wounds, as Olek slashed the bonds away. "Goddess Syltha, help me this night to save this girl. Lend to me your Power and your wisdom."

As her hands began to glow blue, she closed her eyes and touched the girl gently, pulling the pain within herself. A searing pain and the fog of coma almost knocked her out. Rocking gently, trying to retain her Focus, she pulled Power from deeper within herself, her own life force. Swirling the healing power around the girl, she whimpered in pain as she felt bones knit and the torn flesh and muscle mend. As the girl woke groggily, Dii herself passed out. Archos moved fast and caught her, feeling the pull of her Power as she healed. Cradling her, he stroked her face and called her back until her eyes fluttered open. Kissing her softly, he said, "Rest a moment, she is out of danger. You have expended much Power."

Dii shook her head. "No, my lord, I am needed. I will be alright in a moment. I must tend to the girl."

Slowly and somewhat stiffly, she moved to the girl and comforted her. "I am Dii. You are safe now. I know you have suffered greatly, but we are friends and will help you."

Removing her cloak, she wrapped up the injured girl. "Here, take my cloak to cover yourself. I will set a fire to warm you and I have herbs to make you strong. Do not be afraid. That is Lord Archos, and the half-elf is Olek, we are here to assist you. No one will harm you."

The girl gripped her hand, barely able to hold as the battered and bruised flesh slowly healed. "Please, miss, don't leave me. My name is Emmae. The men might come back… I am so frightened they will return. The others… What of the others?" came in whispers from the thin and frail form.

Dii slowly let a comfort spell warm her and replied, "Those men will not hurt you again, do not be afraid. I know what you have endured, but it is over and you live and be strong. The others…were not as strong as you. I am so very sorry. We will take you from this awful place and see you safe." Dii sat for a while and held her hand, then moved to make a fire and using remnants of the wine and herbs and honey from her pack, she produced a warming tea. She checked that she had the correct herbs for later to supply the contraceptive and cleansing wash the girl would need.

Archos went to examine the larger mound. Removing the cloth, he saw the body of a human woman, her long black hair matted with blood and the deep scar of a Baneblade in her back. One arm was bent and broken, and her arms and legs were a mass of bruises, not to mention the livid mark across her face. A pool of blood lay beneath her and soaked both her ripped clothing and the child beneath, but she lay across the elfchild as a shield; a small elven girl of twelve or so summers whose snow white hair was stained pink. The body of the elfchild was still warm, as though life had recently left, yet left it had. The woman too was just cooling, not long dead, but she too had passed to the Other World.

"Amena," Olek murmured. "Oh gods, this will break Ozena's heart. We are too late!" Angrily he stabbed a blade into the wall. In silence and with tenderness, he moved the woman away from her, seeing the broken body of the elfchild Amena Lyn. Gently he lifted the child into his arms and held her close. Tears were in his eyes for her plight, and for the suffering and sadness this news would cause Ozena.

Archos looked around the room angrily and with despair. "Indeed, it would appear we have failed. I had hoped we would find these girls yet living. This will be avenged. I swear this on the storm." As he said this, another bolt of lightning forked from the sky and cleaved a tree in two.

The storm rolled over the village, bringing fire, flood and terror. Archos looked at the small, broken corpse in Olek's arms, the white hair matted in places but flowing over her face. Softly, he touched her. Even after death, he felt a tiny spark of her Power. He paused thoughtfully as he looked at the small elf. Searching his mind for the lore, he wondered whether she had possessed enough Power for what he hoped. He sighed at the loss of another mage, and a Spirit Child at that. As he brushed the hair from her face again, he once more felt a tiny spark, like the prick of a pin. Something called to his magic, just on the edge of his awareness.

As the storm raged outside, Dii turned to Archos with tears in her eyes, but then saw the body of the human woman. Growing pale, she ran forward crying, "Malana, Mama. No, please, no!"

Falling to the floor, she took the hand of the dead woman and began to cry as Olek gently wrapped Amena in a soft velvet drape torn from the wall.

Archos asked gently, "You know this woman?"

Dii nodded, the tears making her eyes bright. "She was my foster mother…the mistress of my Keeper. She was a mage and kind to me; the closest to a mother I ever knew. She would have fought for these girls. I know to whom this house belongs, I remember now. This is the house of my Keeper, Lord Joset Tremayne of Reldfield. He keeps it for his…entertaining. I have been here, not often but sometimes I was forced to attend, to…participate in their pleasures." Trembling with emotion, she pulled the body of Malana closer, looking for signs of life and knowing she would find none.

"He has done these things. Oh, by the gods, I should have known. If I had not fled, would this have happened?" Dii said with cracking voice and breaking heart, almost to herself.

The human girl sat up weakly. "The woman, the mage, she died trying to help us. Those men, they…they…hurt us. She fought them, used her magic, put herself in the path of them. One was a Witch-Hunter, or so they called him. He struck her down, yet still she tried to fight them, protect the young one there; protect all of us, even though her strength and her magic failed her."

Dii sobbed quietly as Archos spoke in a voice laced with the rolling storm beyond. "Lord Joset Tremayne. Yes, I have heard that name before. He shall pay for this; he and the others. Dii, you could not have known. There are many slavers and cruel men in this dark world. Had you stayed, it would have been your body beaten such. It is not your fault. He is the one who has done this and will suffer for it."

Pulling Dii to her feet and kissing her, he said, "I am sorry for the loss you have suffered; for the loss of the elves and the treatment of the girl yonder. Had we arrived earlier, we may have been able to prevent this, yet we did what we could with the information we had. The village yonder will know of this and see what has occurred."

Surveying the tragedy of the room, he sighed. "Dii, will you stay with the girl and sit with the dead? I leave them to your care, if you are able. You have great strength and I know it is so. There must be water and fire, shrouds for the dead, clothes for the girl. There may be food, she needs to eat and so do you. Rest there and Olek will stay with you and make arrangements for our return. I am sure he would care to pay a visit to the constable or steward of the village. He will be appraised of what has occurred here. We will check the rest of the house, and then later, I will pay a visit to the Lord of Reldfield. I will ward the house. No one will harm you."

Olek checked the remainder of the house and barn buildings, finding no more bodies but an abundance of evidence for the party that had occurred. Rooms at the back were more comfortable and less full of reminders, and it was decreed that the women would be moved there and the three dead would also be moved and washed. Olek would visit the village and acquire a wagon in which to take them home. The living quarters would also provide some food and warmth, and could be locked. Other than the housekeeper, there were no servants currently in residence.

Looking at him with her dark eyes full of grief, Dii said quietly, "You would go to Reldfield alone? Joset's guards are nasty. I…I would come with you. I know the house. I can be useful."

Archos kissed her, a soft comforting kiss. "No, I would not make you visit that place again. You are needed here. Care for Emmae and see to your foster mother. His guards are nothing. He will be nothing. It will end, I promise you. Olek can visit the constable. You have expended much Power; that healing was difficult and I see how tired and upset you are. I will be fine. I have dealt with far worse scum than such as Joset Tremayne; if you wish to help, tell me the layout of the house and grounds."

Dii sighed and stroked his face. "I must confess, I would certainly not wish to return to that house. Now Malana is gone, there is nothing for me there. She was a good woman, far too good for him, far more than he deserved. Yet she was so afraid he would send her to the prison Enclave or give her to the Witch-Hunters that she put up with all he did. In her way, she loved him, or had done. She had nothing of her own. As a Kept, all property was his. She felt it better to live as she did than to starve in the Enclave. She protected me also, or at least tried. Told me once her daughter was stillborn and Joset had brought me from the Enclave for her, in the days when he was still kind to her. May we take her home to Tremellic, bury her there? Then I can be close to her again. She can find peace somewhere she would have been happy."

Archos held her close, replying softly, "Of course, did you think I would leave her here? I will not have you return to that man. Malana and the elves shall return with us, and the young human girl also, if she has not somewhere else, a family to miss her."

"Thank you." Dii nodded. "Now, the manor at Reldfield, let me see. There is a gated wall, it will be guarded, but there is a gap in the wall close to some trees, Joset was mean with money and would not repair it. A person could slip through. His suite of rooms is at the back, on the second floor in the East Wing. There is a manservant who tends him and Ulric has one. There are servants there, but mostly they would be afraid of him. The manservant, though, has served him for as long as I remember. It is possible Ulric would have returned by now, although I cannot see Ulric allowing his mother to be brought here. The manor is away from the main village, quite far. He was not known for good management of the lands and the village disliked him, although he had his minions there. There is a small river and some caves nearby in the east hills. He is a late sleeper. He likes to sit and drink in his parlour."

Archos kissed her softly once more. "Do not concern yourself for my safety, my love. My business will not take many days. Once the arrangements are made for transport of the bodies, and you and Emmae are rested, Olek will take you home and I will join you on route. It may take a day or so to make arrangements in a small village such as this, anyway. Olek will know what to do, how to contact me. You are kind and comforting; I know you will see to what must be done here."

Kissing her again, he breathed her scent. He saw the sadness in her eyes, a grief for the woman who lay slain and the children who were strangers to her. The anger within him tempered to a slow burn to be used when he needed it. He felt her tremble in his arms and his heart beat faster for her.

"Come, there are rooms yonder. Settle the girl, find her some clothing and then you know the herbs she will need to ensure there are no on-going symptoms from her ordeal. We will rest this night and tomorrow, the Lord of Reldfield will feel the wrath of the Oncoming Storm."

CHAPTER 23

Olek had risen early, finding a note from Archos waiting for him. He had heard the Archmage leave well before dawn and grinned, hoping Lord Joset would suffer. He found a small cooking pot and decided to make porridge. He knew Dii was tired and would be worried about Archos; she also had the young human girl to care for. He had heard her moving about and, knocking softly, said, "There is porridge cooking for you, Dii. I will visit the village to make arrangements. I will make sure the place is secure and I am not intending to be long. Have you need of anything?"

Dii opened the door. He could see the redness of her eyes from weeping and grief, the sadness in her face, yet she was polite and kind. "Olek, how kind of you to make breakfast. I will look around the place to see if I can find something more suitable for the…er…bodies; something to dress Malana and the girls in, maybe. Perhaps you could fetch something anyway?"

Olek bowed slightly. "Of course. I am sorry you had to find…what we found, your foster mother."

Dii looked away for a moment and replied quietly, "Yes, and I am sorry for Ozena. I should go see to Emmae. I should find out if she has somewhere to go or whether she will return with us."

Olek agreed and locked the doors behind him, heading to the village.

* * *

Olek saw the tiles split on the roof of the cottage, the beam below cleaved almost through. Had the roof been thatch, as many of the cottages were, the building would surely have burned. The storm had been angry indeed last night. The far wall of the cottage had suffered a crack that ran halfway down its length. Olek grinned as he saw the tree split in two and idly wondered what Archos would do to Lord Tremayne. He hoped that whatever it was would make the man suffer. Archos could be creative in his vengeance, and Olek knew he would not hold back in his rage against this man.

The village was beginning to go about its business for the day, wading through the flood water, retrieving boats, and dowsing the minor smoulders that still smoked. Folk muttered about the severity of the storm, ignoring this stranger and going about their tasks after the strange weather. Olek made his way to the small way-point, paying the fee to dispatch the letters Archos had left. Enquiring about the whereabouts of the local constable, he was directed to the gaol where he found the constable sitting at breakfast, surprised by the early morning visit. Olek glanced around the small building, noting the layout: the small table and cupboard in the office, and the small cell beyond. Keeping his face shadowed by the cowl of his cloak, he locked the door behind him and sat down.

"You would be constable of this village? I request both assistance and information," asked the cowled figure.

Martis looked over to the shadowy figure. "Yes, I am Constable Martis. You would be a stranger in these parts, sir. How may I help you?"

"I require provision to be made for caskets for some that have passed to the Other World who lay up at the large cottage yonder. That one owned by the Lord of Reldfield," came the reply.

He saw the constable briefly tense then say, "Dead? Who is dead? I was not aware there was anyone at the dwelling yonder. This is not the Lord of Reldfield's land."

Olek steepled his gloved hands over the table, letting his cloak fall to reveal the swords. Evenly yet with an edge of steel to his voice, he replied, "The dead are two elven children and a human woman; murdered by the hands of those who use yonder dwelling for their disgusting vices. In my care there is a girl, raped and almost killed. You will provide such arrangement to transport those who were killed away from here."

"I know of no such murders. It is not my concern!" the constable snapped, beginning to tire of the conversation and hoping this stranger would leave sooner rather than later; preferably before asking any inconvenient questions.

Angry, Olek moved like the wind and the constable found himself pinned between two drakeswords. "So three people are murdered brutally, a young woman raped and left for dead, and it is not your concern! You are the constable! It is your duty to uphold the law and protect those who cannot protect themselves. I expect the lord pays you well enough not to notice such events, yes? Well, they have been noticed."

Slowly the constable moved his hand towards the sword at his side and Olek's arm moved in a blur, slicing through the scabbard until it dropped to the floor. "You really are a bloody fool. You think you can move faster than I, that you can beat me? I think you were hired for your complacency and not your sword arm, old man. I can kill you and be gone from here before anyone arrives. Believe me when I say I have killed better men than you for a good deal less than you have done, or rather allowed to be done."

"Elves are not people. If a man chooses to take his sport with an elf, it is not against the law. You cannot murder property."

Olek growled and then thumped the man square in the face with the hilt of his sword, breaking the man's nose and spurting blood across the desk. Grabbing the fellow's shirt, he pulled him close and hissed, "They were children! What of the human girl and the woman? That *is* illegal. Now you will provide for us: caskets in which to transport the dead, and a horse and wagon on which to carry them. Unless, of course, you wish to join them in the Other World?"

His eye spotted the drawer in the table across the room and, sheathing one sword, he pulled it open to find bags of gold coins. "So this was your blood money? Either that or the pay for a village constable has significantly improved recently. There is a good deal of coin here," he said, snatching a handful and tossing it into the man's face.

Close, Olek hissed into his ear. "She was but twelve summers old…a child, she lies defiled and broken up at the house yonder. My lady waits for a kinswoman who will return in a shroud, and a sweet, gentle woman weeps for one of the only people to show her kindness. Yet you sit in your rooms with the bloody gold of slavers in your possession. This gold could do much for your village. Now, you will provide what I request and then you will announce to the village what you have allowed to occur."

The constable turned his head. "You can prove nothing. I did not kill those people."

Olek grabbed his hair and pulled his head back sharply. "Perhaps not…yet you did nothing to prevent it. Not through fear, but through greed and apathy. What if your women had been taken, your daughter, your sister? Now perhaps we should see what your villagers say. You accepted a bribe to ignore a crime that has occurred. Do not even think to call the Witch-Hunters. Your lord is not here. What is your life worth to you: a bag of gold now and then, or a slow painful death? Trust me, the treatment you receive from your village may be a lot less…unpleasant."

Binding him tightly, Olek forced him at sword point out to the small square that served as a meeting place. The fishermen turned to look, muttering amongst themselves.

"You have something to say?" Olek hissed.

The constable stood mute and someone called, "What means this? Who are you?"

Olek looked around the group slowly, scrutinising each one, his face still cowled. "I come on behalf of the children and woman that lie in yonder house on the hill. Defiled and murdered for the pleasures of a local nobleman and his friends. Two elven children lie dead, a human girl defiled and beaten almost to death, and a woman who gave her life to defend them. Bloody, broken and ravaged. The constable here has a drawer full of gold in his office, a bribe from the nobleman to look the other way. He claims it is not his concern that someone's daughter, someone's sister, someone's mother, someone's mistress lie dead. The Lord Tremayne would take any woman who took his fancy, Elfkind or human alike, for his pleasure and then cast her aside. How many of you have a daughter, a sister, a wife or mistress upon whom he would cast his eye? The constable here refuses to assist with providing suitable arrangement for transportation of the dead to a place they may rest in peace. He sits alone in his rooms with his hands full of the bloody gold of slavers, whilst children lie slain and your village falls to ruin. Would you have this man as protector of this village?"

"Martis, is this true?" asked a villager. More folk had arrived to see what was happening and now there was quite a crowd.

Martis shook his head. "He lies… What could I gain?"

Olek simply replied, "Go look for yourselves, in the drawer in the gaol office. I will take you to the house yonder where stays a woman of my household, who even now mourns her foster mother."

The villager who had spoken before replied, "I will go and see the truth of this. I have a young daughter." He motioned to another man and they went to the gaol, returning a moment later with a handful of gold. Holding his hand up so the group could it shining, he cried, "The fellow speaks the truth! A drawer of gold, from whence I know not! Let us go to the house, see if he speaks more truths."

Motioning to a couple of the burly fishermen to take the constable, he strode to Olek and held out his hand. "Arian, I keep the tavern here, such as it is. Take us to the house there."

Olek hesitated, concerned for Dii being discovered. "There is an elf woman of my household there. She is in mourning. It would distress her to be disturbed by a group at such a time. These people, they trust you?"

"Aye… I don't short change and I don't piss in the ale. 'Tis a hard living here and an honest man is appreciated. I will come with you, and another to verify. We will just see with our own eyes. We do not wish to cause your woman more upset."

Olek assented and motioned towards the house, accompanied by Arian and a fisherman named Barton, another respected soul among the simple folk of Bornlea. Dii had cleaned and dressed the bodies with clothing she had found, and Emmae cowered behind her when she saw two large, strange men. Grabbing for Dii's hand, she whispered something and Dii squeezed her hand protectively.

"Do not worry, they just wish to see for themselves what has occurred," Olek told her, trying to reassure.

The two men saw the two elven children laid close together. Washed and dressed but still marked from their ordeal, and Malana lay close by with the livid bruise on her face. "See there, two elf children defiled and slain and the woman murdered in defence of them. See the room in which we found them, much evidence of violence plain to behold," Olek said, leading them into the large room they had first discovered.

"I have seen enough. You tell the truth, stranger. A tragedy has occurred in this place and it seems our constable cares not for anything but gold. It could be my daughter next that is taken. I would suggest reporting this to the Order, if I thought they actually gave a damn. As this is not the case, we will deal with this matter ourselves. You shall have your wagon and suitable caskets to transport your dead. The gold... Well, there is much good that can do. Better fishing boats, repairs to the buildings after the storm. There is quite the amount of gold there. It would seem that deflowering young girls calls a goodly price and silence a better one. A dowry perhaps for the poor girl there. It will not make amends, but it may some way go to ease her," Arian suggested.

"And the constable?" asked Olek.

Arian turned to him. "Oh, he well be dealt with well enough for taking bribes, complicity to murder, putting the village at risk. He will be punished, no doubt on that."

"Miss, I am sorry for the loss of your kinswoman. The village will make amends, such as they can be," Arian said to Dii, eyeing the bodies. With that, he left to assist with arrangements and to recount what he had seen to the rest of the village. Olek smiled at Dii and bowed his head slightly to her, then followed to assist.

Later that day, a wagon decked in cloth and flowers was taken to the cottage, and the next day would see three caskets of wood set on it to receive the dead for transport. The cart horse was offered and gold taken from the gaol drawer to provide a replacement. The tavern keeper and two of the fishermen lifted the caskets tenderly onto the wagon and bowed their heads in shame and sadness that such a terrible event had occurred in their village.

The tavern keeper Arian was announced as constable until such time as a new one could be found, and the former constable Martis found himself swinging from the trees nearby at dawn the next day. The housekeeper had been released from the cupboard, still bound, and was taken to the cell behind the gaol. Some argued for her to join the constable on the gallows tree and the others just for her to be run from the region, or taken to the Enclave in chains, the latter of which was agreed upon.

The next morning at dawn, a sad, slow procession of the wagon and Olek leading the convoy left the village. The fishermen, their wives and the tavern keeper Arian watched as the convoy slowly moved towards Tremellic. Dii rode with Emmae, who had barely left her side and gratefully accepted the offer of sanctuary in Tremellic.

Shortly after the convoy left, the house on the hill suffered a fire and was all but destroyed. So it was that Amena Lyn the Spirit Child, Malana the mage who had died in defence of strangers, and the elfchild Roshi began their last journey.

* * *

Archos had ridden hard to Reldfield, resting overnight when he had to for the sake of the horse. He arrived in the evening and for a while, simply walked around, finding the trees, the caves and familiarising himself with the land. At the caves, he had a brief conversation with the two men who stood waiting, advising them to take refuge from the storm. As darkness fell, he walked to the trees and, wishing he had brought his staff, scratched a Circle in the dirt with a thick wooden branch. As he walked the line, it flared and he grinned. Rolling his sleeves up, he slashed deep into the flesh and as the blood began to run, he called, "I am Archos, Lord of the Arcane Realms. I am Archos, Skychild, and Lord of the Storm. This night, by my Power and blood, I call to my will the storm, the elements, the fury of the earth and sky. By the spirits of magic and by the gods, this night I seek revenge, vengeance for a Spirit Child, for the mage Malana, for my love, the sorceress Dii, and the elves of Szendro. By my blood, I vow that I will not leave this area until that vengeance has been sought."

Dark clouds rolled in and he felt the power of the storm fill him. The magic crackled around and the Circle flared high, lighting the trees for a moment in blue light. Lightning struck him as he held the oak branch above his head and as the electricity struck, it burst into flame. Around him, the lightning earthed and scorched the ground, yet the Lord of the Storm stood unharmed. The oak branch glowed red, infused with magic, and a powerful weapon in itself.

Archos grinned, the Power energising him after the long ride. Even though he was a not an elf, his night vision was relatively good. Murmuring a confusion spell and a healing spell, he walked silently to the gap in the wall. The wall was high but in need of repair, and the area where it had crumbled was wide enough to admit a person, though it was a bit of a squeeze. The manor within the walls was lit. Keeping in the shadow of the wall, he saw a guard by the door; a burly man with the bored look of guards everywhere. For a while, Archos simply watched and then muttered something, watching as the guard tumbled to the floor asleep. Archos stepped over the unconscious man and, putting his hand against the door, felt the iron below his fingers lose the fight against his will. The door swung open.

Dii had said that Lord Joset kept his rooms in the East Wing. Dragging the storm-born staff along the wooden threshold, he watched as the door closed quietly. "I command this house to stillness, all but the Lord Tremayne who resides here. The door will open at no will but mine until I leave this place. All who reside within these walls will simply wake and remember nothing."

For a moment, the Power swirled around the house and the wound in his arm burst into blood, the flesh still knitting split and the wound reopened. He dripped blood across the floor and, looking down, dragged the staff through it, pulling the blood within. The staff crackled and sparked, and he gave a terrible smile.

Around the house, the servants stopped what they were doing, frozen in whatever attitude their task required. Outside, he heard thunder and a furious wind roaring. Swiftly, the Magelord moved to the stairs that led to the East Wing, noting as he did so a few elven relics, no doubt stolen from the slaves. The rooms were well furnished, though not his own taste as they were rather gaudy and coarse. The items being overtly expensive, a show of wealth that left nothing to taste.

Within his chambers, Joset Tremayne rose and pulled the casement window shut as the wind and rain beyond vented their fury. He called for his manservant to bring him refreshment, yet received no answer. Calling again, he swore. How dare this man not heed his request! Opening the door, he looked around. The house was silent, the only noise the storm that raged. Bellowing his manservant's name, he stomped to the top of the stairs and rang the bell pull angrily, still receiving no answer. Turning on his heel, he returned to his room to find within a cloaked man leaning on a glowing staff. The fire in the grate roared behind this man and small bolts of lightning cracked around him.

The door slammed shut and Joset reached for the sword on the table, to find as he did so that it was as hot as fire and burned his hand. As the sword clattered to his feet, he yelled for his guard and his servant.

"Do not waste your breath, Slaver-lord, for your guards and your servant will not come unless I will it. Tonight, it is just you and I…" the cloaked figure informed him with a voice that chilled the blood.

"Who are you? What purposes have you here? Get out of my house, Sorcerer!" Joset yelled warily, afraid, and knowing magic when he saw it.

"I have many names, but for now, I am the Oncoming Storm. As to my purpose, well, that is a good question. I trust you remember a red-haired girl you kept for a slave, to use as and when you chose, to share amongst your friends like a whore. A woman who still wakes crying in the night, from the treatment she received in your house and at the hands of the Witch-Hunters when she ran for her life from this place. I trust you remember the elven children you bought and defiled, the girl whom you ruined and was called back from the brink of death; the woman who was your mistress and bore your son, and ended her days in a pool of blood. I doubt you remember the names of the elves you destroyed, the village that lies in ruins due to your greed and sick lusts. My purpose is to make you suffer the pain you have wrought upon others, to take the vengeance for those who cannot." The voice echoed around him.

Joset glanced behind him, checking the door. "What right have you to tell me these things, to seek this vengeance for elves and Witch whores? I have influence. I will call upon you the Witch-Hunters, see you in their dungeon."

Archos laughed and a bolt of white light shot from the staff and knocked Joset back into the wall, pain searing across him. Archos moved like the lightning he controlled and picked him up, his grip like a vice. "I have fought with demons and creatures you cannot comprehend, slaver. Do you really think I fear the Order? As for right... Well, it is simple enough I take that right. To defend those who cannot find defence from what passes for law. I take the right to avenge what you have done because I can, because it disgusts me that you defile, steal, rape, and destroy simply for your own pleasure, because you see elves as less than property or beasts. How dare you take a non-consenting woman for your pleasure simply because she cannot defend herself!"

He growled, the sparks crackling from him close to Joset's face, as the Archmage's eyes glowed silver and beyond the window, the storm raged, terrible, unrelenting. Man and beast with sense within them trembled in their bed or burrow, and the horses in the stable kicked down their stalls and fled from the House of Tremayne.

"Dii, poor sweet girl whom you abused so badly, who could not defend herself through fear of the Witch-Hunters, raised in your house and almost foster daughter to she who lived as your wife. Yet you think this is acceptable and you dare to ask me by what right I am here."

Close to him, Archos let the lightning ripple across them both, and Joset cried in pain as the heat of it scorched him. "Elves and Witches have no rights; I am lord of this region. It is my right!" he managed with surprising courage and a good deal more arrogance, hoping his servant would come to his assistance.

"You will give me the names of your…companions who attended the orgy at the house in Bornlea. Where lay the defiled and murdered sister of a woman of my household and the corpse of your mistress," Archos snarled.

Archos stepped back, dropping Joset in a heap and walking to the other side of the room as he tried to control his anger and not just kill the man there and then.

"You think I would betray my friends to you, Sorcerer? What sort of man do you think I am? My son will find you. He will hunt you."

Archos turned and a powerful wind blew across the room, tearing through the drapes, rattling the casement and sending items tumbling to the floor. From the staff, a bolt of lightning landed at the feet of Joset Tremayne. "Oh, I know what sort of man you are. I will simply take the information from you." Another bolt followed and then a strange, dark, twisting light that snaked and crawled. It crept like a snake and, hitting its mark, made Joset arch in agony and twitch as in a seizure.

Joset whimpered in pain. He found himself barely able to move as the Magelord easily lifted him, pinning him as he sifted his mind; roughly pulling forth memories and thoughts, tearing them from him. As the thoughts and memories surfaced, the pain racked through him. It was a pain like fire in his mind, as though hot oil was pouring in, that made him cry and writhe, the blood spurting from his ears and nose. As the names of his companions rose and were taken by the Magelord, he clawed at his head. He tried to push Archos away, to no avail.

"Your son?" Archos said icily. "That would be the whelp Ulric? Your son is dead. Your House fails and falls. You have nothing, you are nothing."

"Ulric is dead?" Joset whimpered. "Oh, my boy…my son..." Suddenly feeling what it was like to lose someone for whom he cared, the pain eclipsed that which he felt from the magic.

"See how easy that was?" Archos released him. "Now, what to do with you?"

Joset crawled to him, suddenly broken with grief. "You have taken from me the one thing I loved… Is that not enough? Take my house and lands; I care not for them now."

Archos crouched and gripped the man's now bloody shirt, pulling him up. "No, it is not enough. Perhaps you will learn what it is to mourn, to despair, to suffer the pain you have wrought upon others. I did not take your son. He made his own choice when he attempted to take by force one that I love, when he did not stop you in your vile pleasures, when he took his own pleasures from she who was his foster sister. Oh, I have seen and felt her pain and shame. As for your house and lands, they will be mine, but not in the way that you think. I have my own domain to care for; I do not need or wish for another."

The Archmage reached down and roughly tore the Seal Ring of the House of Tremayne from Joset's finger. He noticed another, an ancient amber ring of fine Elvish design on the little finger of the man.

"You dare to wear the items of the elves to which you were so cruel, a pretty trinket that is a spoil of war?" he snapped, holding the ring which began to tingle as it met his Power.

"Take it, it was hers." Joset sniffled. "Now either kill me, or go and let me mourn my son."

Archos slipped the ring into his pocket and dragged Joset to the door. "You may mourn your son, for I will not kill you, at least not directly. I have something far worse than a reasonably quick death for you, slaver. Time to mourn, to contemplate your life and what you have done, the choices you make and have made. Now you tire me, for I have expended much Power and do not wish for conversation."

Joset limped downstairs, his head pounding and feeling now like it was full of needles, his burned skin painful and tight, and the muscles beneath bruised and twisted.

Yet he was unable to resist as Archos dragged him from the house and towards the caves. The rain was freezing and fell about them, although the Magelord remained dry. The storm clouds rumbled and in the distance, smoke rose from a group of trees that had suffered in the storm. Joset was soaked and shivering, yet powerless to resist. As they entered the cave, he felt the darkness pressing upon him and the cold air made him shiver. The Lord of Reldfield saw the two men who bowed to Archos, lit by glowglobes and leaning on rather nasty looking swords. He trembled, his mind providing an assortment of unpleasant scenarios.

The Magelord forced him into a narrow cavern at the back and snapping his fingers, a glowglobe flickered into life. Behind Joset was a vast crevasse that fell deep into the rock. The ceiling of the cave was low and armed with sharp rocks and slimy with water. Archos threw him just short of the edge of the crevasse. He motioned to a bucket and a blanket.

"The guard will feed you, well, assuming he remembers. The glowglobe will last a while. You may have light to survey your prison. Do not try to bribe the guard, for he is my man. You could not possibly offer him anything he could use. He will not betray me, for he knows what would become of him if that were so. He is not the conversationalist, as he lost his tongue in a street fight. You will not escape, for I will find out and then I assure you, your death will be a good deal worse than this."

Joset looked around in horror. "You would leave me to rot here, like a criminal?"

Archos shrugged. "Well, it is similar to the cell in which I found Dii, although she had been tortured and raped also. She had not the luxury of a little movement, for she was shackled with Baneshackles and carries the scars still. You will experience a little of her torment, her fear. She was a criminal simply because she was a mage and an elf, and had dared to use magic against those who tried to torment and force themselves upon her and to use her magic to help and heal."

With that, he turned and left. As he got to the entrance, he dragged the staff along the ceiling and cried, "I am Archos, Lord of the Elements, and this night the stone obeys my will. This cavern will be sealed, not completely, but enough that the man yonder may be entrapped. I call upon the rock to become a prison, unable to be broken."

With a terrifying crack, the rock split and began to tumble down, sealing all but a small gap in the floor just after Archos stepped though into the chamber beyond where the two men waited. Addressing the elven guard, he said, "Feed him once a day if he behaves, if he is quiet. If he tries to threaten or bribe, withhold his food for a day. I do not want him to die…at least not for a while. If he, somehow, manages to escape, you will take his place."

The mute guard made a sign in acknowledgement and then another complex sign. "He was instrumental in destroying an elven village; he took for his pleasure slaves from the village; defiled and murdered two young elven maidens; abused the woman I love; and he stole from elves," Archos told the gaoler.

The elf pulled a face and made another sign angrily. "Yes, I know. Here is some money to buy what you need, Renell. Ealdet will help you. Furnish the cavern yonder and you should be comfortable enough. If you need more money or supplies, apply to Ealdet, he will supply you. You know one another well enough. The Thiefmaster trusts you, and I trust his judgement, Renell. You may keep your cats here – there is hunting enough in the trees and lands for them."

Renell bowed and went to look in the small cavern that he was to inhabit. It, was he concluded, better than the tiny shack he had been forced to live in during his old life. There was a tavern not so far away and besides he was not a man for much company, besides his felines. It would do, and it would please the Thiefmaster, a man whom Renell revered.

Archos handed Ealdet the ring. "Here is the Seal Ring of the House. Lord Tremayne is indisposed after the shock of learning of the untimely death of his son and heir. Apparently the villages all hate him and the servants are afraid of him, so I would hope that will make transition to your Stewardship easier. Lord Tremayne has managed to appoint you Steward to act in his name. If needed, I can arrange forged papers confirming this."

Ealdet bowed and asked, "What are your requests regarding the lands, my lord? The house yonder and such?"

"The house is yours if you want it. Simply manage the lands fairly, do not get greedy, and I will receive my dues in good time. I think, perhaps, ten percent; ten for the House of Thieves, the rest to manage the lands and for bribes to keep the Witch-Hunters away. As much as I despise them, they are easily bribed. You will make more than enough, if the lands hereabouts are managed correctly, to be comfortable. What you choose to do with the contents of the house is yours, however any elven items you do not want, send to me or the Enclave. There is, apparently, a manservant loyal to him, so you may need to deal with that.

"I trust you will do your duty. You have talent and you are clever, so it should not be too much of a challenge for you to run these lands effectively. I know you have experience of managing a household and estate. See that Renell has what he needs and keep him stocked with beer. Now, it has been a long ride here and a long evening, and I find myself in need of rest. I will stay in Reldfield this night and leave at dawn. You may contact me via the House of Thieves if needed. If it's urgent send a rider to the waypoint at Eleiry."

He tossed a small bag of coin to the new Steward of Reldfield, continuing with, "I have the unpleasant task of breaking the heart of a good woman when the body of her sister arrives, and a charming mistress who requires my attention."

The man bowed again. "As you wish, my lord. I will see these lands prosper."

Archos smiled and, very tired, returned to the village, seeking refuge in the tavern as the storm slowly abated. Famished he polished off two plates of food, and most of a bottle of wine. As he supped in his room, he removed the amber ring from his pocket. Turning it over, he examined it and felt the powerful tingle of magic. The ring was old, an ancient amber woven in a strange eternal knot, carved and ornate. Silver had been cast into the stone, a strange twisting symbol he did not recognise. It was an item of some value, that he knew and surely magical. Rare, illegal and elven. What had the Lord of Reldfield to do with such a ring?

As he turned it over, he saw something carved on the underside: ancient High Elvish words, weaving across the amber. He could, of course, read Elvish, but this was old and he would need to consult his library. For now, he put it in his pocket and settled to sleep before his long ride home. He hoped he would not be called upon to use his magic before arriving in Tremellic, for the Archmage felt the drain, and longed for his own bed and the arms of the woman he adored.

CHAPTER 24

The sad funeral procession arrived in Tremellic Valley some days later. Archos had caught up and rode at the head of the procession, progress was slow but unhindered. His note had arrived before them and he found the Steward waiting.

"My lord, I am pleased you have returned. I had hoped that the news would be good regarding the young elf, but I see, alas, it is not. Miss Ozena returned some days ago with the four new elves, but she may tell you herself of that, and the bandit attack on the way back. As you see, new dwellings are swiftly being built, but perhaps we may discuss this on another day. What sort of man could do this? The ruined elven village was tragic enough, but to have to bring these poor children home in a box, that truly is a tragedy."

Archos surveyed the scene briefly and nodded, his face grim. "Indeed, it pains me every day that we were too late. The lady Malana will find her rest in the gardens of the manor, where Dii may be close to her. The elves perhaps may lay with their kin and ancestors. I have yet to break the news to Ozena. Perhaps we may have a ceremony after dawn tomorrow?"

Slowly, the wagon and its burden rolled its way to the manor and Ozena, watching from the windows, saw Archos and Olek ahead. She bounded outside and then her eyes saw the wagon and the three covered boxes. The young hunter stopped in her tracks as Olek hastily dismounted. Shaking her head, she looked around, disbelieving, to see if Amena was somewhere behind them. Archos and Dii also dismounted and exchanged a look when they saw the realisation in Ozena's face; the shock, disbelief, and an almost heart-breaking grief. She ran towards them, the tears stinging her eyes so that she could barely see and she stumbled. Olek moved fast and took her into his arms. "No, no, no. Please, tell me no!" She sobbed, shaking in his arms.

Olek kissed her with a soft tender kiss and his own amber eyes stung as he whispered, "I am so very sorry. We were too late. I wish so much it was different. She is home now, and at peace."

Archos softly touched her arm. "I am sorry. I had truly hoped we would find her alive. I wish I could have done more. Let us take her inside, so you may sit with her awhile. Say goodbye. I know it is little consolation now, but the man who did these things will never again hurt anyone."

As she turned her tear-filled green eyes to him, even the Magelord felt his eyes prick with sadness as he watched her heart break. As his hand lay on her arm, he let a comfort spell ease her. It could not stop the grief, but would calm a little of the pain. He felt her tremble beneath his hand. Patting her arm, he softly said, "Anything I can do to ease your burden and your grief, I will do for you."

She whispered, heart breaking with grief and anger, "I hope he suffered! To kill a child, like that, I hope he felt some of the fear my sister felt."

Archos looked at her, seeing the steel in the normally gentle green eyes. In her head, she heard him say, "Oh, yes. Do not doubt that she was avenged and those slavers who remain alive will fall."

As they stood outside, Old Thomas the gardener approached with a mass of rare flowers in his arms. He nodded to Archos respectfully, yet with the familiarity of a well-established and well-liked servant. Turning to Ozena and Dii, he said with sadness, "I am sorry for your losses, my lady and Miss Ozena. These flowers are from the glass houses, rare Elvish blooms, and ones from the valley and plains, to lie on the caskets; a gift for them to take to the Other World." With reverence, he laid the flowers upon the wagon and then spoke in low tones to Archos, who had moved toward him at his sign.

Bowing his head, he addressed the two elven women once more. "Miss Ozena, my lady, would you permit me to make an offer to you? There is a rose garden yonder, beyond the maze. There are many beautiful flowers, and in the summer, butterflies fill the air with their colour. Even in winter there are roses on the trellises and a soft fragrance hangs in the air. My lord has agreed if you would take the offer, for the ladies you have lost to lie there. You may visit them and be close. They will grow as roses and the earth will embrace them in her arms. It is not much, I know, but the gardens are fine and a fitting tomb for them."

Dii slid her arm into Archos' and nodded mutely, the tears in her eyes threatening to overflow. Ozena hesitated and quietly said, "It is not an elven place. She would be alone there. Yet she loved flowers and plants, I...I could sit there in the summer... I do not know. I would like to think on it, get guidance from the Elder. It may not be correct."

Old Thomas nodded. "As you wish, Miss Ozena. I would not wish to offend."

Ozena bit back tears, both of grief and gratitude. "You do not offend, not at all. It is so kind of you, but I must seek guidance for her to be buried apart from elves."

Archos said, "I will speak to him if you wish, but she will never be alone."

Ozena nodded, overcome by her feelings. As the caskets and flowers were taken to lie in the manor, Dii took her hand and they walked slowly, sisters in grief. As the caskets were laid out, Archos went and fetched brandy while Olek simply stood and held Ozena. Comforting, listening to her sobs, his arms circling her and wishing he knew the words that would take the pain from her.

* * *

Dii quickly appraised the housekeeper of what had happened and she wisely kept the boy Dai'Rohdin out of sight. Silently, she moved to prepare a room for Emmae until such accommodation could be found in the village the next day. Emmae tried to stay out of the way. She had survived, yet two elven children and the mage that defended them lay in coffins. When she saw the grief Ozena felt, she knew not what to say.

"Your friend, it is her sister that is lost? Yet I live and they are gone. I have no one, no family but an aunt who finds me a burden, yet I live and the mage-child had a sister who loved her and has such pain of grieving. I am ashamed I live and Amena does not. You have been so kind to me. My presence here surely causes her more pain," she said quietly to Dii.

Taking her hands and tenderly stroking a blond hair from her face, Dii replied, "My dear, you have no reason to be ashamed. It is a miracle you live, for the sadness would indeed be increased were it otherwise. Her grief is great, but she would not wish for you to not be here, or to have fallen also. Tomorrow, we will see what can be found for you in the village. Perhaps someone will need an apprentice. Did you not say your aunt kept a small shop? There are traders yonder and with more mouths to feed, they may be looking for assistance. I think I heard Marrissa tell me the widow Helena the baker needs someone."

Emmae gripped her hand. "Miss Dii, I will do what you ask, but can I not stay here?"

Dii smiled. "You would be better in the village, unless the housekeeper could find a use for you. There are more people there and Lord Archos likes his privacy. There are others your age and you will be close enough to visit.

"No one will hurt you or be unkind. I promise you will be safe, you will find a place."

* * *

Ozena touched the coffin that held her sister and whispered to Olek, who stood with his arms around her. Trying to comfort her, he held close. "Did she suffer, her and the others?"

"Do not ask such questions. Suffice it to say she was, and will be, avenged. She lies at peace now, back where she belongs."

"She would have been so frightened. She is, was, such a shy child. The others? What of the others?"

Olek sighed. "The woman was…Dii's foster mother. The other was a child from the village. Roshi."

The grieving elf stared at him. "Dii's foster mother? She is grieving too, oh gods, yet still she comforted me in my own grief. It hurts. It hurts so much, Olek."

Kissing her, he whispered, "Yes. The pain will ease, not yet but it will. Cry, let out your feelings. I am here. You are not alone. You will never be alone. Tonight, I will sit up with you. I do not know the correct elven rituals, but I will be here, for both of you."

* * *

Just after dawn the next day, after a night spent watching the dead, the caskets containing the elven children were settled on a cloth of leaf green silk and decked with flowers. Ozena had decided that Amena should be buried with elves. Her mother and father lay in the Garden of Souls, and although the offer was very kind, she felt that it would not be correct for her to lie with strangers. The Elder had advised Archos that he believed elves should lie with elves. Tradition should be maintained, especially in the light of the ruined village.

Slowly, the wagon made its way to the town square. The villagers, both Elfkind and Mankind, watched in sadness as it passed by. Archos led with his staff across his back, while Olek rode with Ozena, his arms protectively around her waist, and Dii beside him, leading a spare horse.

Archos announced as the procession halted, "This day we go to send to the Other World these elven children. This day we will walk the route to the Garden of Souls in the fallen village of Szendro. We go as friends of the elves and as those who care for what has happened here; to mourn with the elves for the lost children and to offer support. We go to mourn those not yet found and those who lie beneath the earth already, and to remember what has been done that we may ensure it is never repeated in these lands. The slavers blight Erana with their foul trade and the Order of Witch-Hunters do nothing to stop the trade in flesh, the murder and the sorrow. At their door too I place the deaths of these people. For inaction is as great a crime."

Elder Loresh emerged with a couple of the women and Archos helped him onto the spare horse. "Elder, will you lead us and the dead to the Garden of Souls?"

The Elder nodded solemnly and moved off slowly. Behind the cortege walked Archos and his household, the rescued elves and a good number of the village. The track to Szendro had been kept clear and as they approached the Garden of Souls, the villagers stood back in respect, not familiar with elven customs. A number of women wept, thinking if things had been different that it could have been their own daughters. Slavers were not averse to taking human cargo and the citizens of Tremellic Valley were not fools, they knew the risks their lord took, and the dangers which lurked beyond their haven. Ozena stood watching, her hand clasped in Olek's. Sad but strong, her tears having been shed, she now stood with the grief within her raw but silent.

A number of the village men lifted down the small caskets and as they were lowered into the earth beneath the trees, the Elder spoke in Elvish. "Guardians of the gates to Other World, allow these children entrance. They are Elfkind and taken from us too soon, guide their journey and give them peace. Let us remember them as we remember all elves, as children of the forest, to lie with their kin and the spirit of Elfkind. We return them to the forest, to the earth and trees, to the sky, the rain and the soil."

As the correct gifts for the Guardians were added and flowers laid in the graves, they were slowly covered. The Elder turned to the assembly and spoke in the Common tongue, "I see here before me friends, kin and those who have risked much for us; elves and humans standing together to see these children given to the earth; these humans who have shown us kindness, sympathy and hospitality, even though this was not their misfortune. The Lord Archos and his household who have returned to us both those alive here and those that lay yonder, at some risk. On this sad day, it comforts me to see such friends before us. I wish it were so throughout this land but, alas, our land is shackled by lies and hatred. Do we not all walk beneath the same sun? Do we not all love in the same way? Do we not all grieve for those we lose? Do we not all bleed when we are wounded? The Order of Witch-Hunters says it is not so. They say we are different, elves are nothing more than property, to be used and discarded. They say elves bring the Plague and corrupt the lands and the slavers who walk in their shadow poison it with their filthy trade. The trade of flesh. The trade of people."

Archos smiled sadly and bowed, knowing what Loresh said was true. Once the elven burials were done, they returned to the manor to lay within the garden the body of Malana. A grave had been dug at the edge of a wall, roses climbed over the stone and the rose bushes had carefully been uprooted. Slowly, the box was laid within and the soft scent of roses filled the air. Malana would lie beneath rare and beautiful flowers, and have the company of bees and butterflies. Ozena took Dii's hand. "I am so sorry for your loss. I have been wrapped in my own grief and you have been so kind. I apologise."

"And I am sorry for yours. Your loss is greater, as she was a child, and kin to you. I have mourned on the journey back. Lord Archos tells me the man who did these things has been punished and those we loved avenged. I will be here for you if you want to cry or yell, and together we will be stronger. Malana was a kind woman, a mage, and as much a slave as I, although perhaps she did not know it. I will not forget her.

* * *

Archos sat in the parlour with Olek, Simon and the Thiefmaster Darius, and they shared fine brandy. The women had gone to bed and the menfolk were talking about business. Simon began his account, savouring the fire of the brandy.

"Much has been salvaged from Szendro, my lord. Foodstuffs - mainly smoked meat, cheese and preserved fruits and wine, wood, trade items, some beasts, such as those small goats the elves favour, a few tame deer, some fowls and a couple of dogs and cats. Oh and a few small weapons concealed in one of the houses. As can be expected, the women are wary, especially around the menfolk, but trust increases every day. The cabins are coming along and hopefully, the elves can be settled amongst their own belongings soon. It would seem we have gained some skilled new citizens, including a weaver, a candle maker and cheesemaker. All trades which can boost our own citizens and bring in a bit of wealth. The old man is a lore-keeper – but he writes well enough and has offered to school the children in the ways of the forest. Although his health will never be strong.

"That lad you returned from the city, Istvan, is a clever lad. Good with numbers and letters, good with business, and trustworthy. He is thoughtful and not prone to rash decisions. Already he is devoted to you, my lord. He speaks of your kindness to him and his woman. He will certainly be of use to us.

"There were three small children rescued by Olek. It seems your housekeeper has taken quite a shine to one lad, the other two are brothers and a little older. I believe the smith will take one for apprentice, as he has only daughters, and the other will live nearby and assist with the market stalls. They are young enough to pick up a trade. Maurice, the carter always needs the help, what with his less than robust health. They will find a place soon enough. The woman Gis'Ellah, she is the woman who kept the goats, she has promised to sell the cheeses and to teach the craft to the others. She is a fine woman and seems to have been appointed as spokeswoman for the elven women. A handsome woman, and not grieving, she cares much for her elven sisters; a handsome, intelligent woman with spirit," Simon said thoughtfully.

"It would seem you are taken with the maker of cheeses, Simon. There will be jealous human women in the village if you are not careful," Olek teased.

"Indeed, I return home to find a small elven boy hiding behind the skirts of my housekeeper. It seems she is rather fond of him, and both she and Old Thomas seem to think he will be of use around the house and gardens. I cannot turn away an elf orphan when I expect the village to do their share. Besides, now we have the ladies to think of and perhaps as Marrissa says, she needs further help. I do not think anything would separate Marrissa from that small boy. Every time he calls her grandmother,

her eyes mist over. Now, Darius, what was it I heard of a bandit attack?" Archos said, rather intrigued.

"Well, my lord," Darius replied, "we were perhaps a day out of the city and your scout, Ozena, who it seems has better eyes than I, spotted something across the road long before I saw it. A wagon that was overturned, crates scattered about, a typical roadblock trap. There were bandits in the trees and undergrowth. Seeing the carriage of what they assumed to be a rich fellow, they began to threaten and menace."

Olek laughed. "That would have been somewhat of a shock when their prey turned out to be the Thiefmaster and an Elvish hunter adept."

Darius grinned. "Aye, it was not what they were expecting at all. Your Ozena is quite the bow mistress; she had dispatched two before the carriage wheels stopped rolling. She is fast and was not afraid to defend those inside. She would make an excellent thief. The bandits-- well, the ones that survived--were persuaded easily enough to reveal their leader and to take themselves elsewhere. I will deal with the leader later. I shall return to the city in the morning. We will maintain the lookout for any further elves and check the whereabouts of the remaining slavers."

After Simon and Darius had left, Archos retired to the library, intending to answer one or two questions that required his attention and Olek headed to his bedchamber. Ozena lay in his bed, wearing a shirt of his and wrapped tight in a blanket. Slipping in next to her, Olek pulled her close, gently snuggling her hair and neck. Softly, he kissed the back of her neck. "Lie here, safe in my arms. I will take care of you, my pretty forest nymph; my poor grieving girl."

Ozena began to cry, tears of grief, tears of despair. Olek held her, whispering comfort and letting her cry until she had no more tears. "You could not have done anything more than you did, none of us could, but we can see her death is not unpunished. She lies close, and at least she is found and returned to us.

"You are not alone. I am here, and you have Dii and Lord Archos. You are safe here and have people who care for you. You are strong and will come through this sadness. Lay safe here with me, sleep in my arms." Together they lay quietly in the darkness, both lost in their own thoughts.

CHAPTER 25

After Amena had returned in such a tragic way, Ozena had been contemplating a great many things. Among which was how easy it had been for the slavers to assault her village and how unprepared they had been. She was, of course, happy that a number of her elven companions had been rescued, but a good number had not and those returned had lost kin, neighbours, friends and their sense of identity. Although she was devastated over Amena's death, part of her was relived the poor girl had not survived to live with what had been done to her. Such a sensitive, shy child would not have been able to ever come to terms with what had occurred.

She sat with Olek in the hills beyond the manor where they had spent the morning hunting. Sitting under a tree, they were now sharing a basket of food when she announced, "I want you to train me, to be like you, move like you...kill like you. I have seen how you move, silently like a cat, calling the shadows to you. I hesitated when we found that slaver in the forest. I wish to be able to do what is necessary and not be afraid. The village, we were so unprepared and complacent. Life in the Shimmering Forest is sheltered and relatively safe, apart from the odd bear or wolf, or so I thought. That man who tried to attack me would have succeeded had you not appeared. I never want to be that afraid or unprepared again. Please teach me what you know, Olek."

Olek looked at her for a while seeing the determination, then rising to his feet, he back-flipped over her to land behind her, sword drawn before she even had a chance to register that he had moved. "You are sure of this? To kill without mercy, to steal and bribe, to live beyond the law, to defend your family no matter what it takes to do so?"

"Yes... Yes. I will never be unprepared again. If I have learned anything from Amena's death and what has occurred, it is that we must protect each other and ourselves. This world is dark. Thus to survive in that darkness, one must be willing to do many things, to kill to protect. Elves have no law to protect them, so we must make our own."

Sheathing his sword, Olek kissed her. "I will happily teach you what I know. You are good with a bow, in fact very good, and you are fast. You have good eyesight and can learn to track men as well as beasts. I think you need to learn to use a sword or dagger; a melee weapon of some sort. Sometimes there is simply not the time to load a bow, or the space to fire one. You will be a good sniper, but there are many things you need to learn and to unlearn. I am sorry every day that we were not able to save Amena, but if one cannot seek justice then revenge must suffice. In a dark world, learn to take that darkness and use it. I expect Lord Archos will readily agree. He appreciates talent and skill, and he knows you are a good scout."

Ozena looked slightly uncomfortable. "I never know how to behave around him. He is kind to me, but he is not my master. He is a human lord. I do not know what to do or say. The elven nobles are dead or hidden from the knowledge of elves and men alike. They are gone from us, along with much history, now only myth and tale from the times when elves were great and held mighty Citadels. If they exist now, we know not where. I do not know what he expects of me. I am afraid to make him angry or frustrated. I do not even know what to call him."

Olek laughed. "Well, his name is Archos, so that's a good start. As for what he expects, well, I think he expects you to be who you are, forest elf Ozena Lyn and a good scout and ranger. I doubt he expects submission. Respect, yes, but submission, no. You have his affection, why would you make him angry? Respect him and his house, tolerate his odd ways and moods, and most importantly do not share his secrets beyond those who already know them... That is what he expects. That and be all that you can be. Magic can be hard to understand and, well, he has lived a long time and doesn't much care for people beyond his house and his valley. He has seen and done many things which even I do not understand. Magic like his can make someone a little strange."

"I am sorry. I have never encountered such a man before. I did not mean to be disrespectful. He has done so much for me," she responded, looking down in shame.

Olek grinned and waggled his finger at her. "Aye, well, best you remember that!"

"You act, at times, well, not how I would expect a servant to act around his master. Yet you call him "my lord." I do not understand. Why?"

He looked at her, wondering slightly at the question, "Respect, affection, or habit perhaps; I have known him many years and in reality, I suppose I am no longer a servant. He is my family; my father, my brother, my friend and my master, all the family I have known for a long time. I serve him because I choose to. He saved my life so many years ago and my life belongs to him. Yet that choice is mine now, and freely given. That is the way things are; an arrangement that suits us both."

"But you are not free? What would he do if you told him you wanted to leave, have your own life?" Ozena asked, curious.

With a laugh, Olek replied, "Oh, Ozena, my sweet forest nymph, there are no free elves. The forest Elfkind hides what is left of their people in the wilds of the forest, yet still they fall prey to the slavers. Have you not seen enough to know this is so? No elf, forest elf or Enclave elf, is free to live where and how he or she pleases. We are adepts; if caught, at best you would be taken to the Enclave Prison, forced to work as a mercenary, or worse. As for leaving, I have no idea. It is never something I have considered. Why would I leave? I am a half-elf; I can never be truly free, at least not beyond these lands. A servant I am, it is true, and it is unlikely I would be allowed to be more, at least not officially. Here, I have wealth, I have influence and respect, and I have a great friend and mentor. My life is far easier and far more comfortable than a good deal of humans, and certainly most elves. You have seen the world beyond the Tremellic Valley."

Ozena looked down. "I am just a foolish elf who knows nothing of the world beyond the forest. I served the village and my kin, but they are gone."

Olek knelt close beside her and taking her face in the cup of his hand, he kissed her. "My dear Ozena, you are young and lived a sheltered life. Why should you know what this world is like? There is no shame to serve a man, when that man is a good man, a powerful man. If you were a human girl, the situation would be the same. He would not ask for your loyalty and service because you are an elf and he is human, but because that is what he asks from those he trusts. He may be powerful, but such men have powerful enemies. Even Archos cannot fight every Witch-Hunter. The Order is nasty. They would know to hit him where he would suffer: the people he cares about, this valley. He is still vulnerable to Banecrystal, as are all mages. Do you not understand the risks he took in bringing to Tremellic the elves from your village, to allow them to live as free citizens in his lands? He is a mage, therefore he is a Forbidden, he is powerful, and therefore he has those who are jealous of that power. He has interfered in politics, annoyed the Witch-Hunters and a good number of important men to save these elves. He risked his life to find Amena, for had the Order arrived in number, he was alone. He is fond of you. Service to such a man is not a burden, it is an honour."

Ozena melted in his embrace. "I am sorry. It is just not what I am used to. Lord Archos has been generous to me. Dii is very kind and like a sister to me. What use would he have of me?"

The half-elf smiled, kissing her hands. "There is always a use for those skilled in stealth and with a sharp eye, a wicked blade and a fast bow. You know a little herb lore, you can create poisons and potions, and you can climb and run. You are a scout, you can track and follow, and you speak Elvish better than I do, which has its uses. Certainly you know elven lore and history better. Learn to pick locks, to hide and walk in the shadow; learn to kill with a blade and to intimidate. Even the smallest can threaten with a sharp blade and a swift arm. You are good with the beasts, perhaps

Archos may buy you a hawk or a hunting dog. You have many skills that are of great use and you can learn. You will learn…by my side. I will seek out the other slavers soon enough and you can have your vengeance and your training; swift vengeance in the dark and the shadow."

He kissed her softly and continued, "The Thiefmaster was impressed by you. He told me of the encounter with the bandits, how you defended the carriage and the elves. You are an accomplished bow-woman and an excellent scout, Ozena. You would be an excellent sniper."

With that, he rolled her back onto the blanket and kissed her passionately. "I will teach you many things, Ozena," he breathed into her ear.

Nuzzling her neck, he began to pull at the ties of her blouse and unstrapping his sword, he cast it aside. "I want you, Ozena Lyn, right here, right now!" Olek whispered huskily.

She kissed him back, the light autumn breeze playing in the turning leaves above them. As he revealed her breasts to his hungry lips, she sighed and arched towards him. Her hands moved beneath his shirt, caressing his back and moaning as he suckled her. "Take me…free beneath the trees and sky."

Olek let his fingers run over her face, her skin was soft and carefully he kissed the lines of her tattoo. Taking her into his arms, he nuzzled into her neck and murmured, "You smell nice, very…edible." As he nibbled her collar bone, she sighed and ran her fingers across his back. Lying back with her in his arms, he sighed happily and gave her a long lingering kiss that sent little sparks down to her groin.

Ozena ran her hands down his chest, letting them play over the muscles, and softly kissed the tattoo.

She stroked the red scar on his belly, gently asking him, "How did you acquire such a scar? This one looks to be the result of a bad wound."

"Oh, you do not want to hear the story…it is nothing of note," he snapped, suddenly defensive.

"I am sorry, Olek… It is not my business," she said and turned away from him, hurt from the sudden snap, sensing the tension.

Olek snaked his arm about her waist and kissed her. "I am sorry. I should not have snapped. It is just that it is not a nice story."

"I would like to hear it. I know so little of you. I did not mean to upset you. It would take my mind from Amena to know you, hear about your life." Her fingers traced the scar and softly, persuasively, Ozena kissed him.

Sighing at the memory, he began, "I told you my mother was a whore in the Enclave, well, such is true. Life in such…establishments is not easy. Mother was, to all intents I suppose, a slave, certainly not free. Thus, of course, nor was I. A child of a whore slave is a slave. We did not reside in the actual place. There were a few small shacks close by that were rented by the women and that is where we lived. A small, cold, often leaking shack, ours was better than some but still terrible. There are many such dwellings in the Enclave. The brothel keeper was a ruthless human woman. She herself lived beyond the Enclave walls and employed a number of equally ruthless guards. Mother was often ill and unable to work. By that point, I was quite an accomplished pickpocket. Trust me when I say it's easy to pick through the belongings of a man when he is…otherwise occupied.

"Mother died, as I told you, in childbirth, leaving me alone in the world. Unbeknownst to me at the time, leaving a debt to the whorehouse. Although she did well enough and I supplemented our income, it is easy to fall into such traps. The brothel mistress was a greedy woman and thus she informed me, the day my mother died, that the debt fell to me. She had allowed mother to keep me, instead of the usual practice of children being sold. I had not been, at that point, forced to work in the whorehouse. However, this woman now informed me that to pay the debts, I must work. Not only women were used as whores and a good looking elven boy would cater for many tastes. I refused. I told her I would acquire what was owed by other means. She agreed I had a set time to pay, and after that time, I became at her mercy to do with as she pleased. She did not want a thief, for that was not her line of work. Even then I showed as an adept and could have been sent to the Enclave prison. It is not only mages who end there.

"For a while I managed to steal enough to placate her, but one night, after the… takings had been meagre, she announced the remaining debt was due and thus I found myself to be at the mercy of one of the many clients. I will not go into details, but suffice it to say once he started to beat me, I decided to be elsewhere very fast. In making my escape, I was forced to jump from a window and, in my haste as the glass broke, a shard sliced into me. As I landed in a ditch behind the building, I had enough presence of mind and strength to crawl into the safety of a dwelling."

"Fortunately, I was found by a friend of my mother's, not a whore but a woman who worked as a servant. I almost bled to death and if it had not been for Villicia, I would have. She paid for a healer, such as they were…herbalists, apothecaries, street surgeons. The woman cared for me until I was strong enough to leave. After that, I mainly lived in the human side of the city. There are places to hide, to conceal one's self beyond the Enclave. So I lived until Archos found me.

"The other scar, the one in my chest, was the result of carelessness. I was acquiring back a couple of Elvish items for the master. Items he knew to have been taken from Enclave elves. He tasked me to fetch them back. Unfortunately, the items were in the possession of a rich merchant. This man had taken the trinkets from some elves in his employ and then simply dispensed with the elves' services when he no longer needed them. He did not believe the elves should have items of value or sentiment and, liking the items for himself, he took them. I suppose he was not cruel in the fact that he did not mistreat them, but his indifference meant he took from them that which was dear to them.

"Archos found the elves employment elsewhere, in a house he knew they would be treated with some respect, and tasked me to fetch back their items. A small ring belonging to a dead sweetheart of one--the only item he retained of hers--and, I think, an old elven statue carved of ivory; an odd little thing, old or perhaps ancient. Anyway, I was acquiring back these items to be returned to their owners and I was discovered by the guard of this merchant. Apparently, he had suffered the attentions of thieves before and decided to employ an adept as a house guard. This fellow managed to spot me. I was not as adept at Shadowplay then as now, and to those others skilled in its use, it is not nearly as effective. I had not been as cautious as I might have been and this adept saw me. We fought, and though I bested him, it was a close victory and his skill with a dagger was formidable. I managed to get back to the townhouse before passing out and the housekeeper patched me up. The guard used a slow poison on his blade that made the wound slow to heal, but as I knew the recipe for the antidote and Valeria is a good nurse, it was not nearly as bad as it might have been."

Ozena smiled. "That at least is a nice story…that the elves had their belongings returned, that is. I…I am sorry for your other treatment. I did not wish to drag up unpleasant memories. What has happened in Szendro is terrible, but life within the village was never as cold and dark, or as dangerous, as the city…or life beyond. At least, that is what I used to think."

Olek kissed her and ran his fingers through her hair. "Aye. The city is not a pleasant place for many elves, or indeed, many humans. It did, however, teach me a great deal, and in our way, we can make a few lives better. Even Lord Archos does not have the wealth or power to openly support or change the lot of the Enclave Elves against the Witch-Hunters and the law. So we work, around and beneath the law, and help where we can. The mage underground is his and the House of Thieves. Maybe one day things will be better. It was not always bad there, the Enclave elves look after each other and there is much kindness there. Anyway, for me at least that life is far away, just memories. Now what can we think of to do to take my mind off such dark memories, I wonder?"

He grinned and kissed the hollow of her neck. His hands found her breasts and began to softly circle her nipples, rubbing and caressing until her breath quickened. "Hmm, now, thinking about your beautiful breasts and your soft skin, your arms around me, that is something worth thinking about; memories of you, those are things I treasure."

He unlaced her leathers and bodice swiftly, letting his hands caress and his eyes feast upon her. Olek kissed her with passion, trailing kisses down to her breasts. Exhaling warm breath, he licked a line around her nipple as she arched back. He bent down and kissed her belly then, sliding to the edge of the blanket, he began to ever so slowly kiss his way up her body; nibbling, kissing, licking, tasting her skin until her breath was ragged and she trembled with desire.

Slowly, he let his fingers run across her with one hand, the other unlacing his breeches. He kissed her, tongue exploring her mouth and his fingers caressing, stroking. Finding her wet and warm, his fingers entered her cleft, thumb circling her button until she began to wriggle and writhe. Quickly he entered her, and she gasped as he thrust fast and deep within her. Hitting the spot that made her moan loudly, she buried her face into his shoulder. Her arms around him, she moved with him faster and almost uncontrolled. Olek pulled her up to sit in his lap and as he worked her, they both felt the pleasure rising within them. Fast and intense was the feeling, and the climax built quickly then suddenly burst, leaving both breathless and trembling with its intensity.

Panting, Olek lay next to her and softly kissed her. "You are so desirable…such a sexy nymph. Here, together, we may be free."

Ozena grinned and snuggled close, beginning to shiver as the breeze blew across them. Olek pulled his cloak over them and lay with her in his arms, now warm and content. Dark thoughts and memories banished, at least for now.

CHAPTER 26

Dii's heart was filled with sorrow. Malana had been kind to her and most certainly had not deserved the violent death she had received. The woman had been the closest person to a mother Dii had and now she was gone. Dii had hoped to have seen Malana again, perhaps even asked Archos to bring her to Tremellic, and regretted not having done so before. She had been too afraid, especially after the meeting with Ulric, that Joset would discover where she hid, and send his men, or worse the Order into the Tremellic Valley.

The young mage felt guilty, if she had not left the house of Tremayne those children, and her foster mother might yet live. Dii had seen the grief in Ozena's eyes and had felt some of her sorrow. At least Ozena had been spared viewing Amena the way she had been found and had not known what she had suffered. Archos had held Dii close as she had cried, and been even more attentive and kind than usual. Although he tried to tell her it was not her fault Dii felt responsible, at least in part. Her life, she felt, was not worth that of two elven children and Malana, not to mention any other victims of the terrible slaver-lord.

Archos was worried – although she had survived her own terrible ordeal Dii was still fragile, especially emotionally. He knew she had a strength within but as yet did not have the confidence in it. He stayed close, offering comfort and advice, reading and studying. They both worked hard focussing on the future and what could be done for the new Tremellic elves and those unfortunates in the Enclave. Much time was spent learning new spells, producing potions and salves to take to the Enclave and House of Thieves. Occupying her mind meant Dii could not dwell on other matters, and she felt useful. Yet when she was alone, or thought she was alone the tears misted those dark, midnight blue eyes.

The Magelord had been examining and contemplating the amber ring he had taken from Joset Tremayne. What had he said? 'Take it – it belongs to her'. Taking Dii's hand, he placed the ring into it and as he did so, it began to glow with a soft golden light that brightened until they were both bathed in it, then suddenly it faded back to a soft glow. Archos looked at it with surprise. He knew it was magical and ancient, but he had not expected such a reaction. Wrapping her fingers over it, he said to her, "I believe this belongs to you. That bastard Tremayne told me he had taken it from you."

Dii was trembling, not sure what to make of the Power she had just felt. "Mine? I…do not understand. Joset used to taunt me with a ring. He told me it was Elvish. He used to say it was all that was left of my elven kin, but he used to say many unkind things to me. I am not sure of the truth of it."

Archos caressed her face. "Flower, did you not see how it reacted? It is an ancient Elvish item. It is yours. At least, it would seem that the ring certainly thinks so. Joset took it from you when you were taken from your mother; a pretty and valuable elven artefact, the last link to your family, I would suppose. What better way to remove your Elfishness? It is yours, Dii, and was it not so, the ring has chosen you."

For a moment, he paused, wondering whether to tell her what he suspected, then decided it would only bring her more pain. He slid the ring onto a chain of silver and hung it about her neck, for her fingers were slim and he was afraid it would fall from her hand. Dii closed her hand over it and felt it tingle.

"It is a pretty Elvish item, for a pretty elf. Now I wish to show you something else, a little ride away."

Dii looked at him, still wondering about the ring. "Where are we going?"

Sweeping Dii into his arms, he spun her around and kissed her soundly. "That would spoil the surprise! Fetch your cloak. It is not far, but we may be gone a while."

The night was dark, but the moon shone and stars filled the sky as they rode to the cave. Getting close, he lifted her off the horse and let Storm wander. Archos took her hand and whispered, "Look at the sky, my love. The stars shine their light upon you this night. Now I would like to show you something…a place I keep for magic, the magic I need that I cannot use in the manor; a cave of crystals that shine like the stars, a place of Power. Now, come with me."

Archos removed the bag he had brought and led her through the cave. The crystals shone and glittered, and both could feel the Power. He heard her gasp as the Power ran through her, heady and exhilarating. Together they entered the central cave and she saw around them soft rugs, furs and cushions. There were a couple of chests in the corner. Gently, he put the bag down and pushed aside the rugs to reveal the Circle. Archos led her to the centre of the Circle and kissed her deeply as the Power washed over them both. He ran his hands over her softly, taking in the curves of her body; the dress she wore was long and flowing, and the tight bodice accentuated her curves. Holding her close, he breathed in her scent and slowly unwound her hair from its braid, letting it fall around her. As she stood, eyes wide and glittering in the ethereal light Archos knew he had never seen such a sight, such a beautiful woman, or one with such potential. So fragile, yet so strong; so gentle, yet so full of Power and such a hunger to learn.

"Dii'Athella, light of my life, I would prove to you that you are not just a pretty toy to grace my arm and warm my bed. You make me feel young and so very alive… I would share with you all I am, all I have, for all time. I would bind myself to you this night, if you would have me. I will be your servant, your worshipper and your teacher. Two as one, unbreakable. Two as one, magic forged."

He stroked her hair as the tears welled in her eyes and she trembled with emotion. Dii laid her head on his chest and nodded, unable to speak. As she trembled, a light began to sparkle around her like stars, and colours began to dance around them both, spinning and weaving.

Archos raised his hands until the fires of the Circle glowed with a deep crimson fire and, taking her hand, he said, "In this place of magic, before the spirits, before the gods, I pledge to this woman everything I am."

He saw the love in her eyes and felt the Power of her, of them both, pulsing around them. He bowed to her and took her hand, peeling from her the soft glove she wore and slowly drawing the kris across it, scoring the flesh and dropping a few crimson drops to the floor. He placed the knife in her hand and whispered softly, "Now you, my love…my light….my soul." Slowly she took the knife and scored the hand he held out to her. Slowly, the blood dripped on to the Circle as the lights and fire spun around them. He kissed her bleeding palm and then took her hand to his own. As their blood mixed, he said softly, "As blood falls this night upon this magical Circle, let the spirits see this ritual bind us, as blood is shared and blood is shed, let us become one. As she is mine, I am hers. Two as one, magic forged."

Dii clasped his hand and replied, looking deep into those silver-grey eyes, "As blood falls this night, I pledge to this man all that I am. Let the spirits see this ritual, as blood is shed and blood is shared, and let us become one. As he is mine, I am his. Two as one, magic forged."

Pulling her close, he murmured his love into her ear as he took in the scent of her. His pulse raced as her magic and the warmth of her in the cold cave enveloped him. "Now we are bound as one, you are my life, my soul. I swear this to you, in this place, I will never leave you. Where ever you are shall I be, where ever you go shall I follow."

The Power pulsed around them and through them; it was almost painful, yet filled them with such intense feelings; desire, love and the magic around them. Archos whirled her around and slowly began to unlace the ribbons of her dress, kissing her, running his fingers through her hair, taking his time. "You are mine, my love, and I am yours. Here in this place of magic, let us seal our love with our bodies as well as our blood."

Archos ran his fingers down her spine and nibbled her neck, nipping her soft skin. He slipped his hands under the soft fabric of her dress and freed her breasts. Behind her, as he stood close, she felt his desire for her and leaned back into him as beneath her soft gown his hands explored, making her sigh.

As he caressed her, he murmured into her ear, still nipping and nibbling. The Circle around them flared as he slipped off her dress and swept her into his arms, carrying her to a soft fur. Kneeling next to Dii, the Archmage kissed her belly, her breasts, her thighs, in slow sensual kisses; full of desire, full of love. As he began to peel from her the soft glove she still wore, she whispered, "No, leave it." With that, she slowly let her gloved fingers run down his chest beneath his robe. Swirling, circling with velvet, soft and warm. It sent shivers across him and he pulled her into a hungry kiss.

He reached out to stroke and caress her breasts, and she told him cheekily, "No. You may not touch…until I say."

Dii smiled wickedly, eyes shining with mischief. Pushing him gently onto his back, she wriggled to hover above him; allowing him to look his fill of her naked body, the strange swirling tattoo stark and bright against her pale skin. Archos again thought this woman was the most beautiful creature he had ever seen; sensual and quite astonishingly desirable. Even with the faint scars, now barely visible, she looked perfect and in the light of the crystals, she almost glowed. Dii moved his hands behind his head, then pulled his robe apart and gently sat on his chest; letting him see her, watching him watching her.

He laughed, settling himself on a pillow and feeling her warmth on him. "Well then…it would seem I am at your whim."

Kissing him again, she pulled his lip into her mouth then slid down and bit his neck. Slowly, she slithered down him and with her ungloved hand, she scored a line across his chest with her nails. The gloved hand rubbed her nipple, flicked, and squeezed until it became hard and pointed. He watched her, eyes never leaving her as his chest fell and rose more quickly with desire. Dii could feel his heart racing beneath her and she gave him another wicked smile. Leaning to his ear, she breathed, "You desire me, you want me…yet you must wait… Not yet, my love. You may not move… not yet."

Archos sighed with pleasure, resisting the urge to take her there and then. Resisting the urge to move as he felt the magic around him and the pleasure and desire in him build.

Dii crackled magic over him, and in the Circle, it rippled over them both, pulsing and sparking. Little shocks of desire that made Dii shiver and moan. As he watched her, she slithered down his chest, nipping and teasing him, down lower until with her gloved hand she slowly unlaced his breeches. The velvet glove was soft and tantalising on his firm manhood, and the other hand scratched and scored with nails, the opposite sensations making him squirm. Slowly she licked and nibbled him, pulling the skin into her mouth. Her eyes never left his as he watched her. Her tongue was warm and wet, and he moaned as her lips circled him, her hand rising and falling expertly.

Archos groaned and managed to resist reaching for her, although it took him a great deal of willpower, heightened his need for her. Moving her ungloved hand to her own cleft, she stroked herself as he watched, sighing and moaning as she did so. Fingers wet with her own juices, she licked the end of her fingers before swirling them around her nipples, and then across his chest. Back she moved to pleasure herself as she sat on his chest, and he watched her, moaning with desire. The gloved hand still stroking him grew faster and firmer as she began to writhe, pleasuring herself before him. Feeling him close to the edge, Dii paused and pressed with her thumb, halting his climax and denying him release. As his eyes rolled back, he moved beneath her, the moan an almost primal rumble in his throat. Removing her hand from him, she began to flick at her nipple, panting and writhing as she pinched and squeezed.

He watched her. The more he tried to resist moving, the more he desired her, and the more he knew that she knew it. Again excruciatingly slowly, she began to stroke and squeeze his manhood until his eyes closed and he breathed heavily, listening to her cries as she stroked herself to climax. Suddenly she stopped her attentions on his member and began to kiss and nip his chest, wriggling and squirming on him. Her body was warm on his and the magic crackled over her, almost bringing him to the edge. Teasing, denying him, and making him yearn for her more than he had ever yearned for anything as she whispered her love into his ear.

Taking the end of his manhood to the edge of her lips, she flicked her tongue across the end, then took him deep into her mouth, tasting him as the muscles in his arms and chest tightened with the sheer willpower of staying still. As he continued to moan beneath her, she chuckled; the sensations teasing and tormenting him. He tried to reach for her.

"No… You must not touch, naughty Archos!" Dii teased, pulling away from him for a moment. For punishment, she scratched a red line across his chest, the rune tattoo glowing as her Power crossed it. She looped her tongue around the ring in his nipple, tugging and licking until he groaned from the pleasure and pain.

"Gods, woman… have you no mercy on a man?" he managed. His voice a hoarse croak and his hands clenched behind him, thrust into the heart of the cushion behind his head. "Gods, you'll be the death of me, but I'll die a happy man." Tilting his head back the Magelord moaned beneath her touch.

Slowly, she slithered back to his groin and returned to her former occupation, knowing it sent him close to the edge. Flicking her tongue down his length, she chuckled as he squirmed. She took him into her mouth once more, slowly pumping and sucking enough to make him moan harder, almost bringing him to a peak before she stopped, and Archos made a low sound, a primal sound of need. Pulling away, she slowly slid up to his ear. "Now you may touch… I am yours…"

He growled and rolled her onto her back, roughly holding her down. "You are a wicked temptress, my exquisite flower. You drive me to the edge then deny me… Now how shall I get my revenge on you, wicked girl?"

Reaching for a soft rope from the bag and sitting on her legs, Archos tied her hands together, not tightly but enough to bind, and he chuckled. She moaned and tried to reach for a kiss. Archos let her lips touch his before he pulled away and tied her bound wrists to a rock.

He pulled the bag he had brought close to him and removed a scarf and tied it over her eyes. "Now you are at my mercy, my delightful and wicked girl. You will beg me to let you come… You will beg me to take you again and again. Two can play this game."

Dii grinned, anticipating pleasures and tried to reach up for a kiss. "Oh no, do not think I will allow you to move, my little tease," he said, pushing her down with a laugh.

Archos slowly and tantalisingly began to kiss her. He nipped and bit and licked until the flush built and then as he sucked her nipples hard, he slid his fingers into her. Beginning to rub and flick and stroke until she gasped. Dii was warm and wet, aroused and slick. Suddenly Archos stopped and moved away from her. In her darkness, she felt a sharp pain like a needle as he dragged it across her. Not deep but scratching, and little pinpricks of pain that with the magic and the desire she felt made her squirm. In the darkness and bound, she was all but helpless, yet filled with such intense desire. The whole scene triggered her pleasure-pain response and she moaned for him. It was a strange erotic pain as it scored her. As it left tiny little beads of blood, he slowly licked them from her, sweet and warm and she wriggled and pulled against her bonds. Being unable to see, her other senses were heightened and his touches on her were intense, almost overwhelming.

She felt a burning pain as he pierced her nipple and then sealed it with a silver hoop set with a sapphire, silver and blue against the painted, tattooed skin. He kissed the nipple gently, then with his lips around it, he tugged with his tongue, spearing lust and need down her. As the blood trickled down, he followed the line with his tongue. Lower and lower he went, until he feasted on her. Flicking, licking, tasting, he breathed into her quim; hot breath teasing. Slowly, Archos tantalised her with a rhythm that was intended for her to need and him to savour her taste, her reactions, a tease until she almost screamed. Dii writhed and squirmed and moaned under his touch and his tongue, until close to the edge as she was, he pulled away and slithered up to her ear.

"Have you something to say, my love?" he growled in a husky voice. Nipping and sucking the skin on her neck before his hot mouth moved back to flick his tongue across her nipple.

As he did so, he rippled a spark over her, hot, almost painful, but somehow deeply erotic and she breathed, "By the gods…I beg you! Archos, I am yours…take me…"

Archos laughed and slid away from her, loosening the bonds but not releasing. Moving Dii so she was on all fours, still lightly bound and blindfolded, Archos knelt behind her and slapped her behind, a sharp slap which left a red mark. Again he slapped her bum as slowly he entered her warmth, burying himself within her. Deep he plunged with a groan and began to thrust hard as he drilled her. One hand twisting in her hair and the other slapping her, snaking around, flicking her pip and scratching and stroking her thighs. Harder he plunged into his breathless, moaning lover until he felt the climax threaten to burst from her.

As she knelt, bound lightly and in darkness, the soft fur underneath her and almost bursting and trembling with desire, she felt the Power around her. The pain and the pleasure from his slaps and hard plunges made her moan and cry in ecstasy. Like a wave, the climax took her and she cried and screamed and writhed as it built and then washed over every part of her. A wave of Power burst from her and enveloped them both as she came again as he continued to pump hard, his hands now clutching her hips, pulling her back into his rhythm.

The Circle flared a deep crimson and the light and sparks crackled in the cave, the light reflected from a thousand crystals. Feeling his own climax close, she pulsed and tightened around him as she peaked once more. Dii screamed and trembled as he burst within her, crying out her name, intense, almost overwhelming. Breathless, he bent and kissed her neck, then unbound her eyes and wrists as she fell in a trembling, shivering heap in the flaring Circle. "My love…my beautiful, desirable flower. You are mine…we are bound as one, in blood and love and Power. I love you and you drive me wild, beyond desire."

Exhausted but happy, he pulled her into a firm embrace, her soft skin flushed and warm against him. "Perhaps we could have a more formal wedding in a few months. You are my light and my love, and I want everyone to see that. You are not just my pretty toy, but my wife, my lady and my love."

She rolled onto her belly and snuggled close to him. "Really? You would publicly have me as your wife?"

Archos smiled and kissed her. "Yes, of course, as much as you can be. At least within the lands here, you will be my wife. I love you, Dii'Athella. Why should I not show you off as my wife, my beautiful and bewitching Flower of the Dawn? Perhaps a solstice wedding and a feast?"

Dii smiled with tears of happiness in her eyes. Softly she kissed him and lay in his arms.

"I am yours, forever, my lord. I would be honoured to be your wife."

As they snuggled happily beneath the rug, he whispered, "Then it is settled."

* * *

Far away, the elf dozed. The Mirror next to him was dim and silent in its frame. It was small and hung inside a glass globe, still and quiet, as it had been for many years. He did not even know why they watched it anymore, but watch it they did. Suddenly the Mirror flared with a bright crimson glow and began to sing, softly at first then with a strange ethereal song. It spun, shining light around the room, waking the Watcher with a start. Checking he was not dreaming, he rushed outside yelling. "It's active! The Mirror, it sings…the ring has found someone. The Heir of the House of Light returns!"

The Keeper of Lore himself came to see and hastily, he made preparations. Summoning the Elders, he announced the Mirror sang and a search party should be dispatched to find the one who wore the Ring of Light. There were many questions and much disbelief, but eventually, after several days debate, it was decreed that a scouting party would go to seek her. They had planned for this, but not believing it would happen, they were caught unawares. The Lore Keeper suggested the mage M'alia, her sister Th'alia, who was a scholar and keeper of history, and two guards. The twins were the descendants of the notable historian El'Thois, and Th'alia was the Lore Keeper's best student. El'Thois had been a survivor of the Shining Citadel and servant to the House of Light, thus his kin were given the honour.

The mage M'alia was a scryer, having perfected the difficult art at an early age. Twins were rare for elves, and to have one as a mage and the other as a Keeper of Lore and History, and an adept in her own right, was almost unheard of. M'alia used her art to search for the Ring of Light, and even though she was adept, she could only find the rough area. The elves of Ilthendra were not familiar with the human lands beyond the forest and, believing that such an elf as she would not go unnoticed, perhaps city kin would know of her and thus the scouting party was sent forth.

The elves could, with luck, avoid the Witch-Hunters and find the one they sought without too much trouble, if they travelled at night and used the lesser roads, or so they believed. Th'alia, though a scholar, could use a blade to some degree, the Elders having decreed that all elves should have some knowledge of weapons. She hoped it would be enough, with luck and courage. She was to soon find out.

CHAPTER 27

A rchos had been pondering the strange spark he had felt from the dead Spirit Child Amena. Sitting in the library alone one night after Dii had gone to bed, he pulled an ancient tome written in Elvish from a little used shelf. He read for a while, confirming what he thought he knew.

In the workshop, the glowglobes cast their pale light on the floor and walls. Pushing aside the rugs that covered the Circle, he walked its line until the edges roared. He set out the items: the small enchanted Emerald Crystal from the mines of Helmerri, an item in itself of great value, the obsidian bowl on the tripod, a strange twisted horn, and a bottle of black viscous liquid and a water skin. Finally, he fetched a pale blue bottle from the shelf. From his robe he took the silk handkerchief that contained the long white hair he had taken from the dead child.

He murmured softly and a small flame appeared under the obsidian bowl. Pouring in half the water, he waited for it to begin steaming. He held the Emerald above it, concentrating until the stone hovered above the bowl. Picking up the horn, Archos poured half the remaining water into it. Unstopping the black bottle, he sniffed the contents. An unpleasant sickly smell, like the inside of a deep, rank cave, assailed his nostrils. Steeling himself for the ritual, he emptied half the bottle into the horn and resealed it. The poison was needed to allow access to the Spirit Realm, even for mages such as he the journey was difficult unless they were dying. Even a mage as Powerful as Archos needed to drink the vile liquid to enter the Realm. The offer of such pain as the poison brought was enough, but the poison was potent enough to leave even one so Powerful in extreme pain and difficulty, if not take him to the edge of death, if he was slow to reach the antidote. Needless to say, Archos visited the Realm rarely and not unless he felt the magic worth a substantial risk of death. Normally he would warn Olek, but this time he preferred to keep his intentions secret, as he was not sure of success. He was, however, confident enough that he would reach the antidote in time.

Taking the kris from his belt, he slashed deep into his arms, first one then the other, letting the blood flow into the Circle until it surrounded him and the fire. He dropped a few drops into the bowl and then sat close to the fire. "I am Archos, Lord of the Arcane Realms. I am Archos, Sky Child. This night I walk in the Spirit Realm to seek the Spirit Child who was Amena Lyn, Elfkind child. I offer to the Spirit Realm my blood and drink of the poison of the Shimmering Spider, that I may offer my pain to call this Spirit."

As the Circle roared around him, he lifted the horn to his lips and drank the contents, feeling the burn of the poison as it flowed down his throat. As his muscles cramped and he grunted in pain, he felt the cold winds of the Astral Realm swirl around him, chilling him until he shivered. As his stomach twisted and the pain tore through him, his Astral Self stepped into the roaring winds and, raising his arms, he calmed them. He felt the strange arcane creatures claw at him and as he walked the paths, he let his Focus search for the Spirit.

As the water bubbled with the blood in the bowl and the steam rose, he saw a thin trail of light. Reaching to touch it, he felt a little spark and a soft voice in his head whispered, "Follow…Lord of Magic…follow." He let his fingers touch the thread and followed for a while, the Astral Winds roaring behind him. Suddenly his muscles cramped again and as he fell back, pain washed over him. His Focus was lost as he cried out. He heard the whisper again and, pulling himself up, felt the thread before him. As he forced himself forward, he saw before him the soft light of the Spirit hovering.

"I seek the Spirit that was Amena Lyn, the elfchild murdered by the slaver Lord Tremayne, for I seek to make an offer." His slightly shaky voice echoed softly.

The Spirit before him swirled around. "I see you have great Power and I feel your pain. Speak your offer, Lord of Magic," said the soft feminine voice.

Holding up the Astral Essence of the Emerald Crystal, he spoke, "I have the Power to return you, to grant you rebirth in a mortal child; a child that may be born to the sister of Amena Lyn. Not yet, but soon…before your Power weakens that you may never be free of this Realm. To be torn as you were from the body of the child in such a manner, I see your Power has been diminished. Come to me, let me bind you in this Crystal until such time as the child is conceived, then should you choose to return, you may. To be close to she who loved you as Amena, and to offer comfort to her. Here, in this Realm, you will remain, unable to grow, unable to be free. I offer a chance of rebirth, to learn and grow, to impart the knowledge that all Spirits hold. This is the choice I offer; a gift for you and for Ozena."

The Spirit hesitated for a short moment, swirling around him, feeling his Power and the pain that racked him. She knew the cost of magic, how much this would cost him and the strength and Power it took. The whisper in his head murmured, "I accept your offer, Lord of Magic. To you I give myself until such time as the child is made that will be a Spirit Child."

She fluttered around him once more, then softly she became a bright light that filled the Crystal; casting its light in glittering green around him. He closed his hand around the Crystal and, falling to the floor, managed to shift his Focus back into the real world. As the poison continued its course, he began to twitch. Trying to reach for the bottle, his vision clouded, he missed and knocked over a glass flask. He swore under his breath and reached again.

Dii felt the ripple of Power and a searing pain within her. Waking, she saw the bed next to her was empty. Suddenly worried, she pulled on her robe and headed for the workshop. As she entered, she saw the Circle flare, the strange arcane flames roaring high. Archos lay in a pool of blood, pale as death, his body twitching as he tried to reach the bottle.

"Oh, my love, what have you done? Why did you not let me help?" she cried, moving quickly to him.

"Poison, spider poison…antidote," Archos croaked. Dii reached for the bottle and slid close to him, cradling his head as she poured it down his throat. Stroking his face, she kissed him and gently let a heal wash over him, feeling his pain as she did so. As she watched the wounds in his arms began to heal, she found a cloth and some spring water. She gently washed the blood from him and wiped his face with the cool water. Carefully and lovingly, she helped him drink, concern in her eyes. As the antidote began to counteract the poison, he weakly took her hand. "My love… the ritual was dangerous, I was not sure it would succeed, but I should have known I would wake to find you there, my pretty flower. I am sorry. I should have told you what I planned."

Dii wiped the sweat from his face and kissed him longingly. "I would face any danger for you, my lord, my love, my husband in magic. I would give my life for you. You should have told me… I could help, lend you my Power."

Archos lay in her arms and the Circle around them eased. "Oh, my love, that is why I did not ask you. You think I would risk you? It was a dangerous ritual, but successful. I sought the Spirit of Amena. There is a chance she could be reborn in a child. Spirit Children are rare and can be Powerful, able to walk the Spirit Realm and to call to their aid those that dwell there as easily as you call forth the fire. She would have been trapped, lost in the Spirit Realm and unable to return. She is bound until such time as she can be born in a mortal baby. You could not go there, at least not yet. One day, you will move as you please amongst the Arcane Realms."

He touched her face softly, feeling her Power envelope him with warmth and love. Managing to sit up, he held up the Crystal which glowed with a soft green light. "A Spirit Crystal, to return to the elves and to Ozena the Spirit Child murdered. Now, my love, help me to rest. I feel weak as a kitten and need you close to me. My beautiful flower, light of my life, I love you. You heal me and bring me a strength I had not before. Please, do not say anything to Ozena."

Slowly, he felt his strength returning. Leaning on her, he allowed her to lead him to their chamber.

"May I get you something? How may I ease you?" Dii asked as she settled him.

Archos grinned. "Well, now…I can think of one or two things, but for now, I am thirsty and hungry, perhaps a little refreshment and then perhaps we can think of other ways you may ease me."

Laughing, she replied, "Well, I see it does not take you long to recover your strength, perhaps we may be gentle tonight. I will fetch you something from the kitchen in the meantime."

* * *

Archos had the Spirit Crystal bound in silver filigree and attached to a silver chain. It glowed softly and he held it to the light, smiling as the glow brightened. Ozena had just returned from training with Olek, and they sat at ease with a small meal. Apparently she was becoming an excellent pupil in the arts of Shadowplay and stealth. She was yet to excel with a blade, but could certainly hold her own in a fight. Every day, she and Olek grew closer and it pleased Archos to see her smile after such a tragedy had befallen her. He was growing fond of the forest elf. He knew Olek adored her and Dii was deeply attached to her.

"Ozena, I have a gift for you: a Spirit Crystal. It is old magic, but contains a Spirit. This is the Spirit of Amena Lyn, called from the Spirit Realm to be returned to you, to the elves. She consented to return to offer you comfort. I was too late to save her as a living child, yet she may reside with you, close to you; my gift to you, and to her."

Ozena saw the Emerald Crystal glowing and held out her hand to touch it. "This is Amena?" she whispered in awe, knowing the myths of her people regarding the Spirit Children, told to her when Amena had been born.

"It is what remains of her, the Spirit that was her. Most of the dead pass to the Other World, which cannot be accessed, even by me. Some mages and Spirits can dwell in the Spirit Realm, and sometimes they return to the mortal world to share their knowledge. She could pass to a child. Care for the Crystal, keep her safe, and one day she may return to your care."

Gently, he put the silver chain around her neck and watched as the pale green light flared for a moment. Smiling, he said softly in her head, "Your future daughter could be a Spirit Child, Ozena, a gift from the Realms of Magic."

Ozena took his hands and kissed them. "It is a wonderful gift to have her close to me. I will treasure the Crystal and keep it close always. I can never repay what you have done for me."

He smiled and tilted her face up. "My dear, I do not ask for repayment. A gift for which payment is sought is not a gift. You and Olek are my family, or as close as makes little difference. I would not have done such as I have done if I did not choose to. All I ask is that you care for her and be all that you can be, Ozena."

With that, he turned on his heel and returned to the library to leave Ozena with her thoughts, and Olek to wonder what price of pain he had paid to get that gift.

Olek kissed her and touched the Crystal. "It is a fine gift indeed, for that is old and dangerous magic. Now you have her back within your care, the Spirit of her at least."

* * *

The whole of Harkenen was decorated. Ribbons adorned the houses, and stalls and booths were set with fine food and drinks. A large pig, game birds, and the sweet local potatoes roasted on the fire. Bottles of wine, spiced cider and barrels of beer were set around decorated tables. Delicacies from the Far Isles were arranged on tables next to the more local sweetmeats, pies, baskets of breads and cheeses. Elven fruit wine and a soft elven pudding made of oats, goat's milk, dried fruit and honey were set on a cloth the colour of buttercups. Musicians were organised to play on a small raised stage and the green area close to the market square had been hung with garlands, with boards laid to provide a dancing stage.

The morning was a bright spring day, the dawn of the equinox. The weather was cold but clear, with the sky blue like a forget-me-not, and the new growth in the trees and flowers bright green and bursting with life. The general energy of spring and renewal was all around and the villages were set to celebrate.

The elves had settled in as well as could be expected over the months that had passed, and the first elf child had been born in the village: a bonny daughter born to the woman rescued some months ago from the slaver wagons. One or two of the woman had found companionship with the human men, including Gis'Ellah, who had been courted in earnest by Steward Simon and had just announced her pregnancy. Everyone, elf and human alike, had turned out to watch the marriage of their beloved Lord Archos and his beautiful elven bride on this fine spring day.

The carriage rolled slowly down towards the village. Archos himself, mounted on his favourite horse, rode alongside, the mount decorated with dark blue and silver. Olek was dressed in black and red and sat proudly on the driving plate, delighted to be here on this day. As the Lord of Tremellic and the carriage arrived, the Steward Simon took the reins of his lord's horse and bowed to Archos, clad in a silver robe that fell to the floor and was edged with black fur, a sash of sapphire blue around his waist. Breeches of deep dark blue covered his legs and his long blond hair fell down his back, loose and flowing. Around his neck he wore the snake torc, gold, silver and bronze glittering in the sun, the bloodstone eyes blinking. He dismounted and gave his Steward a smile. Simon bowed.

As the carriage stopped, Olek opened the door and held his hand for Dii and Ozena to take. First Ozena climbed down, her mahogany hair braided and set with a flower, and dressed in a dark green silk dress that clung to her, tight and flattering; a yellow cord at her waist striking against the dark green. Pale green shoes of soft leather set upon her feet and a velvet wrap of pale and leaf green triangles covered her shoulders under which lay the green scarf Olek had bought her so many months ago. As she stepped down, Olek said softly, "I hope you look as beautiful on our wedding day, my love."

The young huntress moved aside to wait for Dii, who emerged looking radiant, like a summer dawn or the first flower of spring. Dii's hair shone in the sun, the thin braids studded with stones of blue and silver and the corresponding ribbons entwined therein flowing with the red. As the braids ended, the curls twisted down her back like liquid fire. Her gown was a deep blue silk and velvet, studied with silver beads at the bodice. Shoulder-less and low, it set off her alabaster skin and intriguing tattoos. The sleeves fell, long and flowing, and the gold and jewelled serpents around her wrists glinted in the sun. The amber ring lay on its chain around her neck and the light from it shone a pale yellow circle on her skin.

A weaving tattoo of the rare dii'athell rose covered the scar in her shoulder, red and yellow petals and leaves of green disappearing from her collar bone and down beyond the bodice, finishing for those who were privileged enough to see at her waist where it curled around her belly button. A silver cord of woven Shimmering Spider silk sat around her slender waist, the long tassels falling before her in a spray of silver. Around her shoulders was a black fur trimmed with silver to warm her in the cool spring air and pinned with the silver enamelled brooch from Celine.

When she dismounted the coach, the elves exchanged glances and the Elder nodded to Gis'Ellah, who had been appointed to deliver the presents and was uncharacteristically nervous. Approaching Dii, she bowed her head and held out the bundle. "My lady, the elves wish to mark your wedding with a traditional elven present. It is a wedding shawl, woven from the soft wool of forest goats. It can be worn around the shoulders, over the head, or around the waist. I hope you like the colour, one of the women embroidered it for you and we all added the beads. They are elven jewellery and sacred beads, tokens from the forest gods."

The scarf was large, soft and a deep green like ivy leaves, decorated with glass beads the colour of honey, small hollowed ambers and carved bone, horn and polished wood; a multitude of browns, greens and amber that shone and clicked together. The edges were woven with Elvish symbols in blue thread that swirled towards a centre in which someone had carefully embroidered the dii'athell flower in red, light green and gold.

Dii looked at it. Her eyes filled with delight at the gentle craftsmanship and care that had obviously been used to create such an item. "It is very beautiful. I shall treasure it. I thank you and all those involved with its making. I think it is a very special item and I shall proudly wear it," she said, tears in her eyes at the kindness.

Carefully she wrapped it around her waist in a triangle so the beads shone and clicked when she walked. The flower covered her beautiful behind and the dark green and bright blue complimented her dark blue dress. She found attached to one corner a small silver pin topped with a polished stone of grey. With nimble fingers she pinned it closed.

"It is so soft, and so much care has gone into it, Gis'Ellah. I am truly touched that you hold me in such esteem as to give me such a wonderful gift."

Gis'Ellah glanced back at the Elder, who nodded again, and she held out to Archos another bundle.

"It is a cloak, sir; soft wool and lined with fur. The Elvish script is a blessing from the gods of the forest for all you have done for us, and the fur is that of a white wolf."

Archos bowed and replied, "I was not expecting such a gift. I am honoured."

Removing the wrapping, he let the cloak fall about his shoulders, the dark grey blurring to black at the foot. The lining was a soft, thick white fur that he saw could be removed by use of the attaching buttons. The shoulders were sewn with feathers that were iridescent in the bright spring sunshine, and long woven tassels threaded with white and black beads tied it at the neck. The edges were trimmed with a black ribbon on which were sewn elven letters.

He kissed her cheek and said in Elvish, "It is an excellent cloak. I am honoured that you gift me such an item."

Archos turned to Dii and took her hand. Kissing it softly, he murmured to her, "I have never seen one as beautiful as you. You truly are radiant as the sun, a perfect light in this dark world, my love."

Together they walked, as one, to the centre of the town square where an awning had been erected. Olek and Ozena stood close, arm in arm, and the Steward and the members of the household watched from the festival benches set around close to the centre. One of the elven women began to play a small harp, and Archos turned to the assembly.

"This day this woman and I come to be joined before the gods and before the people here. As we have been joined in blood, so shall we be joined as one for all to see. My love, my light is she."

Dii smiled a radiant smile and kissed his hand. "My lord, my love is he. This day I come to be joined to the man who stands with me before the gods and before those here; our friends, our family, those to whom we devote our protection. As we have been joined in blood, so we be joined for all to see."

Softly, he took her hand and slipped onto her finger a woven band of red gold that looped into a flower of amber and rubies, in the centre of which lay a red bloodstone.

"All I am I give to you…all I have I share with you, so we are bound as one."

Kissing her hand that now wore the ring, he felt her Power ripple close around him, soft warmth meant only for him.

Dii looked into the silver-grey eyes that watched her and replied softly, "All I am I give to you…all that I have I share with you, we are bound as one."

She gave to him a ring of woven white gold with a piece of crystal at its heart. It glowed a faint coppery light as she had bound within it a lock of her hair and a tiny wisp of light.

He pulled her close and kissed her long and hard, until Simon coughed and yelled, good naturedly, "There is enough of that later, my lord! May we start the dancing and feasting?"

Archos pulled away from Dii and laughed. "Oh, I am sorry, my beautiful wife distracted me. Of course I decree the festivities under way."

The watching crowd gave a cheer and someone cracked open one of the barrels of beer. A fiddle and pipes were produced, and soon dancing and merrymaking ensued. Elves and humans both danced and feasted. Archos and Dii led the dance. In their happiness, they spun and wove among the crowd; almost as though they were the only people in the world.

As the sun set on proceedings, and Archos rested as Dii was surrounded by the womenfolk, Simon handed a flagon of ale to his lord. "I never thought to see you marry, my lord, but she shines like the stars and the village adores her."

Archos smiled. "Oh yes, she is the most beautiful creature in the world, and I think, I hope at least, finally happy and free. Here, at least, within this valley. For someone who suffered so much, she is remarkable in her kindness. And what of you Simon? I see you married and Gis'Ellah blooms in her pregnancy. It is good to see the elves mingling, and part of the community. The valley prospers and is finally settled."

Simon bowed his head. "Aye, well, Gis'Ellah is a resourceful woman and an excellent housekeeper. Her young daughter comes along fine and is, so I am told, becoming an excellent hunter. It was a good idea of Olek's to suggest the training. The militia are becoming a force to be reckoned with, and I think next year, we may have the best archers outside the forest, thanks to Miss Ozena. The Witch-Hunters become ever bolder, and should they be foolish enough to arrive in force, they will be surprised in the resistance they would meet. Young Kaia leads the training for the youngsters and hopes, so she tells me, to have a brother when the child comes."

Archos grinned. "Yes. Olek and Ozena have been busy, not only dealing with the remaining slavers that were involved in the attack on Szendro, but in training, and Ozena has certainly been helpful in settling in the elves. They are wary of dealing with me, but will ask her. She is becoming the ambassadress for them. As for you, soon to be a father, now stepfather and husband. So many years of resisting the advances of the widow Lillia and then you take for wife an elven widow with a daughter."

Simon laughed. "Lillia has not spoken more than two words to me since. Young Istvan will deal with more business for you, my lord, when the child comes. He was a good find, he and his young lady. Now I should go and tend to my wife and you to yours."

Archos rested as he saw Simon move off to find Gis'Ellah, who saw him and bowed her head. He ran his fingers down the edge of the cloak, admiring its soft wool, and he touched the embroidered edges, the blessings of the elven gods, quite the honour for one not an elf. He smiled as Dii returned to him and, taking her into an embrace, he kissed her.

"Perhaps, my pretty wife, we should leave the villagers to their entertainment and return home to make our own. I need you alone for a while, my love. I have been looking for an opportunity to get you out of that beautiful gown all afternoon."

Dii smiled a wicked smile and kissed his fingers, sucking each one slowly. "Well, my lord and husband, how can I refuse?"

He led her to the horse and lifted her onto his back. "Olek can return the carriage later. Now, my love… Would you like me to take you to the cave, or the waterfall, or the manor…?"

Climbing up behind her, he snaked his hands about her waist and the beads on the scarf clicked and shimmered as he nibbled her neck. "I leave the choice to you, my lord and my husband, I am yours," Dii whispered as she snuggled happily into his arms.

He kissed her neck and nudged Storm, and slowly they rode towards the cave.

* * *

Olek pulled Ozena around in the dance. Amongst the other things she had learned were the dances favoured in the village. He had barely taken his eyes off her all day and as they danced close, he said softly, "I think you are the prettiest girl here by far, Ozena. None of the other women come close to you. Today, you look like a goddess of the forest, the Nymph Oeliana, is that not her name?"

"Yes, that is her name. She is a goddess of the forest pools. I find myself fatigued by the dancing, these shoes are somewhat uncomfortable and this dress is most impractical," Ozena grumbled good-naturedly as she pulled him away.

Olek grinned and kissed the bare skin revealed by the dress, just below the Emerald Crystal. Taking her hand, he led her away from the crowd. With an arm about her waist, he said, "I have a gift for you, and a question. I was going to wait as this was the day for Lord Archos and Dii, but perhaps now is the correct time."

Pilfering a bottle of wine and a basket of fruit, he took her hand and walked with her, away from the village and to the hills now covered in bright green grass, up to the waterfall. Kissing her passionately, he pulled her close.

"I need some time away from the crowd, just the two of us. Archos has disappeared off with his lady, and I suspect they will make their own way back."

"What about the carriage, Olek?" Ozena asked.

"Oh, stuff the carriage. Kiss me, woman. It will be there later…or tomorrow. Simon can bring it back, we do not need it."

He pulled her into an embrace, feeling the soft fabric of her gown over her curves. He led her slowly to a copse of trees near to the waterfall and set down his cloak. Pulling her down beside him, he tossed the wine and the food to one side and kissed her, his lips full of fire. He pulled away and from his pocket, he produced a bracelet of dark green jade, carved with ivy leaves. The jade shone; the carving exquisite. "I would like you to have this… I love you, Ozena Lyn, and I ask you to be my wife, to be by my side every day, to be part of me."

He slipped the band on her wrist and kissed the palm of her hand. "Yes… Yes, please! Oh, Olek, do you mean that?" she asked, rather surprised.

"Of course I mean it. Why would I not? I love you. You make me a better person and the world a less dark place."

She looked down, fingers running over the bracelet. "But what of Archos, and Dii?"

"Archos knows. We live in his house anyway, why should that change? Ozena, we have our own rooms and may come and go as we please. He has Dii. The manor is more than large enough for several families, you know that. I am still his man, nothing will change that, but I would like you to live as my wife, not just my lover. Lord Archos and Dii are my family, I would like them to be yours also." He nuzzled her neck until she sighed at the attention.

"Yes, I will be your wife. I will live with you as we do now. I would live wherever you choose, so long as we are together. Now tell me, how shall we celebrate?"

His hand crept up her thigh under the beautiful dress. "Oh, I can think of a couple of ways…"

EPILOGUE

Far away from Tremellic, in the deep dungeon of a Witch-Hunter fort, M'alia the mage hung in chains and her sister Th'alia knelt, bloody and beaten, at the feet of a Witch-Hunter Commander.

"Your companions were…persuaded to talk, elf. Most informative they were too. So you seek this red-haired mage to lead you to the lost City of Light. This sorceress, she is the key, is she not? There is an elven Citadel, full of treasure, no doubt. An excellent way to bring the elves to their knees when I take it from them, do you not think? You believe this mage can lead you there, has some magic you need to open the doors."

Th'alia said nothing and the Witch-Hunter spun round and brought the whip down across the chained mage, who screamed in pain from the Banecrystal tip of the whip. "How much more can she live through, do you think? Perhaps…perhaps if you were to…cooperate, for we too seek this mage and her lover. For some time, they have been inconvenient to us, but he is Powerful. Maybe a trap could be arranged? Lead them to this elven city full of treasure, and then, well, perhaps the forest will take them in a most unfortunate accident; their lives for that of your sister, and you, of course. She will remain here, but in more comfortable surroundings. She is, I believe, an adept at scrying. She can find this magic ring the Witch wears? You will be watched. If you fail, she dies. If you lead us to them, and this place, then we will turn our attentions away from two elves. If, of course, you refuse, her death will be very slow and very, very painful. As will yours. Would you not save your sister from such pain?"

Th'alia turned her blood-stained face towards her twin and, closing her eyes, whispered, "Yes."

To be continued…

AUTHOR BIO

A. L. Butcher is the British author of the Light Beyond the Storm Chronicles fantasy series, and several short stories in the fantasy and fantasy romance genres. She is an avid reader and creator of worlds, a poet and a dreamer. When she is grounded in the real world she likes science, natural history, history and monkeys. Her work has been described as 'dark and gritty' and her poetry as evocative.

Blog: http://libraryoferana.wordpress.com/
Goodreads: https://www.goodreads.com/author/show/6430414.A_L_Butcher
Twitter:@libraryoferana
Facebook: https://www.facebook.com/DarkFantasyBeyondTheStorm

Also by this author:
The Shining Citadel – The Light Beyond the Storm Chronicles – Book II
The Stolen Tower – The Light Beyond The Storm Chronicles – Book III

Tales of Erana: Myths and Legends (also in audio)
Tales of Erana: The Warrior's Curse (also in audio)
Tales of Erana Volume One (paperback only)

Anthology work:
Heroika: Dragon Eaters
Nine Heroes
Wyrd Worlds
Wyrd Worlds II
A Splendid Salmagundi
Bellator
Kiss and Tales- A Romantic Collection (The Indie Collaboration Presents)
Tales from Darker Places (The Indie Collaboration Presents)
Spectacular Tales (The Indie Collaboration Presents)
Summer Shorts (The Indie Collaboration Presents)

Printed in Great
Britain
by Amazon